The Hollywood Nightmare

The Hollywood Nightmare

**TALES OF FANTASY AND HORROR
FROM THE FILM WORLD**

Edited by Peter Haining

Introduced by Christopher Lee

TAPLINGER PUBLISHING COMPANY
NEW YORK

First Published in the United States in 1971 by
TAPLINGER PUBLISHING CO., INC.
New York, New York

Library of Congress Catalog Card Number: 76-145543

ISBN 0-8008-3921-8

For Robert Bloch

with thanks
for the best nightmares
of my sleep

Contents

Acknowledgements

The editor wishes to express his gratitude to the following authors, agents and publishers for allowing copyright material to appear in this collection:

The Prehistoric Producer by Ray Bradbury. Copyright © 1962 by the Curtis Publishing Company and reprinted by permission of the author's agent, Messrs. A. D. Peters Ltd.

The Plot is the Thing by Robert Bloch. Copyright © 1966 by Mercury Press Inc. and reprinted by permission of the author's agent, Scott Meredith Literary Agency.

The Shadow On The Screen by Henry Kuttner. Copyright © 1939 by *Weird Tales* and reprinted by permission of the author's executors.

Return To The Sabbath by Tarleton Fiske. Copyright © 1945 by Robert Bloch and reprinted by permission of Scott Meredith Literary Agency.

A Wig for Miss DeVore by August Derleth. Copyright © 1943 by *Weird Tales* and reprinted by permission of the author's agent, Scott Meredith Literary Agency.

The Man Who Wanted To Be In The Movies by John Jakes. Copyright © 1962 and reprinted by permission of the author.

The Perfect Plot by Frank Fenton. Copyright © 1955 and reprinted by permission of the author.

Death Double by William F. Nolan. Copyright © 1963 by Paperback Library Inc. and reprinted by permission of the author.

Booked Solid by Ray Russell. Copyright © 1961 by Ray Russell and reprinted by his permission.

The Hollywood Horror Man by Boris Karloff. Copyright © 1968 by Boris Karloff and reprinted by permission of the author's estate.

The New People by Charles Beaumont. Copyright © 1965 by Fawcett Publications Inc. and reprinted by permission of the author.

Gavin O'Leary by John Collier. Copyright © 1945 by H. Allen Smith and reprinted with his permission.

Faed-Out by Avram Davidson. Copyright © 1964 by Mercury Press Inc. and reprinted by permission of the author.

Mantage by Richard Matheson. Copyright © 1961 by Richard Matheson and reprinted with his permission.

Technical Adviser by Chad Oliver. Copyright © 1953 by Fantasy House Inc. and reprinted by permission of the author.

The Screen Game by J. G. Ballard. Copyright © 1963 by Ziff-Davis Publishing Company and reprinted by permission of the author.

Death Warmed Over by Ray Bradbury. Copyright © 1968 by Ray Bradbury and reprinted by permission of his agent, A. D. Peters Ltd.

Editor's Preface

Anyone describing Hollywood as the "Fantasy Capital of America" is probably not going to run into much opposition. Indeed, it may well be an understatement, for where else in the world have so many celluloid dreams and legends of our times been created? Where else has a community so dedicated itself to the making of illusions and the begetting of myths?

It is true to say, too, that you don't actually need to go to Hollywood to become aware of this aura of fantasy. For many of us the feeling first stirs in the darkened auditorium of some local neighbourhood cinema as we sit, still as the "unborn" monster in Frankenstein's laboratory, dreaming dreams of courage and nightmare. For others the absorption may come a little later as we fall hopelessly in love with a twelve-foot beauty who soon becomes more real in the secret part of our imagination than even those with whom we pass our everyday lives. . . .

The Hollywood Nightmare developed, as have a number of my other anthologies, from a fascination with macabre fiction which is linked with a specific theme: in this case it resulted from an observation of the numbers of horror story writers who had been "recruited" by Hollywood to become script and scenario writers. Like others devoted to the genre, I watched with delight as the talents of such as Ray Bradbury, Robert Bloch and Richard Matheson (whom *we* had first read and encouraged with fan letters through the pages of fantasy magazines) were being deployed with increasing regularity to create films for the world's dreaming millions.

Some of these men, we were pleased to see, continued to work in the area they knew best: helping produce pictures to which they brought a special understanding of the sense of unease. Others struck out into the fields of thrillers, westerns and even romances. But—and it is a truism that no man can live by film scripts alone —all these writers have retained their affection for the macabre, for the supernatural, for all those dark mysteries from which they derived their literary beginnings.

So it has been gratifying to note how from time to time they have forsaken the demands of the screen to again write an outre story or two. And what could be more natural, either, than for some of their tales to be set in the city in which they now work? Nothing, of course—and what they've given us over recent years constitutes the collection now in your hands. To be fair, I must add that there are one or two contributors not so employed—but like so many of us they share a fascination with the Hollywood myth and have some special thoughts to impart on the subject. . . .

Together, then, the stories herein present what I believe is a unique look at the many faces of Hollywood and its people. To the city itself I owe a debt of gratitude for providing the inspiration for the book (apart from a lot of personal cinema pleasure) while my thanks are also due to the following "citizens" for the parts they played in its compilation: Christopher Lee for making time during a hectic filming schedule to compose the excellent Introduction; Ray Bradbury for his unfailing courtesy; August Derleth as ever generosity personified; and Robert Bloch for suggestions and advice above and beyond the call of request. Also the many agents and publishers who assisted so magnificently in the complicated business of copyright clearance. Without any of these people my job would have been impossible—and this book would not now be awaiting your approval.

Peter Haining
New York—Essex, England
January 1971

Introduction

By Christopher Lee

The late Boris Karloff once said to me when we were discussing the best way of putting horror across: "Leave it to the audience." And there, in a nutshell, he summed up not only the secret of the success of horror films but of horror stories, too. For it is what the viewer in a cinema conjures up in his mind's eye, or the reader in his thoughts, that makes for real horror—no amount of acting or brilliant writing can quite match up to the inventive power of the mind.

What causes us to react in this way? I suppose it is what Shakespeare called the "secret, black and midnight" aspects of our character. The strange part of our make-up which makes us react in one way or another to the supernatural, the macabre, the fantastic and the weird. And I don't believe that the reason why we go to see this kind of film—or read this type of story—is out of an excessive urge of morbidity. It is simply that we enjoy them.

As an actor who has specialised lately in "graveyard" films (I dislike the word horror—"shock" or "terror" pictures as Boris Karloff used to define them, is so much better) I am convinced that my audience like a jolt from time to time. They like to escape into a fantasy world of evil and corruption for a shudder of pleasure. And when people ask me if I think audiences laugh at these sort of films I reply that they do not; if they do, we have made them badly. Sometimes you'll hear laughter in a cinema—but that's just bravado by people trying to convince themselves they're not really frightened at all!

I don't think it is mere coincidence, either, that over the years the macabre film has been a source of continual popularity—it serves a very real need in allowing people to blow off an emotional steam valve. These films were popular right from their beginnings in the 1930's and 40's in Germany through the Universal Pictures' heyday in Hollywood just before and after the war and right into our highly sophisticated society today. I am told by some people that there will be another big revival soon—as if something which has never died could possibly be revived!

Of course, I know from *personal experience* just how popular the films are because everywhere I go I am recognised. I hear a lot of comments both for and against the films, needless to say, but, speaking from my own point of view, I have no time for people who consider these films "suspect" or even dangerous to impressionable minds. I am convinced that they do not harm at all—and I have said this many times both in private and public. This is by no means an attempt at justifying my work, let me hasten to add; I really believe they don't do any damage to people's minds, unless, of course, the people are already unbalanced and fortunately that group form a very small minority.

This, then, is the world of the fantasy film—and it is not surprising that there are many elements of fantasy about the place where a large number of the pictures are made: Hollywood. Ours is a business both strange and unique, a business of starlight and glamour—one moment a place of dreams, the next of nightmares.

I have to confess that I have never been anywhere else where I was so conscious of two rather alarming characteristics: fear and ignorance. Hollywood is a hallucinatory dream city—as Sheila Graham remarked (and I quote) "This world of dwarfs casting a long shadow"; and one can almost smell the fear that everyone has of losing their jobs or taking a decision or doing anything that means they must *think*. This is a very real kind of horror—and in many cases not all that far removed from the stories you are going to read about in this book.

It alarms me, too, to see the standard which is apparently acceptable amongst the leading performers of today—and it doesn't seem necessary at all to gain a background of experience or a real knowledge of one's field. I don't think there is any other business in the world in which it is possible to get to the very top, both in the executive and in the creative and performing sides, without knowing anything about one's job at all. In every other profession that I know people have to go through the mill; they have to learn their jobs. You can't be a shipbuilder if you don't know how to lay a keel, but you *can* be a film star if you don't know how to act and you *can* be an executive responsible for millions of dollars even if you don't know anything about stories and scripts. This, in a few words, is what I consider the frightening side, the nightmarish side, the horrific side of the film world. Fiction we have in plenty—it is the fact that can make you really scream!

However, I have dwelt too long on films and what I have said doesn't really constitute an introduction to a group of stories. The tales of fantasy and horror which follow all feature the world of films and film making, and Hollywood in particular. There is, as I have intimated, a great deal of fantasy in this world and a great deal of horror, too. Ask anybody who is intimately connected with it and you will soon learn of deals which verge on the fantastic, productions straight from the realms of the extraordinary and not infrequently results which are horrible!

I am in the fortunate position of having read widely from the work of many of the writers to be found in this book—in particular Ray Bradbury, who is a close personal friend of mine, Richard Matheson, who wrote the script for *The Devil Rides Out* from the book by Dennis Wheatley which I filmed a few years ago, and Robert Bloch of *Psycho* fame. I have also been an admirer of Ray Russell for years. He wrote *Sardonicus* which was made into a film, and *Saggitarius* which is a story I have always wanted to film.

Another story with which I have been intimately concerned is "Return To The Sabbath". I played in this for Alfred Hitchcock on his television series about five or six years ago—and it was, in fact, the first time I had been to Hollywood to work. It was the first time, too, that I came face to face with the "Hollywood Nightmare".

I think that almost every writer I have ever met has wanted to write a macabre story—and similarly, practically all actors want to do a macabre film, and that includes some of the greatest names in the business. When you look at the list of actors who have made themselves famous from appearing in this type of story—Basil Rathbone, Lon Chaney, Boris Karloff, Bela Lugosi, Peter Lorre, Vincent Price and Peter Cushing to mention just a few—I am sure you will agree with me that their very names repudiate the statement that horror films are mere gimmicks. These are great actors playing great parts and I am honoured to be in such good company.

To conclude, then, let me say that I am convinced that the stories which are appearing in this book will have tremendous appeal because they are all written by craftsmen—people who are masters of their own field and have worked for years perfecting this skill. People like Bradbury with his extraordinary verbal imagery, or Bloch with his gallows humour, and Derleth with his associations with H. P. Lovecraft—certainly the most unique writer in the field of the macabre. And from England, J. G. Ballard, of course, with his extraordinary allegorical stories of the world turning to crystal, the world drowned, the world splitting up.

I think you will find the titles of the stories very evocative, too—they all seem to me to conjure up the smell of grease-paint, the celluloid and the febrile atmosphere of the studios.

Now it is my turn, in Mr. Karloff's words, to "leave it to the audience". The writers have done their part in creating tales which I think will convince you, when you have finished reading them, that you *need* to look into that dark corner and peep under the bed to make quite sure that there is nothing there after all. And I'm bearing in mind, too, that your imagination may well outstrip that of the writers to create *things* even more ghastly still. . . .

Finally, I hope that all of you about to enter *The Hollywood Nightmare* will enjoy reading the stories as much as I did. I hope, too, that perhaps the day will soon come when it is possible to produce them in film form for the further entertainment and pleasure of an even greater number of people. And until we meet again on either side of the screen—SLEEP WELL!

London
May 1969

"In Hollywood primitive magical thinking exists side by side with the most advanced technology."

Dr. Hortense Powdermaker
Hollywood – The Dream Factory

The Prehistoric Producer

BY RAY BRADBURY

Ray Bradbury is surely the most appropriate person to begin a collection such as this as he is unquestionably the finest screen-writer to have emerged from the ranks of the macabre storytellers. In recent years he has not only scripted a truly outstanding "general" film in John Huston's Moby Dick, *but also helped create one of the most controversial Science Fantasy movies from his own novel* Fahrenheit 451. *The energetic and likeable Ray lives close to Film City and has of late also extended his writing to the stage (a play called* The Anthem Sprinters) *and television. But it is in the realms of literary fantasy that many consider he is to be seen at his very best—as here, for example, weaving a wholly unique story around that king-pin figure in the film world, the Hollywood producer. . . .*

He opened a door on darkness. A voice cried, "Shut it!" It was like a blow in the face. He jumped through. The door banged. He cursed himself quietly. The voice, with dreadful patience, intoned, "Jesus. You Terwilliger?"

"Yes," said Terwilliger. A faint ghost of screen haunted the dark theater wall to his right. To his left, a cigarette wove fiery arcs in the air as someone's lips talked swiftly around it.

"You're five minutes late!"

Don't make it sound like five years, thought Terwilliger.

"Shove your film in the projection room door. Let's *move.*"

Terwilliger squinted.

He made out five vast loge seats that exhaled, breathed heavily as

19

amplitudes of executive life shifted, leaning toward the middle loge where, almost in darkness, a little boy sat smoking.

No, thought Terwilliger, not a boy. That's him, Joe Clarence. Clarence the Great.

For now the tiny mouth snapped like a puppet's, blowing smoke. "Well?"

Terwilliger stumbled back to hand the film to the projectionist, who made a lewd gesture toward the loges, winked at Terwilliger and slammed the booth door.

"Jesus," sighed the tiny voice. A buzzer buzzed. "Roll it, projection!"

Terwilliger probed the nearest loge, struck flesh, pulled back and stood biting his lips.

Music leaped from the screen. His film appeared in a storm of drums:

TYRANNOSAURUS REX: *The Thunder Lizard.*
Photographed in stop-motion animation with miniatures created by John Terwilliger. A study in life-forms on Earth one billion years before Christ.

Faint ironic applause came softly patting from the baby hands in the middle loge.

Terwilliger shut his eyes. New music jerked him alert. The last titles faded into a world of primeval sun, mist, poisonous rain and lush wilderness. Morning fogs were strewn along eternal seacoasts where immense flying dreams and dreams of nightmare scythed the wind. Huge triangles of bone and rancid skin, of diamond eye and crusted tooth, pterodactyls, the kites of destruction, plunged, struck prey, and skimmed away, meat and screams in their scissor mouths.

Terwilliger gazed, fascinated.

In the jungle foliage now, shiverings, creepings, insect jitterings, antennae twitchings, slime locked in oily fatted slime, armor skinned to armor, in sun glade and shadow moved the reptilian inhabitors of Terwilliger's mad remembrance of vengeance given flesh and panic taking wing.

Brontosaur, stegosaur, triceratops. How easily the clumsy tonnages of name fell from one's lips.

The great brutes swung like ugly machineries of war and dissolution through moss ravines, crushing a thousand flowers at one footfall, snouting the mist, ripping the sky in half with one shriek.

My beauties, thought Terwilliger, my little lovelies. All liquid latex, rubber sponge, ball-socketed steel articulature; all night-dreamed, clay-molded, warped and welded, riveted and slapped to life by hand. No bigger than my fist, half of them; the rest no larger than this head they sprang from.

"Good Lord," said a soft admiring voice in the dark.

Step by step, frame by frame of film, stop motion by stop motion, he, Terwilliger, had run his beasts through their postures, moved each a fraction of an inch, photographed them, moved them another hair, photographed them, for hours and days and months. Now these rare images, this eight hundred scant feet of film, rushed through the projector.

And lo! he thought. I'll never get used to it. Look! They come *alive!*

Rubber, steel, clay, reptilian latex sheath, glass eye, porcelain fang, all ambles, trundles, strides in terrible prides through continents as yet unmanned, by seas as yet unsalted, a billion years lost away. They *do* breathe. They *do* smite air with thunders. Oh, uncanny!

I feel, thought Terwilliger, quite simply, that there stands *my* Garden, and these my animal creations which I love on this Sixth Day, and tomorrow, the Seventh, I must rest.

"Lord," said the soft voice again.

Terwilliger almost answered, "Yes?"

"This is beautiful footage, Mr. Clarence," the voice went on.

"Maybe," said the man with a boy's voice.

"Incredible animation."

"I've seen better," said Clarence the Great.

Terwilliger stiffened. He turned from the screen where his friends lumbered into oblivion, from butcheries wrought on architectural scales. For the first time he examined his possible employers.

"Beautiful stuff."

This praise came from an old man who sat to himself far across the theater, his head lifted forward in amazement toward that ancient life.

"It's jerky. Look there!" The strange boy in the middle loge half rose, pointing with the cigarette in his mouth. "Hey, was *that* a bad shot. You *see?*"

"Yes," said the old man, tired suddenly, fading back in his chair. "I see."

Terwilliger crammed his hotness down upon a suffocation of swiftly moving blood.

"Jerky," said Joe Clarence.

White light, quick numerals, darkness; the music cut, the monsters vanished.

"Glad that's over," Joe Clarence exhaled. "Almost lunchtime. Throw on the next reel, Walter! That's all, Terwilliger." Silence. "Terwilliger?" Silence. "Is that dumb bunny still here?"

"Here." Terwilliger ground his fists on his hips.

"Oh," said Joe Clarence. "It's not bad. But don't get ideas about money. A dozen guys came here yesterday to show stuff as good or better than yours, tests for our new film, *Prehistoric Monster*. Leave your bid in an envelope with my secretary. Same door out as you came in. Walter, what the hell are you waiting for? Roll the next one!"

In darkness, Terwilliger barked his shins on a chair, groped for and found the door handle, gripped it tight, tight.

Behind him the screen exploded: an avalanche fell in great flourings of stone, whole cities of granite, immense edifices of marble piled, broke and flooded down. In this thunder, he heard voices from the week ahead:

"We'll pay you one thousand dollars, Terwilliger."

"But I need a thousand for my equipment alone!"

"Look, we're giving you a break. Take it or leave it!"

With the thunder dying, he knew he would take, and he knew he would hate it.

Only when the avalanche had drained off to silence behind him and his own blood had raced to the inevitable decision and stalled in his heart, did Terwilliger pull the immensely weighted door wide to step forth into the terrible raw light of day.

Fuse flexible spine to sinuous neck, pivot neck to deaths-head skull, hinge jaw from hollow cheek, glue plastic sponge over lubricated skeleton, slip snake-pebbled skin over sponge, meld seams with fire, then rear upright triumphant in a world where insanity wakes but to look on madness—Tyrannosaurus Rex!

The Creator's hands glided down out of arc-light sun. They placed the granuled monster in false green summer wilds, they waded it in broths of teeming bacterial life. Planted in serene terror, the lizard machine basked. From the blind heavens the Creator's voice hummed, vibrating the Garden with the old and monotonous tune about the footbone connected to the . . . anklebone, anklebone connected to the . . . legbone, legbone connected to the . . . kneebone, kneebone connected to the. . . .

A door burst wide.

Joe Clarence ran in very much like an entire Cub Scout pack. He looked wildly around as if no one were there.

"My God!" he cried. "Aren't you set up yet? This costs me money!"

"No," said Terwilliger dryly. "No matter how much time I take, I get paid the same."

Joe Clarence approached in a series of quick starts and stops. "Well, shake a leg. And make it real horrible."

Terwilliger was on his knees beside the miniature jungle set. His eyes were on a straight level with his producer's as he said, "How many feet of blood and gore would you like?"

"Two thousand feet of each!" Clarence laughed in a kind of gasping stutter. "Let's look." He grabbed the lizard.

"Careful!"

"Careful?" Clarence turned the ugly beast in careless and nonloving hands. "It's my monster, ain't it? The contract—"

"The contract says you use this model for exploitation advertising, but the animal reverts to me after the film's in release."

"Holy cow." Clarence waved the monster. "That's wrong. We just signed the contracts four days ago—"

"It feels like four years." Terwilliger rubbed his eyes. "I've been up two nights without sleep finishing this beast so we can start shooting."

Clarence brushed this aside. "To hell with the contract. What a slimy trick. It's my monster. You and your agent give me heart attacks. Heart attacks about money, heart attacks about equipment, heart attacks about—"

"This camera you gave me is ancient."

"So if it breaks, fix it; you got hands? The challenge of the shoe-string operation is using the old brain instead of cash. Getting back to the point, this monster, it should've been specified in the deal, is my baby."

"I never let anyone own the things I make," said Terwilliger honestly. "I put too much time and affection in them."

"Hell, okay, so we give you fifty bucks extra for the beast, and throw in all this camera equipment free when the film's done, right? Then you start your own company. Compete with me, get even with me, right, using my own machines!" Clarence laughed.

"If they don't fall apart first," observed Terwilliger.

"Another thing." Clarence put the creature on the floor and walked around it. "I don't like the way this monster shapes up."

"You don't like *what?*" Terwilliger almost yelled.

"His expression. Needs more fire, more . . . goombah. More mazash!"

"Mazash?"

"The old bimbo! Bug the eyes more. Flex the nostrils. Shine the teeth. Fork the tongue sharper. You can *do* it! Uh, the monster ain't mine, huh?"

"Mine." Terwilliger arose.

His belt buckle was now on a line with Joe Clarence's eyes. The producer stared at the bright buckle almost hypnotically for a moment.

"God damn the goddam lawyers!"

He broke for the door.

"Work!"

The monster hit the door a split second after it slammed shut.

Terwilliger kept his hand poised in the air from his overhead throw. Then his shoulders sagged. He went to pick up his beauty. He twisted off its head, skinned the latex flesh off the skull, placed the skull on a pedestal and, painstakingly, with clay, began to reshape the prehistoric face.

"A little goombah," he muttered. "A touch of mazash."

They ran the first film test on the animated monster a week later. When it was over, Clarence sat in darkness and nodded imperceptibly.

"Better. But . . . more horrific, bloodcurdling. Let's scare the hell out of Aunt Jane. Back to the drawing board!"

"I'm a week behind schedule now," Terwilliger protested. "You keep coming in, change this, change that, you say, so I change it, one day the tail's all wrong, next day it's the claws—"

"You'll find a way to make me happy," said Clarence. "Get in there and fight the old aesthetic fight!"

At the end of the month they ran the second test.

"A near miss! Close!" said Clarence. "The face is just almost right. Try again, Terwilliger!"

Terwilliger went back. He animated the dinosaur's mouth so that it said obscene things which only a lip reader might catch, while the rest of the audience thought the beast was only shrieking. Then he got the clay and worked until 3 A.M. on the awful face.

"That's it!" cried Clarence in the projection room the next week. "Perfect! Now *that's* what I call a monster!"

He leaned toward the old man, his lawyer, Mr. Glass, and Maury Poole, his production assistant.

"You *like* my creature?" He beamed.

Terwilliger, slumped in the back row, his skeleton as long as the monsters he built, could feel the old lawyer shrug.

"You seen one monster, you seen 'em all."

"Sure, sure, but this one's special!" shouted Clarence happily. "Even *I* got to admit Terwilliger's a genius!"

They all turned back to watch the beast on the screen, in a titanic waltz, throw its razor tail wide in a vicious harvesting that cut grass and clipped flowers. The beast paused now to gaze pensively off into the mists, gnawing a red bone.

"That monster," said Mr. Glass at last, squinting. "He sure looks familiar."

"Familiar?" Terwilliger stirred, alert.

"It's got such a look," drawled Mr. Glass in the dark, "I couldn't forget, from someplace."

"Natural Museum exhibits?"

"No, no."

"Maybe," laughed Clarence, "you read a book once, Glass?"

"Funny . . ." Glass, unperturbed, cocked his head, closed one eye. "Like detectives, I don't forget a face. But, that Tyrannosaurus Rex—where before did I meet *him*?"

"Who cares?" Clarence sprinted. "He's great. And all because I booted Terwilliger's behind to make him do it right. Come on, Maury!"

When the door shut, Mr. Glass turned to gaze steadily at Terwilliger. Not taking his eyes away, he called softly to the projectionist. "Walt? Walter? Could you favor us with that beast again?"

"Sure thing."

Terwilliger shifted uncomfortably, aware of some bleak force gathering in blackness, in the sharp light that shot forth once more to ricochet terror off the screen.

"Yeah. Sure," mused Mr. Glass. "I almost remember. I almost know him. But . . . *who*?"

The brute, as if answering, turned and for a disdainful moment stared across one hundred thousand million years at two small men hidden in a small dark room. The tyrant machine named itself in thunder.

Mr. Glass quickened forward, as if to cup his ear.

Darkness swallowed all.

With the film half finished, in the tenth week, Clarence summoned thirty of the office staff, technicians and a few friends to see a rough cut of the picture.

The film had been running fifteen minutes when a gasp ran through the small audience.

Clarence glanced swiftly about.

Mr. Glass, next to him, stiffened.

Terwilliger, scenting danger, lingered near the exit, not knowing why; his nervousness was compulsive and intuitive. Hand on the door, he watched.

Another gasp ran through the crowd.

Someone laughed quietly. A woman secretary giggled. Then there was instantaneous silence.

For Joe Clarence had jumped to his feet.

His tiny figure sliced across the light on the screen. For a moment, two images gesticulated in the dark: Tyrannosaurus, ripping the leg fom a Pteranodon, and Clarence, yelling, pumping forward as if to grapple with these fantastic wrestlers.

"Stop! Freeze it right there!"

The film stopped. The image held.

"What's wrong?" asked Mr. Glass.

"Wrong?" Clarence crept up on the image. He thrust his baby hands to the screen, stabbed the tyrant jaw, the lizard eye, the fangs, the brow, then turned blindly to the projector light so that reptilian flesh was printed on his furious cheeks. "What goes? What *is* this?"

"Only a monster, Chief."

"Monster, hell!" Clarence pounded the screen with his tiny fist. "That's *me*!"

Half the people leaned forward, half the people fell back, two people jumped up, one of them Mr. Glass, who fumbled for his other spectacles, flexed his eyes and moaned, "So *that*'s where I saw him before!"

"That's where you what?"

Mr. Glass shook his head, eyes shut. "That face, I *knew* it was familiar."

A wind blew in the room.

Everyone turned. The door stood open.

Terwilliger was gone.

They found Terwilliger in his animation studio cleaning out his desk, dumping everything into a large cardboard box, the Tyrannosaurus, machine-toy model under his arm. He looked up as the mob swirled in, Clarence at the head.

"What did I do to deserve this!" he cried.

"I'm sorry, Mr. Clarence."

"You're sorry?! Didn't I pay you well?"

"No, as a matter of fact."

"I took you to lunches—"

"Once. I picked up the tab."

"I gave you dinner at home, you swam in my pool, and now *this*! You're fired!"

"You can't fire me, Mr. Clarence. I've worked the last week free and overtime, you forgot my check—"

"You're fired anyway, oh, you're *really* fired! You're blackballed in Hollywood. Mr. Glass!" He whirled to find the old man. "Sue him!"

"There is nothing," said Terwilliger, not looking up any more, just looking down, packing, keeping in motion, "nothing you can sue me for. Money? You never paid enough to save on. A house? Could never afford that. A wife? I've worked for people like you all my life. So wives are out. I'm an unencumbered man. There's nothing you can do to me. If you attach my dinosaurs, I'll just go hole up in a small town somewhere, get me a can of latex rubber, some clay from the river, some old steel pipe, and make new monsters. I'll buy stock film raw and cheap. I've got an old beat-up stop-motion camera. Take that away, and I'll build one with my own hands. I can do anything. And that's why you'll never hurt me again."

"You're fired!" cried Clarence. "Look at me. Don't look away. You're fired! You're fired!"

"Mr. Clarence," said Mr. Glass, quietly, edging forward. "Let me talk to him just a moment."

"So talk to him!" said Clarence. "What's the use? He just stands there with that monster under his arm and the goddam thing looks like me, so get out of the way!"

Clarence stormed out the door. The others followed.

Mr. Glass shut the door, walked over to the window and looked out at the absolutely clear twilight sky.

"I wish it would rain," he said. "That's one thing about California I can't forgive. It never really lets go and cries. Right now, what wouldn't I give for a little something from that sky? A bolt of lightning, even."

He stood silent, and Terwilliger slowed in his packing. Mr. Glass sagged down into a chair and doodled on a pad with a pencil, talking sadly, half aloud, to himself.

"Six reels of film shot, pretty good reels, half the film done, three hundred thousand dollars down the drain, hail and farewell. Out of the window all the jobs. Who feeds the starving mouths of boys and girls? Who will face the stockholders? Who chucks the Bank of America under the chin? Anyone for Russian roulette?"

He turned to watch Terwilliger snap the locks on a briefcase.

"What hath God wrought?"

Terwilliger, looking down at his hands, turning them over to examine their texture, said, "I didn't know I was doing it, I swear. It came out in my fingers. It was all subconscious. My fingers do everything for me. They did *this*."

"Better the fingers had come in my office and taken me direct by the throat," said Glass. "I was never one for slow motion. The Keystone Cops, at triple speed, was my idea of living, or dying. To think a rubber monster has stepped on us all. We are now so much tomato mush, ripe for canning!"

"Don't make me feel any guiltier than I feel," said Terwilliger.

"What do you want, I should take you dancing?"

"It's just," cried Terwilliger. "He kept at me. Do this. Do that. Do it the other way. Turn it inside out, upside down, he said. I swallowed my bile. I was angry all the time. Without knowing, I must've changed the face. But right up till five minutes ago, when Mr. Clarence yelled, I didn't see it. I'll take all the blame."

"No," sighed Mr. Glass, "we should *all* have seen. Maybe we did and couldn't admit. Maybe we did and laughed all night in our sleep, when we couldn't hear. So where are we now? Mr. Clarence, he's got investments he can't throw out. You got your career from this day forward, for better or worse, you can't throw out. Mr. Clarence right now is aching to be convinced it was all some horrible dream. Part of his ache, ninety-nine per cent, is in his wallet. If you could put one per cent of your time in the next hour convincing him of what I'm going to tell you next, tomorrow morning there will be no orphan children staring out of the want ads in *Variety* and the *Hollywood Reporter*. If you would go tell him—"

"Tell me *what?*"

Joe Clarence, returned, stood in the door, his cheeks still inflamed.

"What he just told me." Mr. Glass turned calmly. "A touching story."

"I'm listening!" said Clarence.

"Mr. Clarence." The old lawyer weighed his words carefully. "This film you just saw is Mr. Terwilliger's solemn and silent tribute to you."

"It's *what?*" shouted Clarence.

Both men, Clarence and Terwilliger, dropped their jaws.

The old lawyer gazed only at the wall and in a shy voice said, "Shall I go on?"

The animator closed his jaw. "If you want to."

"This film—" the lawyer arose and pointed in a single motion towards the projection room— "was done from a feeling of honor and friendship for you, Joe Clarence. Behind your desk, an unsung hero of the motion picture industry, unknown, unseen, you sweat out your lonely little life while who gets the glory? The stars. How often does a man in Atawanda Springs, Idaho, tell his wife, 'Say, I was thinking the other night about Joe Clarence—a great producer, that man?' How often? Should I tell? Never! So Terwilliger brooded. How could he present the real Clarence to the world? The dinosaur is there; boom! It hits him! This is it! he thought, the very thing to strike terror to the world, here's a lonely, proud, wonderful, awful symbol of independence, power, strength, shrewd animal cunning, the true democrat, the individual brought to its peak, all thunder and big lightning. Dinosaur: Joe Clarence. Joe Clarence: Dinosaur. Man embodied in Tyrant Lizard!"

Mr. Glass sat down, panting quietly.

Terwilliger said nothing.

Clarence moved at last, walked across the room, circled Glass slowly, then came to stand in front of Terwilliger, his face pale. His eyes were uneasy, shifting up along Terwilliger's tall skeleton frame.

"You said *that*?" he asked faintly.

Terwilliger swallowed.

"To me he said it. He's shy," said Mr. Glass. "You ever hear him say much, ever talk back, swear? Anything? He likes people, he can't say. But, immortalize them? That he can do!"

"Immortalize?" said Clarence.

"What else?" said the old man. "Like a statue, only moving. Years from now people will say, 'Remember that film, *The Monster from the Pleistocene*?' And people will say, 'Sure! why?' 'Because,' the others say, 'it was the one monster, the one brute, in all Hollywood history had real guts, real personality. And why is this? Because one genius had enough imagination to base the creature on a real-life, hard-hitting, fast-thinking businessman of A-one caliber.' You're one with history, Mr. Clarence. Film libraries will carry you in good supply. Cinema societies will ask for you. How lucky can you get? Nothing like this will ever happen to Immanuel Glass, a lawyer. Every day for the next two hundred, five hundred years, you'll be starring somewhere in the world!"

"*Every* day?" asked Clarence softly. "For the next—"

"Eight hundred, even; why not?"

"I never thought of that."

"Think of it!"

Clarence walked over to the window and looked out at the Hollywood Hills, and nodded at last.

"My God, Terwilliger," he said. "You really like me *that* much?"

"It's hard to put in words," said Terwilliger, with difficulty.

"So do we finish the mighty spectacle?" asked Glass. "Starring the tyrant terror striding the earth and making all quake before him, none other than Mr. Joseph J. Clarence?"

"Yeah. Sure." Clarence wandered off, stunned, to the door, where he said, "You know? I always *wanted* to be an actor!"

Then he went quietly out into the hall and shut the door.

Terwilliger and Glass collided at the desk, both clawing at a drawer.

"Age before beauty," said the lawyer, and quickly pulled forth a bottle of whisky.

At midnight on the night of the first preview of *Monster from the Stone Age*, Mr. Glass came back to the studio, where everyone was gathering for a celebration, and found Terwilliger seated alone in his office, his dinosaur on his lap.

"You weren't *there*?" asked Mr. Glass.

"I couldn't face it. Was there a riot?"

"A riot? The preview cards are all superdandy extra plus! A lovelier monster nobody saw before! So now we're talking sequels! Joe Clarence as the Tyrant Lizard in *Return of the Stone Age Monster*, Joe Clarence and/or Tyrannosaurus Rex in, maybe, *Beast from the Old Country*—"

The phone rang. Terwilliger got it.

"Terwilliger, this is Clarence! Be there in five minutes! We've done it! Your animal! Great! Is he mine now? I mean, to hell with the contract, as a favor, can I have him for the mantel?"

"Mr. Clarence, the monster's yours."

"Better than an Oscar! So long!"

Terwilliger stared at the dead phone.

"God bless us all, said Tiny Tim. He's laughing, almost hysterical with relief."

"So maybe I know why," said Mr. Glass. "A little girl, after the preview, asked him for an autograph."

"An *autograph*?"

"Right there in the street. Made him sign. First autograph he ever gave in his life. He laughed all the while he wrote his name. Somebody knew him. There he was, in front of the theater, big as life. Rex Himself, so sign the name. So he did."

"Wait a minute," said Terwilliger slowly, pouring drinks. "That little girl . . . ?"

"My youngest daughter," said Glass. "So who knows? And who will tell?"

They drank.

"Not me," said Terwilliger.

Then, carrying the rubber dinosaur between them, and bringing the whisky, they went to stand by the studio gate, waiting for the limousines to arrive all lights, horns and annunciations.

The Plot is the Thing

BY ROBERT BLOCH

Robert Bloch became inextricably bound-up with Hollywood after creating one of its most famous thriller films—Alfred Hitchcock's Psycho. *Bloch's interest in pictures, however, goes right back to his childhood when he was introduced to the world of the macabre in a cinema seat watching Lon Chaney in* The Phantom of the Opera. *Inspired—not to say a little scared—by the story, he took to writing horror stories and after a string of successes in weird and fantasy magazines finally graduated through radio shows and T.V. to scripting for film companies. In recent years he has penned a number of horror films, numerous screen adaptations of Edgar Allan Poe stories and condensed a series of his own tales into a grim shocker,* Torture Garden. *He is himself at present working on a collection of stories about the Hollywood "nightmare".*

When they broke into the apartment, they found her sitting in front of the television set, watching an old movie.

Peggy couldn't understand why they made such a fuss about that. She liked to watch old movies—the Late Show, the Late, Late Show, even the All Night Show. That was really the best, because they generally ran the horror pictures. Peggy tried to explain this to them, but they kept prowling around the apartment, looking at the dust on the furniture and the dirty sheets on the unmade bed. Somebody said there was green mould on the dishes in the sink; it's true she hadn't bothered to wash them for quite a long time, but then she hadn't eaten for several days, either.

It wasn't as though she didn't have any money; she told them about the bank accounts. But shopping and cooking and housekeeping was just too much trouble, and besides, she really didn't like going outside and seeing all those *people*. So if she preferred watching TV, that was her business, wasn't it?

They just looked at each other and shook their heads and made some phone calls. And then the ambulance came, and they helped her dress. Helped her? They practically *forced* her.

In the end it didn't do any good, and by the time she realized where they were taking her it was too late.

At first they were very nice to her at the hospital, but they kept asking those idiotic questions. When she said she had no relatives or friends they wouldn't believe her, and when they checked and found out it was true it only made things worse. Peggy got angry and said she was going home, and it all ended with a hypo in the arm.

There were lots of hypos after that, and in between times this Dr. Crane kept after her. He was one of the heads of staff and at first Peggy liked him, but not when he began to pry.

She tried to explain to him that she'd always been a loner, even before her parents died. And she told him there was no reason for her to work, with all that money. Somehow, he got it out of her about how she used to keep going to the movies, at least one every day, only she liked horror pictures and of course there weren't quite that many, so after a while she just watched them on TV. Because it was easier, and you didn't have to go home along dark streets after seeing something frightening. At home she could lock herself in, and as long as she had the television going she didn't feel lonely. Besides, she could watch movies all night, and this helped her insomnia. Sometimes the old pictures were pretty gruesome and this made her nervous, but she felt more nervous when she didn't watch. Because in the movies, no matter how horrible things seemed for the heroine, she was always rescued in the end. And that was better than the way things generally worked out in real life, wasn't it?

Dr. Crane didn't think so. And he wouldn't let her have any television in her room now, either. He kept talking to Peggy about the need to face reality, and the dangers of retreating into a fantasy world and identifying with frightened heroines. The way he made it sound, you'd think she *wanted* to be menaced, *wanted* to be killed, or even raped.

And when he started all that nonsense about a "nervous disorder" and told her about his plans for treatment, Peggy knew she had to escape. Only she never got a chance. Before she realized it, they had arranged for the lobotomy.

Peggy knew what a lobotomy was, of course. And she was afraid of it, because it meant tampering with the brain. She remembered some mad doctor—Lionel Atwill, or George Zucco?—saying that by tampering with the secrets of the human brain one can change reality. "There are some things we were not meant to know," he had whispered. But that, of course, was in a movie. And Dr. Crane wasn't mad. *She* was the mad one. Or was she? He certainly looked insane— she kept trying to break free after they strapped her down and he came after her—she remembered the way everything gleamed. His eyes, and the long needle. The long needle, probing into her brain to change reality—

The funny thing was, when she woke up she felt fine. "I'm like a different person, Doctor."

And it was true. No more jitters; she was perfectly calm. And she wanted to eat, and she didn't have insomnia, and she could dress herself and talk to the nurses, even kid around with them. The big thing was that she didn't worry about watching television any more. She could scarcely remember any of those old movies that had disturbed her. Peggy wasn't a bit disturbed now. And even Dr. Crane knew it.

At the end of the second week he was willing to let her go home. They had a little chat, and he complimented her on how well she was doing, asking her about her plans for the future. When Peggy admitted she hadn't figured anything out yet, Dr. Crane suggested she take a trip. She promised to think it over.

But it wasn't until she got back to the apartment that Peggy made up her mind. The place was a mess. The moment she walked in she knew she couldn't stand it. All that dirt and grime and squalor—it was like a movie set, really, with clothes scattered everywhere and dishes piled in the sink. Peggy decided right then and there she'd take a vacation. Around the world, maybe. Why not? She had the money. And it would be interesting to see all the *real* things she'd seen represented on the screen all these years.

So Peggy dissolved into a travel agency and montaged into shopping and packing and faded out to London.

Strange, she didn't think of it in that way at the time. But looking back, she began to realize that this is the way things seemed to happen. She'd come to a decision, to go somewhere and do something, and all of a sudden she'd find herself in another setting—just like in a movie, where they cut from scene to scene. When she first became aware of it she was a little worried; perhaps she was having blackouts. After all, her brain *had* been tampered with. But there was nothing really alarming about the little mental blanks. In a way they were very convenient, just like in the movies; you don't particularly want to waste time watching the heroine brush her teeth or pack her clothing or put on cosmetics. The plot is the thing. That's what's *real*.

And everything was real, now. No more uncertainty. Peggy could admit to herself that before the operation there had been times when she wasn't quite sure about things; sometimes what she saw on the screen was more convincing than the dull grey fog which seemed to surround her in daily life.

But that was gone, now. Whatever that needle had done, it had managed to pierce the fog. Everything was very clear, very sharp and definite, like good black and white camera work. And she herself felt so much more capable and confident. She was well-dressed, well-groomed, attractive again. The extras moved along the streets in an orderly fashion and didn't bother her. And the bit players spoke their lines crisply, performed their functions, and got out of the scene. Odd that she should think of them that way—they weren't "bit players" at all; just travel clerks and waiters and stewards and then, at the hotel, bellboys and maids. They seemed to fade in and out of the picture on cue. All smiles, like in the early part of a good horror movie, where at first everything seems bright and cheerful.

Paris was where things started to go wrong. This guide—a sort of Eduardo Cianelli type, in fact he looked to be an almost dead ringer for Cianelli as he was many years ago—was showing her through the Opera House. He happened to mention something about the catacombs, and that rang a bell.

She thought about Erik. That was his name, Erik—The Phantom of the Opera. *He* had lived in the catacombs underneath the Opera House. Of course, it was only a picture, but she thought perhaps the guide would know about it and she mentioned Erik's name as a sort of joke.

That's when the guide turned pale and began to tremble. And then he ran. Just ran off and left her standing there.

Peggy knew something was wrong, then. The scene just seemed to dissolve—that part didn't worry her, it was just another one of those temporary blackouts she was getting used to—and when Peggy gained awareness, she was in this bookstore asking a clerk about Gaston Leroux.

And this was what frightened her. She remembered distinctly that *The Phantom of the Opera* had been written by Gaston Leroux, but here was this French bookstore clerk telling her there was no such author.

That's what they said when she called the library. No such author —and no such book. Peggy opened her mouth, but the scene was already dissolving. . . .

In Germany she rented a car, and she was enjoying the scenery when she came to this burned mill and the ruins of the castle beyond. She knew where she was, of course, but it couldn't be—not until she got out of the car, moved up to the great door, and in the waning sun of twilight, read the engraved legend on the stone. *Frankenstein*.

There was a faint sound from behind the door, a sound of muffled, dragging footsteps, moving closer. Peggy screamed, and ran. . . .

Now she knew where she was running to. Perhaps she'd find safety behind the Iron Curtain. Instead there was another castle, and she heard the howling of a wolf in the distance, saw the bat swoop from the shadows as she fled.

And in an English library in Prague, Peggy searched the volumes of the library biography. There was no listing for Mary Wollstone-craft Shelley, none for Bram Stoker.

Of course not. There wouldn't be, in a *movie* world, because when the characters are real, their "authors" do not exist.

Peggy remembered the way Larry Talbot had changed before her eyes, metamorphizing into the howling wolf. She remembered the sly purr of the Count's voice, saying, "I do not drink—wine." And she shuddered, and longed to be far away from the super-stitious peasantry who draped wolfbane outside their windows at night.

She needed the reassurance of sanity in an English-speaking country. She'd go to London, see a doctor immediately.

Then she remembered what was *in* London. Another werewolf. And Mr. Hyde. And the Ripper. . . .

Peggy fled through a fadeout, back to Paris. She found the name of a psychiatrist, made her appointment. She was perfectly prepared to face her problem now, perfectly prepared to face reality.

But she was not prepared to face the baldheaded little man with the sinister accent and the bulging eyes. She knew him—Dr. Gogol, in *Mad Love*. She also knew Peter Lorre had passed on, knew *Mad Love* was only a movie, made the year she was born. But that was in another country, and besides, the wench was dead.

The wench was dead, but Peggy was alive. "*I am a stranger and afraid, in a world I never made.*" Or had she made this world? She wasn't sure. All she knew was that she had to escape.

Where? It couldn't be Egypt, because that's where *he* would be—the wrinkled, hideous image of the Mummy superimposed itself momentarily. The Orient? What about Fu Manchu?

Back to America, then? Home is where the heart is—but there'd be a knife waiting for that heart when the shower curtains were ripped aside and the creature of *Psycho* screamed and slashed. . . .

Somehow she managed to remember a haven, born in other films. The South Seas—Dorothy Lamour, John Hall, the friendly natives in the tropical paradise. There *was* escape.

Peggy boarded the ship in Marseilles. It was a tramp steamer but the cast—crew, rather—was reassuringly small. At first she spent most of her time below deck, huddled in her berth. Oddly enough, it was getting to be like it had been *before*. Before the operation, that is, before the needle bit into her brain, twisting it, or distorting the world. *Changing reality,* as Lionel Atwill had put it. She should have listened to them—Atwill, Zucco, Basil Rathbone, Edward Van Sloan, John Carradine. They may have been a little mad, but they were good doctors, dedicated scientists. They meant well. "There are some things we were not meant to know."

When they reached the tropics, Peggy felt much better. She regained her appetite, prowled the deck, went into the galley and joked with the Chinese cook. The crew seemed aloof, but they all treated her with the greatest respect. She began to realize she'd done the right thing—this *was* escape. And the warm scent of tropic nights beguiled her. From now on, this would be her life; drifting through nameless, uncharted seas, safe from the role of heroine with all its haunting and horror.

It was hard to believe she'd been so frightened. There were no phantoms, no werewolves in this world. Perhaps she didn't need a doctor. She was facing reality, and it was pleasant enough. There were no movies here, no television; her fears were all part of a long-forgotten nightmare.

One evening, after dinner, Peggy returned to her cabin with something nagging at the back of her brain. The captain had put in one of his infrequent appearances at the table, and he kept looking at her all through the meal. Something about the way he squinted at her was disturbing. Those little pig-eyes of his reminded her of someone. Noah Beery? Stanley Fields?

She kept trying to remember, and at the same time she was dozing off. Dozing off much too quickly. Had her food been drugged?

Peggy tried to sit up. Through the porthole she caught a reeling glimpse of land beyond, but then everything began to whirl and it was too late. . . .

When she awoke she was already on the island, and the woolly-headed savages were dragging her through the gate, howling and waving their spears.

They tied her and left her and then Peggy heard the chanting. She looked up and saw the huge shadow. Then she knew where she was and what *it* was, and she screamed.

Even over her own screams she could hear the natives chanting, just one word, over and over again. It sounded like, "Kong."

The Shadow on the Screen

BY HENRY KUTTNER

Henry Kuttner had the right kind of start for a career as a script-writer, being born in Hollywood. In the grand tradition, he began his writing in the pages of fantasy and science fiction magazines and then made his big break-through with a series of novelettes about the film industry of the future. Kuttner and his wife Catherine Moore—another highly skilled and imaginative writer of science fiction—both worked on film and T.V. scripts—including an abortive attempt by Warner Brothers to film Nathaniel Hawthorne's weird tale Rappaccini's Daughter. *Sadly the promise they displayed of becoming one of the most successful husband-and-wife writing teams was destroyed by Henry's death after a heart attack in 1958.*

Torture Master was being given a sneak preview at a Beverly Hills theatre. Somehow, when my credit line, "Directed by Peter Haviland," was flashed on the screen, a little chill of apprehension shook me, despite the applause that came from a receptive audience. When you've been in the picture game for a long time you get these hunches; I've often spotted a dud movie before a hundred feet have been reeled off. Yet *Torture Master* was no worse than a dozen similar films I'd handled in the past few years.

But it was formula, box-office formula. I could see that. The star was all right; the make-up department had done a good job; the dialogue was unusually smooth. Yet the film was obviously box-office, and not the sort of film I'd have liked to direct.

After watching a reel unwind amid an encouraging scattering of

43

applause, I got up and went to the lobby. Some of the gang from Summit Pictures were lounging there, smoking and commenting on the picture. Ann Howard, who played the heroine in *Torture Master,* noticed my scowl and pulled me into a corner. She was that rare type, a girl who will screen well without all of that greasepaint that makes you look like an animated corpse. She was small, and her hair and eyes and skin were brown—I'd like to have seen her play *Peter Pan.* That type, you know.

I had occasionally proposed to her, but she never took me seriously. As a matter of fact, I myself didn't know how serious I was about it. Now she led me into the bar and ordered drinks.

"Don't look so miserable, Pete," she said over the rim of her glass. "The picture's going over. It'll gross enough to suit the boss, and it won't hurt my reputation."

Well, that was right. Ann had a fat part, and she'd made the most of it. And the picture would be good box-office; Universal's *Night Key,* with Karloff, had been released a few months ago, and the audiences were ripe for another horror picture.

"I know," I told her, signaling the bartender to refill my glass. "But I get tired of these damn hokumy pics. Lord, how I'd like to do another *Cabinet of Doctor Caligari!*"

"Or another *Ape of God,*" Ann suggested.

I shrugged. "Even that, maybe. There's so much chance for development of the weird on the screen, Ann—and no producer will stand for a genuinely good picture of that type. They call it arty, and say it'll flop. If I branched out on my own—well, Hecht and MacArthur tried it, and they're back on the Hollywood payroll now."

Someone Ann knew came up and engaged her in conversation. I saw a man beckoning, and with a hasty apology left Ann to join him. It was Andy Worth, Hollywood's dirtiest columnist. I knew him for a double-crosser and a skunk, but I also knew that he could get more inside information than a brace of Winchells. He was a short, fat chap with a meticulously cultivated moustache and sleekly pomaded black hair. Worth fancied himself as a ladies' man, and spent a great deal of his time trying to blackmail actresses into having affairs with him.

That didn't make him a villain, of course. I like anybody who can carry on an intelligent conversation for ten minutes, and Worth could do that. He fingered his mustache and said, "I heard you talking about *Ape of God*. A coincidence, Pete."

"Yeah?" I was cautious. I had to be, with this walking scandal-sheet. "How's that?"

He took a deep breath. "Well, you understand that I haven't got the real lowdown, and it's all hearsay—but I've found a picture that'll make the weirdest movie ever canned look sick."

I suspected a gag. "Okay, what is it? *Torture Master*?"

"Eh? No—though Blake's yarn deserved better adaptation than your boys gave it. No, Pete, the one I'm talking about isn't for general release—isn't completed, in fact. I saw a few rushes of it. A one-man affair; title's *The Nameless*. Arnold Keene's doing it."

Worth sat back and watched how I took that. And I must have shown my amazement. For it was Arnold Keene who had directed the notorious *Ape of God*, which had wrecked his promising career in films. The public doesn't know that picture. It never was released. Summit junked it. And they had good cause, although it was one of the most amazingly effective weird films I've ever seen. Keene had shot most of it down in Mexico, and he'd been able to assume virtual dictatorship of the location troupe. Several Mexicans had died at the time, and there had been some ugly rumors, but it had all been hushed up. I'd talked with several people who had been down near Taxco with Keene, and they spoke of the man with peculiar horror. He had been willing to sacrifice almost anything to make *Ape of God* a masterpiece of its type.

It was an unusual picture—there was no question about that. There's only one master print of the film, and it's kept in a locked vault at Summit. Very few have seen it. For what Machen had done in weird literature, Keene had done on the screen—and it was literally amazing.

I said to Worth, "Arnold Keene, eh? I've always had a sneaking sympathy for the man. But I thought he'd died long ago."

"Oh, no. He bought a place near Tujunga and went into hiding.

He didn't have much dough after the blow-up, you know, and it took him about five years to get together enough *dinero* to start his *Nameless*. He always said *Ape of God* was a failure, and that he intended to do a film that would be a masterpiece of weirdness. Well, he's done it. He's canned a film that's—unearthly. I tell you it made my flesh creep."

"Who's the star?" I asked.

"Unknowns. Russian trick, you know. The real star is a—a shadow."

I stared at him.

"That's right, Pete. The shadow of something that's never shown on the screen. Doesn't sound like much, eh? But you ought to see it!"

"I'd like to," I told him. "In fact, I'll do just that. Maybe he'll release it through Summit."

Worth chuckled. "No chance. No studio would release that movie. I'm not even going to play it up in my column. This is the real McCoy, Pete."

"What's Keene's address?" I asked.

Worth gave it to me. "But don't go out till Wednesday night," he said. "The rough prints will be ready then, or most of them. And keep it under your hat, of course."

A group of autograph hunters came up just then, and Worth and I were separated. It didn't matter. I'd got all the information I needed. My mind was seething with fantastic surmises. Keene was one of the great geniuses of the screen, and his talent lay in the direction of the macabre. Unlike book publishers, the studios catered to no small, discriminating audiences. A film must suit everybody.

Finally I broke away and took Ann to a dance at Bel-Air. But I hadn't forgotten Keene, and the next night I was too impatient to wait. I telephoned Worth, but he was out. Oddly enough, I was unable to get in touch with him during the next few days; even his paper couldn't help me. A furious editor told me the Associated Press had been sending him hourly telegrams asking for Worth's copy; but the man had vanished completely. I had a hunch.

It was Tuesday night when I drove out of the studio and took a short cut through Griffith Park, past the Planetarium, to Glendale. From there I went on to Tujunga, to the address Worth had given me. Once or twice I had an uneasy suspicion that a black coupé was trailing me, but I couldn't be sure.

Arnold Keene's house was in a little canyon hidden back in the Tujunga mountains. I had to follow a winding dirt road for several miles, and ford a stream or two, before I reached it. The place was built against the side of the canyon, and a man stood on the porch and watched me as I braked my car to a stop.

It was Arnold Keene. I recognized him immediately. He was a slender man under middle height, with a closely cropped bristle of grey hair; his face was coldly austere. There had been a rumor that Keene had at one time been an officer in Prussia before he came to Hollywood and Americanized his name, and, scrutinizing him, I could well believe it. His eyes were like pale blue marbles, curiously shallow.

He said, "Peter Haviland? I did not expect you until tomorrow night."

I shook hands. "Sorry if I intrude," I apologized. "The fact is, I got impatient after what Worth told me about your film. He isn't here, by any chance?"

The shallow eyes were unreadable. "No. But come in. Luckily, the developing took less time that I had anticipated. I need only a few more shots to complete my task."

He ushered me into the house, which was thoroughly modern and comfortably furnished. Under the influence of good cognac my suspicions began to dissolve. I told Keene I had always admired his *Ape of God*.

He made a wry grimace. "Amateurish, Haviland. I depended too much on hokum in that film. Merely devil-worship, a reincarnated Gilles de Rais, and sadism. That isn't true weirdness."

I was interested. "That's correct. But the film had genuine power—"

"Man has nothing of the weird in him intrinsically. It is only the hints of the utterly abnormal and unhuman that give one the true feeling of weirdness. That, and human reactions to such supernatural phenomena. Look at any great weird work—*The Horla*, which tells of a man's reaction to a creature utterly alien, Blackwood's *Willows*, Machen's *Black Seal*, Lovecraft's *Color Out of Space*—all these deal with the absolutely alien influencing normal lives. Sadism and death may contribute, but alone they cannot produce the true, intangible atmosphere of weirdness."

I had read all these tales. "But you can't film the indescribable. How could you show the invisible beings of *The Willows*?"

Keene hesitated. "I think I'll let my film answer that. I have a projection room downstairs—"

The bell rang sharply. I could not help noticing the quick glance Keene darted at me. With an apologetic gesture he went out and presently returned with Ann Howard at his side. She was smiling rather shakily.

"Did you forget our date, Pete?" she asked me.

I blinked, and suddenly remembered. Two weeks ago I had promised to take Ann to an affair in Laguna Beach this evening, but in my preoccupation with Keene's picture the date had slipped my mind. I stammered apologies.

"Oh, that's all right," she broke in. "I'd much rather stay here— that is, if Mr. Keene doesn't mind. His picture—"

"You know about it?"

"I told her," Keene said. "When she explained why she had come, I took the liberty of inviting her to stay to watch the film. I did not want her to drag you away, you see," he finished, smiling. "Some cognac for Miss—eh?"

I introduced them.

"For Miss Howard, and then *The Nameless*."

At his words a tiny warning note seemed to throb in my brain. I had been fingering a heavy metal paperweight, and now, as Keene's attention was momentarily diverted to the sideboard, I slipped it, on a sudden impulse, into my pocket. It would be no defense, though, against a gun.

What was wrong with me, I wondered? An atmosphere of distrust and suspicion seemed to have sprung out of nothing. As Keene ushered us down into his projection room, the skin of my back seemed to crawl with the expectation of attack. It was inexplicable, but definitely unpleasant.

Keene was busy for a time in the projection booth, and then he joined us.

"Modern machinery is a blessing," he said with heavy jocularity. "I can be as lazy as I wish. I needed no help with the shooting, once the automatic cameras were installed. The projector, too, is automatic."

I felt Ann move closer to me in the gloom. I put my arm around her and said, "It helps, yes. What about releasing the picture, Mr. Keene?"

There was a harsh note in his voice. "It will not be released. The world is uneducated, not ready for it. In a hundred years, perhaps, it will achieve the fame it deserves. I am doing it for posterity, and for the sake of creating a weird masterpiece on the screen."

With a muffled click the projector began to operate, and a title flashed on the screen: *The Nameless.*

Keene's voice came out of the darkness. "It's a silent film, except for one sequence at the start. Sound adds nothing to weirdness, and it helps to destroy the illusion of reality. Later, suitable music will be dubbed in."

I did not answer. For a book had flashed on the gray oblong before us—that amazing tour de force, *The Circus of Doctor Lao.* A hand opened it, and a long finger followed the lines as a toneless voice read:

"These are the sports, the offthrows of the universe instead of the species; these are the weird children of the lust of the spheres. Mysticism explains them where science cannot. Listen: when that great mysterious fecundity that peopled the worlds at the command of the gods had done with its birth-giving, when the celestial midwives all had left, when life had begun in the universe, the primal womb-thing found itself still unexhausted, its loins still potent. So that awful fertility tossed on its couch in a final fierce outbreak of life-giving and gave birth to these nightmare beings, these abortions of the world."

The voice ceased. The book faded, and there swam into view a mass of tumbled ruins. The ages had pitted the man-carved rocks with cracks and scars; the bas-relief figures were scarcely recognizable. I was reminded of certain ruins I had seen in Yucatan.

The camera swung down. The ruins seemed to grow larger. A yawning hole gaped in the earth.

Beside me Keene said, "The site of a ruined temple. Watch, now."

The effect was that of moving forward into the depths of a subterranean pit. For a moment the screen was in darkness; then a stray beam of sunlight rested on an idol that stood in what was apparently an underground cavern. A narrow crack of light showed in the roof. The idol was starkly hideous.

I got only a flashing glimpse, but the impression on my mind was that of a bulky, ovoid shape like a pineapple or a pine-cone. The thing had certain doubtful features which lent it a definitely unpleasant appearance; but it was gone in a flash, dissolving into a brightly lighted drawing-room, thronged with gay couples.

The story proper began at that point. None of the actors or actresses was known to me; Keene must have hired them and worked secretly in his house. Most of the interiors and a few of the exteriors seemed to have been taken in this very canyon. The director had used the "parallel" trick which saves so much money for studios yearly. I'd often done it myself. It simply means that the story is tied in with real life as closely as possible; that is, when I had a troupe working up at Lake Arrowhead last winter, and an unexpected snowfall changed the scene, I had the continuity rewritten so that the necessary scenes could take place in snow. Similarly, Keene had paralleled his own experiences—sometimes almost too closely.

The Nameless told of a man, ostracized by his fellows because of his fanatical passion for the morbid and bizarre, who determined to create a work of art—a living masterpiece of sheer weirdness. He had experimented before by directing films that were sufficiently unusual to stir up considerable comment. But this did not satisfy him. It was acting—and he wanted something more than that. No one can convincingly fake reaction to horror, not even the most talented actor, he contended. The genuine emotion must be felt in order to be transferred to the screen.

It was here that *The Nameless* ceased to parallel Keene's own experiences, and branched out into sheer fantasy. The protagonist in the film was Keene himself, but this was not unusual, as directors often act in their own productions. And, by deft montage shots, the audience learned that Keene in his search for authenticity had gone down into Mexico, and had, with the aid of an ancient scroll, found the site of a ruined Aztec temple. And here, as I say, reality was left behind as the film entered a morbid and extraordinary phase.

There was a god hidden beneath this ruined temple—a long-forgotten god, which had been worshipped even before the Aztecs had sprung from the womb of the centuries. At least, the natives had considered it a god, and had erected a temple in its honor, but Keene hinted that the thing was actually a survival, one of the "off-throws of the universe," unique and baroque, which had come down through the eons in an existence totally alien to mankind. The creature was never actually seen on the screen, save for a few brief glimpses in the shadowed, underground temple. It was roughly barrel-shaped, and perhaps ten feet high, studded with odd spiky projections. The chief feature was a gem set in the thing's rounded apex—a smoothly polished jewel as large as a child's head. It was in this gem that the being's life was supposed to have its focus.

It was not dead, but neither was it alive, in the accepted sense of that term. When the Aztecs had filled the temple with the hot stench of blood the thing had lived, and the jewel had flamed with unearthly radiance. But with the passage of time the sacrifices had ceased, and the being had sunk into a state of coma akin to hibernation. In the picture Keene brought it to life.

He transported it secretly to his home, and there, in an underground room hollowed beneath the house, he placed the monster-god. The room was built with an eye for the purpose for which Keene intended it; automatic cameras and clever lighting features were installed, so that pictures could be shot from several different angles at once, and pieced together later as Keene cut the film. And now there entered something of the touch of genius which had made Keene famous.

He was clever, I had always realized that. Yet in the scenes that were next unfolded I admired not so much the technical tricks—which were familiar enough to me—as the marvelously clever way in which Keene had managed to inject realism into the acting. His characters did not act—they *lived*.

Or, rather, they died. For in the picture they were thrust into the underground room to die horribly as sacrifices to the monster-god from the Aztec temple. Sacrifice was supposed to bring the thing to life, to cause the jewel in which its existence was bound to flare with fantastic splendor. The first sacrifice was, I think, the most effective.

The underground room in which the god was hidden was large, but quite vacant, save for a curtained alcove which held the idol. A barred doorway led to the upper room, and here Keene appeared on the screen, revolver in hand, herding before him a man—overall-clad, with a stubble of black beard on his stolid face. Keene swung open the door, motioned his captive into the great room. He closed the barred door, and through the grating could be seen busy at a switchboard.

Light flared. The man stood near the bars, and then, at Keene's gesture with his weapon, moved forward slowly to the far wall. He stood there, staring around vaguely, dull apprehension in his face. Light threw his shadow in bold relief on the wall.

The another shadow leaped into existence beside him.

It was barrel-shaped, gigantic, studded with blunt spikes, and capped by a round dark blob—the life-jewel. The shadow of the monster-god! The man saw it. He turned.

Stark horror sprang into his face, and at sight of that utterly ghastly and realistic expression a chill struck through me. This was almost too convincing. The man could not be merely acting.

But, if he was, his acting was superb, and so was Keene's direction. The shadow on the wall stirred, and a thrill of movement shook it. It rocked and seemed to rise, supported by a dozen tentacular appendages that uncoiled from beneath its base. The spikes—changed. They lengthened. They coiled and writhed, hideously worm-like.

It wasn't the metamorphosis of the shadow that held me motionless in my chair. Rather, it was the appalling expression of sheer horror on the man's face. He stood gaping as the shadow toppled and swayed on the wall, growing larger and larger. Then he fled, his mouth an open square of terror. The shadow paused, with an odd air of indecision, and slipped slowly along the wall out of range of the camera.

But there were other cameras, and Keene had used his cutting-shears deftly. The movements of the man were mirrored on the screen; the glaring lights swung and flared; and ever the grim shadow crawled hideously across the wall. The thing that cast it was never shown—just the shadow, and it was a dramatically effective trick. Too many directors, I knew, could not have resisted the temptation to show the monster, thus destroying the illusion—for papier-maché and rubber, no matter how cleverly constructed, cannot convincingly ape reality.

At last the shadows merged—the gigantic swaying thing with its coiling tentacles, and the black shadow of the man that was caught and lifted, struggling and kicking frantically. The shadows merged— and the man did not reappear. Only the dark blob capping the great shadow faded and flickered, as though strange light were streaming from it; the light that was fed by sacrifice, the jewel that was—life.

Beside me there came a rustle. I felt Ann stir and move closer in the gloom. Keene's voice came from some distance away.

"There were several more sacrifice scenes, Haviland, but I haven't patched them in yet, except for the one you'll see in a moment now. As I said, the film isn't finished."

I did not answer. My eyes were on the screen as the fantastic tale unfolded. The pictured Keene was bringing another victim to his cavern, a short, fat man with sleekly pomaded black hair. I did not see his face until he had been imprisoned in the cave, and then, abruptly there came a close-up shot, probably done with a telescopic lens. His plump face, with its tiny mustache, leaped into gigantic visibility, and I recognized Andy Worth.

It was the missing columnist, but for the first time I saw his veneer of sophistication lacking. Naked fear crawled in his eyes, and I leaned forward in my seat as the ghastly barrel-shaped shadow sprang out on the wall. Worth saw it, and the expression on his face was shocking. I pushed back my chair and got up as the lights came on. The screen went blank.

Arnold Keene was standing by the door, erect and military as ever. He had a gun in his hand, and its muzzle was aimed at my stomach.

"You had better sit down, Haviland," he said quietly. "You too, Miss Howard. I've something to tell you—and I don't wish to be melodramatic about it. This gun"—he glanced at it wryly—"is necessary. There are a few things you must know, Haviland, for a reason you'll understand later."

I said, "There'll be some visitors here for you soon, Keene. You don't think I'd neglect normal precautions!"

He shrugged. "You're lying, of course. Also you're unarmed, or you'd have had your gun out by now. I didn't expect you until tomorrow night, but I'm prepared. In a word, what I have to tell you is this: the film you just saw is a record of actual events."

Ann's teeth sank into her lip, but I didn't say anything. I waited, and Keene resumed.

"Whether you believe me or not doesn't matter, for you'll have to believe in a few minutes. I told you something of my motive, my desire to create a genuine masterpiece of weirdness. That's what I've done, or will have done before tomorrow. Quite a number of vagrants and laborers have disappeared, and the columnist, Worth, as well; but I took care to leave no clues. You'll be the last to vanish—you and this girl."

"You'll never be able to show the film," I told him.

"What of it? You're a hack, Haviland, and you can't understand what it means to create a masterpiece. Is a work of art any less beautiful because it's hidden? I'll see the picture—and after I'm dead the world will see it, and realize my genius even though they may fear and hate its expression. The reactions of my unwilling actors—that's the trick. As a director, you should know that there's no substitute for realism. The reactions were not faked—that was obvious enough. The first sacrifice was that of a clod—an unintelligent moron, whose fears were largely superstitious. The next sacrifice was of a higher type—a vagrant who came begging to my door some mont is ago. You will complete the group, for you'll know just what you're facing, and your attempt to rationalize your fear will lend an interesting touch. Both of you will stand up, with your hands in the air, and precede me into this passage."

All this came out tonelessly and swiftly, quite as though it were a rehearsed speech. His hand slid over the wall beside him, and a black oblong widened in the oak paneling. I stood up.

"Do as he says, Ann," I said. "Maybe I can—"

"No, you can't," Keene interrupted, gesturing impatiently with his weapon. "You won't have the chance. Hurry up."

We went through the opening in the wall and Keene followed, touching a stud that flooded the passage with light. It was a narrow tunnel that slanted down through solid rock for perhaps ten feet to a steep stairway. He herded us down this, after sliding the panel shut.

"It's well hidden," he said, indicating metal sheathing—indeed, the entire corridor was lined with metal plates. "This lever opens it from within, but no one but me can find the spring which opens it from without. The police could wreck the house without discovering this passage."

That seemed worth remembering, but of little practical value at the moment. Ann and I went down the stairway until it ended in another short passage. Our way was blocked by a door of steel bars, which Keene unlocked with a key he took from his pocket. The passage where we stood was dimly lighted; there were several chairs here; and the space beyond the barred door was not lighted at all.

Keene opened the door and gestured me through it. He locked it behind me and turned to Ann. Her face, I saw, was paper-white in the pale glow.

What happened after that brought an angry curse to my lips. Without warning Keene swung the automatic in a short, vicious arc, smashing it against Ann's head.

She saw it coming too late, and her upflung hand failed to ward off the blow. She dropped without a sound, a little trickle of blood oozing from her temple. Keene stepped over her body to a switchboard set in the rock wall.

Light lanced with intolerable brilliance into my eyes. I shut them tightly, opening them after a moment to stare around apprehensively. I recognized my surroundings. I was in the cave of sacrifice, the underground den I had seen on the screen. Cameras high up on the walls began to operate as I discovered them. From various points blinding arc-lights streamed down upon me.

A grey curtain shielded a space on the far wall, but this was drawn upward to reveal a deep alcove. There was an object within that niche —a barrel-shaped thing ten feet high, studded with spikes, and crowned with a jewel that pulsed and glittered with cold flame. It was grey and varnished-looking, and it was the original of Keene's Aztec god.

Somehow I felt oddly reassured as I examined the thing. It was a model, of course, inanimate and dead; for certainly no life of any kind could exist in such an abnormality. Keene might have installed machinery of some sort within it, however.

"You see, Haviland," Keene said from beyond the bars, "the thing actually exists. I got on the trail of it in an old parchment I found in the Huntington Library. It had been considered merely an interesting bit of folk-lore, but I saw something else in it. When I was making *Ape of God* in Mexico I discovered the ruined temple, and what lay forgotten behind the altar."

He touched a switch, and light streamed out from the alcove behind the thing. Swiftly I turned. On the wall behind me was my own shadow, grotesquely elongated, and beside it was the squat, amorphous patch of blackness I had seen on the screen upstairs.

My back was toward Keene, and my fingers crept into my pocket, touching the metal paperweight I had dropped there earlier that evening. Briefly I considered the possibility of hurling the thing at Keene, and then decided against it. The bars were too close together, and the man would shoot me at any sign of dangerous hostility.

My eyes were drawn to the shadow on the wall. It was moving.

It rocked slightly, and lifted. The spikes lengthened. The thing was no longer inanimate and dead, and as I swung about, stark amazement gripping me, I saw the incredible metamorphosis that had taken place in the thing that cast the shadow.

It was no longer barrel-shaped. A dozen smooth, glistening appendages, ending in flat pads, supported the snake-thin body. And all over that greyish upright pole tentacles sprouted and lengthened, writhing into ghastly life as the horror awakened. Keene had not lied, and the monstrous survival he had brought from the Aztec temple was lumbering from the alcove, its myriad tentacles alive with frightful hunger!

Keene saved me. He saw me standing motionless with abysmal fear in the path of that gigantic, nightmare being, and realizing that he was being cheated of his picture, the man shouted at me to run. His hoarse voice broke the spell that held me unmoving, and I whirled and fled across the cave to the barred door. Skin ripped from my hands as I tore at the bars.

"Run!" Keene yelled at me, his shallow eyes blazing. "It can't move fast! Look out—"

A writhing, snake-like thing lashed out, and a sickening musky stench filled my nostrils. I leaped away, racing across the cave again. The arc-lights died and others flared into being as Keene manipulated the switchboard. He was adjusting the lights, so that our shadows would not be lost—so that in the climax of *The Nameless* the shadow of that ghastly horror would be thrown on the cave wall beside me.

It was an infernal game of tag we played there, in those shifting lights that glared down while the camera lenses watched dispassionately. I fled and dodged with my pulses thundering and blood pounding in my temples, and ever the grim shadow moved slowly across the walls, while my legs began to ache with the strain. For hours, perhaps, or eons, I fled.

There would come brief periods of respite when I would cling to the bars, cursing Keene, but he would not answer. His hands flickered over the switchboard as he adjusted the arc-lights, and his eyes never paused in their roving examination of the cave. In the end it was this that saved me.

For Keene did not see Ann stir and open her eyes. He did not see the girl, after a swift glance around, get quietly to her feet. Luckily she was behind Keene, and he did not turn.

I tried to keep my eyes away from Ann, but I do not think I succeeded. At the last moment I saw Keene's face change, and he started back; but the chair in Ann's hands crashed down and splintered on the man's head. He fell to his knees, clawing at the air, and then collapsed inertly.

I was on the far side of the cave, and my attention was momentarily diverted from the monster. I had been watching it from the corner of my eye, expecting to be able to dodge and leap away before it came too close; but it lumbered forward with a sudden burst of speed. Although I tried to spring clear I failed; a tentacle whipped about my legs and sent me sprawling. As I tried to roll away another smooth grey coil got my left arm.

Intolerable agony dug into my shoulder as I was lifted. I heard Ann scream, and a gun barked angrily. Bullets plopped into the smooth flesh of the monster, but it paid no attention. I was lifted through a welter of coiling, ropy tentacles, until just above me was the flaming jewel in which the creature's life was centered.

Remembrance of Keene's words spurred me to action; this might be the monster's vulnerable point. The paperweight was still in my pocket, and I clawed it out desperately. I hurled it with all my strength at the shining gem. And the jewel shattered!

There came a shrill vibration, like the tinkling of countless tiny crystalline bells. Piercingly sweet, it shrilled in my ears, and died away quickly. And suddenly nothing existed but light.

It was as though the shattering of the gem had released a sea of incandescent flame imprisoned within it. The glare of the arc-lights faded beside this flood of silvery radiance that bathed me. The cold glory of Arcturus, the blaze of tropical moonlight, were in the light.

Swiftly it faded and fled away. I felt myself dropping, and pain lanced into my wrenched shoulder as I struck the ground. I heard Ann's voice.

Dazedly I got up, expecting to see the monster towering above me. But it was gone. In its place, a few feet away, was the barrel-shaped thing I had first seen in the alcove. There was a gaping cavity in the rounded apex where the jewel had been. And, somehow, I sensed that the creature was no longer deadly, no longer a horror.

I saw Ann. She was still holding Keene's gun, and in her other hand was the key with which she had unlocked the door. She came running toward me, and I went swiftly to meet her.

I took the gun and made sure it was loaded. "Come on," I said, curtly. "We're getting out of here."

Ann's fingers were gripping my arm tightly as we went through the door, past the prone figure of Keene, and up the stairway. The lever behind the panel was not difficult to operate, and I followed Ann through the opening into the theater. Then I paused, listening.

Ann turned, watching me, a question in her eyes. "What is it, Pete?"

"Listen," I said. "Get the cans of film from the projection booth. We'll take them with us and burn them."

"But—you're not—"

"I'll be with you in a minute," I told her, and swung the panel shut.

I went down the stairs swiftly and very quietly, my gun ready and my ears alert for the low muttering I had heard from below.

Keene was no longer unconscious. He was standing beside the switchboard with his back to me, and over his shoulder I could see the shadow of the monster-god sprawling on the wall, inert and lifeless. Keene was chanting something, in a language I did not know, and his hands were moving in strange gestures.

God knows what unearthly powers Keene had acquired in his search for horror! For as I stood there, watching the patch of blackness on the cave wall, I saw a little shudder rock that barrel-shaped shadow of horror, while a single spike abruptly lengthened into a tentacle that groped out furtively and drew back and vanished.

Then I killed Arnold Keene.

Return to the Sabbath

BY TARLETON FISKE

Tarleton Fiske is the pen-name of Robert Bloch, whose career has already been outlined earlier. The name was utilised by Bloch during his early writing years when editors would only accept a certain number of stories under his real name and to keep up the sales from his prodigious output he sought this other literary identity. This particular story, as Christopher Lee described in his introduction, has been made into a T.V. play by Alfred Hitchcock with Lee in the title role. It has also deservedly earned itself the stature of a minor classic in the horror story genre.

It's not the kind of story that the columnists like to print; it's not the yarn press-agents love to tell. When I was still in the Public Relations Department at the studio, they wouldn't let me break it. I know better than to try, for no paper would print such a tale.

We publicity men must present Hollywood as a gay place; a world of glamor and stardust. We capture only the light, but underneath the light there must always be shadows. I've always known that—it's been my job to gloss over those shadows for years—but the events of which I speak form a disturbing pattern too strange to be withheld. The shadow of these incidents is not *human.*

It's been the cursed weight of the whole affair that has proved my own mental undoing. That's why I resigned from the studio post, I guess. I wanted to forget, if I could. And now I know that the only way to relieve my mind is to tell the story. I must break the yarn, come what may. Then perhaps I can forget Karl Jorla's eyes. . . .

The affair dates back to one September evening almost three years ago. Les Kincaid and I were slumming down on Main Street in Los Angeles that night. Les is an assistant producer up at the studio, and there was some purpose in his visit; he was looking for authentic types to fill minor roles in a gangster film he was doing. Les was peculiar that way; he preferred the real article, rather than the Casting Bureau's ready-made imitations.

We'd been wandering around for some time, as I recall, past the great stone Chows that guard the narrow alleys of Chinatown, over through the tourist-trap that is Olvera Street, and back along the flophouses of lower Main. We walked by the cheap burlesque houses, eyeing the insolent Filipinos that sauntered past, and jostling our way through the usual Saturday night slumming parties.

We were both rather weary of it all. That's why, I suppose, the dingy little theatre appealed to us.

"Let's go in and sit down for a while," Les suggested. "I'm tired."

Even a Main Street burlesque show has seats in it, and I felt ready for a nap. The callipygy of the stage-attraction did not appeal to me, but I acceded to the suggestion and purchased our tickets.

We entered, sat down, suffered through two striptease dances, an incredibly ancient black-out sketch, and a "Grand Finale." Then, as is the custom in such places, the stage darkened and the screen flickered into life.

We got ready for our doze, then. The pictures shown in these houses are usually ancient specimens of the "quickie" variety; fillers provided to clear the house. As the first blaring notes of the sound-track heralded the title of the opus, I closed my eyes, slouched lower in my seat, and mentally beckoned to Morpheus.

I was jerked back to reality by a sharp dig in the ribs. Les was nudging me and whispering.

"Look at this," he murmured, prodding my reluctant body into wakefulness. "Ever see anything like it?"

I glanced up at the screen. What I expected to find I do not know, but I saw—*horror*.

There was a country graveyard, shadowed by ancient trees through which flickered rays of mildewed moonlight. It was an old graveyard, with rotting headstones set in grotesque angles as they leered up at the midnight sky.

The camera cut down on one grave, a fresh one. The music on the sound-track grew louder, in cursed climax. But I forgot camera and film as I watched. That grave was reality—hideous reality.

The grave was *moving!*

The earth beside the headstone was heaving and churning, as though it were being dug out. Not from above, but from *below*. It quaked upward ever so slowly; terribly. Little clods fell. The sod pulsed out in a steady stream and little rills of earth kept falling in the moonlight as though there were something clawing the dirt away . . . something clawing from beneath.

That something—it would soon appear. And I began to be afraid. I—I didn't want to see what it was. The clawing from below was not natural; it held a purpose not altogether *human*.

Yet I had to look. I had to see him—it—emerge. The sod cascaded in a mound, and then I was staring at the edge of the grave, looking down at the black hole that gaped like a corpse-mouth in the moonlight. Something was coming out.

Something slithered through that fissure, fumbled at the side of the opening. It clutched the ground above the grave, and in the baleful beams of that demon's moon I knew it to be a human hand. A thin, white human hand that held but half its flesh. The hand of a lich, a skeleton claw. . . .

A second talon gripped the other side of the excavation top. And now, slowly, insidiously, arms emerged. Naked, fleshless arms.

They crawled across the earth-sides like leprous white serpents. The arms of a cadaver, a rising cadaver. It was pulling itself up. And as *it* emerged, a cloud fell across the moon-path. The light faded to shadows as the bulky head and shoulders came into view. One could see nothing, and I was thankful.

But the cloud was falling away from the moon now. In a second the face would be revealed. The face of the thing from the grave, the resurrected visage of that which should be rotted in death—what would it be?

The shadows fell back. A figure rose out of the grave, and the face turned toward me. I looked and saw—

Well, you've been to "horror pictures." You know what one usually sees. The "ape-man," or the "maniac," or the "death's-head." The papier-mâché grotesquerie of the make-up artist. The "skull" of the dead.

I saw none of that. Instead, there was *horror*. It was the face of a child, I thought, at first; no, not a child, but a man with a child's soul. The face of a poet, perhaps, unwrinkled and calm. Long hair framed a high forehead; crescent eyebrows tilted over closed lids. The nose and mouth were thin and finely chiseled. Over the entire countenance was written an unearthly peace. It was as though the man were in a sleep of somnambulism or catelepsy. And then the face grew larger, the moonlight brighter, and I saw—more.

The sharper light disclosed tiny touches of evil. The thin lips were fretted, maggot-kissed. The nose had *crumbled* at the nostrils. The forehead was flaked with putrefaction, and the dark hair was dead, encrusted with slime. There were shadows in the bony ridges beneath the closed eyes. Even now, the skeletal arms were up, and bony fingers brushed at those dead pits as the rotted lids fluttered apart. The eyes opened.

They were wide, staring, flaming—and in them was the grave. They were eyes that had closed in death and opened in the coffin under earth. They were eyes that had seen the body rot and the soul depart to mingle in worm-ravened darkness below. They were eyes that held an alien life, a life so dreadful as to animate the cadaver's body and force it to claw its way back to outer earth. They were *hungry* eyes—triumphant, now, as they gazed in graveyard moonlight on a world they had never known before. They hungered for the world as only Death can hunger for Life. And they blazed out of the corpse-pallid face in icy joy.

Then the cadaver began to walk. It lurched between the graves, lumbered before ancient tombs. It shambled through the forest night until it reached a road. Then it turned up that road slowly . . . slowly.

And the hunger in those eyes flamed again as the lights of a city flared below. Death was preparing to mingle with men.

I sat through all this entranced. Only a few minutes had elapsed, but I felt as though uncounted ages had passed unheeded. The film went on. Les and I didn't exchange a word, but we watched.

The plot was rather routine after that. The dead man was a scientist whose wife had been stolen from him by a young doctor. The doctor had tended him in his last illness and unwittingly administered a powerful narcotic with cataleptic effects.

The dialogue was foreign and I could not place it. All of the actors were unfamiliar to me; and the setting and photography was quite unusual; unorthodox treatment as in *The Cabinet of Dr. Caligari* and other psychological films.

There was one scene where the living-dead man became enthroned as arch-priest at a Black Mass ceremonial, and there was a little child. . . . His eyes as he plunged the knife. . . .

He kept—*decaying* throughout the film . . . the Black Mass worshippers knew him as an emissary of Satan, and they kidnapped the wife as sacrifice for his own resurrection . . . the scene with the hysterical woman when she saw and recognized her husband for the first time, and the deep, evil whispering voice in which he revealed his secret to her . . . the final pursuit of the devil-worshippers to the great altar-stone in the mountains . . . the death of the resurrected one.

Almost a skeleton in fact now, riddled by bullets and shot from the weapons of the doctor and his neighbors, the dead one crumbled and fell from his seat on the altar-stone. And as those eyes glazed in second death the deep voice boomed out in a prayer to Sathanas. The lich crawled across the ground to the ritual fire, drew painfully erect, and tottered into the flames. And as it stood weaving for a moment in the blaze the lips moved again in infernal prayer, and the eyes implored not the skies, but the earth. The ground opened in a final flash of fire, and the charred corpse fell through. The Master claimed his own. . . .

It was grotesque, almost a fairy-tale in its triteness. When the film had flickered off and the orchestra blared the opening for the next "flesh-show" we rose in our seats, conscious once more of our surroundings. The rest of the mongrel audience seemed to be in a stupor almost equal to our own. Wide-eyed Japanese sat staring in the darkness; Filipinos muttered covertly to one another; even the drunken laborers seemed incapable of greeting the "Grand Opening" with their usual ribald hoots.

Trite and grotesque the plot of the film may have been, but the actor who played the lead had instilled it with ghastly reality. He *had* been dead; his eyes *knew*. And the voice was the voice of Lazarus awakened.

Les and I had no need to exchange words. We both felt it. I followed him silently as he went up the stairs to the manager's office.

Edward Relch was glowering over the desk. He showed no pleasure at seeing us barge in. When Les asked him where he had procured the film for this evening and what its name was, he opened his mouth and emitted a cascade of curses.

We learned that *Return to the Sabbath* had been sent over by a cheap agency from out Inglewood way, that a Western had been expected, and the "damned foreign junk" substituted by mistake. A hell of a picture this was, for a girl-show! Gave the audience the lousy creeps, and it wasn't even in English! Stinking imported films!

It was some time before we managed to extract the name of the agency from the manager's profane lips. But five minutes after that, Les Kincaid was on the phone speaking to the head of the agency; an hour later we were out at the office. The next morning Kincaid went in to see the big boss, and the following day I was told to announce for publication that Karl Jorla, the Austrian horror-star, had been signed by cable to our studio; and he was leaving at once for the United States.

I printed these items, gave all the build-up I could. But after the initial announcements I was stopped dead. Everything had happened too swiftly; we knew nothing about this man Jorla, really. Subsequent cables to Austrian and German studios failed to disclose any information about the fellow's private life. He had evidently never played in any film prior to *Return to the Sabbath*. He was utterly unknown. The film had never been shown widely abroad, and it was only by mistake that the Inglewood agency had obtained a copy and run it here in the United States. Audience reaction could not be learned, and the film was not scheduled for general release unless English titles could be dubbed in.

I was up a stump. Here we had the "find" of the year, and I couldn't get enough material out to make it known!

We expected Karl Jorla to arrive in two weeks, however. I was told to get to work on him as soon as he got in, then flood the news agencies with stories. Three of our best writers were working on a special production for him already; the Big Boss meant to handle it himself. It would be similar to the foreign film, for that "return from the dead" sequence must be included.

Jorla arrived on October seventh. He put up at a hotel; the studio sent down its usual welcoming committee, took him out to the lot for formal testing, then turned him over to me.

I met the man for the first time in the little dressing-room they had assigned him. I'll never forget that afternoon of our first meeting, or my first sight of him as I entered the door.

What I expected to see I don't know. But what I did see amazed me. For Karl Jorla was the dead-alive man of the screen *in life*.

The features were not fretted, of course. But he was tall, and almost as cadaverously thin as in his role; his face was pallid, and his eyes blue-circled. And the eyes were the dead eyes of the movie; the deep, *knowing* eyes!

The booming voice greeted me in hesitant English. Jorla smiled with his lips at my obvious discomfiture, but the expression of the eyes never varied in their alien strangeness.

Somewhat hesitantly I explained my office and my errand. "No pub-leecity," Jorla intoned. "I do not weesh to make known what is affairs of mine own doeeng."

I gave him the usual arguments. How much he understood I cannot say, but he was adamant. I learned only a little; that he had been born in Prague, lived in wealth until the upheavals of the European depression, and entered film work only to please a director friend of his. This director had made the picture in which Jorla played, for private showings only. By mischance a print had been released and copied for general circulation. It had all been a mistake. However, the American film offer had come opportunely, since Jorla wanted to leave Austria at once.

"After the feelm app-ear, I am in bad lights weeth my—friends," he explained, slowly. "They do not weesh it to be shown, that ceremonee."

"The Black Mass?" I asked. "Your *friends*?"

"Yes. The wor-ship of Lucifer. It was real, you know."

Was he joking? No—I couldn't doubt the man's sincerity. There was no room for mirth in those alien eyes. And then I knew what he meant, what he so casually revealed. He had been a devil-worshipper himself—he and that director. They had made the film and meant it for private display in their own occult circles. No wonder he sought to escape abroad!

It was incredible, save that I knew Europe, and the dark Northern mind. The worship of Evil continues today in Budapest, Prague, Berlin. And he, Karl Jorla the horror-actor, admitted to being one of them!

"What a story!" I thought. And then I realized that it could, of course, never be printed. A horror-star admitting belief in the parts he played? Absurd!

All the features about Boris Karloff played up the fact that he was a gentle man who found true peace in raising a garden. Lugosi was pictured as a sensitive neurotic, tortured by the roles he played in the films. Atwill was a socialite and a stage star. And Peter Lorre was always written up as being gentle as a lamb, a quiet student whose ambition was to play comedy parts.

No, it would never do to break the story of Jorla's devil-worship. And he was so damnably reticent about his private affairs!

I sought out Kincaid after the termination of our unsatisfactory interview. I told him what I had encountered and asked for advice. He gave it.

"The old line," he counseled. "Mystery man. We say nothing about him until the picture is released. After that I have a hunch things will work out for themselves. The fellow is a marvel. So don't bother about stories until the film is canned."

Consequently I abandoned publicity efforts in Karl Jorla's direction. Now I am very glad I did so, for there is no one to remember his name, or suspect the horror that was soon to follow.

The script was finished. The front office approved. Stage Four was under construction; the casting director got busy. Jorla was at the studio every day; Kincaid himself was teaching him English. The part was one in which very few words were needed, and Jorla proved a brilliant pupil, according to Les.

But Les was not as pleased as he should have been about it all. He came to me one day about a week before production and unburdened himself. He strove to speak lightly about the affair, but I could tell that he felt worried.

The gist of his story was very simple. Jorla was behaving strangely. He had had trouble with the front office; he refused to give the studio his living address, and it was known that he had checked out from his hotel several days after first arriving in Hollywood.

Nor was that all. He wouldn't talk about his part, or volunteer any information about interpretation. He seemed to be quite uninterested—admitting frankly to Kincaid that his only reason for signing a contract was to leave Europe.

He told Kincaid what he had told me—about the devil-worshippers. And he hinted at more. He spoke of being followed, muttered about "avengers" and "hunters who waited." He seemed to feel that the witch-cult was angry at him for the violation of secrets, and held him responsible for the release of *Return to the Sabbath*. That, he explained, was why he would not give his address, nor speak of his past life for publication. That is why he must use very heavy make-up in his film debut here. He felt at times as though he were being watched, or followed. There were many foreigners here . . . too many.

"What the devil can I do with a man like that?" Kincaid exploded, after he had explained this to me. "He's insane, or a fool. And I confess that he's too much like his screen character to please me. The damned casual way in which he professes to have dabbled in devil-worship and sorcery! He believes all this, and—well, I'll tell you the truth. I came here today because of the last thing he spoke of to me this morning.

"He came down to the office, and at first when he walked in I didn't know him. The dark glasses and muffler helped, of course, but he himself had changed. He was trembling, and walked with a stoop. And when he spoke his voice was like a groan. He showed me—this."

Kincaid handed me the clipping. It was from the London *Times*, through European press dispatches. A short paragraph, giving an account of the death of Fritz Ohmmen, the Austrian film director. He had been found strangled in a Paris garret, and his body had been frightfully mutilated; it mentioned an inverted cross branded on his stomach above the ripped entrails. Police were seeking the murderer. . . .

I handed the clipping back in silence. "So what?" I asked. But I had already guessed his answer.

"Fritz Ohmmen," Kincaid said, slowly, "was the director of the picture in which Karl Jorla played; the director who, with Jorla, knew the devil-worshippers. Jorla says that he fled to Paris, and that *they* sought him out."

I was silent.

"Mess," grunted Kincaid. "I've offered Jorla police protection, and he's refused. I can't coerce him under the terms of our contract. As long as he plays the part, he's secure with us. But he has the jitters. And I'm getting them."

He stormed out. I couldn't help him. I sat thinking of Karl Jorla, who believed in devil-gods; worshipped, and betrayed them. And I could have smiled at the absurdity of it all if I hadn't seen the man on the screen and watched his evil eyes. He *knew*! It was then that I began to feel thankful we had not given Jorla any publicity. I had a hunch.

During the next few days I saw Jorla very seldom. The rumors, however, began to trickle in. There had been an influx of foreign "sight-seers" at the studio gates. Someone had attempted to crash through the barriers in a racing-car. An extra in a mob scene over on Lot Six had been found carrying an automatic beneath his vest; when apprehended he had been lurking under the executive office windows. They had taken him down to headquarters, and so far the man had refused to talk. He was a German. . .

Jorla came to the studios every day in a shuttered car. He was bundled up to the eyes. He trembled constantly. His English lessons went badly. He spoke to no one. He had hired two men to ride with him in his car. They were armed.

A few days later news came that the German extra had talked. He was evidently a pathological case . . . he babbled wildly of a "Black Cult of Lucifer" known to some of the foreigners around town. It was a secret society purporting to worship the Devil, with vague connections in the mother countries. He had been "chosen" to avenge a wrong. More than that he dared not say, but he did give an address where the police might find cult headquarters. The place, a dingy house in Glendale, was quite deserted, of course. It was a queer old house with a secret cellar beneath the basement, but everything seemed to have been abandoned. The man was being held for examination by a specialist.

I heard this report with deep misgivings. I knew something of Los Angeles' and Hollywood's heterogeneous foreign population; God knows, Southern California has attracted mystics and occultists from all over the world. I've even heard rumors about stars being mixed up in unsavory secret societies, things one would never dare to admit in print. And Jorla was afraid.

That afternoon I tried to trail his black car as it left the studio for his mysterious home, but I lost the track in the winding reaches of Topanga Canyon. It had disappeared into the secret twilight of the purple hills, and I knew then that there was nothing I could do. Jorla had his own defenses, and if they failed, we at the studio could not help.

That was the evening he disappeared. At least he did not show up the next morning at the studio, and production was to start in two days. We heard about it. The boss and Kincaid were frantic. The police were called in, and I did my best to hush things up. When Jorla did not appear the following morning I went to Kincaid and told him about my following the car to Topanga Canyon. The police went to work. Next morning was production.

We spent a sleepless night of fruitless vigil. There was no word. Morning came, and there was unspoken dread in Kincaid's eyes as he faced me across the office table. Eight o'clock. We got up and walked silently across the lot to the studio cafeteria. Black coffee was badly needed; we hadn't had a police report for hours. We passed Stage Four, where the Jorla crew was at work. The noise of hammers was mockery. Jorla, we felt, would never face a camera today, if ever.

Bleskind, the director of the untitled horror opus, came out of the Stage Office as we passed.

His paunchy body quivered as he grasped Kincaid's lapels and piped, "Any news?"

Kincaid shook his head slowly. Bleskind thrust a cigar into his tense mouth.

"We're shooting ahead," he snapped. "We'll shoot around Jorla. If he doesn't show up when we finish the scenes in which he won't appear, we get another actor. But we can't wait." The squat director bustled back to the Stage.

Moved by a sudden impulse, Kincaid grasped my arm and propelled me after Bleskind's waddling form.

"Let's see the opening shots," he suggested. "I want to see what kind of a story they've given him."

We entered Stage Four.

A Gothic Castle, the ancestral home of Baron Ulmo. A dark, gloomy stone crypt of spidery horror. Cobwebbed, dust-shrouded, deserted by men and given over to the rats by day and the unearthly horrors that crept by night. An altar stood by the crypt, an altar of evil, the great black stone on which the ancient Baron Ulmo and his devil-cult had held their sacrifices. Now, in the pit beneath the altar, the Baron lay buried. Such was the legend.

According to the first shot scheduled, Sylvia Channing, the heroine, was exploring the castle. She had inherited the place and taken it over with her young husband. In this scene she was to see the altar for the first time, read the inscription on its base. This inscription was to prove an unwitting invocation, opening up the crypt beneath the altar and awakening Jorla, as Baron Ulmo, from the dead. He was to rise from the crypt then, and walk. It was at this point that the scene would terminate, due to Jorla's strange absence.

The setting was magnificently handled. Kincaid and I took our places beside Director Bleskind as the shot opened. Sylvia Channing walked out on the set; the signals were given, lights flashed, and the action began.

It was pantomimic. Sylvia walked across the cobwebbed floor, noticed the altar, examined it. She stooped to read the inscription, then whispered it aloud. There was a drone, as the opening of the altar-crypt was mechanically begun. The altar swung aside, and the black gaping pit was revealed. The upper cameras swung to Sylvia's face. She was to stare at the crypt in horror, and she did it most magnificently. In the picture she would be watching Jorla emerge.

Bleskind prepared to give the signal to cut action. Then—
Something emerged from the crypt!
It was dead, that thing—that horror with a mask of faceless flesh. Its lean body was clothed in rotting rags, and on its chest was a bloody crucifix, inverted—carved out of dead flesh. The eyes blazed loathsomely. It was Baron Ulmo, rising from the dead. *And it was Karl Jorla!*

The make-up was perfect. His eyes were dead, just as in the other film. The lips seemed shredded again, the mouth even more ghastly in its slitted blackness. And the touch of the bloody crucifix was immense.

Bleskind nearly swallowed his cigar when Jorla appeared. Quickly he controlled himself, silently signaled the men to proceed with the shooting. We strained forward, watching every move, but Les Kincaid's eyes held a wonder akin to my own.

Jorla was acting as never before. He moved slowly, as a corpse must move. As he raised himself from the crypt, each tiny effort seemed to cause him utter agony. The scene was soundless; Sylvia had fainted. But Jorla's lips moved, and we heard a faint whispering murmur which heightened the horror. Now the grisly cadaver was almost half out of the crypt. It strained upward, still murmuring. The bloody crucifix of flesh gleamed redly on the chest . . . I thought of the one found on the body of the murdered foreign director, Fritz Ohmmen, and realized where Jorla had gotten the idea.

The corpse strained up . . . it was to rise now . . . up . . . and then, with a sudden rictus, the body stiffened and slid back into the crypt.

Who screamed first I do not know. But the screaming continued after the prop-boys had rushed to the crypt and looked down at what lay within.

When I reached the brink of the pit I screamed, too.

For it was utterly empty.

I wish there were nothing more to tell. The papers never knew. The police hushed things up. The studio is silent, and the production was dropped immediately. But matters did not stop there. There was a sequel to that horror on Stage Four.

Kincaid and I cornered Bleskind. There was no need of any explanation; how could what we had just seen be explained in any sane way?

Jorla had disappeared; no one had let him into the studio; no make-up man had given him his attention. Nobody had seen him enter the crypt. He had appeared in the scene, then disappeared. The crypt was empty.

These were the facts. Kincaid told Bleskind what to do. The film was developed immediately, though two of the technicians fainted. We three sat in the projection booth and watched the morning's rushes flicker across the screen. The sound-track was specially dubbed in.

That scene—Sylvia walking and reading the incantation—the pit opening—and God, when *nothing* emerged!

Nothing but that great red scar suspended in mid-air—that great inverted crucifix cut in bleeding flesh; no Jorla visible at all! That bleeding cross in the air, and then the mumbling. . . .

Jorla—the thing—whatever it was—had mumbled a few syllables

on emerging from the crypt. The sound-track had picked them up. And we couldn't see anything but that scar; yet we heard Jorla's voice now coming from nothingness. We heard what he kept repeating, as he fell back into the crypt.

It was an address in Topanga Canyon.

The lights flickered on, and it was good to see them. Kincaid phoned the police and directed them to the address given on the sound-track.

We waited, the three of us, in Kincaid's office, waited for the police call. We drank, but did not speak. Each of us was thinking of Karl Jorla the devil-worshipper who had betrayed his faith; of his fear of vengeance. We thought of the director's death, and the bloody crucifix on his chest; remembered Jorla's disappearance. And then that ghastly ghost-thing on the screen, the bloody thing that hung in midair as Jorla's voice groaned the address. . .

The phone rang.

I picked it up. It was the police department. They gave their report. I fainted.

It was several minutes before I came to. It was several more minutes before I opened my mouth and spoke.

"They've found Karl Jorla's body at the address given on the screen," I whispered. "He was lying dead in an old shack up in the hills. He had been—murdered. There was a bloody cross, inverted on his chest. They think it was the work of some fanatics, because the place was filled with books on sorcery and Black Magic. They say—"

I paused. Kincaid's eyes commanded. "Go on."

"They say," I murmured, "that Jorla had been dead for at least three days."

A Wig for Miss DeVore

BY AUGUST DERLETH

August Derleth, one of the great names in the horror story genre, has a long and abiding interest in Hollywood—particularly the period just after the Second World War when it really was the film capital of the world. His insight into the particular star-system that operated then and its method of creating sex-symbols like Marilyn Monroe and Jayne Mansfield is well demonstrated in this tale. Derleth, both as writer and publisher, has played a major part in introducing talented writers to the genre, as well as giving us some of the most eerie and gruesome stories since the heyday of Algernon Blackwood and M. R. James.

Sheila DeVore was a glamor girl whose platinum blonde hair and languorous smile outshone any other's on the silver screen. Quite a girl! She occupied more attention in the minds of more thousands of young and old men than she had any right to occupy. She had eyes of baby blue with a come-on slant, and she had curves that haunted many an uneasy dreamer. Her pictures were in the screen magazines, on the cigarette ads ("Miss DeVore smokes nothing but Flambeaux! 'I never assume a role until I am assured my supply of Flambeaux is at hand to protect my throat, my bronchial tubes, and my photogenic value.' "), even on the confession magazine covers; and she was the subject of an oft-reprinted biography telling all about her beginnings, her debut into society, her escape from the rich home that had been hers, her longing for fame, to do her part for society by entertaining the millions of underprivileged, etc., etc.

A beautiful story! Unfortunately, it sprang full-bodied from the imagination of her publicity agent.

Actually, Sheila DeVore was born plain Maggie Mutz in a little Missouri town whose chief claim to fame was that an Indian chief had once stopped there on his way to be massacred. She was a mistress of false frontage, and knew how to hog any picture in which she took part, throwing around her curves (which were the only genuine thing about her) in a way calculated to distract the attention of anything human from the only real acting in the picture—not Miss DeVore's, of course. She had a background which would have put Herbert Asbury's Hatrack into a wild scramble for her humble fame, and even now she was the subject and the object of plenty of gossip—some self-initiated. Publicity, after all, being what it is, and considered so necessary. Among her intimates in Hollywood she was fondly known by a four-letter word which the law says it is illegal to call anyone no matter how many witnesses are ready to testify.

She forgot her parents and let her father die in the poor-farm. She divorced her first—and only—husband, and ruined his reputation. She could not bear to let alone the poor deluded promoter who was responsible for putting her on the road to fame, but managed to shorten his life by a prolonged suit for the return of such money as she had paid him in that first flush of gratitude which accompanied sight of her name in bright lights. She was as selfish as an inhibited pack-rat, and had never heard of moral scruples. As for ethics—there was no room for ethics in her profession. She was, in short, one of those people for whom there does not seem to be any excuse for permitting them to continue an existence which is giving them no pleasure, and is burdening others far too much. However, on the other side of the ledger, there were those countless thousands of palpitating hearts in the darkened theatres of the land, watching that curvaceous morsel of femininity fling her weight around in picture after picture, loving and being loved, as if it were all the real thing and Miss DeVore were not getting a cool four grand a week to play roles which women like her and all female cats are by nature fully qualified to play without acting.

And at the moment, too, there was Herbert Bleake. Herbert was a good-natured, addle-pated playboy, who saw Sheila DeVore's tooth-some face in a screen magazine and immediately took a plane out to Hollywood to see her. Sheila would never have seen him, but her publicity agent saw him first. After all, that story about the attempted robbery of her apartment had already been forgotten, and that touching release about how Sheila had given a ten thousand dollar home to her old mother (complete with picture, posed by an underpaid extra and a rented house, her real mother having been dead five years) was getting pretty well around, and it was time for something new in the life of the darling of America's repressed males. So Herbert was it; he was seized upon by the publicity agent, photographed descending from a liner of the air, shown with a great armful of flowers, and finally, with Sheila DeVore, all for the purpose of screaming head-lines: "RICH PLAYBOY MAKES BEELINE FOR HOLLYWOOD AFTER SEEING DEVORE'S PIX!"

What a story!

For weeks Sheila DeVore's publicity agent could count upon seeing that inane and rather vacuous face looking out from behind that armful of roses, or fatuously at Sheila, staring up from the newspapers and magazines, and after that, there was always the runaround that could be given the gossip columnist, Arabella Bearst. She would be good for a couple of hundred lines about the tantalizing possibilities of Sheila DeVore's engagement, wedding to, and break with Herbert Bleake to keep the matter running through all the yellow sheets for two months thereafter—if Sheila DeVore could hold out that long—which was doubtful.

In any case, there was Herbert, and Sheila had to treat him with a modicum of decency, however difficult it might be, while she devised some way to get rid of him. Preferably something spectacular—like a brawl at the Actors' Lagoon, when the photographers were present. Alas! for Herbert—he had his coming, and he might have known.

Sheila DeVore would never have believed that she had hers coming too—long overdue, to be sure. And she would have burst into raucous Maggie Mutz laughter if someone had told her that Herbert was the instrument of her fate, her nemesis, and so on. But there it was; the

Fates had cut the pattern, and there was nothing to do but for the unwitting actors to play their parts.

Sheila had been cast in the role of Meg Peyton, the Soho murderess: four dead men, a leg show for the jury, and acquittal. A color picture for which she would need red hair, for the real Meg Peyton had worn red hair, and, moreover, she had worn a wig—brighter than auburn. She stamped her pretty foot and said she could not go into the role without the proper accoutrements—by which she meant the wig; and she ranted and raved for a day or so about the necessity of having it. She would have forgotten all about it, had her director not rebelled and said she should shut her silly mouth and get on to the work in hand. That was too much for her, and that night she poured her heart's desire into Herbert's flapping ears, and before dawn there was a cablegram on the way to Herbert's London agent, and within forty-eight hours more, Meg Peyton's wig had been leased for a huge sum from a London exhibitor and was on its way to Sheila DeVore.

Her publicity agent went into ecstasies.

Herbert was childishly happy.

Sheila preened herself and posed for some sober-faced pictures and gave out noble statements: "I could not feel that I could do my best work without something of this nature to inspire me!"

The wig arrived, was duly photographed on and off Sheila DeVore (good for several hundred rotogravure shots, and a dragged-out existence in the screen magazines), and the picture went into production, Sheila DeVore in SOHO MEG, or THE TITIAN MURDERESS.

Not a word about the letter that came with the wig. Sheila read it, committed it to memory, and destroyed it without saying anything about it. She did not think it important, and memorized it only because it was reasonably short and a little curious. Her publicity agent would have torn his hair if he could have realized what a first-rate story she was passing up. The letter concerned the real Meg Peyton, and said of her that she had not originally been anything more than a poor artist's model, but that, after the loss of her hair, she had acquired her red wig, and her change of character more or less coincided with that date. Moreover, there were certain suggestions which went over Sheila DeVore's head like a balcony. For instance— that the wig should not be worn more than a few minutes at a time; that it should be kept out of sight; that it had certain "properties" not subject to reasonable explanation. And so forth. Naturally, the fancies of its present owner were no concern of Sheila DeVore's.

The wig was really a beauty. It was made of real hair, beyond question; indeed, it seemed to have come from a single head—in what manner a sensitive person would not have wanted to guess. Moreover, it was beautifully preserved; in age, it was said to date far back, to certain Central American Indians—which was completely beyond Sheila DeVore's limited ken. In fact, it was such a striking thing that Sheila DeVore painted her eyebrows and announced that, in the custom of Charles Laughton and other notables, she was going to wear the wig and impregnate herself with the character of Meg Peyton, so that she could more effectively portray her role—which she insisted upon treating as something to stand beside the roles of Lady Macbeth, Portia, and Ophelia. With the co-operation of her agent, of course, and of Herbert—though he was getting the brush-off, but was not at the moment sufficiently alert to correctly interpret the signs. After all, he had done his work, and there was no reason to be obtuse about it.

But Herbert was obtuse. He was so fatuous as to believe he had won Sheila DeVore, and actually gave himself airs on the strength of it. Sheila admitted to herself that he was rapidly becoming a nuisance with whom she would have to cope sooner or later. Fortunately—or unfortunately, as the case may be—for Herbert, she was at the time much too wrapped up in the titian wig, both figuratively and literally.

She went everywhere in the wig—with an entire new wardrobe to go along. She was photographed from Hollywood to New York, getting out of the plane in Chicago, eating at the Savoy, dancing at the Trianon, and, of course, in various stills from the picture. It was wonderfully exciting, and she felt an exhilaration she had never known before. She felt something more, too—something that took possession of her in the few hours during which she was alone.

It was a curious delusion, or rather, a succession of delusions, beginning with the conviction that she was not alone in her rooms, that someone was there with her, someone she could only fancy that she saw. Her fancies were real enough, at any rate; once or twice she was certain she saw someone lurking in the vicinity of the stand where she kept the wig; so that presently she was convinced that someone meant to steal her titian treasure. This hallucination made a wonderful press release, though there was one annoying aftermath, when the story got around to Meg Peyton's home town; that was an urgent cablegram from Grigsby Heather, the owner of the wig, that it be returned immediately.

Naturally, Sheila DeVore ignored Heather's unreasonable demand.

The hallucinations, however, increased, and one evening, when the picture had got about half way along, she had a particularly strange experience. She was sitting at her dressing table preparing to go out, and had just adjusted the titian wig over her closely-cropped platinum hair, when she saw bending above her someone she at first took to be her maid. Indeed, she went so far as to give a casual order, when something about the creature's dress caught her eye: a colorful, spangled costume worn loosely over the shoulder in a kind of ceremonial manner, a band about its head; and at the same moment she was conscious of the face of a very old man, seamy with wrinkles, horny and swarthy, like a gypsy's face, and of the man's long, gnarled, titian hair. For just one instant she had this vision; then the creature at her back seemed to dissolve like a fog and settle down upon her to vanish into her own shapely chassis.

The most extraordinary thing about it was that, while at the moment of her vision, Sheila DeVore was frightened out of her small allotment of wits, as soon as the creature had made its strange disappearance, she was not at all disturbed: a transition so rapid that she had actually put out her hand to ring for her maid, and arrested her movement in mid-air, as the vision at her back vanished.

It was at about this time, too, that her intimates began to notice a change in Sheila DeVore. Her claws seemed to have grown sharper and more expert, even her most casual glance seemed dangerously predatory, and her manner, when she walked into a public place, was cat-like, as if she were a huntress after bigger game than that which formerly interested her. But, of course, the most startling mutation which took place in the character of Sheila DeVore was a sudden, unprecedented craving for raw meat, preferably the comparatively fresh hearts of such fowl and animals as she was normally accustomed to eat in a more civilized fashion.

Even her publicity agent could not make use of this. Indeed, he did everything in his power to hush the matter up, but of course, there was Arabella Bearst, who had had her feelings hurt by Sheila (as who hadn't!), and she hinted at it in her column, so that millions of Americans read it and began to wonder.

By this time, Grigsby Heather was in a dither. He sent Herbert a long message saying flatly that Herbert must get the wig away from Miss DeVore at once, without delay, under pain of the gravest consequence. "The thing carries a revenant with it," he wrote. "And there is great danger in wearing it. I should never have permitted it to leave my possession, but I was assured that Miss DeVore would wear it only a short time each day." And so on. Herbert, being a rich playboy, looked upon any matter of the "gravest consequence," as something like a court battle; he had survived many of them, and estimated that he could survive this one, especially since it could be fought at long range. As for the "revenant," he wondered about that. Frankly, Herbert was far more educated in biological lines than in words of three syllables. He looked it up in the dictionary. "One returned from the dead or from exile, &c." Not very illuminating, he thought. Undoubtedly Heather had got the wrong word.

Nevertheless, he asked his valet what a revenant was.

Unlike Herbert, his valet had several degrees, on the strength of which he had been hired. "A revenant is something left over," he explained. "Well, sort of like a ghost—if you know what I mean."

"No I don't," admitted Herbert with that characteristic bluntness he could afford to manifest before those whose wages he paid.

"Well, it's like this. If I died, and left something of my character or personality in this room—why, that would be a revenant."

"I see," said Herbert.

He pondered this for a week, and then returned to his original hypothesis: that Heather had got hold of the wrong word—the imbecile!

Soon there came another letter from Heather, via Clipper. He said frankly that if it had not been for wearing the wig, Meg Peyton would never have committed those murders. Moreover, there was much more to those murders than ever got into print—a peculiarly horrible feature which was a common practise among the priesthood of the Aztec Indians of Mexico in making the blood sacrifice to the Sun God. Herbert's knowledge of the Aztecs was about as profound as the average man's knowledge of outermost cosmos.

That lack was unfortunate for Herbert.

Things had come to a pretty pass indeed, insofar as Sheila DeVore was concerned. Her passion for raw meat was unabated—indeed it was getting quite out of hand. Moreover, she was becoming a veritable tower of selfishness: she was not to be crossed, not to be thwarted, not to be gainsaid in anything. She fired her maid, her cook, her housekeeper, her butler, and her gardener, and she was alone on that fateful night when Herbert came to remonstrate with her about this revolting habit of hers.

He rang the bell, but no one answered.

He peered in through the window, and saw her sitting at her dressing-table, titian wig and all. But that was not all he saw. In the glass beyond her he saw a most awful caricature of a face: not the face of a woman at all—but that of a horrible, wrinkled old man, with incredibly evil eyes—and worse—it was in that place where the face of Sheila DeVore ought to have been. He cried out, and Sheila turned. Fortunately for Herbert's sanity, it was the familiar face that looked out at him.

She came to let him in, rather petulantly, and then went back to her dressing-table, Herbert dogging her heels. But she was not dressing. She was fascinated by a curious stone intrument, like a horseshoe with a handle on it, which she said she had been compelled to buy in an antique shop in San Francisco only the previous day. It was like nothing Herbert had ever seen before, but since Herbert's attention had been exclusively for banks, women, yachts, and high life in general, that was no wonder.

It was like nothing Sheila had ever seen before, either—and yet, she could not help thinking, she had known the feel of this tool before. She would know what to do with it if the time came.

Clearly, it was psychologically the wrong moment for Herbert to open up about his complaint. But he did, with a witlessness characteristic of him. Sheila said not a word. She turned slowly and looked at him. One look out of those eyes was enough to stop his words in his throat; they were not the eyes of Sheila DeVore—they were the eyes he had seen in the glass. He swallowed hard and got up.

With paralyzing rapidity Sheila struck.

Then, with the utmost composure, she proceeded to put to its designed use the curious instrument from the antique shop.

And she was sly. It was not until a week after the disappearance of her publicity agent, who made something of the same mistake Herbert did, that Herbert's body was discovered, and two days later, the agent's. That discovery rocked Hollywood, and then California, and then the nation, with repercussions that spread across the seas. One headline after the other—STAR OF SOHO MEG INVOLVED IN MURDER MYSTERY; DEATHS RECALL MEG PEYTON MURDERS—and so on.

But always there was something concealed, something secret: a kind of hush-hush. Something that did not get out, though Arabella Bearst hustled her 350-pound self around to dig it out. Some juicy morsel of scandal that Arabella might miss. "The condition of the bodies. . . ." Something about the condition of the bodies. But no one would talk. Miss DeVore was clapped into quod, and from there was taken quietly to an asylum for the rest of her days.

Arabella Bearst was furious about being tied. And then Grigsby Heather came on to the scene. At first he would say nothing. He got his wig; he shipped it back to London. But Arabella was not to be put off forever, and she was a master of the trip-up. She cornered Heather one day at the railroad station and flashed the instrument "found in Miss DeVore's possession."

"How curious!" exclaimed Heather excitedly. "Wherever did you find it?"

"What is it?" asked Arabella, with her dimples at their best.

"Why, it's a sacrificial tool of the Aztec priests. Mexico, you know. That's the instrument with which they cut out the living hearts of their human sacrifices."

Arabella was a woman who never forgot a slight, however unimportant. And she had it in for Sheila DeVore, no matter where she was. As soon as possible her column blossomed out with a cutting little line: "Ask Sheila DeVore, one-time screen star, how she enjoyed the heart of Herbert Bleake!"

That was too much for even her employer. If Sheila DeVore had been in any position to appreciate it, she would have enjoyed knowing that Arabella Bearst was in the market for a job, thanks to Sheila's titian wig.

Arabella Bearst's employer was needlessly impulsive. No one would have guessed from her column that, far from captivating the heart of Herbert Bleake—or for that matter, of her publicity agent —Sheila DeVore had followed the prevailing custom among the Aztecs—and eaten it, raw.

The Man who wanted to be in the Movies

BY JOHN JAKES

John Jakes appropriately follows August Derleth in this collection for it was Derleth who first published his work. Now an established writer with numerous books to his credit—including a larger-than-life swords and sorcery character, Brak the Barbarian—Jakes is breaking into the script-writing arena and has film and T.V. work lined up for the future. His particular slant on the "Hollywood Obsession" is finely executed in this extraordinary tale.

George Rollo stepped away from the mirror and surveyed his scrupulous grooming. His hair was neatly brushed back, his suit freshly pressed, and his maroon tie with the white polka dots was artfully knotted. His face was almost eclipsed by the carefully planned sartorial perfection.

George Rollo was in love. He happened to be in love with a young woman who received his attention with reserve. But he went right on pursuing her, doing anything within his power to win her affections. Because of her, he dressed carefully.

He picked up the expensive box of candy secured from the drug store. He was able to afford a large box because he was a pharmacist in the drug store and could get the candy wholesale.

He locked the door of his room soundly behind him and clattered down the stairs. On the second landing a young and rather pretty woman with big amber eyes stood leaning on the doorjamb, next to a sign that announced, *Yolanda Fox, Licensed Thaumaturgist, Helpful and Benevolent Spells of All Types.*

"Hello, George," she said warmly as he came banging down the stairway.

"Oh. Hello, Yolanda, how are you?" His voice was strained, absent.

A large furry white thing rushed past the girl's legs and began lapping affectionately at the young man's shoes.

"Down, Faust," Yolanda said sharply. "Come here."

The familiar, who resembled a large and pugnacious bull dog with amber eyes quite like the girl's, crept back to a position at the side of his mistress, whining helplessly.

"Going out?" Yolanda asked yearningly.

"Yes," George replied in a nervous tone, "with Mabel."

"Oh." Sadness dropped like a curtain across her face.

"Well," he said nervously, "well, I guess I'd better be going."

He hurried off down the stairs. Yolanda caught a glimpse of the candy box and her amber eyes narrowed with faint jealous anger.

Faust growled, displaying bulldog teeth.

She shrugged then, as if winning out against an impulse to injure George, who shot a hasty glance at her from the bottom of the stairs just as she returned to her apartment.

Out in the street, George shivered. He knew Yolanda liked him, even though he had a distinct fear of witches. Even white witches licensed by the State Thaumaturgy Board. They could only conjure helpful spirits or make hexes to ward off illness. The law said they could do no more, but George was certain many of them had darker, half-forgotten powers.

He put Yolanda from his thoughts and hurried on down the street.

Miss Mabel Fry sat in her dirty armchair, surrounded by piles of magazines. Their glazed covers blanketed the rugs, made colorful landscapes even in the small dinette. The walls of the apartment were covered with pictures of male movie idols, wearing hound's tooth jackets or holding a golf club or smiling at starlets.

The doorbell clacked with a noise of sad disrepair.

Mabel reached for another peppermint, shoved it into her red mouth and went on reading her magazine: *It's the Simple Home Girl For Me, by Rodney de Cord, Rising Young Parafilm Star.*

The doorbell clacked a second time.

Mabel lifted her large body and moved disconsolately to the alcove. She opened the door and said in a bored manner, "Oh. George."

"Hello . . . uh . . . Mabel."

He burst eagerly into the room, presenting his candy. She accepted it with mumbled thanks. She was a perfume clerk in a local department store, but she didn't much like the idea of accepting candy from an ordinary druggist.

"Where are we going tonight?" she asked, slipping into her coat.

"Anyplace," George replied casually. "There's a fine concert at the Music Hall. . . ."

She ignored him. "The Royal has a wonderful new picture, *I'll Slay My Love,* with Todd St. Bartholomew. He's *so* masculine. When he played a private detective and slapped Lona Lawndale in *Bodies to Burn,* I just couldn't stand it, it was so thrilling."

George didn't argue. "Anything you say," he mumbled.

As they walked to the theatre she babbled about the latest gossip from Hollywood. Who was marrying whom. Who was divorcing whom. Who was in bed with whom when who came home with who's perfume all over him. George listened with resignation.

Mabel waited under the glaring lights of the marquee while he bought the tickets. She rolled her eyes ecstatically at Todd St. Bartholomew staring belligerently from the poster, gun in hand. A caption balloon from his lithographed lips announced, *I'll Slay My Love.*

As they passed through the door, Terry Silver, the aging owner of the theatre, waved to Mabel.

"Evening," he called affably. "Next week we're showing *Husbands and Paramours* with Michale Yarven."

"Ooooooo," Mabel exclaimed loudly. "How wonderful!"

She allowed George to take her hand as they approached the main aisle. Just then a young man in a bright red sport coat sauntered over.

" 'Lo, Mabel," said Bertie Wallen.

George swore in a whisper. Bertie Wallen was a bit actor on local television shows. He dressed and looked like a movie actor.

"Thought I might find you here," Bertie said to Mabel. "Got big news. Friend of mine in Hollywood just wired me that I should fly out there right away. Metropole wants to test me."

Mabel squealed with delight.

George stood by impotently, glaring at Bertie as if he were a liar.

"Like to see the wire?" Bertie asked in broadly humorous tones.

"Sure, Bertie," Mabel cooed.

"Come on out to my car. Only take a minute."

Mabel started away, then turned to George. "Be a sweetie and go inside and wait for me. I'll be right in. The usual seats."

He started to protest feebly, hesitated, and stumbled into the auditorium. He found the customary seats, saving the adjacent chair for Mabel.

For two hours he sat woodenly, alone, watching Todd St. Bartholomew consuming quarts of alcohol and being pounded by assorted mobsters. George rather enjoyed the picture. One of Hollywood's better character actors, a man named Tab something or other, played a kindly old judge. George liked Tab whatever-it-was, although he doddered a bit. He must have been at least seventy-five. He had a sympathetic rugged face. He did not impress George as a professional lover.

George tapped on Yolanda Fox's door at eleven-thirty that evening. The door opened after a moment and she invited him in, surprised and pleased. Slipping out of a black robe and erasing a chalk pentagram from the floor, she turned up the lights.

"Just practicing a hay fever prevention spell," she explained. "Pollen season coming on."

He sank down on her sofa, staring moodily at the floor. Faust nuzzled his leg.

"Yolanda," he said at last as she bustled out of the kitchen with two steaming cups of tea, "you're the one for me."

She almost dropped the cups. Quickly she set them down and hurried to his side. "Oh, George. . . ."

"Yes sir," he added gloomily, "you're the one to help me get Mabel."

"Oh."

Her face smoothed out. She seemed quite calm. She served the tea and inquired in a helpful tone, "What can I do?"

"I love Mabel Fry. I'll do anything to make her love me. But she . . . well . . . she likes movie stars. Isn't there any kind of a spell to make me lucky?" He paused, deliberated and plunged on. "Can't you get me into the movies?"

"I don't know," she answered, thinking.

"I'll pay anything," he offered. "That is, anything I can."

"It won't be necessary to pay me," she replied carefully. "I'll be glad to help you. In fact, I think I can get you into the movies tonight."

"You . . . can?" He was startled.

"Certainly." She picked up a valise, began to stuff it with the paraphernalia of demonology. "But we must have the right atmosphere."

"Atmosphere?"

"A theatre. The Royal is near. I guarantee that before morning you'll be in the movies. Come, Faust."

They hurried through the dark streets.

The Royal was a mound of shadow, closed for the night. The street was relatively deserted. Only a drunk reeled from a cocktail lounge opposite the theatre.

"Sssssh," Yolanda cautioned, finger to lips. "We've got to get inside."

They crept through the vacant lot adjoining the theatre. Before the brick wall, Yolanda halted and made several passes in the air, murmuring something about Asmodeus, and a cold wind shoved George forward through grey fog.

He looked about. They were in the middle of the darkened theatre lobby.

Faust yipped with satanic glee. His large amber eyes glowed with strange delight. Yolanda's eyes glowed in the same fashion. George didn't notice.

They made their way down one aisle of the auditorium. Above them, the screen was a formless patch of silver-white.

Yolanda opened her valise, pulling forth her black robe. She lit two small braziers that gave off pungent fumes. She drew circles on the rug, remembering all of the bits of black magic the law had forced her to forget.

George watched the screen in fascination, because if Yolanda proved successful, he would be up there, and soon!

Yolanda moaned and waved her hands in the air and chanted. The braziers smouldered with oily bronze fire. Faust capered up and down the aisle, barking. And then Yolanda tapped George on the shoulder. Her face was illuminated by some unholy light.

"All right, George," she whispered. "Here you go."

He was strangely lifted.

Yolanda erased her marks, put out her braziers, repacked her valise and departed. Faust cavorted behind her, bulldog face aglow with strange humor.

For a long time George Rollo didn't know what had happened, or where he was. If this was the way to get into the movies, it was certainly a peculiar way.

When he tried to move his hands or feet he found it was impossible. In fact, he was unable even to feel them at the ends of his arms or legs. That is, he amended in his thoughts, he would have been, if he could have felt his arms or legs.

Everything was strangely dark. Then suddenly it was as though a curtain had been swept away from his eyes.

He saw rows of white staring faces. Two of them belonged to Mabel Fry and Bertie Wallen. Suddenly it began to dawn on him just what Yolanda had done. Blinding lights hit him. He screamed.

The only sound that came out was a ruffle of drums and a snatch of vaguely familiar music.

He wasn't George Rollo. *God in heaven!* . . . he wasn't even a *man! He was flat . . . and from one end of him to the other, in gigantic letters, he said* IN CINEMASCOPE . . . .

The Perfect Plot

BY FRANK FENTON

*Frank Fenton has been a Hollywood screenwriter for many years
with a score of top credits to his name. One of a whole host of young
hopefuls who flocked to the Film City more full of hope than experience in the twenties, he has graduated into the top flight through
a deft ear for dialogue and excellent plotting. The story here is, by
his own admission, more than a little autobiographical—except in
the one aspect that will become abundantly clear as you read....*

His name was Francis Cary. He lived in a small studio apartment
just off Sunset Strip in Hollywood, and he made a somewhat pre-
carious living by writing occasional scripts for the films. He was a
good-looking man and quite personable in a faintly sardonic way. But
though he had many acquaintances, he had few actual friends. And
this can only be accounted for by the fact that he was an egghead.

In the unhappy jargon of these unhappy times, an egghead, of
course, is a synonym for an intellectual, and as such a creature,
Francis Cary was inevitably tagged. In Hollywood, of late, many
such fellows have become marked and lonely men. It is easy to say
that Cary was marked for this designation because he had worked
his way through Harvard in sprightlier days as a bus-boy and later
as a waiter. It is also easy to point to his several degrees and the Phi
Beta Kappa key he wore. But his true difficulty was that he had not
got over these things. In fact he had gone from bad to worse and
subsequently written a novel castigating the capitalist system. Since
no more than five hundred people had ever bought or read this book,

the capitalist system was not seriously damaged by his assault. In fact, the failure of the book had driven Cary out of the chill and heartless East and into the sunny and listless environs of southern California. In this balmy clime he eventually lost his fervour for the working class and for working itself. And after serving his country for three years in the South Pacific he returned to become a true dilettante. He wrote a play about the sex life of the Polish fishermen south of Ventura, and although this drama was a relative flop on Broadway, it remained on that fabled street long enough for Cary to earn considerable theatrical repute. And this enabled him to gain employment in the studios as a writer.

To him, this was a grim ordeal. But it paid the rent and it bought books. It was also a stake with which he could afford to go prospecting for another novel—a novel about the despair of the intellectual, the plight of the egghead. When at some bar he was asked the title of his work in progress, he would answer bitterly, *The Chicken or the Egghead,* and the inquirer would thereupon drop the subject, having had practically no interest in it in the first place. "What goes on with you?" Hollywood asks, and the actor out of work says, "The rent!" The idle writer replies, "I'm doing a book."

Actually, he was not writing so much as reading. The condition of the world so confused him that he sought explanations for its lunacy in Santayana, Russell, Toynbee and Schweitzer. And during this period Arod Summer borrowed the books after he had read them.

Arod is Dora spelled backward, while Summer once had been spelled Loudermilk. But she was beautiful to see. Her hair was golden blonde and her eyes were sky blue. Her body was exquisitely proportioned, and half the male adults of the United States and Canada lusted after her. Whenever she appeared on the great new screens of the cinema, the box office enjoyed a rare enrichment. Unhampered by any thespian talent whatever, she simply moved across the screen and became the delight of mankind.

To Cary she was an incredible phenomenon. Not because of her sensual allure and radiance, which were obvious, but because, for reasons impenetrable by him, she worshipped him. His cash was low and his best suit was becoming frayed and he showed her no special interest, yet she adored him. She was a great and rising star and oil millionaires knelt at her feet; beautiful actors, famed athletes, powerful industrialists, clamoured for her favour, but she smiled and scorned them all.

She would sneak away from a glamorous première or any such exclusive brawl of celebrities and knock at Cary's door, however late the hour might be, and despite the would-be-lovers she had left in the lurch. If he let her in, she was happy just to be there and near him. She would make coffee and browse among his tumbled books. She would admire the prints he had collected and pinned to the wall, and his one original, a painting called the "Beast of Alamogordo", that presumed to symbolize the meaning of the A bomb. She knew he prized this concept and so would stand admiring it, while he sat trying not to admire her magnificent figure. "It's marvellous, utterly marvellous," she would say, though he knew she did not understand it, since he found it completely incomprehensible himself. It was that kind of art known to *aficionados* as Abstract, and for all of its craft and cunning it still reminded him of something trapped on a microscope slide.

Once he said as much and she laughed merrily with a kind of practised theatrical mirth—not at the painting, but at his wit. She laughed merrily every time she imagined that he said something witty and superior. And it disgusted him.

"What did you think of Toynbee?" he asked when she brought the book back.

"He's awful deep," she said. "Awful."

"Do you think that Western civilization has a chance?" he asked.

"Don't be silly!" she said and laughed merrily, and there came to him the strange feeling that she knew more about it than Toynbee. She knew the world would go on, in spite of the beast of Alamogordo.

"Why do you come here," he said, indicating the studio walls and the scrambled volumes, "when you can have anything in the world by holding up your little finger?"

She held it up smiling. "I can't," she said. "See?"

"What is it you want?" he asked curiously.

"You," she said.

"What is there about me?" he asked coldly.

"I love you," she said simply and picked up Dostoevsky's *The Idiot*, turning the pages idly and with a little frown of pretended interest.

He stared at her thoughtfully and wondered why it should matter so much to him that she was a boob, that her stupidity and ignorance were as spectacular as her physical splendour. The uneasy notion that he had become an eccentric and queer accosted him, so that he even wondered if some latent homo-sexuality might not be creeping over him in his middle years. He thrust the notion aside and regarded her purely—or impurely—from the neck down, becoming at once reassured by a powerful impulse to cart her off to the bed in the other room. The impulse was so powerful that he raised his eyes to her face and as though divining what had just occurred to him, she smiled. But when she spoke the urge swiftly vanished. "I kinda think," she said, "that people ought to be honest about their feelings, and that's what's wrong with the world today. If some guy is cute and a girl goes for him in a big way, I don't think she oughta hide her true feelings—not for just the sex bit, but for character and that kind of thing. A guy sending a girl is one thing, but when she finds he's for real, that's different."

"It's two o'clock, Arod," he said, "and you ought to go home and get some sleep. I'll take you."

"No, I'll go alone," she said. And she looked gravely at him. "Sometimes I like to be alone, so I can dream."

And so she left him, and through the window he saw her yellow Cadillac swerve down the hill and turn the corner like a police car in hot pursuit of a traffic violator.

He sighed and wondered whether or not she should see a psychiatrist—or whether he should himself. He turned back from the window. The expensive perfume she wore still haunted the air and her cigarette still burned in the ash-tray, red from her mouth. He laughed out loud and sat down to read in peace, but the perfume of Chanel overcame the prose of Marcel Proust.

It was at this time that he bought a small television set from a stuntman who was broke, and for many nights he did not read a book but stared at the little screen, at once revolted and fascinated. It was peopled by clowns and pitchmen, detectives and vaudevillians. Garish blondes, all looking like Arod Summer, delivered opinions on the problems of mankind. In this satanic theatre, mayhem seemed to be the most staple commodity and almost every half-hour, on one channel or another, a murder was being done or a beating administered. And during the interludes between these crimes came unctuous newscasters telling, with a kind of morbid relish, the disasters of the day.

And it was during this period that the Great Communist Conspiracy was brought to bay and summarily demolished. One after another, the conspirators appeared on the television screen and were excoriated and exposed by the Congressional Committee. Most of them seemed to be writers of one sort or another, and Cary had known several of them personally. They appeared scornful and defiant, like the French aristocrats of old, riding in their tumbrels to the guillotine.

It was a kind of shocking exposé, and as the list of names lengthened daily, a kind of fear went through the town. Men spoke carefully about it and wondered who would be next.

Arod Summer said to Cary, "They won't get you for this, will they?"

"For what?" he said.

"For a Red."

"A Red," he said, "a Spic, a Wop, a Hebe, a Pict, a Jute, a Nig. It's a matter of semantics."

"But you were never a Commie?" she pressed, looking at him, for the first time fearfully.

"No," he said coldly.

"What is it?" she asked with relief.

"Communism?"

She nodded and brought him his coffee.

He said thoughtfully, "Lenin thought it was a million little paths finally making a human highway. He neglected to add that it was necessary to pave them with human skulls."

"Is he head of it?"

"He's dead. He was a sardine trying to rationalize the ocean in terms of sardines."

"What's it about?" she asked. "Almost everybody's talking about it."

He looked at her with a kind of pity. "It's for the masses," he said, "the people, the *mobile vulgus*. It's a political pitch like trying to get everybody to smoke the same God-damned cigarette. It's another con game and the people are the mark, the big mark."

"Why don't we go to Las Vegas for the week-end?" she said.

"I have no money," he said.

"I could lend you some."

"No," he said, and at that moment he heard his name mentioned on the screen and stared with surprise. It was mentioned quite casually by a writer, Milton Gay, who was at the moment naming names for the Committee, and apparently listing all persons to whom he had ever been introduced.

"Well, I'll be damned," Cary murmured.

"See!" Arod cried. "There you are! You lied to me!"

"All right," he said, seizing the golden opportunity, "you better get out of here. Get to Las Vegas. Say that you never knew me. Say I was just one of thousands trying to seduce you."

She looked at him wildly a moment. Then a great calm came over her. "No," she said quietly, "I'm sticking with you—whatever you've done, whatever you are. I have faith."

"You want to ruin a great career?"

"It doesn't matter," she said. And she walked to the window and stood there, looking out on the vista of Hollywood, a lake of neon lights in the valley below.

The psychiatrist's name was Davison Funck. He was very fat and extraordinarily brilliant. He smoked one pipe after another and had the same wistful, ironic smile for all circumstances, however tragic or absurd or banal. A profound and devious man, he had a remarkable talent for listening to anybody and understanding what was not being said. He looked benignly at Cary, who was his friend, and said, "I see no reason why you should be upset. When there is a net out for sharks, surely a few tuna and minnows will also be hauled in."

"I am not upset," Cary said calmly. "This dreamy idiot named me and as a consequence I had to appear and be questioned. To my amazement I found they had gotten hold of a copy of a novel I once wrote damning the system. Aside from the fact that I was an amateur and the book was roasted by experts, I was flabbergasted to find that it still existed. I even read it again, and found it very bad."

"And what was the outcome?" Funck asked, reloading his huge pipe.

"Nothing," Cary said. "What outcome could there be?"

"How would I know?" Funck said.

"Why not—you know everything," Cary said.

Funck smiled but did not disagree.

"I was cleared." Cary went on.

"Then what disturbs you?"

Cary shook his head.

Funck smiled. "I will tell you, Francis," he said, "You are really disturbed because you are an intellectual, and the times are very unfortunate for this type of affliction. Being an intellectual, it is difficult for you to belong to the right wing. Being intelligent, it is impossible for you to belong to the extreme left. So you have no wings. You are a bird reduced to the limitations of a biped, and therefore extremely vulnerable. You will be suspected by both the right and the left. To use a colloquialism, you are caught dead in the middle."

"What would you advise then?"

"One of two things," Funck said urbanely. "Find a cave and become a recluse, or conform. I would suggest conforming. Become innocuous. Do innocuous things. Write innocuous movies and novels. Marry an innocuous woman and have innocuous children. The world will have to do this some day, and then it will become happy, innocuously happy. I see it as the final Utopia, the true aspiration of man. In fact, I have concocted, I believe, a small pill for just such a purpose—a medicament that will induce normalcy in a human being much as certain potions induce sleep."

Cary stared at him curiously.

Funck smiled confidently. "No, I have not become insane," he said. "I really think I have accomplished it. And why not? It's no more miraculous than the antibiotics or the fission of the uranium atom—or the pathology of love."

Cary suddenly laughed. Then he asked. "What do you call this nostrum?"

Funck pronounced it carefully, a long Latin hyphenate.

"It sounds very important," Cary said.

"That's why it's in Latin," Funck said. "That's why all prescriptions are in Latin."

"Have you ever tried this on anybody?"

"On one of my cats," said Funck, "an extremely eccentric ringtail cat and a brilliant animal. In a few days he was killing birds, scratching the furniture, and caterwauling at night just like his companions. We achieved perfect feline normalcy."

"Normalcy?"

"A word that should not deceive us," Funck said.

"And what would you regard as a normal human being?" Cary asked.

"A normal North American in the United States?"

Cary nodded.

"Simple," Funck said, "In my definition normalcy is that state of mind and being that finds abstract ideas both nonsensical and revolting—and this is what my nostrum should bring about in you. For instance, if it works, you will feel a revulsion for those aspirations and aesthetics that the world's philosophers and artists have deemed most admirable in the character of man."

"And what supplants these aspirations?"

"All that you have heretofore regarded as vulgar and banal," Funck said, smiling.

"Such as murder, embezzlement, adultery?" Cary's tone was sarcastic.

"Not at all," Funck said calmly. "Such things are committed by men of imagination—psychopaths, misfits, rebels."

"Then what will I be?"

Funck's smile was broad and sunny. "A regular guy," he said. "A bundle of the most approved clichés, fair and square, who minds his p's and q's and earns his bread and board by the sweat of his brow—especially when things are at sixes and sevens you'll keep the world safe and sound for democracy."

"How enviable," Cary murmured. "The comic strips, the sports pages, the straight Republican ticket. What a dream!"

"A reality," Funck said eagerly, "to which I am able to transport you. Not only will you unravel the knots of your soul, but you will be making a contribution to science. You will be Exhibit A for what may be the panacea for all humanity's ills, or at least its profoundest —imagination. Remember this: imagination is all that separates the pig from the poet, the ape from the artist, the great hanging sloth from the tycoon."

Cary rose and strode to the window. He gazed out across the boulevard to the low blue hills of the Sierra Madre. "Contract bridge, Arthur Godfrey—perhaps even love," he murmured. Then he turned resolutely and faced Funck with an ironical smile. "I am your man," he said. "I am your human guinea pig."

For days it seemed that the pills were not working. Funck had advised him not to fight against any inclination toward a tolerance for mediocrity after taking them. And he had not done so. In fact, in a complete effort towards co-operation, he had gone to the other extreme. He had attended a baseball game between Hollywood and Seattle and had eaten two hot dogs—his first in years—during the seventh inning. Then, the same evening he had gone to a movie, after which he had bought a beer at the Cock and Bull saloon and bet fifteen to ten against the PCC in the Rose Bowl with a bookmaker named Maurice.

He had begun to suspect Davison Funck of playing a practical joke on him—or having committed a scientific blunder—when a curious thing happened. He was sitting in his studio apartment reading Liddell's history of the fall of Carthage when he felt a powerful impulse to put this tale into a scenario. There and then he put the book down, went to the typewriter, and wrote furiously, deep into the night. As he wrote he visualized his scenes in technicolour on huge, wide screens. Cato crying *"Delenda est Carthago!"* And Rome's treachery. He saw his hero as young Scipio the peacemaker, falling in love with a Carthaginian princess. He saw the desperate women of Carthage cutting their long hair and twisting it into strings for the catapults that defended the city. He saw the fierce and ancient Masinissa leading the Numidian horse against the walls. He saw the city burnt at last and salt strewn on the earth so that it would never rise again. He saw his Roman hero and his Carthaginian princess joined in death, with love triumphant—an eternal poem rising from the ashes of conquest. He saw and wrote it all, and at dawn he was finished. He went to bed with a kind of exultation, and as he lay there he visualized Arod Summer in the role of the princess. He saw her as magnificent in the part and a tremendous asset at the box office, and then dimly, for the first time, he knew that Funck's chemistry had begun its work.

The following day his transition was in full blossom. He found himself displeased with the usual disarray of his room and so he rearranged and cleaned it neatly. He took down the "Beast of Alamogordo" from the wall and put it in a closet. He could no longer bear to look at it. Then, instead of his usual coffee and orange juice, he went down the street to the Scandia and breakfasted on wheat cakes and bacon, gorging himself.

He felt curiously well. As he carried the manuscript down the street to his agent's office he carried his hat in his hand so that the warm sun could shine on his face. Passing an alley he suddenly glanced at the hat and threw it away. Passing a haberdasher, he stopped in and bought two flowered sport shirts, wearing one and leaving his old shirt behind. A breeze blew mildly down the boulevard and brought the slight tang of the sea. He looked at the white and yellow stucco houses that clustered on the brown and green hillsides and thought what a lovely land California was. Wonderful and beautiful—the land of Portola and Crespi. Perhaps Hollywood was to America what Athens had been to ancient Greece. Perhaps it would make another Golden Age for America, particularly with the wide screens and the inevitable fusion with TV.

He wondered where Arod was this day, and felt a happy yearning for her. In spite of her magnificent beauty, she was a simple soul, and therein he thought, lay her charm. She was unspoiled, in spite of a tremendous Press. She was still the girl next door beneath the surface of her indescribable loveliness. What an idiot he had been not to perceive this and to regard her as a common boob!

He laughed and went on. He noted the pallor of the skin of his hands and told himself he needed to get in the open more, go swimming or perhaps take up golf, get out in the sun and God's fresh air that was so plentiful and available in this summery land.

When he greeted Sam Feilman, his agent, with a cheery hello, the dark little man gave him a startled look.

"What's the matter?" Cary asked.

"Your shirt."

"What's wrong with it?"

"Nothing," Feilman said hastily. "It's colourful. It's magnificent."

Cary laid the script on the desk. "So is this," he said. "Read it and call me at Arod Summer's." He waved to Feilman and walked out.

He drove west on Sunset Boulevard into Beverly Hills. He found Arod sunning herself beside her swimming-pool, having orange juice and coffee. She was almost as startled as Feilman had been to see him, but incalculably more delighted.

"I thought I'd take a dip," he said.

She was stunned. "There's suits in the locker," she said.

He went to the bath-house and put one on. Then he returned to the swimming-pool and plunged into the water. She watched him with amazement, thinking, despite her love, that he swam like a drowning spider. He had never been in the pool before. His skin was white and the muscles of his long body were soft and flabby. When at last he crawled panting out of the pool, she poured him some coffee and he drank it gratefully.

"I've got to do more of this," he said, rubbing his hair with a huge green towel.

"Do you have a hang-over?" she asked.

He shook his head. "I worked all night on a movie," he said. "I was inspired."

"Would it be right for me?"

"I wrote it for you," he said quietly.

She stared at him blankly. One strange thing had succeeded another too swiftly for her. The flowered shirt, the plunge into the pool, the writing of a movie for her, to say nothing of his pleasant, smiling manner. It was an overwhelming combination of the incredible. She poured some coffee and drank it black. He lay back in the canvas chair to bathe in the sun and closed his eyes. She watched him and her heart pounded wildly. For the first time he had come to her, and joy sang through her blood. She wanted to kneel beside him and kiss his limp wet hand. But she restrained herself and was contented to gaze at him with tears forming in her eyes. In repose he looked at once absurd and splendid. His body was lean and angular, his black hair long and awry. He did not remotely resemble any of the tanned and bemuscled young actors or the brown and pot-bellied producers who usually were her guests at this poolside. She saw how tired he was and how the sun and water had relaxed him. She knew the moment he fell asleep and a great motherly pity and happiness pervaded her. He was asleep and the dark and bitter poetry of his soul was now mute. She had never seen him sleeping before and she found it delightful. She sat and stared at his face that was the face of a poet and an artist, an eternal outcast. He belonged to the black sheep that God, if He did not love them more, wanted most. Hollywood was filled with vain idiots who made or inherited fortunes, Texas Midases whose touch had turned everything to oil, nepots in cashmere and jaguars, soda-jerks who had been ballooned to fame by a publicity as ceaseless as it was banal, just as she herself had been. Only *she* knew it. She had not worked seven years in an Ohio brewery not to have learned something of life and truth—and now, an immense success in this world capital of boobs and posturers, she still had not lost her ancient values. She knew that the gaunt, pale man sleeping beside her was different. He despised the entire kingdom in which she was now a princess, and if only for this reason, she thought that he was great. Great not as a performance or a picture is called great, but as a work of art is great. And as she pondered this, the phone rang. She picked it up quickly so that it would not awaken him.

It was Feilman. He had read the script and his voice was hushed as with awe. "You can tell him when he wakes up," Feilman said. "I have finished it and it's great. It is the greatest story I have ever read. It is the love story of all time. It is history, spectacle, passion, humanity, and tragedy. I laughed and I cried. It will cost four million to make. If you will play it, I will now go out and sell it for five hundred thousand dollars rock bottom cash—and a percentage of the gross."

"I will, I will," Arod said breathlessly.

"If he sleeps six hours, he will wake up a rich man," Feilman said. "God bless you both."

Arod put the phone down and gazed at Cary. He was snoring softly. Her eyes filled again with tears, but so great was the delight in her heart that she could not sit still but longed to embrace him. Instead, because he was weary and exhausted by his masterpiece, she ran to the diving-board and for the first time actually entered the waters of her pool. It was a great day for first things.

The rise of Francis Cary began with *The Fall of Carthage*. Cary himself wrote the screen play and he wove into the drama an irreproachable *more*, by inference likening ancient Rome to the modern Soviet Russia, inasmuch as both yearned to conquer and enslave the world. He showed how, by offerings of peace, Carthage was tricked into unpreparedness and then destroyed. The young Roman consul and the lovely Carthaginian princess died in each other's arms, somehow proving that love eternally dissolves the antipathies of great nations.

It became an epic. It cost the studio four million dollars. It was shown on a huge wide screen and it took New York by storm. It was a smash in Boston, socko in Chicago, terrific in Philadelphia, mighty in Minneapolis. It stormed the Bastille of television, freed the half-blinded prisoners, and led them back to the movie theatres. It satisfied everybody except the highbrow critics—and these curious creatures lambasted it unmercifully. They called it banal, uninspired, a distortion of historical fact. They called it trite, dull, maudlin, and inept. But their small dissenting voices were drowned in the vast public roar of approval.

As Francis Cary sat in a small neighbourhood theatre and gazed at the thing he had wrought, a strange doubt began to fill his mind; but even as it did so, he reached in his pocket and took out one of the precious pills that Davison Funck had supplied, and devoured it. In a moment or two his qualms disappeared and he bought a bag of popcorn and returned to his seat to view the remainder of the film with infinite relish.

And as the days passed, he realized, also with infinite relish, that he had become a man of great importance—what the columnists called a VIP, a very important person. It was, indeed, a splendid importance, as warm and relaxing as a sunbath. Wherever he went, he felt like a man walking in a spotlight. He could almost hear people turning to each other and whispering, "There is the author of *The Fall of Carthage.*"

He felt that his appearance should be commensurate with this importance, and so he bought a half-dozen suits from an important tailor named Arnold Cohn, who catered only to the most distinguished people. And in these suits he appeared at the most expensive and celebrated restaurants to loll and drink and dine, and chat with other celebrities.

He hired a publicity agent named Resner, a huge fat man of incredible cunning and duplicity. It was this Resner who persuaded him to buy a dark and conservative Cadillac rather than a Jaguar. It was Resner who counselled him to be serious and earnest in his behaviour and manner.

"You're a writer," he said wisely, "and you're selling dignity and knowledge and serious talent. You look like a solid capable man and you should wind up a big producer. I have made ambassadors out of bigger boobs than you!"

And so, by the shrewd manipulations of Resner, his public career began. He appeared at luncheons and spoke with grave wit to Rotarians, Kiwanians, Optimists, and Legionnaires, and they were all impressed by his appearance and his manner of speech. He seemed to achieve, almost exactly, a delicate balance of rigid conservatism and yet humane philosophy. He became a dedicated man, in the great Roosevelt tradition. He appealed to all the little people, or, appealing to their needs, he lifted them up by *his* bootstraps. Fattened somewhat by the savoury viands of Chasen's, Romanoff's, the Stork Club, and Twenty-One, Cary was now no longer Lincolnesque but seemed only the more solid and successful because of the added flesh that bulked his body. But what gave him his greatest influence was the gravity and solid common sense behind his sometimes seemingly light and humorous comments. And this too could be credited to Resner, who knew only too well that no man could become a Great American who could not tell a joke.

Perhaps achieving fame is like planning a chess game properly. And if this is so, Resner was a master strategist. For in a relatively short time Francis Cary was a *name*—a man who the least script girl knew was destined for high places. Even as the gross of *The Fall of Carthage* reached ten million, Cary's second picture was in production and promised to be another hit. At its preview the audience stood up and cheered and there could no longer be doubt in anyone's mind that Francis Cary knew what the public wanted. Perhaps no man since Cecil B. De Mille had shown such promise. Any head waiter could have predicted that soon he would be head of a major studio. It was no secret. It was hinted at elegant cocktail-parties. It was muttered at meetings of boards of directors. It was a blind item in a dozen movie gossip columns. And in the steam room at the Hillcrest Country Club, where all the powers that be relax after playing good gin rummy and bad golf, it was an absolute cinch.

It was also part of the dream of Francis Cary, and it would all have made him gloriously happy but for one strange and unaccountable thing—Arod Summers had cooled toward him.

As soon as he realized this, he redoubled his efforts to please her. He sat under the stars with her at the Hollywood Bowl and smiled as he realized that the music of Debussy, which he had once admired, now bored him immeasurably. And it was strange to him that Arod, who knew nothing whatever about music, seemed to love it. But he made no comment, being delighted just to sit close to her, knowing that tomorrow there would be friendly items about them in all the Hollywood columns.

He took her to Palm Springs for the tennis matches and to Mexico for the bullfights. He escorted her to the most exclusive parties. Because she thought it was good, he arranged to buy the latest Book-of-the-Month Club selection as a starring vehicle for her. But her coolness persisted. He found her, frequently, gazing at him, curiously, aloofly, as though trying to analyse something about him that was odd and distasteful.

At last, in a remote corner of Chasen's, over a bottle of vintage champagne, he said bluntly, "Something has happened to us, Arod."

"Something has happened to you," she said calmly, and sipped the wine with exasperating detachment.

"A lot has happened to me," he said, "I've come a long way in a short year."

"A short way in a long year," she murmured. He matched her aloofness, desperately.

"I'm afraid I don't quite understand you," he said.

"I'm afraid you're right," she said.

"God dammit!" he shouted, and then was silent as curious stares were fixed on them.

She laughed in his face and swept the mink stole into her arms and marched out of the restaurant. For a moment he sat there, stunned, and then ordered another bottle of champagne for himself. He sat there for a long time, drinking the wine and thinking. He could not figure it out. He knew there was no other man in her life at the moment. He remembered how wild her infatuation had once been and how definite, though gradual, had been its decline. She was bored with him and he could not understand why.

Then it struck him, deep in the second bottle of champagne, that he had paid her too much attention, too much homage. So he made a shrewd, if drunken, decision. He would play at her own game. He would be aloof himself, fight fire with fire. He would not see

her for a while. He would get somebody else for that part she wanted
—Gardner, Hayward, Jennifer Jones, Audrey Hepburn. He would
teach her a lesson.

Being very drunk now, but delighted with his cleverness, he
decided to go home, and asked the head waiter to call him a cab.
He rode home, slumped in the seat, and gazing amiably at the star-
lighted sky of Hollywood. He decided that one day soon he would
make a great picture about a cab-driver—a real study of the common
man, of the strange, troubled lives of all the little people who made
the world go around. For Francis Cary, right now, the world was
indeed going around. As he gradually passed out, he was smiling at
the thought of Arod coming back to him on her knees, figuratively
speaking, of course. But what white, lovely, elegantly proportioned
knees. . . .

In the hang-over that followed, he awaited her phone call. But
when it did not come, and the hang-over passed, he decided to remain
firm in his decision. Firmness became his *modus operandi*. He
delivered a firm speech before the Committee of Americans for
America. He issued a firm and ringing statement of faith in the
future of the film industry. He was firm with the writers preparing
a screen play for him, scolding them for being on page nineteen
instead of page ninety. Firmness was the straw to which he clung.
It was the whistle in his graveyard.

But he longed for her. He hated the coming of night. He slept
badly and ate little. He lost six pounds. His golf game fell to pieces.
He fought off sudden impulses to buy her automobiles, mink coats,
jewels. He drove through red lights and stop signs like a blind man,
dreaming about her. He began taking sleeping pills, aspirins, Tums,
Benzedrine. And at last he knew that he was pinning all his hopes
on winning the Oscar for *The Fall of Carthage*. He no longer thought
of this great accolade as a personal achievement or badge of merit,
as he had for these many months. He now saw it only as a way of
winning her back, of regaining her respect and admiration, her love.

His heart jumped when he learned that he had won a nomination,
and he began seeking her in all of their old haunts. He would walk
into these places, looking lonely and sad, hoping she might be there

and see him thus and be moved to pity him, to understand that in spite of his position and achievement he was after all a human being, a man who could be moved or hurt as well as the next one.

He saw her several times, but she only glanced at him. Once she was with a wild-haired Armenian author, again with an Italian painter, and then with a defensive line-backer for the Detroit Lions. He was angered and tormented, but he kept a grip on himself and bided his time.

At last the long-awaited night of the Academy Awards arrived and Cary sat in the audience, trembling in spite of the phenobarbital he had taken to quiet his nerves. When his name was called and thunderous applause broke out, he leaped from his seat and strode to the stage like a man in a trance. His forlorn hope was that she were there somewhere in the crowd, watching him. He took the shining Oscar and made a speech of acceptance, quiet, humble, and brief. He had worked on this for many sleepless midnights and thought it just the thing that might win her back. It posed him, in this supreme moment of triumph, as just a simple, humble man bereft of all affectation and pretence—a good and worthy and deserving human being.

But she was not there. He learned why later at Romanoff's where he anxiously sought her. He learned that she had gone deep-sea fishing at Mazatlan with a stuntman named Bud York.

He got drunk. He got drunker than ever before in his life. He got in a fist fight with an actor noted for his night-club combats, and won a draw. Later he side-swiped three parked automobiles and was picked up by the police and booked on a 502, for operation of a motor vehicle while intoxicated. The next day he paid a five-hundred dollar fine and through bleary eyes saw his name headlined in all the papers.

It was a stunning disgrace.

He did not go to the studio, but went straight from the City Hall to the Beverly Hills office of Davison Funck. There he sank into the deep, soft green chair and stared dismally at the benign face of the psychiatrist.

Funck said calmly, "I haven't seen you for a long time, but I have followed your career closely. You've done amazingly well."

"Haven't I?" Cary muttered.

"Are you out of pills?" Funck asked blandly.

"I am out of my mind," Cary said.

"Tell me about it," Funck said, and lighted his pipe.

"I've lost her," Cary said, as though he had gained the world only to lose his soul.

Funck smiled at him with a kind of Olympian pity.

"What have you done?' he asked.

Cary whirled on him. "What have I done? I made her a star! I made her an actress. She is no longer just the creature of Press agents." He walked close to Funck. "What have I done? Don't you read the papers? Don't you know what has happened to me?"

Funck smiled. "I have followed your ascension religiously," he said. "It is my own accomplishment, as well as yours."

"What do you mean?" Cary asked, leaning his hands on the mahogany desk.

"I gave you the great average mind," Funck said gently. "It is the perfect equipment for the motion-picture producer. Whatever you create, that entertains you, will be entertaining to millions. Whatever you say that seems profound and good to you will seem so to millions. I made you a normal human animal, and what could be more delightful and sensible than that?"

"I have never been so miserable in my life," Cary said. "Without Arod none of it makes sense and it is something far short of delightful."

"She despises you?" Funck asked with a strange smile.

"I'm dirt under her feet," Cary said, and sank back into the deep green chair, a tortured man.

Funck looked dreamily through the window. At last he said, "You will have to make a decision."

"Impossible," Cary muttered.

Funck ignored him and went on.

"She has rejected your change of character," he murmured. "In her way, she is a remarkable woman. She paid me a visit, knowing I was your friend. She told me of the monstrous thing you had become—that you had turned from a great poet into a sagacious pig, to a hypocritical monster. I did not tell her why, because I only betray my clients to themselves, not to others." He sighed. "I had not anticipated this."

"Nonsense!" Cary said.

"Not at all," Funck said. "You must now decide. Either you get this girl out of your mind, or you get my pills out of your system. It is up to you."

Cary rose. "I know only one thing," he said in utter misery, "I cannot live without her."

Funck extended his hand. "Give me the pills," he said.

Without a word Cary handed him the little cardboard box. Funck dropped them into the waste-basket. "You'll be all right," he said. He sighed again and smiled. "There is no way," he said. "There is no way to make the world inhabitable."

The change in Francis Cary began slowly but gained momentum swiftly. He went about his usual concerns, sad with the loss of Arod, but grimly fulfilling his commitments. Then it began to happen. Listening to a group of executives discussing budget and exploitation for his own new picture, Cary suddenly burst out laughing. They stared at him in surprise and then one of them asked what the joke was.

"The picture," Cary said. "The picture is the joke." He rose at the table and looked at them with contempt. "How is it possible, in a world like this," he asked, "that five men like you, all rich and serious, old and sick, can foist such an obscenity on the innocent public of the United States? How much money do you need? How elegant do your funerals have to be?"

He was met with the sudden breathless silence that confronts insanity. In the silence he turned and left the huge office.

The next day it was all over town. There were a dozen theories trying to explain it. Cary had gone mad—for love, for ambition, for power. The president of the company, a quiet little man who looked like a gifted chipmunk, called him on the telephone and suggested that he take a vacation, a trip to Mexico or Italy, or a sea voyage.

"Take one yourself," Cary replied, "where the elephants die, or try a voyage to Mars."

That did it.

Three days later Francis Cary was amongst the unemployed. Four days later he delivered a speech at an Optimists' Club luncheon in Englewood, suggesting that these genial fellows disband and remove at least one dismal anachronism from the modern American culture. He was not lynched for this but was very firmly escorted to the door.

The following day he rendered a verdict on the motion-picture business to a group of assembled newspapermen who drank his Scotch and Bourbon and listened with delight to his prognostications. That very night news stories and columns carried his dire predictions. MGM would be turned into an immense bowling alley. Twentieth-Century Fox would once again become an oil field. Warner's would be a riding academy, Paramount a psychiatric clinic for those driven mad by television. The business was doomed and the nation was doomed. Civilization was *in extremis* and perhaps the Bomb was the best solution.

For days after this blast he went around the town, as in the old times, a patron of the second-class bistros. Three times he was punched for what he had said: twice by actors seeking publicity and once by a scenario writer who really resented what he had said— the man was already out of work and worried. He drew with one actor, lost the decision to the other, and scored an easy victory over the writer who, though a hothead, was very small.

But he was ruined. The rats of Hollywood scurried down the gangplank of his sinking ship.

He returned to his old studio apartment and rehung "The Beast of Alamogordo". If he was not happy, he at least experienced a kind of bitter satisfaction. Probably no man holds greater love than for the child he has just whipped and so Cary, having castigated civilization publicly, began to feel a strange warmth for mankind. He felt it so keenly that he began work on a book. He phoned Davison Funck and asked the doctor to destroy his remaining wonder pills as a personal favour to human society.

"They were nothing," Funck said gently. "Only flour and sugar and the power of suggestion. I only enabled you to express yourself honestly. I freed you, temporarily, at least, from the pose you had created for yourself. No man can be completely a boob or a charlatan and be happy. He has to be a mixture of both. The redistribution of these ingredients is the sole function of psychiatry."

He hung up and it never occurred to Cary to wonder if he had lied about the make-up of the pills. Cary sat there for a long time and stared out of the window at the boulevard below. He did not see the yellow Cadillac park at the kerb but he heard the anxious knock at his door. Desperately hoping that it was she, he rushed to the door and opened it.

Like a weeping goddess she stood there, gazing at him through splendid tears. After a brief moment he flung his arms about her and they held each other as though it was their last embrace with life itself. He shut his eyes ecstatically, inhaling her perfume. It was the first time he had ever held her in his arms.

He could hear her saying, "I should never have doubted you, darling. I should have known you could never really change."

But for the first time in his life he realized what piffle and babble mere words can be. He swung her aloft in his arms and carried her triumphantly to the bed where all men begin and end. And there he discovered that all was still well with the world.

Death Double

BY WILLIAM F. NOLAN

William F. Nolan has lived in California all his life and as a result has come to understand the mystique of Hollywood with rare insight. Intimately concerned with the worlds of Science Fiction since his boyhood, he has published a regular appreciation magazine about his mentor, Ray Bradbury, co-authored one of the most notable fantasy novels in recent years, Logan's Run, *which is to be filmed by M.G.M., and produced numerous splendid tales and anthologies.*

Clayton Weber eased himself down from the papier mâché mountain and wiped the artificial sweat from his face. 'How'd I look?' he asked the director.

'Great,' said Victor Raddish. 'Even Morell's own mother wouldn't know the difference.'

'That's what I like to hear,' grinned Weber, seating himself at a makeup table. Thus far, *Courage at Cougar Canyon*, starring 'fearless' Claude Morell as the Yellowstone Kid had gone smoothly. Doubling for Morell, Weber had leaped chasms, been tossed from rolling wagons, dived into rivers and otherwise subjected himself to the usual rigors of a movie stuntman. Now, as he removed his makeup, he felt a hand at his shoulder.

'Mr. Morell would like to see you in his dressing room,' a studio messenger boy told him.

Inside the small room Weber lit a cigarette and settled back on the brown leather couch. Claude Morell, tall and frowning, stood facing him.

'Weber, you're a nosy, rotten bastard and I ought to have you thrown off the lot and blacklisted with every studio in town.'

'Then Linda told you about my call?'

'Of course she did. Your imitation of my voice was quite excellent. Seems you do as well off-camera as on. She was certain that *I* was talking or she never would have—'

'—discussed the abortion,' finished Weber, feet propped on the couch.

Morell's eyes hardened. 'How much do you want to keep silent?' Morell seated himself at a dressing table and flipped open his checkbook.

'Bribery won't be necessary,' smiled Clayton Weber through the spiraling smoke of his cigarette. 'I don't intend to spill the beans to Hedda Hopper. The fact that you impregnated the star of our picture and that she is about to have an abortion will never become public knowledge. You can depend on that.'

Morell looked confused. 'Then . . . I don't—'

'Have you ever heard of the parallel universe theory?'

Morell shook his head, still puzzled.

'It's simply this—that next to our own universe an infinite number of parallel universes exist—countless millions of them—each in many ways identical to this one. Yet the life pattern is different in each. Every variation of living is carried out, with a separate universe for each variation. Do you follow me?'

Obviously, Morell did not.

'Let me cite examples,' said Weber. 'In one of these parallel universes Lincoln was never assassinated; in another Columbus did *not* discover America, nor did Joe Louis become heavyweight champ. In one universe, America *lost* the First World War. . . .'

'But that's ridiculous,' Morell said. 'Dream stuff.'

'Let me approach it from another angle,' persisted Weber. 'You've heard of Doppelgangers?'

'You mean—*doubles*?'

'Not simply doubles, they are exact duplicates.' Weber drew on his cigarette, allowing his words to take effect. 'The reason you never see two of them together, for comparison, is that one of them always knows he is a duplicate of the other—and stays out of the other's life. Or enters it wearing a disguise.'

'You're talking gibberish,' said Claude Morell.

'Bear with me. The true Doppelganger *knows* he is not of this universe—and he chooses to stay away from his duplicate because it is too painful for him to see his own life being lived by another man, to see his wife and children and know they can never be his. So he builds a new life for himself in another part of the world.'

'I don't see the point, Weber. What are you telling me?'

Clayton Weber smiled. 'You'll see my point soon enough.' He continued. 'Sometimes a man or woman will simply vanish, wink out, as it were without a trace. Ambrose Bierce, the writer, was one of these. Then there was the crew of the *Marie Celeste*. . . . They unknowingly reached a point in time and space that allowed them to step through into a separate world, like and yet totally unlike their own. They became Doppelgangers.'

Weber paused, his eyes intent on Morell. '*I'm* one of them,' he said. 'It happened to me as it happened to them, without any warning. One moment I was happily married with a beautiful wife and a baby girl—the next I found myself in the middle of Los Angeles. Sometimes it's impossible to adjust to this situation. Some of us end up in an institution, claiming we're other people.' He smiled again. 'And—of course we *are*.'

Morell stood up, replacing the checkbook in his coat. 'I don't know what kind of word game you're playing, Weber, but I've had enough of it. You refuse my offer—all right, you're fired. And if a word of this affair with Linda Miller ever hits print I'll not only see that you never work again in the industry, I'll also see that you receive the beating of your life. And I have the connections to guarantee a *thorough* job.'

'Do one thing for me, Mr. Morell,' asked Weber. 'Just hold out your right hand, palm up.'

'I don't see—'

'Please.'

Morell brought up his hand. Weber raised his own, placing it beside Morell's. 'Look at them,' he said. 'Look at the shape of the thumbs, the lines in the palm, the whorls on each finger-tip.'

'Good God!' said Claude Morell.

The man who called himself Clayton Weber reached up and began to work on his face. The cheek lines were altered as he withdrew some inner padding, his nose became smaller as he peeled away a thin layer of wax. In a moment the change was complete.

'Incredible,' Morell breathed. 'That's my face!'

'I had to look enough like you to get this job as your double,' Weber told him, 'but of course I couldn't look *exactly* like you. Now, however, we are identical.' He withdrew the Colt from the hip holster of his western costume and aimed it at Morell.

'No blanks this time,' he said.

'But why kill me?' Morell backed to the wall. 'Even if all you said is true, why kill me? They'll send you to the gas chamber. You'll die with me!'

'Wrong,' grinned Weber. 'The death will be listed as a suicide. A note will be found on the dresser in the apartment I rented, stating "Clayton Weber's" intention to do away with himself, that he felt he'd always be a failure, nothing but a stuntman, while others became stars. It will make excellent sense to the police. I will report that you shot yourself in my presence as we discussed the career you could never have.'

'But my face will be the face of Claude Morell, not Clayton Weber!'

'Half of your face will be disposed of by the bullet at such close range. There will be no question of identity. And we're both wearing the same costume.'

Morell leaned forward, eyes desperate. 'But why? Why?'

'I'm killing you for what you did to my wife,' said Weber, holding the gun steady.

'But—I never *met* your wife.'

'In your world, this world, Linda Miller was just another number on your sexual hit parade, but in my world she was my wife. In *my* world that baby girl she carries in her body was born, allowed to live. And that's just the way it's going to happen now. If you'd married Linda I would have disappeared, gone to live in another city, left you alone. But you didn't. So, *I'll* marry her—again.'

Claude Morell chose that moment to spring for the gun, but the bullet from the big Colt sent his head flying into bright red pieces.

The man who had called himself Clayton Weber placed the smoking weapon in Morell's dead hand.

Booked Solid

BY RAY RUSSELL

Ray Russell made his name both in Hollywood and throughout the world in 1961 with Sardonicus, *a Gothic horror film starring Oscar Homolka and Guy Rolfe which he scripted from his own short story. A former editor at* Playboy *magazine, Russell has written widely for the screen and even landed a major international film award. He recently completed a black-humour novel about Hollywood entitled* The Colony.

Ed Keally, sitting next to me in the bar, drinking beer, verified the date: "It was October 10th," he said. "I know because it was the afternoon before we opened in Chicago, and we opened on the 11th."

Ed, at that time, was stage manager for *Brief Candle,* the Virgil Leslie comedy of a few years back. "We were backstage at the Harwyn Theatre. I had just had a run-through for the third-act extras we'd picked up in Chi. This Zebrowski gal was one of them. She was playing the maid: a walk-on, no lines. But after the run-through, she was trying to convince me she should play Julie. You know the play? Well, it's the usual Leslie crap: two acts of triangular dialogue tailor-made for himself, Wynn and Lorraine, with a loud, confused third act that brings in a lot of new people in the inevitable party scene. This Julie is one of the new people—a small part, but kind of cute. You remember the character Dumby in *Lady Winder-mere's Fan?* Doesn't say much, but when he does, it's a gem? Well, this Julie is out of the same box. Sybil Danleigh played it in London.

It *needs* a good comedienne like her, but for New York and the road we had a cretin with a peroxide head and a thirty-eight chest who didn't know a cue from a hole in the ground. Friend of our biggest angel."

At this point, it was just like Ed to deplore the mores of his business in a strangely puritanical manner. When I had agreed with him and had exchanged disapproving grunts and sage nods, he ordered another beer and went on:

"Anyway, this kid thought The Cretin was lousy, and told me so. Then she begged me to give *her* the part. 'Look,' I said, 'I'm only the lowly stage-manager. I don't cast. Talk to the director, not to me.' In this case, of course, the director was also the author and one of the three co-stars: Virgil Leslie himself. 'Do you think he'll see me?' she asked. 'No, I don't,' I told her. Then she says, 'Please help me, Mr. Keally. I'd do anything to get that part!' That was when I first saw him."

"Him?"

"Joe Dunn."

Ah! Now my interview with Ed was bearing fruit: his rambling story began to sharpen focus.

"He slid into the backstage phone-booth. The only reason I noticed him was because he looked kind of familiar. I couldn't place him, but I was sure I'd seen that guy hanging around theatres and bars and handbooks from L. A. to Marblehead. Thin. No lips. Narrow eyes. I pegged him for a racketeer. He was cast for the part! Well, the gal was still beating her gums: 'Don't you think if *you* talked to Mr. Leslie, he'd see me?' I drew pictures for her: 'Kid,' I said, 'I'm nobody. Leslie has to think twice before he remembers my name. Besides, there are such things as contracts: he can't kick her out of the cast: she'd sue him.' I didn't go into the problem of her influential friend in New York. She started to open her yap again, but my phone rang. It was on the other side of the stage, and one of the cast answered it: Bud Gerhardt, an old trouper, played the butler, hell of a nice guy. 'It's for you,' he said. I walked over and took it.

"I recognized the voice right away: from the first word I had an image of a fat, red-faced little guy with not much hair and English tweeds which were just not his type at all. He was The Cretin's benefactor: I'd seen him backstage a lot in New York. He was calling long-distance from there and wanted to speak to his little charge. She was at the stage door, tossing a mink stole around her and all set to walk out with one of the young fellows in the company. I called her over.

"And that's all I know except that about 12:30 that night (the rest of the company were hitting the high spots, but I was in my room with a book) I get a call from Leslie. He just tells me to get some program inserts printed by the next night and to call all the third act people for another rehearsal at eleven A. M. The inserts are to read: *The role of Julie is played by Lilith Kane.*

"Lilith Kane turned out to be the Zebrowski girl. You could have blown me over. At the rehearsal the next morning, she was fine. Good looking, plenty of poise, and what a sense of comedy timing! Man, that night we had laughs we never had before. The whole last act brightened up—and I heard Leslie tell Wynn and Lorraine that he thought that gal was almost as good as Sybil Danleigh."

"How much experience had she had before that, Ed, do you know?"

"Yeah. She told me one night in the green room. Not much experience at all. Three years in a drama school, a couple of summers in stock—which she hated, by the way. She wasn't one of these amateurs who are content to play stock for years. She wanted to make the big time, quick. She'd had enough of playing in barns with tiny stages and squeaking floor-boards and noisy roll-up curtains. Had enough of sleepy summer audiences, too. It was sheer hell to her; she was an ambitious kid." Ed paused to sip a thoughtful dram of beer. "Nothing else to say. That's about all. That's the story of the birth of the late Lilith Kane."

That was not, as Ed claimed, all. But it was all he could tell me. I had to be filled in by the young lady who, although not exactly brilliant, was not—as Ed had described her—a cretin. She was married now, to a prominent producer, and her hair was currently red.

"So I pick up the phone and I hear this voice. Well, it's Bunny! I'd know his voice anywhere. Had a voice like a bull-frog. And he says: 'Listen, my dear. There's a great opening for you here in New York. You're all set for Ophelia in the Raphael Bowman Hamlet, but the reading is next week and rehearsals start week after that. Can you shake *Brief Candle*?' Well, you can imagine how I felt! Ophelia! I mean, after all! I told him I had a contract, but he said: 'Don't worry about that. Without me, that show would fold like a cracker-box. Leslie will listen to reason. Is he there?' Well, Mr. Leslie had just gone, so I said 'No' and he said, 'That's all right. What's his number?' I got his phone number from Ed Keally and Bunny said, 'Get a reservation on the next plane out of Chicago. Then send me a wire and I'll meet you at the airport.' And he hung up.

"Next thing I know Mr. Leslie is telling me that I'm to return to New York immediately, and he's cursing and carrying on about having to rehearse a new girl and maybe even delay the opening. There's a knock at the door. Before Mr. Leslie can even say boo, this tall skinny guy walks in. 'Who the hell are you?' says Mr. Leslie. Mad. 'I'm sorry to interrupt you, Mr. Leslie,' this thin-lipped fellow says. 'But I'm the representative of Lilith Kane, one of the brightest young comediennes on the theatrical horizon . . .' (Mr. Leslie starts to say something, but the guy goes right on:) '. . . who is not only eminently gifted, but who *knows every word and move of the part of Julie*.' Isn't it funny how I remember every word he said, so exact? He was so calm and cool he made an impression on me. Well, Mr. Leslie kind of does a double-take and then says, real polite: 'Will you wait outside a moment, sir? I'll talk to you in a moment.'

"So I fly to New York. And am I mad when Bunny isn't waiting at the airport. But I'm madder when I call him up and he says what the hell am I doing in New York and *what* Ophelia and *whose* Hamlet and am I crazy or something? We swore at each other for ten minutes and finally he drove down to the airport and picked me up. Was *he* mad!"

The lady had more to say, but no more that has any bearing on my story. The following letter, from London, reached me that after-noon:

Dear Sir,

In reply to your request for material concerning Miss Kane, I can tell you that my first contact with her was in Chicago, October of 1946, when I hired her as a last-minute replacement for my play, "Brief Candle." I met her through her agent, a man named Dunn. The actress who had been playing the part had been called back to New York, and—presumably—Mr. Dunn had heard of our pre-dicament.

The next day, however, a call from one of our chief backers con-vinced us that the previous day's New York call was obviously a hoax—possibly on the part of Mr. Dunn. We were angry, of course, but we had no proof, Miss Kane's contract had already been signed, and—to tell the truth—Miss Kane proved so delightful in the role that I would have been loath to dismiss her even had I been able.

After the road tour, we parted and I had no more dealings with her, although, as you know, she went on to a particularly brilliant career.

I hope I have been able to help you.

Very sincerely,
Virgil Leslie

I have dwelt at length on the opening of Lilith Kane's career because my facts on that portion of her life are quite substantial and from many reliable sources. From that point on, however, intimate personal data paradoxically grows scarce and I will be obliged to resort to some "reconstruction" of my own in order to make what-ever shreds and patches I have gathered adhere.

In New York, a major broadcasting company is auditioning young women for a new role in a perennial soap opera. Perhaps twenty women are sitting about the studio on brown metal folding-chairs. Some are alone, others with husbands, boy-friends, agents. Lilith Kane sits next to the steely-eyed Joe Dunn, her agent. On her other side is a pretty girl, nervous with expectation. The girl has started a conversation some minutes before. She has told Lilith that her name is Jane Conway, that she is from Gary, Indiana, and that she has done work in community theatre. Now she is asking, "Where is the lady's room?" Lilith tells her, and the girl rises, saying, "I'll be right back." At the microphone up front, a woman is reading from a mimeographed script.

From a loudspeaker, a disembodied voice says: "Thank you." After a pause, the voice says: "Sorry, ladies, but this next will have to be the last for today." Groans of disappointment fill the studio. "Quiet, please. Conway?" Silence. "Jane Conway? Jane?"

Joe Dunn hisses to Lilith: "Get up there!"

"What? . . ."

"Get up there!"

Puzzled, Lilith walks to the microphone and begins reading.

It is a matter of record that Lilith Kane (pseudonym Jane Conway, which studio officials told her was less glamorous than her real name to which they advised her to revert) played Teresa on *Second Husband* for eight months, the last three months working simultaneously with evening performances of:

> *The Indestructible Mr. Fawcett,* a dismal piece of whimsy which closed the night it opened;
>
> an off-Broadway revival of *Candida* with an odious cast that even Lilith's fine playing of the name-part could not counteract;
>
> and, finally, *Ravishing Strides,* in which she was so successful that she abandoned the radio show.

Ravishing Strides was a dirty, brittle fantasy by Farley York (a Virgil Leslie imitator) in which Lilith played the shade of Catherine the Great with a Russian accent, decolletage down to the navel, and situations that would have made even the real Catherine blush with embarrassment. Except for Lilith's larger-than-life portrayal, the press condemned the piece, but the public found it a riotous evening's entertainment that stretched into a twenty-month bonanza.

In his recent autobiography, Farley York tells it this way:

"Who would play Catherine? All the pretties in town were fluttering about little Farley (and some of the not-so-pretties, too, I recall!). Their shrill cackles bombarded my shell-like ears and expensive perfume rose seductively out of a score of equally expensive necklines to assail my quivering nostrils. I, however, was as stone. I allowed nothing to sway me but the dictates of my oldest flame, The Muse, who sat on my padded shoulder like Mr. Coffee-Nerves. Then, like a bolt from the wild blue yonder, came the inspiration: Sybil Danleigh, of course! I had last seen the old girl in London, playing a clever bit in some trifle of Leslie's, and though I knew her to be an old soak, she was superb. I cabled London, instanter."

Two paragraphs later in Mr. York's book:

". . . Halfway through rehearsal came the blow: Sybil was dead drunk. What could I do? Nonplussed, I told my stage-manager, Joey Dunn, to read the part for the nonce. He passed the task to a lesser member of the company, a good looking girl who was playing Lise, and we started again. *Quel sortilège!* The girl was good! Not only was she a better actress than dear old Sybil, but she was *young,* and the enchanting swell of her sweater promised a cleavage that would nicely complement Rod Condor's daring designs. Need I mention that her name was Lilith Kane?"

It is still a subject of conjecture how a fifth of Scotch got into Miss Danleigh's hotel room that afternoon. It is a fact, however, that Mr. York's stage manager called on her that morning in order to inform her of the afternoon's rehearsal. Although why he couldn't have simply phoned, I wouldn't care to say. . . .

Here I must insert some of that reconstruction I spoke about:

"How do I look, Joe?" asked Lilith, stepping from her bedroom.

"Good enough to take a bite out of," answered Dunn. Her exquisite body was sheathed in black satin so tight it displayed every ripple of her lean and interesting stomach-muscles, while the copious eighty percent of her revealed bosom gleamed its dull, powdered pinkness in almost luminous contrast. "Turn around."

Behind, the satin plunged down to below the small of her back. Heavy perfume, heated by the warmth of her blood, sent its waves of spiced persuasion writhing upward from the cascades of naked flesh.

Dunn was arranging a table with glasses, hors d'oeuvres and a bottle of champagne in ice. "Play your cards right tonight, and you'll be in the chips. Know what to do?"

"You've coached me enough."

"Well," Dunn flashed one of his rare cold smiles, "if you forget your lines, just let that female instinct take over. Steiner saw you in *Ravishing Strides* and can't get his mind off you. He'll do the rest. I'd better get out of here. He's due any minute. Luck, baby." And he vanished into his adjoining suite. Some minutes later, Lilith answered a discreet knock at her door.

The following is a newspaper clipping:

> ### LILITH KANE NAMED IN STEINER SUIT
> Lilith Kane, comely star of "Ravishing Strides," current Broadway hit, was named today by Julia Steiner, wife of Olympia Pictures head Jake Steiner, as co-respondent in a divorce suit. . . .

The next year was a lucrative one for Lilith, and one filled with acclaim. She starred in a hugely successful Technicolor version of *Moll Flanders,* and followed this by the equally successful saga of violence and sex in old Italy called *Blood and Wine.*

Now, Jake Steiner was a canny businessman. He knew what the public liked, and he knew they liked his wife, Lilith, in those low-cut, swashbuckling epics in which it was his wont to cast her. But Lilith had other plans. She was beginning to get artistic yearnings. She wanted Jake to get her Raphael Bowman to star with her in a film *Macbeth.* "I'd make a great Lady Macbeth," she would say.

"Sure you would, honey," Jake would answer, "but who wants to sit and listen to Shakespeare and look at that Bowman guy with that nose? Schoolroom stuff. 'Tomorrow and tomorrow and tomorrow and tomorrow.' I know all about it—I ain't so dumb. No, baby. No *Macbeth.*"

And so, one night, Lilith sat in a dark little Hollywood bar with Joe Dunn.

"Too bad, Lilith," said Joe. "I'd like to see you as Lady Macbeth, too, but Jake's an obstinate guy."

"Can't you talk to him, Joe?" she asked, rolling about the olive in her empty martini glass.

"Me?" Joe almost laughed. "Who am I?"

"You're the guy who got me every break I ever had—right from the time you cornered me backstage at the Harwyn in Chicago and said—"

" 'May I speak to you, Miss Kane?' " Joe mimicked himself.

"That's right. And I said: 'You've got the wrong party. My name's Wanda Zebrowski.' "

"And I replied: 'It *was*. But from now on it's Lilith Kane. With your permission, of course.' Then we went across the street for a drink." Joe laughed in reminiscence. "Lilith . . ." he said, suddenly changing the subject, "Jake willed you his controlling interest in Olympia, didn't he?"

"Of course," she smiled. "I kept after him, just as you told me to. I have ways."

"I know. How old is Jake, anyway?"

"Fifty-five."

"Hmm. You know, when he dies, you'll practically own that studio, and you can make any picture you want: *Macbeth* included."

She frowned. "I can't wait that long, Joe."

"You can't, eh?"

"No."

"Want to listen to a little idea of mine?"

"Why not? Your little ideas haven't steered me wrong yet."

An interlude of solid fact, in the concise form of newspaper column-heads:

STEINER, MOVIE MOGUL, DIES
Coroner Blames Sleeping Pills
SUICIDE HINTED IN STEINER DEATH
LILITH QUESTIONED IN STEINER CASE
(Photo caption:) Lilith Kane, lovely actress-widow of late Jake Steiner, seen leaving coroner's office with Joseph Dunn, friend of Steiner family.
STEINER MURDERED?
D. A. Calls Special Session
D. A. ACCUSES LILITH!
New Evidence Throws Court into Turmoil
JURY STILL OUT IN STEINER TRIAL

LILITH TO DIE!
Actress Guilty; Faints at Sentence
(Photo caption:) Lilith Kane (face hidden) escorted from court-
room by Sheriff.

It is a matter of record that Lilith Kane was sentenced to die at
ten P. M., April 29th, of this year.

And now, patient reader, I am going to ask you to bear with me.
For I am about to indulge in the most flagrant piece of reconstruction in this whole history. You may call it fanciful, absurd, ground-
less. Literally speaking, it is probably all of these. But I can think of
only one way to end this story. You may reject it if you wish.

The last scene of this tale take place on the night of April 29th.

9:58 P. M. The luminous dial of the wristwatch cast a spectral
glow in the thick and heavy gloom. Joe's eyes narrowed, scanning
the murk. They glinted, those eyes. They seemed as luminous as
the watch. Impatient, he sighed and began to pace again. The fog
weaved around him. He was a black and bat-like silhouette.

Then he stopped. He had heard something. The click of a woman's
heel. While he squinted, a shape congealed out of the obscurity. It
was Lilith.

"Over here!" he called, waving. She groped toward him, her
vague outline growing more distinct as she approached. "Joe!" she
breathed with relief.

"You're right on time," he smiled. "Right on time." It was ten
P. M. by his wristwatch.

"Joe, the reprieve! You got it! You must have. But. . . ."

"I said I would, didn't I?"

"Everything happened so quickly, though. I had given up hope.
How did you swing it? One moment I was in the death-house, and
then—"

"No time for chatter now, honey. We're on a tight schedule. Let's
go."

"Where are we going?" She followed him through the mist, her
hand in his.

"You'll see."

"Is it far?"

·

"Far enough."

"Far enough . . ." she echoed, with a trace of despair. "Far enough to live down the disgrace, the humiliation? Joe, you couldn't get me a booking now in summer stock!"

"Don't worry," was his response. He turned, and his eyes looked directly into hers. They were blazing now, those eyes. And Lilith realized, with a suddenly freezing heart, that the hand which held hers possessed a strength far beyond physical force; that the voice which had advised her all these years was the same that had tempted Job and had bargained with Faust.

Inside the prison, the coroner was saying, "I pronounce this woman dead."

While Outside and Beyond, Lilith grew faint at the sight the thinning mists revealed: a converted barn; a shallow stage with creaking floor-boards and a clattering asbestos roll-curtain; in the house, a handful of completely bored auditors. Joe's hand seemed to sink into her very bone.

"Baby, you're booked solid. From now on!"

The Hollywood Horror Man

BY BORIS KARLOFF

For my box-office money the finest of all the Hollywood horror-film stars was Boris Karloff who brought a depth of understanding and a consummate actor's skill to every major horror role he played. No one else was quite his equal and his death in 1969 robbed the genre of its outstanding exponent. For me, too, he personified the Hollywood illusion—the man who before the cameras could terrify any audience, yet off-screen was a quite different person altogether. Born William Henry Pratt in Dulwich, London, in 1878, he moved to Hollywood during the early years of this century, but had to be content with bit-parts until 1931. In that year he was offered the part of the monster in James Whale's production of Frankenstein *(the role having been turned down by Bela Lugosi) and his performance made him an international star overnight. In later years he was to portray other monsters, a great many practitioners of evil and a whole variety of strange half-human creatures—but the Frankenstein monster remained his supreme achievement. In the article which follows (written by Karloff shortly before his death and subsequently only printed in a specialist publication) he discusses his life and work and how it feels to be right at the very heart of the Hollywood Nightmare. . . .*

Being a bogeyman—like baggage carrying and truck driving—is apt to be a rather exhausting occupation. I know, because I've tried all three. But on the whole, I think I would prefer truck driving to house haunting were it not for the fact that the latter job is likely to be more remunerative. And, of course, you meet the most interesting werewolves!

Nevertheless the Hollywood horror man runs into numerous occupational hazards that have nothing to do with the hours of work or the risks run in actual performance.

There is, for example, one's social life to consider. Although actors have long since come to realise that their private lives are everyone's concern but their own, they have at least the comfort of knowing that their public is certain to be reasonably well disposed towards them. Not so in my case.

For, no matter how pleasant the company in which I find myself, there is always that awkward moment when newcomers become aware of the fact that the quiet-spoken man in the corner is actually Boris Karloff. Nor are hostesses ever quite sure what I feed myself upon while other guests are sipping their whisky-and-sodas.

According to the popular impression, my hostesses regard me variously as a zombie, a ghoul, an ogre, a vampire, and a monster.

As a result, they become convinced that a typical dinner for Karloff should consist of (a) one steaming witch's potion, (b) one piece of red raw meat ripped from a live and struggling anatomy, (c) one soothing bowl of fresh blood. But, whatever the jest with which hostesses try to pass off their uneasiness, I am often aware that they look upon me with about the same degree of trust and confidence as they would upon a cobra de capello!

Acquaintances, asking me to their summer homes, fill their medicine cabinets with such niceties as arsenic, old daggers, strychnine, cyanide, and ground glass—somehow feeling that this will make me happy.

For all these reactions I have naturally no one but myself to blame. For years now I have been haunting houses—motion-picture houses and private homes with television—ever since I first strode on the screen in full horrifying armor as the Monster of Frankenstein.

Guilty must I plead likewise to supplying the goose pimples in such pictures as *The Mummy, The Mask of Fu Manchu, The Ghoul, The Black Room, The Raven, Devil's Island, The Man*

They Could Not Hang, *The Man With Nine Lives*, and *The Devil Commands*, each with its full complement of shudders.

My role in *Arsenic and Old Lace* tended to spoof the more serious-minded of the horror films. Yet, all the same, I found myself playing a murderer of considerable distinction, while my fellow players garnered the lion's portion of the laughs. If that all sounds rather sinister, I might add that the author made a good deal of fun of Jonathan Brewster, but that does not prevent the role from being reasonably grim and gruesome.

Typical of the embarrassment attendant upon my sort of career was an incident that occurred shortly after the filming of *Frankenstein*. Mrs Karloff and I had gone up to San Francisco to visit one of her school friends. To our surprise, we found that *Frankenstein*, which we had not yet seen, was playing across the bay, in Oakland. What could be more natural than to invite our friend to a performance?

I had, of course, seen rushes of the picture, but never a connected version, and as the film progressed I was amazed at the hold it was taking upon the audience. At the same time I couldn't help wondering how my own performance would weather all the build-up.

I was soon to know.

Suddenly, out of the eerie darkness and gloom, there swept on the screen, about eight sizes larger than life itself, the chilling horrendous figure of me as the Monster!

And, just as suddenly, there crashed out over the general stillness the stage whisper of my wife's friend. Covering her eyes, gripping my wife by the shoulder, she screamed:

"Dot, how can you live with that creature?"

I was really surprised on arriving in London or New York to find people quite as apt to stare at me on the street as in Hollywood. Even in the theatrical hotel at which I first registered I seemed to attract more than what I consider my share of attention.

But actually not everyone cringes in horror at my approach. On the contrary, I have encountered an amazing amount of sympathy and understanding for parts that seemed to me fairly loathsome. Yet there is always a touch of wonder that I am not given to eating eight or nine orphans for breakfast. People are inclined to take somewhat the attitude of the famous Marquise du Deffand. Once, during the course of a conversation, someone asked her: "My dear madame, do you believe in ghosts?"

And she smiled sagely and replied, "No—but I'm afraid of them!"

Speaking of ghost stories, my presence at any gathering seems to be all that is needed to inspire an endless flood of them. Even when I returned to England, I found myself listening to an entire evening of such tales in my home town of Dulwich.

One of the most famous of all English ghost stories was told again that night. It concerned Harriet Westbrook, unhappy wife of the poet Shelley, who drowned herself more than a century ago in the Serpentine, the famous sheet of water that winds through Hyde Park.

One day, just before the First World War, two elderly English ladies were taking a stroll through the park. It was a chilly, windy afternoon in early autumn. The park was almost deserted. As the ladies paused at the bank of the Serpentine, they noticed a series of curious ripples on the water, which caused them to wonder, for they knew there were no fish in the Serpentine.

As they watched the ripples, fascinated, a hand suddenly pierced the surface of the water—a human hand, thin and white, a woman's hand! It clutched frantically, desperately, at the air. It clutched like the hand of a drowning person. It then disappeared again under the surface of the water.

But on the middle finger of the hand, both elderly ladies had seen a heavy gold ring, flashy and bright against the drabness of the bleak afternoon.

The two old ladies were dumbfounded, petrified in their tracks, for they knew, as all London knew, that according to history Harriet Westbrook Shelley drowned wearing such a ring—a century ago!

By way of a leavening note, I might add that the only time I really enjoyed playing the Monster was at the annual charity baseball game in Hollywood between a team of comedians and a team of leading men. I strode up to the plate for the occasion in my full make-up as Frankenstein's Monster—whereupon the late Buster Keaton, who was catching for the comedians, promptly shrieked at the sight of me, did a backward somersault, and passed out cold behind the plate.

I waved my bat. The pitcher tossed the ball in my direction, and I swung at it as best I could, encumbered as I was with the Monster's metallic overalls. Luckily enough, I managed to tap the ball, which bounced crazily in the general direction of the pitcher's box. It should have been an easy out at first. But as I approached each base the opposing player fainted dead away. And the Three Stooges, who were playing second, all passed out cold. It was a home run—though horrible!

But I can't possibly take leave of you without one last plea for my personal character. I am a normal and quiet soul. My wife will tell you gladly of the time we had guests in the house and the TV blared forth the report of a murderous lunatic who had broken loose and was in the vicinity of our neighborhood. The announcer suggested the forming of a neighborhood posse. Well, one of my guests rose and said:

"Karloff, let's take a quick drink before going out after that murderer."

They all went to the bar and drank—except me.

"Have a drink, Karloff," my friend insisted.

But I wasn't in the mood. "No thanks, not me," I replied. "It gives me too much courage!"

All of which, the reader may surmise, is offered in substantiation of the argument that I am really a mild and harmless sort of fellow who likes his coffee warm and his fruit juice cold; who enjoys nothing more than puttering around his garden or lying in the sun and reading Joseph Conrad.

And, just to prove that I am not alone in this conviction, I might add I appeared as Santa Claus at a party for crippled children. Which I did, successfully!

And on a recent television program I managed to get away with one of the sweetest and most sentimental scenes of Smilin' Through!

But, of course, such performances are as unusual as they are gratifying to a professional horror man. On the whole, I suspect that I am likely to spend the rest of my career as a purveyor of the macabre, constantly adding to the perils of life on the screen.

Actually, my life is nowhere near as bleak as I like to make it sound. For every correspondent who writes that my last picture kept him or her awake all night (obviously an exaggeration intended as flattery) there are a dozen tending from curiosity to sympathy. Whoever said that nobody loves a zombie has never peeked into my fan mail!

So, on balance then, I have no complaints to make about the roles in which I have appeared, and I hope that from what I have written here you will perhaps realise that despite the houses I have haunted, I do have a heart (my own) and I'm not a vicious ghoul.

I'm *really* not, you know!

The Casket-Demon

BY FRITZ LEIBER

In this story the renowned Fritz Leiber spotlights that most important—indeed vital—aspect of film making: publicity. The interest of the public in a projected movie has to be generated right from the start, and the Hollywood PRO has become almost a symbol of the world he represents: flamboyant, verbose and utterly relentless in pursuing his objectives. Leiber, whose father and mother were both actors, in fact first tried to make his living in Hollywood in pictures (his best scene in an Errol Flynn epic ended on the cutting room floor, he says), but disillusioned with his lack of progress turned to writing and is now generally acknowledged as being one of the top half-dozen Science Fiction authors. If ever a man demonstrated an understanding of the headlines-at-all-cost system it is Leiber in this sardonic tale. . . .

"There's nothing left for it—I've got to open the casket," said Vividy Sheer, glaring at the ugly thing on its square of jeweled and gold-worked altar cloth. The most photogenic face in the world was grim as a valkyry's this Malibu morning.

"No," shuddered Miss Bricker, her secretary. "Vividy, you once let me peek in through the little window and I didn't sleep for a week."

"It would make the wrong sort of publicity," said Maury Gender, the nordic film-queen's press chief. "Besides that, I value my life." His gaze roved uneasily across the gray "Pains of the

Damned" tapestries lining three walls of the conference room up to its black-beamed 20-foot ceiling.

"You forget, baroness, the runic rhymes of the Prussian Nostrodamus," said Dr. Rumanescue, Vividy's astrologist and family magician. " '*Wenn der Kassette-Tuefel . . .*'—or to translate roughly, 'When the casket-demon is let out, The life of the Von Sheer is in doubt.' "

"My triple-great grandfather held out against the casket-demon for months," Vividy Sheer countered.

"Yes, with a demi-regiment of hussars for bodyguard, and in spite of their sabres and horse pistols he was found dead in bed at his Silesian hunting lodge within a year. Dead in bed and black as a beetle—and the eight hussars in the room with him as nightguard permanently out of their wits with fear."

"I'm stronger than he was—I've conquered Hollywood," Vividy said, her blue eyes sparking and her face all valkyry. "But in any case if I'm to live weeks, let alone months, I *must* keep my name in the papers, as all three of you very well know."

"Hey, hey, what goes on here?" demanded Max Rath, Vividy Sheer's producer, for whom the medieval torture-tapestries had noiselessly parted and closed at the bidding of electric eyes. His own little shrewd ones scanned the four people, veered to the black gnarly wrought-iron casket, no bigger than a cigar box, with its tiny peep-hole of cloudy glass set in the top, and finally came to rest on the only really incongruous object in the monastically-appointed hall—a lavender-tinted bathroom scales.

Vividy glared at him, Dr. Rumanescue shrugged eloquently, Miss Bricker pressed her lips together, Maury Gender licked his own nervously and at last said, "Well, Vividy thinks she ought to have more publicity—every-day-without-skips publicity in the biggest papers and on the networks. Also, she's got a weight problem."

Max Rath surveyed in its flimsy dress of silk jersey the most voluptuous figure on six continents and any number of islands, including Ireland and Bali. "You got no weight-problem, Viv," he pronounced. "An ounce either way would be 480 grains away from pneumatic perfection." Vividy flicked at her bosom contemptuously. Rath's voice changed. "Now as for your name not being in the papers lately, that's a very wise idea—my own, in fact —and must be kept up. *Bride of God* is due to premiere in four months—the first picture about the life of a nun not to be thumbs-downed by any religious or non-religious group, even in the sticks. We want to keep it that way. When you toured the Florence night-clubs with Biff Parowan and took the gondola ride with that what's-his-name bellhop, the Pope slapped your wrist, but that's all he did—*Bride*'s still not on the Index. But the wrist-slap was a hint—and one more reason why for the next year there mustn't be one tiny smidgin of personal scandal or even so-called harmless notoriety linked to the name of Vividy Sheer.

"Besides that, Viv," he added more familiarly, "the reporters and the reading public were on the verge of getting very sick of the way your name was turning up on the front page every day— and mostly because of chasing, at that. Film stars are like goddesses —they can't be seen too often, there's got to be a little reserve, a little mystery.

"Aw, cheer up, Viv. I know it's tough, but Liz and Jayne and Marilyn all learned to do without the daily headline and so can you. Believe an old timer: euphoric pills are a safer and more lasting kick."

Vividy, who had been working her face angrily throughout Rath's lecture, now filled her cheeks and spat out her breath contemptuously, as her thrice-removed grandfather might have at the maunderings of an aged major domo.

"You're a fool, Max," she said harshly. "Kicks are for nervous virgins, the vanity of a spoilt child. *For me, being in the headlines every day is a matter of life or death.*"

Rath frowned uncomprehendingly.

"That's the literal truth she's telling you, Max," Maury Gender put in earnestly. "You see, this business happens to be tied up with what you might call the darker side of Vividy's aristocratic East Prussian heritage."

Miss Bricker stubbed out a cigarette and said, "Max, remember the trouble you had with that Spanish star Marta Martinez who turned out to be a *bruja*—a witch? Well, you picked something a little bit more out of the ordinary, Max, when you picked a Junker."

The highlights shifted on Dr. Rumanescue's thick glasses and shiny head as he nodded solemnly. He said, "There is a rune in the Doomsbook of the Von Sheers. I will translate." He paused. Then: " 'When the world has nothing more to say, The last of the Sheers will fade away.' "

As if thinking aloud, Rath said softly, "Funny, I'd forgotten totally about that East Prussian background. We always played it way down out of sight because of the Nazi association—and the Russian too." He chuckled, just a touch nervously. " '. . . fade away,' " he quoted. "Now why not just 'die'? Oh, to make the translation rhyme, I suppose." He shook himself, as if to come awake. "Hey," he demanded, "what is it actually? Is somebody blackmailing Vividy? Some fascist or East German commie group? Maybe with the dope on her addictions and private cures, or her affair with Geri Wilson?"

"Repeat: a fool!" Vividy's chest was heaving but her voice was icy. "For your information, Dr. 'Escue's translation was literal. *Day by day, ever since you first killed my news stories, I have been losing weight.*"

"It's a fact, Max," Maury Gender put in hurriedly. "The news decline and the weight loss are matching curves. Believe it or not, she's down to a quarter normal."

Miss Bricker nodded with a shiver, disturbing the smoke wreathes around her. She said, "It's the business of an actress fading out from lack of publicity. But this time, so help me, *it's literal.*"

"I have been losing both *weight and mass*," Vividy continued sharply. "Not by getting thinner, but *less substantial*. If I had my back to the window you'd notice it."

Rath stared at her, then looked penetratingly at the other three, as if to discover confirmation that it was all a gag. But they only looked back at him with uniformly solemn and unhappy—and vaguely frightened—expressions. "I don't get it," he said.

"The scales, Vividy," Miss Bricker suggested.

The film star stood up with an exaggerated carefulness and stepped on to the small rubber-topped violet platform. The white disc whirled under the glass window and came to rest at 37.

She said crisply, "I believe the word you used, Max, was 'pneumatic'. Did you happen to mean I'm inflated with hydrogen?"

"You've still got on your slippers," Miss Bricker pointed out.

With even greater carefulness, steadying herself a moment by the darkly gleaming table-edge, Vividy stepped out of her slippers and again on to the scales. This time the disk stopped at 27.

"The soles and heels are lead, fabric-covered," she rapped out to Rath. "I wear them so I won't blow over the edge when I take a walk on the terrace. Perhaps you now think I ought to be able to jump and touch the ceiling. Convincing, wouldn't it be? I rather wish I could, but my strength has decreased proportionately with my weight and mass."

"Those scales are gimmicked," Rath asserted with conviction. He stooped and grabbed at one of the slippers. His fingers slipped off it at the first try. Then he slowly raised and hefted it. "What sort of gag is this?" he demanded of Vividy. "Dammit, it does weigh five pounds."

She didn't look at him. "Maury, get the flashlight," she directed.

While the press chief rummaged in a tall Spanish cabinet, Miss Bricker moved to the view window that was the room's fourth wall and flicked an invisible beam. Rapidly the tapestry-lined drapes crawled together from either end, blotting out the steep, burnt-over, barely regrown Malibu hillside and briefly revealing in changing folds "The Torments of Beauty" until the drapes met, blotting out all light whatever.

Maury snapped on a flashlight long as his forearm. It lit their faces weirdly from below and dimly showed the lovely gray ladies in pain beyond them. Then he put it behind Vividy, who stood facing Rath, and moved it up and down.

As if no thicker anywhere than fingers, the lovely form of the German film star became a twin-stemmed flower in shades of dark pink. The arteries were a barely visible twining, the organs blue-edged, the skeleton deep cherry.

"That some kind of X-ray?" Rath asked, the words coming out in a breathy rush.

"You think they got technicolor, hand-size, screenless X-ray sets?" Maury retorted.

"I think they must have," Rath told him in a voice quiet but quite desperate.

"That's enough, Maury," Vividy directed. "Bricker, the drapes." Then as the harsh rectangle of daylight swiftly reopened, she looked coldly at Rath and said, "You may take me by the shoulders and shake me. I give you permission."

The producer complied. Two seconds after he had grasped her he was shrinking back, his hands and arms violently trembling. It had been like shaking a woman stuffed with eiderdown. A woman warm and silky-skinned to the touch, but light almost as feathers. A pillow woman.

"I believe, Vividy," he gasped out. "I believe it all now." Then his voice went far away. "And to think I first cottoned to you because of that name Sheer. It sounded like silk stockings—luxurious, delicate . . . *insubstantial*. Oh my God!" His voice came part way back. "And you say this is all happening because of some old European witchcraft? Some crazy rhymes out of the past? How do you really think about it, how do you explain it?"

"Much of the past has no explanation at all," Dr. Rumanescue answered him. "And the further in the past, the less. The Von Sheers are a very old family, tracing back to pre-Roman times. The runes themselves—"

Vividy held up her palm to the astrologist to stop.

"Very well, you believe. Good," she said curtly to Rath, carefully sitting down at the table again behind the ugly black casket on its square of altar cloth. She continued in the same tones, "The question now is: how do I get the publicity I need to keep me from fading out altogether, the front-page publicity that will perhaps even restore me, build me up?"

Like a man in a dream Rath let himself down into a chair across the table from her and looked out the window over her shoulder. The three others watched them with mingled calculation and anxiety.

Vividy said sharply, "First, can the release date on *Bride of God* be advanced—to next Sunday week, say? I think I can last that long."

"Impossible, quite impossible," Rath muttered, still seeming to study something on the pale green hillside scrawled here and there with black.

"Then hear another plan. There is an unfrocked Irish clergyman named Kerrigan who is infatuated with me. A maniac but rather sweet. He's something of a poet—he'd like me light as a feather, find nothing horrible in it. Kerrigan and I will travel together to Monaco—"

"No, no!" Rath cried out in sudden anguish, looking at her at last. "No matter the other business, witchcraft or whatever, we can't have anything like that! It would ruin the picture, kill it dead. It would mean my money and all our jobs. Vividy, I haven't told you, but a majority committee of stockholders wants me to get rid of you and reshoot *Bride*, starring Alicia Killian. They're deathly afraid of a last-minute Sheer scandal. Vividy, you've always played square with me, even at your craziest. You wouldn't . . ."

"No, I wouldn't, even to save my life," she told him, her voice mixing pride and contempt with an exactitude that broke through Maury Gender's miseries and thrilled him with her genuine dramatic talent. He said, "Max, we've been trying to convince Vividy that it might help to use some routine non-scandalous publicity."

"Yes," Miss Bricker chimed eagerly, "we have a jewel robbery planned for tonight, a kitchen fire for tomorrow."

Vividy laughed scornfully. "And I suppose the day after that I get lost in Griffith Park for three hours, next I rededicate an orphanage, autograph a Nike missile, and finally I have a poolside press interview and bust a brassiere strap. That's cheap stuff, the last resort of has-beens. Besides I don't think it would work."

Rath, his eyes again on the hillside, said absently, "To be honest, I don't think it would either. After the hot stuff you've always shot them, the papers wouldn't play."

"Very well," Vividy said crisply, "that brings us back to where we started. There's nothing left for it—I've got to . . ."

"Hey, wait a second!" Rath burst out with a roar of happy excitement. "We've got your physical condition to capitalize on! Your loss of weight is a scientific enigma, a miracle—and absolutely non-scandalous! It'll mean headlines for months, for years. Every woman will want to know your secret. So will the spacemen. We'll reveal you first to UCLA, or USC, then the Mayo Clinic and maybe Johns Hopkins. . . . Hey, what's the matter, why aren't you all enthusiastic about this?"

Maury Gender and Miss Bricker looked toward Dr. Rumanescue, who coughed and said gently, "Unfortunately, there is a runic couplet in the Von Sheer Doomsbook that seems almost certainly to bear on that very point. Translated: 'If a Sheer be weighed in the market place, he'll vanish away without a trace.' "

"In any case, I refuse to exhibit myself as a freak," Vividy added hotly. "I don't mind how much publicity I get because of my individuality, my desires, *my will*—no matter how much it shocks and titillates the little people, the law-abiders, the virgins and eunuchs and moms—but to be confined to a hospital and pried over by doctors and physiologists. . . . No!"

She fiercely brought her fist down on the table with a soft, insubstantial thud that made Rath draw back and set Miss Bricker shuddering once more. Then Vividy Sheer said, "For the last time: There's nothing left for it—I've got to open the casket!"

"Now what's in the casket?" Rath asked with apprehension.

There was another uncomfortable silence. Then Dr. Rumanescue said softly, with a little shrug, "The casket-demon. The Doom of the Von Sheers." He hesitated. "Think of the genie in the bottle. A genie with black fangs."

Rath asked, "How's that going to give Vividy publicity?"

Vividy answered him. "It will attack me, try to destroy me. Every night, as long as I last. No scandal, only horror. But there will be headlines. And I'll stop fading."

She pushed out a hand toward the little wrought-iron box. All their eyes were on it. With its craggy, tortured surface, it looked as if it had been baked in Hell, the peep-hole of milky glass an eye blinded by heat.

Miss Bricker said, "Vividy, don't."

Dr. Rumanescue breathed, "I advise against it."

Maury Gender said, "Vividy, I don't think this is going to work out the way you think it will. Publicity's a tricky thing. I think—"

He broke off as Vividy clutched her hand back to her bosom. Her eyes stared as if she felt something happening inside her. Then, groping along the table, hanging on to its edge clumsily as though her fingers were numbed, she made her way to the scale and maneuvred herself on to it. This time the disk stopped at 19.

With a furious yet strengthless haste, like a scarecrow come alive and floating as much as walking, the beautiful woman fought her way back to the box and clutched it with both hands and jerked it towards her. It moved not at all at first, then a bare inch as she heaved. She gave up trying to pull it closer and leaned over it, her sharply bent waist against the table edge, and tugged and pried at the casket's top, pressing rough projections as if they were parts of an antique combination-lock.

Maury Gender took a step toward her, then stopped. None of the others moved even that far to help. They watched her as if she were themselves strengthless in a nightmare—a ghost woman as much tugged by the tiny box as she was tugging at it. A ghost woman in full life colors—except that Max Rath, sitting just opposite, saw the hillside glowing very faintly through her.

With a whir and a clash the top of the box shot up on its hinges, there was a smoky puff and a stench that paled faces and set Miss

Bricker gagging, then something small and intensely black and very fast dove out of the box and scuttled across the altar cloth and down a leg of the table and across the floor and under the tapestry and was gone.

Maury Gender had thrown himself out of its course, Miss Bricker had jerked her feet up under her, as if from a mouse, and so had Max Rath. But Vividy Sheer stood up straight and tall, no longer strengthless-seeming. There was icy sky in her blue eyes and a smile on her face—a smile of self-satisfaction that became tinged with scorn as she said, "You needn't be frightened. We won't see it again until after dark. Then—well, at least it will be interesting. Doubtless his hussars saw many interesting things during the seven months my military ancestor lasted."

"You mean you'll be attacked by a black rat?" Max Rath faltered.

"It will grow," said Dr. Rumanescue quietly.

Scanning the hillside again, Max Rath winced, as if it had occurred to him that one of the black flecks out there might now be *it*. He looked at his watch. "Eight hours to sunset," he said dully. "We got to get through eight hours."

Vividy laughed ripplingly. "We'll all jet to New York," she said with decision. "That way there'll be three hours' less agony for Max. Besides, I think Times Square would be a good spot for the first . . . appearance. Or maybe Radio City. Maury, call the airport! Bricker, pour me a brandy!"

*   *   *

Next day the New York tabloids carried half-column stories telling how the tempestuous film star Vividy Sheer had been attacked or at least menaced in front of the United Nations Building at 11:59 p.m. by a large black dog, whose teeth had bruised her without drawing blood, and which had disappeared, perhaps in company with a boy who had thrown a stink bomb, before the first police arrived. The *Times* and the *Herald Tribune* carried no stories whatever. The item got on Associated Press but was not used by many papers.

The day after that *The News of the World* and *The London Daily Mirror* reported on inside pages that the German-American film actress Vividy Sheer had been momentarily mauled in the lobby of Claridge's Hotel by a black-cloaked and black-masked man who moved with a stoop and very quickly—as if, in fact, he were more interested in getting away fast than in doing any real damage to the Nordic beauty, who had made no appreciable effort to resist the attacker, whirling in his brief grip as if she were a weightless clay figure. The *News of the World* also reproduced in one-and-a-half columns a photograph of Vividy in a low-cut dress showing just below her neck an odd black clutch-mark left there by the attacker, or perhaps drawn beforehand in india ink, the caption suggested. In *The London Times* was a curt angry editorial crying shame at notoriety-mad actresses and conscienceless press agents who staged disgusting scenes in respectable places to win publicity for questionable films—even to the point of setting off stench bombs—and suggesting that the best way for all papers to handle such nauseous hoaxes was to ignore them utterly—and cooperate enthusiastically but privately with the police and the deportation authorities.

On the third day, as a few eye-witnesses noted but were quite unwilling to testify (what Frenchman wants to be laughed at?) Vividy Sheer was snatched off the top of the Eiffel Tower by a great black paw, or by a sinuous whirlwind laden with coal dust and then deposited under the Arc de Triomphe—or she and her confederates somehow created the illusion that this enormity had occurred. But when the Sheer woman, along with four of her film cohorts, reported the event to the Sureté, the French police refused to do anything more than smile knowingly and shrug, though one inspector was privately puzzled by something about the Boche film-bitch's movements—she seemed to be drawn along by her companions rather than walking on her own two feet. Perhaps drugs were involved, Inspector Gibaud decided—cocaine or mescalin. What an indecency, though, that the woman should smear herself with shoeblacking to bolster her lewd fantasy!

Not one paper in the world would touch the story, not even one of the Paris dailies carried a humorous item about *Le bête noir et énorme*—some breeds of nonsense are unworthy even of humorous reporting. They are too silly (and perhaps in some silly way a shade too disturbing) for even silly-season items.

During the late afternoon of the fourth day, the air was very quiet in Rome—the quiet that betokens a coming storm—and Vividy insisted on taking a walk with Max Rath. She wore a coif and dress of white silk jersey, the only material her insubstantial body could tolerate. Panchromatic make-up covered her black splotches. She had recruited her strength by sniffing brandy—the only way in which her semi-porous flesh could now absorb the fierce liquid. Max was fretful, worried that a passerby would see through his companion, and he was continually maneuvering so that she would not be between them and the lowering sky. Vividy was tranquil, speculating without excitement about what the night might bring and whether a person who fades away dies doubly or not at all and what casket-demons do in the end to their victims and whether the Gods themselves depend for their existence on publicity.

As they were crossing a children's park somewhere near the Piazza dell' Esquilino, there was a breath of wind, Vividy moaned very quietly, her form grew faint, and she blew off Max's arm and down the path, traveling a few inches above it, indistinct as a camera image projected on dust motes. Children cried out softly and pointed. An eddy caught her, whirled her up, then back toward Max a little, then she was gone.

Immediately afterward mothers and priests came running and seven children swore they had been granted a vision of the Holy Virgin, while four children maintained they had seen the ghost or double of the film star Vividy Sheer. Certainly nothing material remained of the courageous East Prussian except a pair of lead slippers—size four-and-one-half—covered with white brocade.

Returning to the hotel suite and recounting his story, Max Rath was surprised to find that the news did not dispel his companions' nervous depression.

Miss Bricker, after merely shrugging at Max's story, was saying,

"Maury, what do you suppose really happened to those eight hussars," and Maury was replying, "I don't want to imagine, only you got to remember that that time the casket-demon wasn't baulked of his victim."

Max interrupted loudly, "Look, cut the morbidity. It's too bad about Vividy, but what a break for *Bride of God*! Those kids' stories are perfect publicity—and absolutely non-scandalous. *Bride*'ll gross forty million! Hey! Wake up! I know it's been a rough time, but now it's over."

Maury Gender and Miss Bricker slowly shook their heads. Dr. Rumanescue motioned Max to approach the window. While he came on with slow steps, the astrologist said, "Unfortunately, there is still another pertinent couplet. Roughly: 'If the demon be baulked of a Von Sheer kill, On henchman and vassals he'll work his will!'" He glanced at his wrist. "It is three minutes to sunset." He pointed out the window. "Do you see, coming up the Appian Way, that tall black cloud with blue lightning streaking through it?"

"You mean the cloud with a head like a wolf?" Max faltered.

"Precisely," Dr. Rumanescue nodded. "Only, for us, it is not a cloud," he added resignedly and returned to his book.

The New People

BY CHARLES BEAUMONT

The tragic death five years ago of Charles "Chuck" Beaumont robbed macabre literature of one of its brightest young talents. Beaumont, in company with Richard Matheson and William Nolan, owed much to the support and encouragement he received as a fledgling magazine writer from Ray Bradbury. His career in Hollywood began at the Preminger-Stuart Agency writing T.V. scripts and it was here, also, that he met Richard Matheson and worked with him on several collaborations. On his own he also wrote The Seven Faces of Dr. Lao *and the wide-screen spectacular,* The Wonderful World of the Brothers Grimm.

If only he had told her right at the beginning that he didn't like the house, everything would have been fine. He could have manufactured some plausible story about bad plumbing or poor construction—something; anything!—and she'd have gone along with him. Not without a fight, maybe: he could remember the way her face had looked when they stopped the car. But he could have talked her out of it. Now, of course, it was too late.

For what? he wondered, trying not to think of the party and all the noise that it would mean. Too late for what? It's a good house, well built, well kept up, roomy. Except for that blood stain, cheerful. Anyone in his right mind. . . .

"Dear, aren't you going to shave?"

He lowered the newspaper gently and said, "Sure." But Ann was looking at him in that hurt, accusing way, and he knew that it was hopeless.

hank-what's-wrong, he thought, starting toward the bathroom.

"Hank," she said.

He stopped but did not turn. "Uh-huh?"

"What's wrong?"

"Nothing," he said.

"Honey. Please."

He faced her. The pink chiffon dress clung to her body, which had the firmness of youth; her face was unblemished, the lipstick and powder incredibly perfect; her hair, cut long, was soft on her white shoulders: in seven years Ann hadn't changed.

Resentfully, Prentice glanced away. And was ashamed. You'd think that in this time I'd get accustomed to it, he thought. *She* is. Damn it!

"Tell me," Ann said.

"Tell you what? Everything is okay," he said.

She came to him and he could smell the perfume, he could see the tiny freckles that dotted her chest. He wondered what it would be like to sleep with her. Probably it would be very nice.

"It's about Davey, isn't it?" she said, dropping her voice to a whisper. They were standing only a few feet from their son's room.

"No," Prentice said; but, it was true—Davey was part of it. For a week now Prentice had ridden on the hope that getting the loco-motive repaired would change things. A kid without a train, he'd told himself, is bound to act peculiar. But he'd had the locomotive re-paired and brought it home and Davey hadn't even bothered to set up the track.

"He appreciated it, dear," Ann said. "Didn't he thank you?"

"Sure, he thanked me."

"Well?" she said. "Honey, I've *told* you: Davey is going through a period, that's all. Children do. Really."

"I know."

"And school's been out for almost a month."

"I know," Prentice said, and thought: *Moving to a neighborhood where there isn't another kid in the whole damn block for him to play with, that might have something to do with it, too!*

"Then," Ann said, "it's me."

"No, no, no." He tried to smile. There wasn't any sense in arguing: they'd been through it a dozen times, and she had an answer for everything. He could recall the finality in her voice . . . "I love the house, Hank. And I love the neighborhood. It's what I've dreamed of all my life, and I think I deserve it. Don't you?" (It was the first time she'd ever consciously reminded him.) The trouble is, you've lived in dingy little apartments so long you've come to *like* them. You can't adjust to a really *decent* place—and Davey's no different. You're two of a kind: little old men who can't stand a change, even for the better! Well, I can. I don't care if *fifty* people committed suicide here, I'm happy. You understand, Hank? Happy."

Prentice had understood, and had resolved to make a real effort to like the new place. If he couldn't do that, at least he could keep his feelings from Ann—for they were, he knew, foolish. Damned foolish. Everything she said was true, and he ought to be grateful.

Yet, somehow, he could not stop dreaming of the old man who had picked up a razor one night and cut his throat wide open. . . .

Ann was staring at him.

"Maybe," he said, "I'm going through a period, too." He kissed her forehead, lightly. "Come on, now; the people are going to arrive any second, and you look like Lady Macbeth."

She held his arm for a moment. "You are getting settled in the house, aren't you?" she said. "I mean, it's becoming more like home to you, isn't it?"

"Sure," Prentice said.

His wife paused another moment, then smiled. "Okay, get the whiskers off. Rhoda is under the impression you're a handsome man."

He walked into the bathroom and plugged in the electric shaver. Rhoda, he thought. First names already and we haven't been here three weeks.

"Dad?"

He looked down at Davey, who had slipped in with nine-year-old stealth. "Yo." According to ritual, he ran the shaver across his son's chin.

Davey did not respond. He stepped back and said, "Dad, is Mr. Ames coming over tonight?"

Prentice nodded. "I guess so."

"And Mr. Chambers?"

"Uh-huh. Why?"

Davey did not answer.

"What do you want to know for?"

"Gee." Davey's eyes were red and wide. "Is it okay if I stay in my room?"

"Why? You sick?"

"No. Kind of."

"Stomach? Head?"

"Just sick," Davey said. He pulled at a thread in his shirt and fell silent again.

Prentice frowned. "I thought maybe you'd like to show them your train," he said.

"Please," Davey said. His voice had risen slightly and Prentice could see tears gathering. "Dad, please don't make me come out. Leave me stay in my room. I won't make any noise, I promise, and I'll go to sleep on time."

"Okay, okay. Don't make such a big deal out of it!" Prentice ran the cool metal over his face. Anger came and went, swiftly. Stupid to get mad. "Davey, what'd you do, ride your bike on their lawn or something? Break a window?"

"No."

"Then why don't you want to see them?"

"I just don't."

"Mr. Ames likes you. He told me so yesterday. He thinks you're a fine boy, so does Mr. Chambers. They—"

"*Please*, Dad!" Davey's face was pale; he began to cry. "Please, please, please. Don't let them get me!"

"What are you talking about? Davey, cut it out. Now!"

"I saw what they were doing there in the garage. And they know I saw them, too. They know. And—"

"Davey!" Ann's voice was sharp and loud and resounding in the tile-lined bathroom. The boy stopped crying immediately. He looked up, hesitated, then ran out. His door slammed.

Prentice took a step.

"No, Hank. Leave him alone."

"He's upset."

"Let him be upset." She shot an angry glance toward the bedroom. "I suppose he told you that filthy story about the garage?"

"No," Prentice said, "he didn't. What's it all about?"

"Nothing. Absolutely nothing. Honestly, I'd like to meet Davey's parents!"

"We're his parents," Prentice said, firmly.

"All right, all right. But he got that imagination of his from *some-body*, and it wasn't from us. You're going to have to speak to him, Hank. I mean it. Really."

"About what?"

"These wild stories. What if they got back to Mr. Ames? I'd—well, I'd die. After he's gone out of his way to be nice to Davey, too."

"I haven't heard the stories," Prentice said.

"Oh, you will." Ann undid her apron and folded it, furiously. "Honestly! Sometimes I think the two of you are trying to make things just as miserable as they can be for me."

The doorbell rang, stridently.

"Now make an effort to be pleasant, will you? This is a *house-warming*, after all. And do hurry."

She closed the door. He heard her call, "Hi!" and heard Ben Roth's baritone booming: "Hi!"

Ridiculous, he told himself, plugging the razor in again. Utterly goddam ridiculous. No one complained louder than I did when we were tripping over ourselves in that little upstairs coffin on Friar. *I'm* the one who kept moaning for a house, not Ann.

So now we've got one.

He glanced at the tiny brownish blood stain that wouldn't wash out of the wallpaper, and sighed.

Now we've got one.

"Hank!"

"Coming!" He straightened his tie and went into the living room.

The Roths, of course, were there. Ben and Rhoda. Get it right, he thought, because we're all going to be pals. "Hi, Ben."

"Thought you'd deserted us, boy," said the large, pink man, laughing.

"No. Wouldn't do that."

"Hank," Ann signaled. "You've met Beth Cummings, haven't you?"

The tall, smartly dressed woman giggled and extended her hand. "We've seen each other," she said. "Hello."

Her husband, a pale man with white hair, crushed Prentice's fingers. "Fun and games," he said, tightening his grip and wheezing with amusement. "Yes, sir."

Trying not to wince, Prentice retrieved his hand. It was instantly snatched up by a square, bald man in a double-breasted brown suit. "Reiker," the man said. "Call me Bud. Everyone does. Don't know why; my name is Oscar."

"*That's* why," a woman said, stepping up. "Ann introduced us but you probably don't remember, if I know men. I'm Edna."

"Sure," Prentice said. "How are you?"

"Fine. But then, I'm a woman: I *like* parties!"

"How's that?"

"Hank!"

Prentice excused himself and walked quickly into the kitchen. Ann was holding up a package.

"Honey, look what Rhoda gave us!"

He dutifully handled the salt and pepper shakers and set them down again. "That's real nice."

"You turn the rooster's head," Mrs. Roth said, "and it grinds your pepper."

"Wonderful," Prentice said.

"And Beth gave us this lovely salad bowl, see? And we've needed *this* for *cen*turies!" She held out a gray tablecloth with gold bordering. "Plastic!"

"Wonderful," Prentice said. Again, the doorbell rang. He glanced

at Mrs. Roth, who had been staring thoughtfully at him, and returned
to the living room.

"How you be, Hank?" Lucian Ames walked in, rubbing his hands
together briskly. "Well! The gang's all here, I see. But where's that
boy of yours?"

"Davey? Oh," Prentice said, "he's sick."

"Nonsense! Boys that age are never sick. Never!"

Ann laughed nervously from the kitchen. "Just something he ate!"

"Not the candy we sent over, I hope."

"Oh, no."

"Well, tell him his Uncle Lucian said hello."

A tan elf of a man, with sparkling eyes and an ill fitting mustache,
Ames reminded Prentice somewhat of those clerks who used to sit
silently on high wooden stools, posting infinitesimal figures in immense yellow ledgers. He was, however, the head of a nationally
famous advertising agency.

His wife Charlotte provided a remarkable contrast. She seemed
to belong to the era of the twenties, with her porcelain face, her thin,
delicately angular body, her air of fragility.

Nice, Prentice told himself.

He removed coats and hung them in closets. He shook hands and
smiled until his face began to ache. He looked at presents and thanked
the women and told them they shouldn't have. He carried out sandwiches. He mixed drinks.

By eight-thirty, everyone in the block had arrived. The Johnsons,
the Ameses, the Roths, the Reikers, the Klementaskis, the Cham-
berses; four or five others whose names Prentice could not remember,
although Ann had taken care to introduce them.

What it is, he decided, looking at the people, at the gifts they had
brought, remembering their many kindnesses and how, already, Ann
had made more friends than she'd ever had before, is, I'm just an
antisocial bastard.

After the third round of whiskeys and martinis, someone turned on
the FM and someone else suggested dancing. Prentice had always
supposed that one danced only at New Year's Eve parties, but he
said the hell with it, finally, and tried to relax.

"Shall we?" Mrs. Ames said.

He wanted to say no, but Ann was watching. So he said, "Sure, if you've got strong toes," instead.

Almost at once he began to perspire. The smoke, the drinks, the heat of the crowded room, caused his head to ache; and, as usual, he was acutely embarrassed at having to hold a strange woman so closely.

But, he continued to smile.

Mrs. Ames danced well, she followed him with unerring instinct; and within moments she was babbling freely into his ear. She told him about old Mr. Thomas, the man who had lived here before, and how surprised everyone had been at what had happened; she told him how curious they'd all been about The New People and how relieved they were to find him and Ann so very nice; she told him he had strong arms. Ann was being twirled about by Herb Johnson. She was smiling.

An endless, slow three-step came on, then, and Mrs. Ames put her cheek next to Prentice's. In the midst of a rambling sentence, she said, suddenly, in a whisper: "You know, I think it was awfully brave of you to adopt little Davey. I mean, considering."

"Considering what?"

She pulled away and looked at him. "Nothing," she said. "I'm awfully sorry."

Blushing with fury, Prentice turned and strode into the kitchen. He fought his anger, thinking, God, God, is she telling strangers about it now? Is it a topic for back-fence gossip? *My husband is impotent, you know. Is yours?*

He poured whiskey into a glass and drank it, fast. It made his eyes water, and when he opened them, he saw a figure standing next to him.

It was—who? Dystal. Matthew Dystal; bachelor; movie writer—lives down the block. Call him Matt.

"Miserable, isn't it?" the man said, taking the bottle from Prentice's hand.

"What do you mean?"

"Everything," the man said. He filled his glass and drained it smartly. "Them. Out there." He filled the glass again.

"Nice people," Prentice forced himself to say.

"You think so?"

The man was drunk. Clearly, very drunk. And it was only nine-thirty.

"You think so?" he repeated.

"Sure. Don't you?"

"Of course. I'm one of them, aren't I?"

Prentice peered at his guest closely, then moved toward the living room.

Dystal took his arm. "Wait," he said. "Listen. You're a good guy. I don't know you very well, but I like you, Hank Prentice. So I'm going to give you some advice." His voice dropped to a whisper. "Get out of here," he said.

"What?"

"Just what I said. Move away, move away to another city."

Prentice felt a quick ripple of annoyance, checked it. "Why?" he asked, smiling.

"Never mind that," Dystal said. "Just do it. Tonight. Will you?" His face was livid, clammy with perspiration; his eyes were wide.

"Well, I mean, Matt, that's a heck of a thing to say. I thought you said you liked us. Now you want to get rid of us."

"Don't joke," Dystal said. He pointed at the window. "Can't you see the moon? You bloody idiot, can't you——"

"Hey, hey! Unfair!"

At the sound of the voice, Dystal froze. He closed his eyes for a moment and opened them, slowly. But he did not move.

Lucian Ames walked into the kitchen. "What's the story here," he said, putting his arm on Dystal's shoulder, "you trying to monopolize our host all night?"

Dystal did not answer.

"How about a refill, Hank?" Ames said, removing his hand.

Prentice said, "Sure," and prepared the drink. From the corner of his eye, he saw Dystal turn and walk stiffly out of the room. He heard the front door open and close.

Ames was chuckling. "Poor old Matt," he said. "He'll be hung over tomorrow. It seems kind of a shame, doesn't it? I mean, you know, of all people, you'd think a big Hollywood writer would be able to hold his liquor. But not Matt. He gets loaded just by staring at the labels."

Prentice said, "Huh."

"Was he giving you one of his screwball nightmares?"

"What? No—we were just sort of talking. About things."

Ames dropped an ice cube into his drink. "Things?" he said.

"Yeah."

Ames took a sip of the whiskey and walked to the window, looking lithe, somehow, as well as small. After what seemed a long time, he said, "Well, it's a fine night, isn't it. Nice and clear, nice fine moon." He turned and tapped a cigarette out of a red package, lighted the cigarette. "Hank," he said, letting the gray smoke gush from the corners of his mouth, "tell me something. What do you do for excitement?"

Prentice shrugged. It was an odd question, but then, everything seemed odd to him tonight. "I don't know," he said. "Go to a movie once in a while. Watch TV. The usual."

Ames cocked his head. "But—don't you get bored?" he asked.

"Sure, I guess. Every so often. Being a C.P.A. you know, that isn't exactly the world's most fascinating job."

Ames laughed sympathetically. "It's awful, isn't it?"

"Being a C.P.A.?"

"No. Being bored. It's about the worst thing in the world, don't you agree? Someone once remarked they thought it was the only real sin a human could commit."

"I hope not," Prentice said.

"Why?"

"Well, I mean—everybody gets bored, don't they?"

"Not," Ames said, "if they're careful."

Prentice found himself becoming increasingly irritated at the conversation. "I suppose it helps," he said, "if you're the head of an advertising agency."

"No, not really. It's like any other job: interesting at first, but then you get used to it. It becomes routine. So you go fishing for other diversions."

"Like what?"

"Oh . . . anything. Everything." Ames slapped Prentice's arm good naturedly. "You're all right, Hank," he said.

"Thanks."

"I mean it. Can't tell you how happy we all are that you moved here."

"No more than we are!" Ann walked unsteadily to the sink with a number of empty glasses. "I want to apologize for Davey again, Lucian. I was telling Charlotte, he's been a perfect beast lately. He should have thanked you for fixing the seat on his bike."

"Forget it," Ames said, cheerfully. "The boy's just upset because he doesn't have any playmates." He looked at Prentice. "Some of us elders have kids, Hank, but they're all practically grown. You probably know that our daughter, Ginnie, is away at college. And Chris and Beth's boy lives in New York. But, you know, I wouldn't worry. As soon as school starts, Davey'll straighten out. You watch."

Ann smiled. "I'm sure you're right, Lucian. But I apologize, anyway."

"Nuts." Ames returned to the living room and began to dance with Beth Cummings.

Prentice thought then of asking Ann what the devil she meant by blabbing about their personal life to strangers, but decided not to. This was not the time. He was too angry, too confused.

The party lasted another hour. Then Ben Roth said, "Better let these good folks get some sleep!" and, slowly, the people left.

Ann closed the door. She seemed to glow with contentment, looking younger and prettier than she had for several years. "Home," she said, softly, and began picking up ash trays and glasses and plates. "Let's get all this out of the way so we won't have to look at it in the morning," she said.

Prentice said, "All right," in a neutral tone. He was about to move the coffee table back into place when the telephone rang.

"Yes?"

The voice that answered was a harsh whisper, like a rush of wind through leaves. "Prentice, are they gone?"

"Who is this?"

"Matt Dystal. Are they gone?"

"Yes."

"All of them? Ames? Is he gone?"

"Yes. What do you want, Dystal? It's late."

"Later than you might think, Prentice. He told you I was drunk, but he lied. I'm not drunk. I'm—"

"Look, what is it you want?"

"I've got to talk with you," the voice said. "Now. Tonight. Can you come over?"

"At eleven o'clock?"

"Yes. Prentice, listen to me. I'm not drunk and I'm not kidding. This is a matter of life and death. Yours. Do you understand what I'm saying?"

Prentice hesitated, confused.

"You know where my place is—fourth house from the corner, right-hand side. Come over now. But listen, carefully: go out the back door. The back door. Prentice, are you listening?"

"Yes," Prentice said.

"My lights will be off. Go around to the rear. Don't bother to knock, just walk in—but be quiet about it. They mustn't see you."

Prentice heard a click, then silence. He stared at the receiver for a while before replacing it.

"Well?" Ann said. "Man talk?"

"Not exactly." Prentice wiped his palm on his trousers. "That fellow Matt Dystal, he's apparently sick. Wants me to come over."

"Now?"

"Yeah. I think I better; he sounded pretty bad. You go on to sleep, I'll be back in a little while."

"Okay, honey. I hope it isn't anything serious. But, it *is* nice to be doing something for *them* for a change, isn't it?"

Prentice kissed his wife, waited until the bathroom door had closed; then he went outside, into the cold night.

He walked along the grass verge of the alleyway, across the small lawns, up the steps to Dystal's rear door.

He deliberated with himself for a moment, then walked in.

"Prentice?" a voice hissed.

"Yes. Where are you?"

A hand touched his arm in the darkness and he jumped, nervously. "Come into the bedroom."

A dim lamp went on. Prentice saw that the windows were covered by heavy tan drapes. It was chilly in the room, chilly and moist.

"Well?" Prentice said, irritably.

Matthew Dystal ran a hand through his rope-colored hair. "I know what you're thinking," he said. "And I don't blame you. But it was necessary, Prentice. It was necessary. Ames has told you about my 'wild nightmares' and that's going to stick with you. I realize; but get this straight." His hand became a fist. "Everything I'm about to say is true. No matter how outlandish it may sound, it's *true*— and I have proof. All you'll need. So keep still, Prentice, and listen to me. It may mean your life: yours and your wife's and your boy's. And, maybe, mine. . . ." His voice trailed off; then, suddenly, he said, "You want a drink?"

"No."

"You ought to have one. You're only on the outskirts of confusion, my friend. But, there are worse things than confusion. Believe me." Dystal walked to a bookcase and stood there for almost a full minute. When he turned, his features were slightly more composed. "What do you know," he asked, "about the house you're living in?"

Prentice shifted uncomfortably. "I know that a man killed himself in it, if that's what you mean."

"But do you know why?"

"No."

"Because he lost," Dystal said, giggling. "He drew the short one. How's that for motivation?"

"I think I'd better go," Prentice said.

"Wait." Dystal took a handkerchief from his pocket and tapped his forehead. "I didn't mean to begin that way. It's just that I've never told this to anyone, and it's difficult. You'll see why. Please, Prentice, promise you won't leave until I've finished!"

Prentice looked at the wiry, nervous little man and cursed the weakness that had allowed him to get himself into this miserably uncomfortable situation. He wanted to go home. But he knew he could not leave now.

"All right," he said. "Go on."

Dystal sighed. Then, staring at the window, he began to talk. "I built this house," he said, "because I thought I was going to get married. By the time I found out I was wrong, the work was all done. I should have sold it, I know, I see that, but I was feeling too lousy to go through the paper work. Besides, I'd already given up my apartment. So I moved in." He coughed. "Be patient with me, Prentice: this is the only way to tell it, from the beginning. Where was I?"

"You moved in."

"Yes! Everybody was very nice. They invited me to their homes for dinner, they dropped by, they did little favors for me; and it helped, it really did. I thought, you know, what a hell of a great bunch of neighbors. Regular. *Real*. That was it: they were real. Ames, an advertising man; Thomas, a lawyer; Johnson, paint company; Chambers, insurance; Reiker and Cummings, engineers—I mean, how average can you get?" Dystal paused; an ugly grin appeared on his face, disappeared. "I liked them," he said. "And I was really delighted with things. But, of course, you know how it is when a woman gives you the business. I was still licking my wounds. And I guess it showed, because Ames came over one evening. Just dropped by, in a neighborly way. We had some drinks. We talked about the ways of the female. Then, bang, out of nowhere, he asked me the question. Was I bored?"

Prentice stiffened.

"Well, when you lose your girl, you lose a lot of your ambition. I told him yes, I was plenty bored. And he said, 'I used to be.' I remember his exact words. 'I used to be,' he said. 'The long haul to success, the fight, the midnight oil: it was over. I'd made it,' he said. 'Dough in the bank. Partnership in a top agency. Daughter grown and away to school. I was ready to be put out to pasture, Matt. But the thing was, I was only fifty-two! I had maybe another twenty years left. And almost everybody else in the block was the same way—Ed and Ben and Oscar, all the same. You know: they fooled around with their jobs, but they weren't interested any more—not really. Because the jobs didn't *need* them any more. They were bored'." Dystal walked to the nightstand and poured himself a drink. "That was five years ago," he murmured. "Ames, he pussy-footed around the thing for a while—feeling me out, testing me; then he told me that he had decided to do something about it. About being bored. He'd organized everyone in the block. Once a week, he explained, they played games. It was real Group Activity. Community effort. It began with charades, but they got tired of that in a while. Then they tried cards. To make it interesting, they bet high. Everybody had his turn at losing. Then, Ames said, someone suggested making the game even *more* interesting, because it was getting to be a drag. So they experimented with strip poker one night. Just for fun, you understand, Rhoda lost. Next time it was Charlotte. And it went that way for a while, until finally, Beth lost. Everyone had been waiting for it. Things became anticlimactic after that, though, so the stakes changed again. Each paired off with another's wife; lowest scoring team had to—" Dystal tipped the bottle. "Sure you won't have a bracer?"

Prentice accepted the drink without argument. It tasted bitter and powerful, but it helped.

"Well," Dystal went on, "I had one hell of a time believing all that. I mean, you know: *Ames,* after all—a little bookkeeper type with grey hair and glasses. . . . Still, the way he talked, I knew—somehow, I *knew*—it was the truth. Maybe because I didn't feel that a guy like Ames could make it all up! Anyway: when they'd tried all the possible combinations, things got dull again. A few of the women wanted to stop, but, of course, they were in too deep already. During one particular Fun Night, Ames had taken photographs. So, they had to keep going. Every week, it was something new. Something different. Swapsies occupied them for a while, Ames told me: Chambers took a two week vacation with Jacqueline, Ben and Beth went to Acapulco, and that sort of thing. And that is where I came into the picture." Dystal raised his hand. "I know, you don't need to tell me. I should have pulled out. But I was younger then. I was a big writer, man of the world. Training in Hollywood. I couldn't tell him I was shocked: it would have been betraying my craft. And he figured it that way, too: that's why he told me. Besides, he knew I'd be bound to find out eventually. They could hide it from just about everybody, but not someone right in the block. So, I played along. I accepted his invitation to join the next Group Activity—which is what he calls them.

"Next morning, I thought I'd dreamed the whole visit, I really did. But on Saturday, sure enough, the phone rings and Ames says, 'We begin at eight, sharp.' When I got to his house, I found it packed. Everybody in the neighborhood. Looking absolutely the same as always too. Drinks; dancing; the whole bit. After a while, I started to wonder if the whole thing wasn't an elaborate gag. But at ten, Ames told us about the evening's surprise." Dystal gave way to a shudder. "It was a surprise, all right," he said. "I told them I wanted nothing to do with it, but Ames had done something to my drink. I didn't seem to have any control. They led me into the bedroom, and . . ."

Prentice waited, but Dystal did not complete his sentence. His eyes were dancing now.

"Never mind," he said. "Never mind what happened! The point is, I was drunk, and—well, I went through with it. I *had* to. You can see that, can't you?"

Prentice said that he could see that.

"Ames pointed out to me that the only sin, the *only* one, was being bored. That was his justification, that was his incentive. He simply didn't want to sin, that was all. So the Group Activities went on. And they got worse. Much worse. One thing, they actually plotted a crime and carried it off: the Union Bank robbery, maybe you read about it: 1953. I drove the car for them. Another time, they decided it would ward off ennui by setting fire to a warehouse down by the docks. The fire spread. Prentice—do you happen to remember that DC-7 that went down between here and Detroit?"

Prentice said, "Yes, I remember."

"Their work," Dystal said. "Ames planned it. In a way, I think he's a genius. I could spend all night telling you the things we did, but there isn't time. I've got to skip." He placed his fingers over his eyes. "Joan of Arc," he said, "was the turning point. Ames had decided that it would be diverting to re-enact famous scenes from literature. So he and Bud went down to Main Street, I think it was, and found a beat doll who thought the whole thing would be fun. They gave her twenty-five dollars, but she never got a chance to spend it. I remember that she laughed right up to the point where Ames lit the pile of oil-soaked rags. . . . Afterward, they re-enacted other scenes. The execution of Marie Antoinette. The murder of Hamlet's father. You know *The Man in the Iron Mask*? They did that one. And a lot more. It lasted quite a while, too, but Ames began to get restless." Dystal held out his hands suddenly and stared at them. "The next game was a form of Russian roulette. We drew straws. Whoever got the short one had to commit suicide—in his own way. It was understood that if he failed, it would mean something much worse—and Ames had developed some damned interesting techniques. Like the nerve clamps, for instance. Thomas lost the game, anyway. They gave him twelve hours to get it over with."

Prentice felt a cold film of perspiration over his flesh. He tried to speak, but found that it was impossible. The man, of course, was crazy. Completely insane. But—he had to hear the end of the story. "Go on," he said.

Dystal ran his tongue across his lower lip, poured another drink and continued. "Cummings and Chambers got scared then," he said. "They argued that some stranger would move into the house and then there'd be all sorts of trouble. We had a meeting at Reiker's, and Chris came out with the idea of us all chipping in and buying the place. But Ames didn't go for it. 'Let's not be so damned exclusive,' he said. 'After all, the new people might be bored, too. Lord knows we could use some fresh blood in the Group.' Cummings was pessimistic. He said, 'What if you're wrong? What if they don't want to join us?' Ames laughed it off. 'I hope,' he said, 'that you don't think we're the only ones. Why, every city has its neighborhoods just like ours. We're really not that unique.' And then he went on to say that if the new people didn't work out, he would take care of the situation. He didn't say how."

Dystal looked out the window again.

"I can see that he's almost ready to give you an invitation, Prentice. Once that happens, you're finished. It's join them or accept the only alternative."

Suddenly the room was very quiet.

"You don't believe me, do you?"

Prentice opened his mouth.

"No, of course you don't. It's a madman's ravings. Well, I'm going to prove it to you, Prentice." He started for the door. "Come on. Follow me; but don't make any noise."

Dystal walked out the back door, closed it, moved soundlessly across the soft, black grass.

"They're on a mystic kick right now," he whispered to Prentice. "Ames is trying to summon the devil. Last week we slaughtered a dog and read the Commandments backward; the week before, we did some chants out of an old book that Ben found in the library; before that it was orgies—" He shook his head. "It isn't working out, though. God knows why. You'd think the devil would be so delighted with Ames that he'd sign him up for the team."

Prentice followed his neighbor across the yards, walking carefully, and wondering why. He thought of his neat little office on Harmon Street, old Mrs. Gleason, the clean, well-lighted restaurant where he had his lunch and read newspaper headlines; and they seemed terribly far away.

Why, he asked himself, am I creeping around back-yards with a lunatic at midnight?

Why?

"The moon is full tonight, Prentice. That means they'll be trying again."

Silently, without the slightest sound, Matthew Dystal moved across the lawns, keeping always to the shadows. A minute later he raised his hand and stopped.

They were at the rear of the Ameses' house.

It was dark inside.

"Come on," Dystal whispered.

"Wait a minute." Somehow, the sight of his own living room, still blazing with light, reassured Prentice. "I think I've had enough for this evening."

"Enough?" Dystal's face twisted grotesquely. He bunched the sleeve of Prentice's jacket in his fist. "Listen," he hissed, "listen, you idiot. I'm risking my life to help you. Don't you understand yet? If they find out I've talked. . . ." He released the sleeve. "Prentice, *please*. You have a chance now, a chance to clear out of this whole stinking mess; but you won't have it long—Believe me!"

Prentice sighed. "What do you want me to do?" he said.

"Nothing. Just come with me, quietly. They're in the basement."

Breathing hard now, Dystal tiptoed around the side of the house. He stopped at a small, earth-level window.

It was closed.

"Prentice. *Softly*. Bend down and keep out of view."

In invisible, slow movements, Dystal reached out and pushed the window. It opened a half inch. He pushed it again. It opened another half inch.

Prentice saw yellow light stream out of the crack. Instantly his throat felt very dry, very painful.

There was a noise. A low, murmurous sound; a susurrus like distant humming.

"What's that?"

Dystal put a finger to his lips and motioned: "Here."

Prentice knelt down at the window and looked into the light.

At first he could not believe what his eyes saw.

It was a basement, like other basements in old houses, with a large iron furnace and a cement floor and heavy beams. This much he could recognize and understand. The rest, he could not.

In the center of the floor was a design, obviously drawn in colored chalks. It looked a bit, to Prentice, like a Star of David, although there were other designs around and within it. They were not particularly artistic, but they were intricate. In the middle was a large cup, similar to a salad bowl, vaguely familiar, empty.

"There," whispered Dystal, withdrawing.

Slightly to the left were drawn a circle and a pentagram, its five points touching the circumference equally.

Prentice blinked and turned his attention to the people.

Standing on a block of wood, surrounded by men and women, was a figure in a black robe and a serpent-shaped crown.

It was Ames.

His wife, Charlotte, dressed in a white gown, stood next to him. She held a brass lamp.

Also in robes and gowns were Ben and Rhoda Roth, Bud Reiker and his wife, the Cummingses, the Chambers, the Johnsons—

Prentice shook away his sudden dizziness and shaded his eyes.

To the right, near the furnace, was a table with a white sheet draped across it. And two feet away, an odd, six-sided structure with black candles burning from a dozen apertures.

"Listen," Dystal said.

Ames' eyes were closed. Softly, he was chanting:

All degradation, all sheer infamy,
  Thou shalt endure. Thy head beneath the mire.
  And dung of worthless women shall desire
As in some hateful dream, at last to lie;
  Woman must trample thee till thou respire
    That deadliest fume:
The vilest worms must crawl, the loathliest vampires gloom . . .

"The Great Beast," chuckled Dystal.

"I," said Ames, "am Ipsissimus," and the others chanted, "He is Ipsissimus."

"I have read the books, dark Lord. *The Book of Sacred Magic of Abra-Melin the Mage* I have read, and I reject it!"

"We reject it!" murmured the Roths.

"The power of Good shall be served by the power of Darkness, always."

He raised his hands. "In Thy altar is the secret of Ankf-f-n-Khonsu; there, also, *The Book of the Dead* and *The Book of the Law,* six candles to each side, my Lord, Bell, Burin, Lamen, Sword, Cup, and the Cakes of Life. . . ."

Prentice looked at the people he had seen only a few hours ago in his living room, and shuddered. He felt very weak.

"We, your servants," said Ames, singing the words, "beseech your presence, Lord of Night and of Life Eternal, Ruler of the Souls of men in all Thy vast dominion. . . ."

Prentice started to rise, but Dystal grasped his jacket. "No," he said. "Wait. Wait another minute. This is something you ought to see."

". . . we live to serve you; grant us . . ."

"He's begging the devil to appear," whispered Dystal.

". . . tonight, and offer the greatest and most treasured gift. Accept our offering!"

"Accept it!" cried the others.

"What the hell is this, anyway?" Prentice demanded, feverishly.

Then Ames stopped talking, and the rest were silent. Ames raised his left hand and lowered it. Chris Cummings and Bud Reiker bowed and walked backwards into the shadows where Prentice could not see them.

Charlotte Ames walked to the six-sided structure with the candles and picked up a long, thin object.

She returned and handed this to her husband.

It was a knife.

"*Killnotshaltthou!*" screamed Ed Chambers, and he stepped across the pentagram to the sheet-shrouded table.

Prentice rubbed his eyes.

"Shhh."

Bud Reiker and Chris Cummings returned to the center of light then. They were carrying a bundle. It was wrapped in blankets.

The bundle thrashed and made peculiar muffled noises. The men lifted it onto the table and held it.

Ames nodded and stepped down from the block of wood. He walked to the table and halted, the long-bladed butcher knife glittering in the glow of the candles.

"To Thee, O Lord of the Underground, we make this offering! To Thee, the rarest gift of all!"

"What is it?" Prentice asked. "What is this gift?"

Dystal's voice was ready and eager. "A virgin," he said.

Then they removed the blanket.

Prentice felt his eyes bursting from their sockets, felt his heart charging the walls of his chest.

"Ann," he said, in a choked whisper. "Ann!"

The knife went up.

Prentice scrambled to his feet and fought the dizziness. "Dystal," he cried. "Dystal, for God's sake, what are they doing? Stop them. You hear me? Stop them!"

"I can't," said Matthew Dystal, sadly. "It's too late. I'm afraid your wife said a few things she shouldn't have, Prentice. You see— we've been looking for a real one for such a long time. . . ."

Prentice tried to lunge, but the effort lost him his balance. He fell to the ground. His arms and legs were growing numb, and he remembered, suddenly, the bitter taste of the drink he'd had.

"It really couldn't have been avoided, though," Dystal said. "I mean, the boy knew, and he'd have told you eventually. And you'd have begun investigating, and—oh, you understand. I told Lucian we should have bought the place, but he's so obstinate; thinks he knows everything! Now, of course, we'll have to burn it, and that does seem a terrible waste." He shook his head from side to side. "But don't you worry," he said. "You'll be asleep by then and, I promise, you won't feel a thing. Really."

Prentice turned his eyes from the window and screamed silently for a long time.

Gavin O'Leary

BY JOHN COLLIER

*John Collier has an assured place in the annals of macabre literature
and over many years has written some of the most unusual—and
terrifying—tales in the genre:* Thus I Refute Beelzy, *to name just
one outstanding example. He describes himself as having no particular obsession with Hollywood, but has always been a devotee of
the cartoon film. In this story he has created an unforgettable insect
character just crying out to be cartooned for the screen.*

There was a young, bold, active, and singularly handsome flea, who
lived as blissful as a shepherd in Arcady upon the divine body of
Rosie O'Leary. Rosie was an eighteen-year-old nursemaid in the
comfortable home of a doctor in Vermont, and no flea has been better
pastured than this one since the beginning of the world. He considered himself a landowner in a country overflowing with milk and
honey, and he delighted in every undulation of the landscape.

Rosie was the merriest, most ardent, laughing, bounding, innocent,
high-spirited creature that ever trod on earth, from which it follows
that our flea was equally blessed in temperament and general physical
tone. It is widely known that the flea imbibes more than half his
weight at a single repast, from which it follows that not only the
bodily health but the nervous conditions, the emotions, the inclina-
tions, and even the moral standards of whoever provides the meal are
very directly transmitted to his diminutive guest.

Thus it came about that this particular flea bounded higher than
most, and ceaselessly extolled his good fortune. All his nourishment

came fresh and ruby from her untroubled heart and there was never such a gay, silly, glossy, high-jumping, well-developed flea as Gavin O'Leary. Gavin was his given name; the other he took from Rosie, as a nobleman takes his title from his domain.

There came a time when Gavin found something a little heady in his drink, and his whole being was filled with delicious dreams. On Thursday evening this sensation rose to a positive delirium. Rosie was being taken to the movies.

Our flea at that time had no great interest in the art of the motion picture. He sat through the first half of the performance in a nook that offered no view of what was going on. At ten o'clock he began to feel ready for his supper, and, as Rosie showed no signs of going home to bed, he resolved to picnic, as it were, on the spot. He inserted his privileged proboscis in the near neighborhood of her heart. His earlier exhilaration should have warned him that great changes were taking place in the nature and quality of the nectar on which he lived, but as Rosie was guileless and heedless, so therefore was Gavin O'Leary. Thus he was taken by surprise when his light and sparkling sustenance changed to a warm and drowsy syrup, with a fire smouldering under its sweetness, which robbed him of all his bounding enterprise. A tremor ran through his body, his eyes half closed, and when his shy retreat was suddenly and inexplicably invaded by an alien hand, he was neither amazed nor hopping mad, but crawled half-reluctantly away, looking over his shoulder with a languid simper, for all the world as if he were a mere bug.

Gavin took refuge in a cranny of the plush seat, and surrendered himself to the throbbing intoxication that filled his veins. He awoke from his drunken sleep several hours later, with a slight sense of shame. It was early morning; Rosie and her companion were gone; the picture house was empty and no food was in sight. Gavin waited eagerly for the place to re-open, for his appetite was of the best. At the proper hour people began to file in. Gavin's seat was taken by a pale youth, who fidgeted impatiently until the performance began, and when the performance began he sighed. Gavin, brushing his forefoot over his proboscis, for all the world like a toper who wipes his lips before taking a swig, entered between a pair of waistcoat buttons, and, without any affectation of saying grace, tapped his new host between the fourth and fifth rib, in order that he might drink as fresh and pure as it came.

I think it is Dante who describes a lover's blood as running pale and fiery like old wine. By this comparison the draught now sucked up by Gavin was vodka or absinthe at the very least. No sooner had he swallowed his potent philter than he began to pant, moan, and roll his eyes like a madman, and he could not clamber up fast enough out of the young man's shirt to where he could catch a glimpse of the object of what was now their joint adoration. It was none other than Miss Blynda Blythe, whose infinitely famous, infinitely glamorous face at this moment filled the greater part of the screen.

Gazing upon her, our flea was in the condition of one who has made a whole meal of a love potion. He felt his host's blood positively boiling within him. He was devoured, wrought-up, hysterical; his proboscis burned, throbbed, and tingled at the sight of that satiny skin; he wept, laughed, and finally began to rhyme like a demon, for his host was a poet, or he could never have been such a lover. In short, no flea has ever loved, longed, and hungered as Gavin did, at his very first sight of Miss Blynda Blythe. (Except that one, dear Madame, which was availing itself of my hospitality, when you passed in your limousine last Thursday.)

All too soon the film came to its end, and Gavin rode home to a hall bedroom, where he spent the night on the young man's coat collar, looking over his shoulder at the fan magazines which this youth incessantly studied. Every now and then he would take a quick shot at that burning brew that was the cause of his furious passion. A number of lesser fleas, and other creatures of a baser sort, refreshed themselves at the same source and shared a night-long bacchanal. Their besotted host, confused between his itches, was too far gone even to scratch. The crazy drinkers were free to take their perilous fill, and the scene was worse than any opium den. Some wept and moaned their lives away in corners; some, dirty, unkempt, lost to the world, lay abandoned in a feverish reverie; others sprang from the window, drowned themselves in the slop-pail, or took Keatings. Many, mad with desire, blunted their proboscises on one or other of

the glossy photographs of Blynda Blythe which adorned the mantel-
piece and the screen.

Gavin, though he sipped and sipped till the potent liquor entered
into the very tissues of his being, was made of sterner stuff. It was
not for nothing that he had spent his youth on the finest flower of
the indomitable immigrant stock. With the dawn his bold plan was
made. His host rose from his uneasy slumbers, dashed off a few lines,
and went out to seek his breakfast at a drugstore. Gavin rode boldly
on the rim of his hat, taking his bearings from the position of the
sun.

The poet walked westward for two or three blocks, and Gavin was
grateful for the lift. But no sooner did the fellow veer off in a
northerly direction in quest of his coffee and doughnut than Gavin
was down on the sidewalk, and hopping furiously on the first stage
of his three-thousand-mile trek to the Coast. He hitch-hiked when
he could, but as he left the town behind him these opportunities grew
fewer. The dust choked him, the hard surface proved lacerating to
those sensitive feet, accustomed to nothing coarser than the silken
skin of Rosie O'Leary. Nevertheless, when the red sunset beaconed
where the long trail crossed the distant hills, a keen eye might have
discerned the speck-like figure of Gavin, jigging lamely but gamely
on.

It was afterwards, and after Heaven knows what adventures by
prairie, desert, and mountain, that a travel-worn, older, and gaunter
Gavin entered Hollywood. He was gaunt, not merely by reason of
his incredible exertions, but because of the knight-errant asceticism
he had practiced through all the hungry miles of the way. Fearing
lest any full meal should fill him with some baser, alien mood, he
had disciplined himself to take the merest semi-sip, except when he
was well assured that his entertainer was also an adoring fan of
Blynda Blythe.

He now hastened along Hollywood Boulevard in search of the
world-famous Chinese Theatre. There, sinking on one knee, he
reverently pressed his long proboscis to a certain beloved footprint
set here in the cement of eternity. A keen-eyed producer noticed the
knightly gesture as he drove by, and instantly conceived the idea of

doing a new version of Cyrano de Bergerac. Gavin, having accomplished this act of homage, took the innocent equivalent of a glass of milk from the dimpled shoulder of a baby star, and began to ponder on how he might make contact with his idol.

He thought at first of striking up an acquaintance with some of the lounging, idle, disappointed fleas of the town, to find out from them which laundry she patronized, so that he might arrive like a male Cleopatra rolled up in some intimate article of her apparel. His wholesome pride rejected this backstairs approach. He dallied for a shuddering moment with the fierce temptation to perch on the cuff of an autograph hunter, and make a Fairbanks leap upon her as she signed the book. "To spring upon her!" he muttered. "To wreak my will upon her regardless of her cries and struggles! To plunge my cruel proboscis into her delicate epidermis!" But Gavin O'Leary was no brutal, cowardly rapist. There was something upright and manly in his nature that demanded he meet his mate as a friend and as an equal. He was fully conscious of the immense social gulf that lay between a poor, unknown flea and a rich and famous film star. Painful as the thought was to him, he did not avert his eyes from the racial barrier. But to Gavin barriers were made to be overleaped. He felt that he must be recognized as a fellow being, and respected as . . . as what? "Why, that's it!" he cried as the inspiration struck him. "Respected as a fellow artist! Who has not heard of performing fleas? Whenever did a troupe of players travel without a numerous companionship of my dark, brittle, and vivacious kin?"

The decision made, nothing remained but to crash the studios, as the ambitious phrase it. Gavin had certain misgivings at the thought of permitting an agent to handle him. The only alternative was to mingle with the ranks of shabby extras who hung about the gates of Blynda's studio in the hope of being called in on some emergency. Fortune favors the brave; he had not been waiting there many weeks when an assistant director dashed out, crying in an urgent voice: "Say! Any of you guys got a performing flea? Anybody know where I can hire one?"

The word was spread. The extras on the sidewalk began to search themselves hastily. Genuine professional flea masters patrolled the boulevards rounding up and corralling their troupes, which they had, with the inhumanity of their kind, turned out to forage for themselves during the bad times. While all this *brouhaha* was spreading through the town, with "Yipee i ay! Yipee i ay!" re-echoing from Gower Street to Culver City, Gavin boldly entered the studio, and took up a point of vantage on the producer's desk. "At least," thought he, "I am first in the queue."

Some flea masters soon entered, carrying their recaptured artistes in pill boxes and phials. Gavin surveyed his rivals, and saw that every one of them bore the indefinable stamp of the bit player. He could hardly suppress a sneer.

When all were assembled: "We've got a part here for the right flea," said the producer. "It's not big, but it's snappy. Listen, this flea's going to have the chance to play opposite Blynda Blythe. It's a bedroom scene, and there's a close two-shot. He's going to bite her on the shoulder in a lodging-house scene. Say, where are your fleas from, feller?"

"Dey're Mex, boss," replied the impresario he had addressed. "Mexican flea, him lively, him jumpa, jumpa. . . ."

"That's enough," replied the producer coldly. "This scene's laid in the East, and when I shoot a scene it's authentic. You can't fool the public these days. Come on, boys, I want a New England flea."

As he spoke he spread the contract out before him. A babble arose from the flea masters, all of whom swore their fleas had been bred on Plymouth Rock and raised on none but Lowells, Cabots, and Lodges. While they still argued, Gavin dipped his proboscis in the ink bottle and scrawled his minute signature on the dotted line.

The effect was electrifying. "The darned little guy!" said the producer. "He's got what it takes. While all you fellers are shooting off your mouths, he muscles right in and gets his moniker on the contract. Reminds me of the time when *I* broke into this industry." he added to a sycophant who nodded smiling agreement. Gavin was hurried on to the set, where his coming was eagerly awaited. "You wouldn't like your stand-in to do this scene, Miss Blythe?" said an over-obsequious assistant. Gavin's heart sank.

"No," said Miss Blythe. "When it's a champagne scene, I want real champagne, and when I get bitten by a flea I stand for a real flea bite."

"Get that written down and over to the publicity department," said the producer to another hanger-on. "O.K., Jack," to the director, "I'll watch you shoot."

"Better run over it once or twice in rehearsal," said the director. "Somebody stand by with a glass of brandy for Miss Blythe."

"It's all right, Benny," said Blynda. "It's for my art."

"Look how it is, Blynda," said the director, taking up the script. "This is where you've walked out on Carew, just because you're nuts about him. You want to see if he'll follow you down to the depths. You're yearning for him. And you're lying on the lodging-house bed, crying. And you feel the bite, just where he kissed you in the scene we're going to shoot when that goddam Art Department get the country-club revel set done. Get the point, Blynda? You feel the bite. For a moment you think it's Carew."

"Yes, Jack. I think I see that. I think I understand."

"And, Jesus! you turn your head, hoping against hope it's him . . ."

". . . and it's only the flea!" she nodded gravely. "Yes, I can feel that. I can play it."

"Bet your life you can play it! Okay, get on the bed. Where's Make-up? Got Miss Blythe's tears ready?"

Blynda waved the crystal vial aside. She shook her head and smiled bravely at the director. "I shan't need phony tears, Jack. Not if it's Carew."

At these words a look and a murmur passed through all the numerous company. Actors and technicians alike felt sympathy and admiration for the plucky girl, for her unrequited real-life passion for the handsome, sneering leading man was no secret. In fact it was the subject of almost hourly bulletins from the Publicity Department.

It was whispered that "Repressed Carew," as he was nick-named by the psychology-conscious younger set of Hollywood, was a man contemptuous of love in any form whatever. Only those who had seen him at his mirror knew that he made an exception in favour of his own supercilious profile. This was the man Blynda hopelessly adored, and Blynda was the girl Gavin was about to bite.

Next moment the director had said a quiet word to his assistant, and the assistant, like a human megaphone, blared the command to the farthest corner of the vast sound stage. "QUIET for Miss Blythe and Mr. Gavin O'Leary rehearsing."

Gavin's heart swelled. To become at one stroke a successful film actor and a happy lover is enough to intoxicate a more down-to-earth personality than a flea's. Blynda pressed her face to the pillow and wept. Her delicious shoulder blades heaved with emotion, and Gavin stood ready for the leap. He wished only that he had a delicate scrap of cambric, that he might wipe his proboscis and fling it into the hands of a nearby grip. He felt the gesture would have shown a nice feeling.

His regrets were cut short by a crisp word: "Mr. O'Leary!" He sprang high into the air, landed, and struck deep.

"Boy! did you see that jump?" cried the director to the producer. "Watch him bite! The little guy gives it all he's got."

"Make a note for me to get him under long-term contract," said the producer to his secretary.

"What the hell am I doing on this floozy's shoulder?" murmured Gavin in a petulant voice. "I wonder when this fellow Carew is going to make his entrance." Forgive him, reader! It was the drink speaking.

At that very moment a deep, rich jocular voice was heard. "Hey, what goes on here? New talent, eh? Stealing my scene!"

All turned to eye the newcomer with respect; Blynda and Gavin with something more. Blynda wallowed as invitingly as she could upon the bed; Gavin, with a leap that approached if not surpassed the world's record, flung himself upon his new idol's breast, sobbing in mingled ecstasy and shame.

"The little fellow seems to take to me," said the actor good-humouredly. "Going to be buddies, eh? Good material that, Jack, for the Publicity Department." These words marked the beginning, and, as far as the speaker was concerned, the motivation, of a friendship between the oddly assorted pair. Soon they became inseparable.

The biographer prefers to draw a veil over the next stage of Gavin's career. To know all is to excuse all, but to know less in a case of this sort is to have less to excuse. Suffice it to say that Carew's love for himself continued what Blynda's love for Carew had begun, and as it was marked by a fervour and a constancy very rare in Hollywood, fervid and constant was Gavin's unhallowed passion for Carew.

It was not long before ugly rumors were in circulation concerning the flea star. People whispered of his fantastic costumes, his violet evening suits, his epicene underwear, his scent-spray shower-bath, and of strange parties at his bijou house in Bel Air. A trade paper, naming no names, pointed out that if individuals of a certain stripe were considered bad security risks by the State Department, they must be even more of a danger in the most influential of all American industries. It seemed only a matter of time before Gavin would be the centre of an open scandal, and his pictures be picketed by the guardians of our morals.

But time works in many ways, and the actor's face withered even faster than Gavin's reputation. Soon he was rejected everywhere for the rôle of the lover, and must either play character parts or go in for production. Character never having been his strong point, he felt himself better fitted to be a producer. Now, producers are known to be God-like creatures, and the chief point of resemblance is that they must either create new stars or have no public.

Carew, of course, had Gavin as an ace up his sleeve. Splendid parts, full of nimble wit and biting satire, were written for the flea actor, but nowhere could a new beauty be found who was worthy to play opposite him. The talent scouts ranged far and wide, but their eulogies carried little conviction. At last, however, a short list was made. Carew read it over, shook his head, and threw it down on his dressing table. "There's not a winner among them," he muttered. "That means I'm not a genius as a producer."

He retired to bed feeling thoroughly dissatisfied with himself for the first time in many years. To Gavin, his supper that night seemed to have a smack of clean and salutary bitterness about it. His nerves steadied themselves, his mind cleared; he saw Carew for what he was, and the hour of his salvation was upon him. At such moments the mind naturally reverts to thoughts of old times, early days, youth, innocence, and the bright faces of the past.

Gavin O'Leary rose and ripped off the flimsy, decadent night attire he had recently affected. He sought, with a leap that was already less mincing and effeminate, the list upon the writing table. The ink-well stood open; to him its sable depths were a positive Jordan, in which, if he dipped seven times, he might yet cease to be a social leper. He immersed himself with a shudder, and, clambering painfully out, he stood for a moment upon the dark rim of the ink-well, nude, shivering, gasping, yet tensing his muscles for a leap to a certain spot at the head of the list. He made it, and made it without splash or blot. With the accuracy of a figure skater, but with all the slow difficulty of a treacle-clogged fly, he described the word "Rosie" in a perfect imitation of the sprawling hand of the chief talent scout.

Another painful leap, and he was back, sobbing and choking, in the bitter, glutinous ink. The hot weather had thickened it. This time he completed the word "O'Leary." Five times more, and her address was written. Gavin, utterly worn out, black as your hat, half-poisoned by ink, sank exhausted on the blotting pad. But a great gladness had dawned in his heart.

The ruse was successful. Rosie was brought to the Coast for a screen test. Needless to say, she passed it triumphantly. Gavin, with a thankful sigh, nestled once more upon her heart, and drank deep of its cleansing, life-giving vintage. With that draught the last of his aberration fell away from him like a shoddy outworn garment. The past was dead. He was a new flea and had earned his right to be the lover of the most beautiful Irish colleen, and the greatest little actress, and the most important human being, in the world. And as Miss O'Leary soon began to think of herself in the same terms, you may be sure they lived happily ever after.

Faed-out

BY AVRAM DAVIDSON

Avram Davidson, author of several much praised novels and short stories, recently captured one of Science Fiction's top prizes, a Hugo Award. A film enthusiast since his childhood, he draws for the story which follows on his early association with the American film and T.V. industry to present a unique—and eerie—slant on the old-time stars and their films.

In an old brown house on Cheromoya in the foothills of the canyon-cut range which parts The Valley from L.A.—in short, in Hollywood —in between a Chiropractic College which had no charter and the premises of an unfrocked rabbi who now practiced as a marriage counsellor, lived Philip Farnel, world-famed star of stage and screen. Farnel was a lovable and God-fearing little man who was so far from chicanery in any form that he even mailed back to the General Telephone System the occasional dimes in extra change which came his way in coin-boxes. Nature, however, had endowed him with a ratty and evil face surmounted by a bulging skull sparsely adorned with hair and divided by a mouthful of irregular and jutting teeth. On the strength of the ancient and time-tested axiom, If Life Hands You A Lemon, Make Lemonade, Phil had sought and obtained work as a moving picture and theatrical villain.

Success on the peripatetic stage had been moderate and full of interest, but when, in 1925, Philip Farnel first saw Hollywood, when he observed the great studios looming like cathedrals amid the orange-groves, when he looked upon the palaces of the great stars, gleaming alabaster and graced with cypresses, roses and bougainvillea, as the villas and latifundia of ancient Rome—seeing the great people themselves riding by like the wind in their great custom-made cars, red, white, mauve, cerise, pearl grey and shocking pink—he said a farewell to the footlights and the one-night stands and even the occasional parts in New York successes. He turned up at the office of a reputable agent with his stills and his scrap-book, and within a week he was playing a disreputable sidekick to Noah Beery in a motion picture involving saloons, stagecoaches, and kidnapped schoolteachers.

He never had more than a secondary role in a Grade A picture, but he often was the lead scoundrel in B films—dishonest guardians, chain-gang captains, corrupt politicians, the boss of the turpentine camp, the brains of the bank robbers. Between 1925 and 1950 Philip Farnel was employed in an average of three pictures a year. He was sober, diligent, amiable, dependable, and he had many friends and no enemies; he knew the great and mingled with them without being one of them, and it did not at any time occur to him to snub or be snide to cameramen or stage-carpenters or wardrobe people or yes-men or writers or script-girls. The wheel turned, those who were low in '25, in '35 were often high (and vice versa). Secure in his many friendships and his own well-deployed if modest talents, Farnel was always in work. In 1950 the wheel made its last turn for him— the television was abroad in the land, the handwriting was on the wall, the doom of the B picture was sealed; in neither spectacles nor horror films was there a place for him.

He accepted the situation calmly and without railing. Farnel was frugal, though never niggardly. He had saved, he had invested, bought and sold. He continued, in his retirement, to do so. He now owned the old brown house on Cheromoya, which was subdivided into apartments; as well as the building occupied by the Chiropractic College and the premises of formerly Reverend Doctor Bernard-son, the marriage counsellor. He collected stamps and coins and science fiction magazines and dealt commercially in all three as well, in a small but profitable way. He had thus enough money for his needs and pleasures and was in some hopes of obtaining more through the re-runs of old films in which he had appeared and which were now on TV, although at too late an hour for Farnel to care to watch.

One beautiful June day when the smog had lifted and it was possible from the hills to see as far as Inglewood or Culver City, Mr. Farnel who had been shopping in the great supermarket on Hollywood Boulevard and was walking home (his one eccentricity), was hailed by a passing motorist whom he recognized with pleasure as Malcolm Morris, an old-time wardrobe man.

'Wait there for me, Phil, will you?' Morris called. 'I'll park and come back.' Farnel replied that he would meet Morris in the coffee-shop nearby, and the latter nodded and drove off.

Over coffee and sweet rolls the two old acquaintances chatted for a while, discussing various friends, living and dead, and then their eyes met full on for a full second. Morris dropped his gaze to the tabletop and began to draw circles out of a little puddle there. It always gave Farnel a small but definite pleasure to encounter in real life a cliché out of the movies, and so it was with a certain sober relish that he inquired, 'What's on your mind, Mal?'

Mal gave a nervous laugh, hesitated, then said, awkwardly but doggedly, 'Couple years ago, Phil, there was an incident in all the papers of a man turned up alive after everybody, including his whole family and the law enforcement agencies, they had all believed him dead. He was out fishing, this man was out fishing and the boat was found overturned and eventually they turned up this body which was identified as his and buried as his and then, after I forgot how many years, he turned up alive in another state and he had run off with this woman who worked for him and they were living as man and wife under an assumed name. And the real body belonged to somebody else and had no connection with the incident. He had faked the over-turned boat so he could run away with the other woman without anyone looking for him.'

Farnel nodded slowly. 'I remember it now. Yes. Didn't the insurance company try to get back the life insurance money they'd paid the legal wife at the time? How did it finally turn out?'

Morris shrugged. 'No idea,' he said. 'I just mentioned it as an example. What I mean is, Phil, do you believe that a similar incident could of been staged here in Hollywood? I mean, it *is* . . . *possible,* isn't it?'

Philip Farnel considered the question as he sipped his coffee. 'Whom did you have in mind?' he asked.

'Ohh . . .' Morris hesitated, made some more circles, joined them to form figure-eights, pursed his mouth, and then dropped the dumb-show altogether by lifting his eyes to Farnel's and saying, rapidly and defiantly, 'S. Maxwell Pierce.'

'No,' said Farnel, at once. 'Absolutely not.'

'You don't think so?' There was a disappointed, almost pleading tone in Morris's voice. Then, challengingly, he demanded, 'Why not? Why is it so impossible? I could tell you—'

Farnel cut in, 'I don't care what you could tell me, Mal, I'll tell you why not. Sam Pierce didn't disappear on any fishing trip, he dropped dead in his home in Beverly Hills the day before Pearl Harbor. He was pronounced dead of a heart attack by his personal physician who had been attending him for his heart condition and for his ulcers, namely Dr. William Allen Albine, a man of the utmost integrity; that's why not.'

Morris wasn't convinced. 'He could have been bribed,' he said.

'Dr. *Albine*? Are you out of your mind? You know better than that! Why, the man is incorruptable. Listen, Mal—*you* know, and *I* know, that a certain actress got down on her bended knees and offered him $10,000 to perform an illegal operation, and he refused, and she offered him fifteen and twenty and finally $25,000, because she trusted him and was afraid to trust anybody else—'

'—I know, I know—'

'And he not only refused but he talked with her the whole night long and he talked her out of it and she had the baby, the delight of her life, and she blesses the name of Dr. Albine every day of her life. So—'

Morris said, 'But that was a different situation.' Farnel went on to point out that they had both attended the funeral services and had seen S. Maxwell Pierce laid out in his casket and that he, at least, Philip Farnel, had accompanied the body to its cremation. Morris's reply was, 'It's possible it was a wax image or something.

I don't *care!*' he concluded, with a defiant cry that was almost a shout.

Farnel threw up his hands. 'The doctor was bribed, the coroner was bribed, the undertaker was bribed, a wax model was made—Mal! For heaven's sake! What's put this extraordinary idea in your mind, the most ridiculous notion I've ever heard, a man of your age—'

Whereupon Malcolm Morris proceeded to tell him that on two successive days in the past week he, M. M., had seen S. Maxwell Pierce and that Pierce had spoken to him. What had he said was Farnel's utterly sceptical question. Morris, pale, half-ashamed, half-distraught, looked at him squarely, and quoted, in a flat and hollow voice, ' "*Help. Help. Help. Help. Help.*" '

Much puzzled, and not a little troubled at his old aquaintance's extraordinary and stubborn delusion, Philip Farnel resumed his walk home. The day continued beautiful, all the more so for the ever-increasing rarity of such days in and around Los Angeles, and by the time he reached his residence the weight upon his mind was almost lifted. He prepared a roast of beef and put it into the oven, set the temperature low, and then went to his office in the rear of the apartment, intending to deal with the day's commercial correspondence, when, acting upon a sudden impulse, he got into his automobile and drove to Beverly Hills.

At the rear of a spacious estate in that city, attending to the fruit trees espaliered against the stone wall, was a small and wiry man in a faded plaid shirt, baggy trousers, and a filthy felt hat. Philip Farnel approached him. 'Doc!' he called. Dr. William Allen Albine turned, squinted, beamed, and advanced to meet him. 'Well, well, well—Phil Farnel!' he exclaimed, greeting him heartily. 'This *is* a surprise. And a very pleasant one, I hasten to add.' The two men shook hands and walked along, chatting of this and that, and took seats in the patio, where an Oriental manservant presently brought them drinks. They toasted one another's health, sipped, and then exchanged a silent look.

After a moment Dr. Albine spoke. 'I'm glad you came, Phil,' he said. 'A great many of my old friends and patients do drop in to see me, from time to time, even though I'm retired, and of course I keep busy—as, I know, do you. But if I'd been asked to name one individual out of all whom I'd be most glad to see today, I'd have named *you*, Phil; I'd have named *you*. And you'll never guess why.' He looked at his visitor; and although Farnel smiled his gratitude at the compliment, nonetheless a shiver passed down his spine.

'You know the individual whom I'm about to name, Phil,' Dr. Albine continued. 'And you were his friend, just as I had the privilege of being. To us he was more than a mere figure of glamor, although far be it from me to deny the immense value of what he did in bringing that glamor into many otherwise drab lives—the public. But I mustn't make a speech. Anyway, I know you will receive what I'm going to tell you, respectfully.'

He took another swallow of his drink without removing his eyes from the face of his guest, then removed the glass from his lips. 'One of the advantages of being retired is that a fellow can catch up on his reading. That's just what I was doing last night, at about ten p.m. I was sitting in my living room with a glass of milk and an apple, and I had some reading matter with me. The lamp was on behind my shoulder, and the rest of the room was in darkness. I had finished looking through Time Magazine and after that I started browsing a bit in the current number of the Journal of the A.M.A.—man named Harrow has been doing some remarkable research at Johns Hopkins into those non-specific micro-organism which so often masquerade as—but I don't want to bore you, you're a layman. I must have dozed off, of *course* I dozed off, and I woke up with a start. But—you know how it is, I didn't at first realize that I was dreaming, I thought I was still awake. . . .'

Dr. Albine told Mr. Farnel that he had looked up, in his dream, and saw S. Maxwell Pierce advancing slowly towards him with a perfectly silent tread.

'He had that gloomy expression upon his face which I'd seen there so often,' the physician continued, sighing, and shaking his head regretfully. 'And I was just going to say to him, "Oh, come on, now,

Sam, you old croaker, cheer up"—when suddenly it hit me: Great Scott! This man is dead! And at that moment he spoke to me.'

Farnel said, 'Don't tell me what he said, just tell me if I'm right. O.K., Doc?' The doctor, astonished, nodded his head. And Farnel repeated the words, ' "*Help. Help. Help. Help. Help,*" ' imitating as best he could the flat and hollow sound.

The color ebbed from Dr. Albine's face, then slowly it returned. He licked his lips. 'My God, Phil,' he whispered. 'How did you know?'

'Because you're the second person today who's told me the same thing. Mal Morris—you remember Mal Morris? A real old-time wardrobe man, used to be with Famous Players, used to be with old Jake Fox, then for years and years he was with C-S—a heavy-set man with a ruddy face. One of the first people I got to know when I started work out here.' And Farnel recapitulated the circumstances of his meeting with Malcolm Morris on Hollywood Boulevard. Doctor Albine listened, nodding slowly.

'Well, you know, Doc, some outfit has leased the old C-S Studio down on Santa Monica, it's been lying empty for years, and they have some sort of a deal whereby independent TV outfits can sublease part of it to make their films, and part of the deal is that the people who took it over from C-S supply wardrobe. To the sub-leasers, I mean. Sub-*lessors*. Anyway, Mal Morris was bringing some items out of storage for the shooting—it was a jungle serial, and he had a bunch of old-time pith helmets and stuff like that. You probably wouldn't remember, but coming from storage along the south end is an L-shaped corridor and Mal says that he noticed as he went down that the lights were flickering in one arm of the L and when he turned the corner coming back they were almost out and that's where—he says—he saw Sam Pierce. Coming toward him. And saying just what I just said. And the next afternoon the same thing happened, only over by where the old dressing-rooms used to be. So tell me, Doc, what do you think it means?'

At first, all that Doctor Albine, who had been physician, friend, and counsellor to the great and near-great among the stars during the Golden Age of Hollywood, could do was shake his head. Then he muttered something to the effect of 'extraordinary coincidence'; and then sat silent for a space of time.

Philip Farnel broke the silence. 'Doc,' he asked, 'what did Sam really die of?'

Albine's benign and wrinkled face turned savage behind his gold-rimmed spectacles. 'I'll tell you what he died of,' he said, almost snarling. 'He died of over-work. Worn out—worn-out at thirty-nine! Isn't that a fine commentary on our so-called Modern Civilization? He died because he was paying alimony to two ex-wives and the only way he could keep up with the payments was to borrow from his agent and the only way he could pay back his agent was to make one picture after another, as fast as he could, with no time out for rest or recreation or leisure or the finer things in life. No wonder he had a heart affliction. No wonder he had an ulcerated stomach. I tell you, Phil, in California a husband has no rights which an ex-wife is bound to respect, and in my opinion, it makes a mockery of our fine, old Anglo-Saxon legal system.'

With these cutting words ringing in his ears, Philip Farnel re-flected, not for the first time, upon the unhappy story of Doctor Albine's sole venture into matrimony; and he did not say a single word, but shook his head.

Farnel drove back home, pensively, and found that his married sister, Mrs. Edna Carter, had arrived in time to rescue the roast from the oven (where he had completely forgotten about it), and had made sandwiches from it for herself and teen-age daughter, Linda. 'You'd forget your head, if it wasn't on your shoulders, Philly,' was her greeting to him. He kissed the two women, mumbled an excuse, and sat down to eat for—truth to tell—the untoward inci-dents of the day and the walks, as well as the ride through the clean air, had combined to give him an appetite perhaps somewhat keener than usual.

After a while he said, 'Edna, you remember Sam Pierce, don't you?'

His sister threw back her head and lifted one hand. 'Do I remem-ber!' she cried, rhetorically. 'I will never forget him as long as I

live! What a loss! What a tragedy! What a handsome man! One
of the greatest actors of our day and age.'

'Oh, come on, Mother,' said Linda, in a scornful tone. 'S. Maxwell
Pierce was a *ham*—and you know it. He wasn't even an *honest* ham,
like Uncle Philly.'

Mrs. Carter said, 'You shut your mouth,' and glared venomously
at her child. 'Just because he doesn't talk with his mouth closed and
scratch himself—'

Farnel swallowed some roast beef. 'Why do you call him a ham,
honey?' he enquired. 'Have you seen any of his pictures in recent
years?'

Linda said that she had. *The Dark Of The Moon* was on the Late,
Late Show. 'What a flop,' she said. 'Not just because he's Pre-
Method, as Mommy seems to think I mean. I mean, some of those
real old-timey actors, like Frank Sinatra, are a gas. But—S. Maxwell
Pierce? Phooey. Strictly from Hamsville.'

It had been many years since Farnel had laid eyes on Roger
Sherman and he was far from sure that the latter would consent
to see him. The ease with which the appointment was made, and the
fact that it was set for the following morning, surprised him. Even
more of a surprise, and a sad one, was the inactivity he saw on all
sides as he entered the offices of Cahan-Sherman Productions in
that so-called New Studio in Culver City. He remembered when
both the newer and the older C-S studios were hives of industry, and
although he had accepted that things were not with the silver screen
as they once were, still, it was a surprise.

The second surprise was what the passing years had done to Rog
Sherman. The Young Lion of Hollywood, he had been called, once
upon a time. The account of how he had wrested control of the
studio from Sam Cahan in the days when the latter was still holding
back cautiously from total conversion to sound, flying his private
biplane across country and interviewing Mrs. Yetta Meredith—
widow of Isidore Meredith, co-founder of the studio—and then
immediately flying his biplane back again with her proxy in his
pocket: this is the stuff from which legend is made.

But time had wrought many changes in the one-time Young Lion of Hollywood, and he now looked like a very old lion indeed, with hollowed eyes, hollowed cheeks, hollowed throat, and his once leonine mane more scanty than otherwise. Little as Philip Farnel was prepared for this, even less was he prepared for the expression on Roger Sherman's face. The head of Cahan-Sherman Productions glared at him, baleful, menacing and hostile. Farnel felt taken aback.

'I'm waiting,' said the movie magnate. 'I. Am. Waiting.'

Realizing that the man's time was valuable and not to be lightly wasted, Farnel plunged right into his narrative. 'It's about S. Maxwell Pierce, C.S.,' he said.

'I'll bet it is,' said Mr. Sherman. 'I'll just bet it is.' Then a flood of scarlet washed across his face and he all but lunged from his desk, pointing his finger and shaking his hand at the astonished visitor. 'Well, let me tell you that you won't get away with it!' he shouted. 'I promise you and your rotten friends that!' And then he sank back into his capacious chair and fumbled a capsule, a pill, and two tablets into his mouth, and reached with a trembling grasp for the carafe of water.

Without even recovering from his astonishment, Farnel pushed the jug within reach, and waited until the medicine had been swallowed. Then he said, 'C.S., I do not understand.'

'You understand, you understand all right,' the tycoon mumbled. A few drops of water glistened on his chin, and he wiped them off on one of the famous linen handkerchiefs with the monograms woven into them especially for him at a factory in Northern Ireland. 'Don't tell me you don't understand. What, are you in cahoots with them— the whole rotten bunch of them? Darnley Mackenzie, Emile Ungar, Richard Rowe, Stella Smith, Sir Q. Fenton Stock, and all the others? I suppose it's just the powers of my imagination, I merely fancied I saw your name on the letter sent to me by that terrible shyster, Leonardo Del Bello? Ha!'

A faint glimmering of light came to Philip Farnel as he recognized the names of other players more famous in the past days than at present. 'Please, C.S.,' he pleaded. 'Don't excite yourself. Why do you take it so personally? It's true, certainly, that I and others have engaged Mr. Del Bello to represent us in discussions—'

'"Discussions,"' sneered Mr. Sherman. 'On the surface, discussion; yes. And behind my back, what? Extortion! That's what it is and you won't get away with it, and when I find out how you're doing it, believe me, my good man, you and all your fine friends will rot in the common jail. The William J. Burns Agency is on the track of your tricks right now, and so soon as they obtain conclusive evidence—the police! That's what. You forget with whom you have to contend. I wouldn't put up with it when the motion picture business was good and I certainly have no intention of submitting to it without a wink of a blink when the motion picture business is no business at all unless a man of my standing is prepared to become a mere hired lackey or errand boy for the Chase Manhattan Bank, the millions and billions of dollars which the so-called "stars" they have nowadays are demanding before they'll consent or condescend to shoot a single frame, and then what happens? All the evil diseases of Egypt, from a hangover to a miscarriage, meanwhile, the money is eaten up, while these temperamental cuties sulk in their tents like Alcibiades and watch television. Twentieth-Century, why *they* deserve such fortune and me not, I couldn't tell you, they strike oil on their lot, and part of the property goes for a high-class housing development. But does C-S strike oil? Do *you* strike oil? That's how C-S strikes oil, and who, may I ask, would be crazy enough to start or even to consider a high-class housing development in Culver City? No one. Meanwhile, the costs continue and the debts mount up and the little shtickle income on Santa Monica wouldn't begin to cover it. So what happens? I rent a few of the old films to television as an experiment and a desperation, they catch on, an offer is made to me by N.B.C. for all the old films in our vaults, an adequate sum of money for the years of service and aggravation which I've given to The Industry, and it would enable me to settle with my creditors for one hundred cents on the dollar and end my career honorably and have a little peace and pleasure in the few years left to me by Our Father in Heaven, so then what happens?'

Barely pausing for breath and a fresh sip of water, the head of Cahan-Sherman continued, 'I'll tell you what happens, as if you didn't know, you snake-in-the-grass. What happens. Every surviving motion picture performer who ever played a bit part in a C-S production hires that Leonardo Del Bello, a money-hungry conniver from the word Go, in the hopes that they'll be able to gouge from me a share in the moneys for the television sales and even the few rentals to the same medium. You know what this means, Mr. Philip Farnel, do you?'

Farnel lowered his eyes from a photo-portrait of the late S. Maxwell Pierce which, among those of other stars both male and female, adorned the walls of Mr. Sherman's still-lavish office.

'Why, Mr. Sherman,' he said, mildly; 'it seems to me that all it means is that all of those who helped create a picture will be able to share in the profits. We were paid, true, don't get me wrong, I'm not complaining that we weren't paid well enough. Maybe some of us were really paid too much. But we were paid for moving pictures intended to be shown in moving picture theaters. Television opens up an entirely—'

A dangerous calm descended on the Lion of Hollywood. A faint smile began its tracings on his distinguished face. 'My friend,' he said, softly, 'let me explain to you. You are proposing to open the dike in order to irrigate certain fields of land. You think the water will flow here, it will flow there, it will flow exactly where you want, and it can be arranged just that way. No. No, my friend. Not so. A flood is a flood. If the actors obtain a share of the proceeds from television sales and rentals, then everybody will obtain a share. The producer.' He began to count on his fingers. 'The director. The assistants. The cameraman. The music arranger. The costumier. The carpenter. The electrician, the wardrobe man, the make-up man, the script-girl, the salad-cook in the commissary, the guard at the gate. Everybody. Literally, ev-er-y-bod-y. So with everybody obtaining a share, what is left? *Bubkis,* that's what's left. Goat-droppings, I'm sorry you oblige me to use such a coarse expression. And C-S Productions dissolves into bankruptcy. So you can understand my position. But what,' and here he began to shout again, 'about *your* position? Sabotage! Espionage! Extortion! Terrorist tactics! And you have the gall to come here and tell me that you're here about S. Maxwell Pierce, yet? Shame! Shame! Ghoul! Vampire! To use the form and the voice of your old friend, you're not ashamed?

'I'd just like to know how you did it! *Why* you did it, that's obvious—to blackmail me and to squeeze your rotten ransom money from our depleted coffers, it's obvious. One single picture we've got in production and it hasn't cost me enough heart-ache, that bitch, Myffanwydd Evans, no—two million dollars, a modest little sum at today's prices—*She Stoops To Conquer,* in modern dress—as if you didn't know, you terrible person—' The mogul's phrases came rapidly, abruptly, his chest heaved. '—and into at least half the scenes we've shot—you and your rotten crew—ruined; ruined—right over the scenes, like double exposure, that fink you hired to masquerade as S. Maxwell Pierce—comes walking, comes walking—and his voice all over the sound track—"*Help! Help! Help! Help! Help!*"—'

This time it was Philip Farnel's turn to reach, with trembling fingers, for the carafe of water.

It was Louella Parsons' column (confused beyond correction, but mentioning both Pierce and Farnel and spelling their names properly) that brought Doody Michaeljohn to the old brown house on Cheromoya. She sat in the living room of his apartment, sun-tanned, healthy, and ill at ease.

'I suppose it's only natural that you were interested,' he said, also a bit nervous. 'Considering that you and Sam were such good friends—'

'He'd been keeping me for years, as well you know, bless you, Phil,' she said. ' "Good friends," yes. I guess we were. He would've married me, too, if it hadn't been for Irma and Dorothy. . . . At least that's what he always said, anyway. I don't know. I just don't know. I never did. However—' Her voice lost its uncertain note and became brisk.

'This happened over a month ago. . . .' She rummaged in her purse, brought out a piece of paper, unfolded it. '. . . but I didn't understand it at the time. Mrs. Mobery told me at the time—'

'Mrs. who?' Philip Farnel squinted, leaned closer. The burden of the entire affair was now weighing down on him; he would very much have liked to be able to get back to his Burmese airmails, his rixdollars, his complete collection of Gernsback *Amazing*, his business block in Chatsworth, and the other familiar items which had occupied his time before all this. 'Mrs. *who?*'

'Mrs. Phyllis Mobery. She's a very well-known Sensitive, Phil, I got to know her at the Spiritual Science Church on Cahuenga Boulevard, in connection with our Friday Night Dutch Suppers, and Phil—I want to tell you—she is marvellous! Simply marvellous! There isn't a thing to which she can't turn her hand, and what she's done for the bedridden and the shut-ins, she can sing, she can paint, she has a pilot's licence and a black belt, and her work with handwriting has attracted world-wide attention.'

Farnel felt himself utterly lost. All he could say was, 'Go on.'

'It was over a month ago, there were only the three of us, Mrs. Mobery, Laura Bender, and me, and it was at my place, Phil, you were never there, I had to give up the bungalow, Phil, it had too many memories. I live in a court in Boyle Heights now. Well, it was about eight o'clock, and suddenly it seemed to have become very quiet and I looked at Laura and she looked at me and then we both looked at Mrs. Mobery and we saw right away that she had slipped into Trance. So I very quickly put a pad of paper and two pencils right by her hands, the soft-lead Eberhard Faber Mongol 480, the kind she prefers, you know. . . .'

Curious soft noises began to escape from the parted lips of the Sensitive, but her hearers knowing that they would never develop into coherent speech, wasted no efforts listening to them, but watched her hands, instead—old hands, strong hands, capable with mahlstick and brush, capable with the organ and the judo-hold, airplane controls and pots and pans—and now, submitting to things utterly removed from any of those others, hands grasping pad and pencils, hands . . . writing.

Farnel took the sheet of yellow paper handed to him, put on his glasses and began to read—or to try to read. He looked up. 'Doody, are you trying to tell me that one person wrote all this?'

'Do you think I'd lie to you, Phil? Laura and I *saw* it. Of course, you have to understand that she was just the medium whereby those who have passed beyond communicated with us. . . . Go, on, Phil—'

'No—I—well, just let me read this. . . .' His voice died away.

In a clear Spencerian hand at the top of the page someone had written, *Mother Mother Mother Dearest Mothe*—and had broken off abruptly without even a trace of the final *r*. Immediately succeeding this an entirely different handwriting began—small, cramped, bearing down heavily, quite incomprehensible: Farnel, looking at it in dismay, was not even sure that it was English. He was certain only that it was very ugly and that, whatever it meant, it did not mean well. It vanished in a swirl of lines, as if there had been a struggle to seize the pencil. After that was a space of about an inch, followed by an address vigorously written—*Mrs H M Stevenson 1327 Franklin Street Reissborough P.A.*—and the words, *Hi, Pipsqueak. 'Hank and Bucky.'* The bottom of the sheet was subscribed in a large, uneven and faltering script, *our Fideral Unon it mus an will be preasarved.* And over this, on the slant, was something else which Farnel could not make out.

He looked up, met her eager glance, shook his head. 'Means nothing to me,' he said. 'I'm sorry.'

Doodie Michaeljohn gave a wordless exclamation, tapped her finger excitedly on the yellow sheet, then clapped her hand to her forehead. 'Oh, of course! Phil! Take it—hold it upside down—and hold it up to a mirror. That one over there. Go *on*, Phil!'

Farnel obeyed. He saw reflected his own face, those irregular and ugly features which had been his misfortune as a boy and his fortune as a man. Many thoughts went rapidly through his mind, but he forced his glance down to the reflection of the paper. All the writing was reversed and incomprehensible, and then part of it jumped suddenly into almost-clarity. He tilted the paper until the slanting words were straight, then jumped, startled, his breath hissing. The woman came up behind him. 'There,' she said. 'Now do you see?'

'Yes,' he said. 'I can see it now.'

Doodie help help Doodie help help stop then or no peace for me darling D flix no Ive got to faed-out hel

His quick and frightened respiration was the only sound for a second or two. Then Doodie said, 'We called up, you know, that Mrs. Stevenson? And she said everybody else used to call her husband 'Henry' and she was the only one who called him "Hank," and "Bucky" was the name they had for their little child before it was born, only it didn't live, and she started to cry—'

'Doodie—'

'—but she managed to tell us that his nick-name for *her* was "*Pip-*" '—

'Doodie—' That the Veil of Oblivion should be lifted to no better end than the exchange of domestic trivia or the proclamation of obsolete political slogans seemed suddenly intolerable to Farnel. 'Doodie, this is Sam's *hand*writing!'

She seemed surprised at his surprise. Very quickly, she said, 'Yes, of course it is, Phil. And I've finally figured out what it means, don't you see, Phil? I've figured out what it *means*. He wouldn't Appear to *me*, Phil, he wouldn't want to even faintly take a chance of frightening me, so this is what he did, you see.' She chuckled, faintly, fondly. 'He never was much of a speller. 'F-a-e-d-o-u-t' That's one mistake he always used to make. And he was probably in a hurry this time, too, because who knows how much time he had. If there's any such thing as Time as we know it, There. . . . Don't you see, Phil, Sam wasn't just a player, a mere mummer, Sam was an artist, Sam was an *actor*. He had oh such a tremendous talent, and he didn't use it in the movies, he couldn't use it in the movies. He was type-cast and he couldn't escape and he needed money, he always needed money, Irma and Dorothy and their alimony, and so he let the studio push him into one piece of tripe after another and that's the reason—'

She stopped abruptly. Looking away from Farnel, she said in a lower tone, 'That's not the reason. It's not the whole reason. He loved the rich living and the big house he lived in and the big houses he visited in and the big cars he drove. He loved the fine, fancy clothes he was always buying and he loved the stupid crowds at the stupid premieres—every few months, another premiere for him because every few months there was another picture.'

Philip Farnel looked at a photograph in a gold frame, showing the beautiful features of S. Maxwell Pierce. The star's arm was around Farnel's shoulders and the latter was looking at him with an affectionate smile which made his face even more than usually ugly, devoid as it was of even the minor dignity of villainy. 'He was always talking of going on the stage,' Farnel recalled. ' "I'm going to throw it all up, Phil," he used to say. "When this contract is up I'm going to tell the Studio where to go, and then it's New York for me. I don't care what parts I have to take at first or how hard I've got to work. Sooner or later Broadway will give me the kind of part I want, and then, Phil, I'll be the happiest man alive." '

Doodie Michaeljohn nodded. S. Maxwell Pierce had told her the same things, too; told them to her often—and often with tears. But he had never made the move, had never been able to bring himself to make the sacrifice, do the hard work required. Not that the screen was easy, no. Sometimes he had to be up at five in the morning after only a few hours' sleep, to be on the set at seven. But once on the set, what did he have to do? Nothing. He just had to stroll through his lines, show his dimples, flash his teeth, take the girl in his arms, and that was it.

'It was easier for you, Phil,' Doodie said. 'Actors like you and Quentin Stock and Emile Ungar and lots of others. You looked on it as a job. You were round pegs and you fitted comfortably into round holes. But with Sam it was *different*. He knew that he was prostituting himself and he hated it but he went right on *do*ing it. He used to talk about "that one talent which is death to hide—" '

Farnel nodded. 'I know. . . . He used to call it "the real Sin against the Holy Ghost. . . ." '

And then Pierce had died, worn-out at thirty-nine, but at least— Doodie said—at least he was at peace, at rest. 'Until they took his old pictures out of the vaults and dusted them off and began showing them on TV. Because, you know, after he died, his popularity faded awfully fast. The pictures dated so quickly, the War and all, and there were newer and younger handsome men to take his place, and the exhibitors just stopped booking his pictures and the distributors didn't even push them. But by now, you see, Phil, they're so old that they're *quaint*—isn't that a terrible thing, Phil? Isn't that *terrible*? People look at those bits and pieces of Sam Pierce's heart and body and soul, that he killed himself making, and they smirk and titter and yawn and reach for another can of beer, because it's only midnight and they aren't sleepy enough to go to bed. It's just killing *time* to them, Phil. And it's just making money, for the studio. But do you know what it is to *Sam*, Phil? Why, you only have to read this desperate plea of his for help, Phil. Each time I read it, it's an arrow in my heart. *Doodie help help stop then*—that should be "stop the*m*," of course—stop the people who're showing his old films. *Flix no*—that's what he used to call the movies, the flics, flickers, you know, English slang, I don't know where he picked it up. Oh, Phil!'

She began to cry and he awkwardly put his arms around her and patted her. 'That's what it means. That's why he's haunting people and the studios. It's why his face and his voice keep coming onto the prints and the sound-tracks of whatever it is they're making there, and why he shows up and appeals to all these people, Phil. Because . . . Phil . . . *as long as his old films keep on being shown, his soul won't be able to rest in peace. . . .*'

The matter was settled, for the time being, at least, without too much difficulty. Roger Sherman, balancing television rentals for *Dark Of The Moon* (starring S. Maxwell Pierce) against the losses being sustained in the making of *She Stoops To Conquer* (starring Myffanwydd Evans), was persuaded to make the experiment. *Dark Of The Moon* was retired to the vaults once more, and, with that, the ghost of S. Maxwell Pierce walked no more.

How long it will last, of course, no one knows. After all, Pierce starred in close to thirty pictures, and appeared in many others made before he reached starhood. Sherman will not remain active in movie-making forever; and when he retires, the complete stock of C-S films passes out of his hands. Only his continuance for the present, plus the law-suit (for it finally came to that) filed by the surviving old movie stars for a share in the TV rights to the films they played in—only these two things continue to keep S. Maxwell Pierce off the TV screen.

Philip Farnel awaits the future with patience, resignation, optimism, and—in this particular instance—no small measure of sadness.

He had held S. Maxwell Pierce to be his close and beloved friend. He had, silently, silently, silently, and very deeply, too—envied S. Maxwell Pierce every atom of personal beauty and personal charm which Pierce had possessed and he, Farnel, had not. He had suffered in the great star's death, and this wound, which time had eventually healed, had been opened again. It had been opened afresh—or was this yet another wound?—and it still pained, and still it bled. For Pierce's shade, drawn from the Valley of Death, had sought out friends, had sought out enemies, had sought out casual acquaintances, and even strangers.

But it seemed to have forgotten, utterly forgotten, that it had ever known Philip Farnel.

Mantage

BY RICHARD MATHESON

Richard Matheson, as Christopher Lee said in his opening remarks, is one of the best of the modern screen-writers in the "horror film genre". Schooled in the demanding medium of T.V., he has of late scripted a number of Edgar Allan Poe films, several nerve-twisting weird movies and an adaptation of his own famous novel, The Incredible Shrinking Man. *He is also a more than accomplished short story writer as he shows here, letting us into some of the secrets of his craft, a craft which would appear to best flourish in the dark corners of the mind.*

Fadeout.

The old man had succumbed. From its movie heaven, an ethereal choir paeaned. Amid roiling pink clouds they sang: *A Moment or Forever*. It was the title of the picture. Lights blinked on. The voices stopped abruptly, the curtain was lowered, the theater boomed with P.A. resonance; a quartet singing *A Moment or Forever* on the Decca label. Eight hundred thousand copies in a month.

Owen Crowley sat slumped in his seat, legs crossed, arms slackly folded. He stared at the curtain. Around him, people stood and stretched, yawned, chatted, laughed. Owen sat there, staring. Next to him, Carole rose and drew on her suède jacket. Softly, she was singing with the record, *"Your mind is the clock that ticks away a moment or forever."*

She stopped. "Honey?"

Owen grunted. "Are you coming?" she asked.

He sighed. "I suppose." He dragged up his jacket and followed her as she edged toward the aisle, shoes crunching over pale popcorn buds and candy wrappers. They reached the aisle and Carole took his arm.

"Well?" she asked. "What did you think?"

Owen had the burdening impression that she had asked him that question a million times; that their relationship consisted of an infinitude of movie going and scant more. Was it only two years since they'd met; five months since their engagement? It seemed, momentarily, like the dreariest of eons.

"What's there to think?" he said. "It's just another movie."

"I thought you'd like it,' Carole said, "being a writer yourself."

He trudged across the lobby with her. They were the last ones out. The snack counter was darkened, the soda machine stilled of technicolored bubblings. The only sound was the whisper of their shoes across the carpeting, then the click of them as they hit the outer lobby.

"What is it, Owen?" Carole asked when he'd gone a block without saying a word.

"They make me mad," he said.

"Who does?" Carole asked.

"The damn stupid people who make those damn stupid movies," he said.

"Why?" she asked.

"Because of the way they gloss over everything."

"What do you mean?"

"This writer the picture was about," said Owen. "He was a lot like I am; talented and with plenty of drive. But it took him almost ten years to get things going. *Ten years*. So what does the stupid picture do? Glosses over them in a few minutes. A couple of scenes of him sitting at his desk, looking broody, a couple of clock shots, a few trays of mashed-out butts, some empty coffee cups, a pile of manuscripts. Some bald-headed publishers with cigars shaking their heads no at him, some feet walking on the sidewalk; and that's it. Ten years of hard labor. It makes me mad."

"But they have to do that, Owen," Carole said. "That's the only way they have of showing it."

"Then life should be like that too," he said.

"Oh, you wouldn't like that," she said.

"You're wrong. I would," he said. "Why should I struggle ten years—or more—on my writing? Why not get it all over with in a couple of minutes?"

"It wouldn't be the same," she said.

"That's for sure," he said.

An hour and forty minutes later, Owen sat on the cot in his furnished room staring at the table on which sat his typewriter and the half-completed manuscript of his third novel *And Now Gomorrah.*

Why not indeed? The idea had definite appeal. He knew that, someday, he'd succeed. It had to be that way. Otherwise, what was he working so hard for? But that transition—that was the thing. That indefinite transition between struggle and success. How wonderful if that part could be condensed, abbreviated.

Glossed over.

"You know what I wish?" he asked the intent young man in the mirror.

"No, what?" asked the man.

"I wish," said Owen Crowley, "that life could be as simple as a movie. All the drudgery set aside in a few flashes of weary looks, disappointments, coffee cups and midnight oil, trays of butts, no's and walking feet. *Why not?*"

On the bureau, something clicked. Owen looked down at his clock. It was 2:43 a.m.

Oh, well. He shrugged and went to bed. Tomorrow, another five pages, another night's work at the toy factory.

A year and seven months went by and nothing happened. Then, one morning, Owen woke up, went down to the mailbox and there it was.

We are happy to inform you that we want to publish your novel Dream Within a Dream.

"Carole! Carole!" He pounded on her apartment door, heart drumming from the half-mile sprint from the subway, the leaping ascent of the stairs. *"Carole!"*

She jerked open the door, face stricken. "Owen, what—?" she began, then cried out, startled, as he swept her from the floor and whirled her around, the hem of her nightgown whipping silkenly. "Owen, what *is* it?" she gasped.

"Look! Look!" He put her down on the couch and, kneeling, held out the crumpled letter to her.

"Oh, Owen!"

They clung to each other and she laughed, she cried. He felt the unbound softness of her pressing at him through the filmy silk, the moist cushioning of her lips against his cheek, her warm tears trickling down his face. "Oh, Owen. *Darling.*"

She cupped his face with trembling hands and kissed him; then whispered, "And you were worried."

"No more," he said. "No more!"

The publisher's office stood aloofly regal above the city; draped, paneled, still. "If you'll sign here, Mr. Crowley," said the editor. Owen took the pen.

"Hurray! Hurroo!" He polkaed amid a debris of cocktail glasses, red-eyed olives, squashed hors d'oeuvres and guests. Who clapped and stamped and shouted and erected monumental furies in the neighbors' hearts. Who flowed and broke apart like noisy quicksilver through the rooms and halls of Carole's apartment. Who devoured regimental rations. Who flushed away Niagaras of converted alcohol. Who nuzzled in a fog of nicotine. Who gambled on the future census in the dark and fur-coat-smelling bedroom.

Owen sprang. He howled. "An Indian I am!" He grabbed the laughing Carole by her spilling hair. "An Indian I am, I'll scalp you! No, I won't, I'll kiss you!" He did to wild applause and whistles. She clung to him, their bodies molding. The clapping was like rapid fire. "And for an encore!" he announced.

Laughter. Cheers. Music pounding. A graveyard of bottles on the sink. Sound and movement. Community singing. Bedlam. A policeman at the door. *"Come in, come in, defender of the weal!"*

"Now, let's be having a little order here, there's people want to sleep."

Silence in the shambles. They sat together on the couch, watching dawn creep in across the sills, a nightgowned Carole clinging to him, half asleep; Owen pressing his lips to her warm throat and feeling, beneath the satin skin, the pulsing of her blood.

"*I love you*," whispered Carole. Her lips on his, wanted, took. The electric rustle of her gown made him shudder. He brushed the straps and watched them slither from the pale curving of her shoulders. "Carole, *Carole*." Her hands were cat claws on his back.

The telephone rang, rang. He opened an eye. There was a heated pitchfork fastened to the lid. As the lid moved up it plunged the pitchfork into his brain. "*Ooh!*" He winced his eyes shut and the room was gone. "Go away," he muttered to the ringing, ringing; to the cleat-shoed, square-dancing goblins in his head.

Across the void, a door opened and the ringing stopped. Owen sighed.

"Hello?" said Carole. "Oh. Yes, he's here."

He heard the crackle of her gown, the nudging of her fingers on his shoulder. "Owen," she said. "Wake up, darling."

The deep fall of pink-tipped flesh against transparent silk was what he saw. He reached up but she was gone. Her hand closed over his and drew him up. "The phone," she said.

"More," he said, pulling her against himself.

"The phone."

"Can wait," he said. His voice came muffled from her nape. "I'm breakfasting."

"Darling, the *phone*."

"Hello?" he said into the black receiver.

"This is Arthur Means, Mr. Crowley," said the voice.

"*Yes!*" There was an explosion in his brain but he kept on smiling anyway because it was the agent he'd called the day before.

"Can you make it for lunch?" asked Arthur Means.

Owen came back into the living room from showering. From the kitchen came the sound of Carole's slippers on linoleum, the sizzle of bacon, the dark odor of percolating coffee.

Owen stopped. He frowned at the couch where he'd been sleeping. How had he ended up there? He'd been in bed with Carole.

The streets, by early morning, were a mystic lot. Manhattan after midnight was an island of intriguing silences, a vast acropolis of crouching steel and stone. He walked between the silent citadels, his footsteps like the ticking of a bomb.

"Which will explode!" he cried. "*Explode!*" cried back the streets of shadowed walls. "Which will explode and throw my shrapnel words through all the world!"

Owen Crowley stopped. He flung out his arms and held the universe. "You're mine!" he yelled.

"*Mine,*" the echo came.

The room was silent as he shed his clothes. He settled on the cot with a happy sigh, crossed his legs and undid lace knots. What time was it? He looked over at the clock. 2:58 a.m.

Fifteen minutes since he'd made his wish.

He grunted in amusement as he dropped his shoe. Weird fancy, that. Yes, it was exactly fifteen minutes if you chose to ignore the one year, seven months and two days since he'd stood over there in his pajamas, fooling with a wish. Granted that, in thinking back, those nineteen months seemed quickly past; but not *that* quickly. If he wished to, he could tally up a reasonable itemization of every miserable day of them.

Owen Crowley chuckled. Weird fancy indeed. Well, it was the mind. The mind was a droll mechanism.

"Carole, let's get married!"

He might have struck her. She stood there, looking dazed.

"What?" she asked.

"*Married!*"

She stared at him. "You mean it?"

He slid his arms around her tightly. "Try me," he said.

"Oh, Owen." She clung to him a moment, then, abruptly, drew back her head and grinned.

"This," she said, "is not so sudden."

It was a white house, lost in summer foliage. The living room was large and cool and they stood together on the walnut floor, holding hands. Outside, leaves were rustling.

"Then by the authority vested in me," said Justice of the Peace Weaver, "by the sovereign state of Connecticut, I now pronounce you man and wife." He smiled. "You may kiss the bride," he said.

Their lips parted and he saw the tears glistening in her eyes.

"How do, Miz Crowley," he whispered.

The Buick hummed along the quiet country road. Inside, Carole leaned against her husband while the radio played, *A Moment or Forever*, arranged for strings. "Remember that?" he asked.

"Mmmm-hmmm." She kissed his cheek.

"Now where," he wondered, "is that motel the old man recommended?"

"Isn't that it up ahead?" she asked.

The tires crackled on the gravel path, then stopped. "Owen look," she said. He laughed. *Aldo Weaver, Manager,* read the bottom line of the rust-streaked wooden sign.

"Yes, brother George, he marries all the young folks around about," said Aldo Weaver as he led them to their cabin and unlocked the door. Then Aldo crunched away and Carole leaned her back against the door until the lock clicked. In the quiet room, dim from tree shade, Carole whispered, "Now you're mine."

They were walking through the empty, echoing rooms of a little house in Northport. "Oh, *yes*," said Carole happily. They stood before the living room window, looking out into the shadow-dark woods beyond. Her hand slipped into his. "Home," she said, "*sweet home*."

They were moving in and it was furnished. A second novel sold, a third. John was born when winds whipped powdery snow across the sloping lawn; Linda on a sultry, cricket-rasping summer night. Years cranked by, a moving backdrop on which events were painted.

He sat there in the stillness of his tiny den. He'd stayed up late correcting the galleys on his forthcoming novel *One Foot in Sea*. Now, almost nodding, he twisted together his fountain pen and set it down. "My God, my God," he murmured, stretching. He was tired.

Across the room, standing on the mantel of the tiny fireplace, the clock buzzed once. Owen looked at it. 3:15 a.m. It was well past his—

He found himself staring at the clock and, like a slow-tapped tympani, his heart was felt. Seventeen minutes later than the last time, thought persisted; thirty-two minutes in all.

Owen Crowley shivered and rubbed his hands as if at some imaginary flame. Well, this is idiotic, he thought; idiotic to dredge up this fantasy every year or so. It was the sort of nonsense that could well become obsession.

He lowered his gaze and looked around the room. The sight of time-won comforts and arrangements made him smile. This house, its disposition, that shelf of manuscripts at his left. These were measurable. The children alone were eighteen months of slow transition just in the making.

He clucked disgustedly at himself. This *was* absurd; rationalizing to himself as if the fancy merited rebutal. Clearing his throat, he tidied up the surface of his desk with energetic movements. There. And there.

He leaned back heavily in his chair. Well, maybe it was a mistake to repress it. That the concept kept returning was proof enough it had a definite meaning. Certainly, the flimsiest of delusions fought against could disorient the reason. All men knew that.

Well, then, face it, he decided. Time was constant; that was the core. What varied was a person's outlook on it. To some it dragged by on tar-held feet, to others fled on blurring wings. It just happened he was one of those to whom time seemed overly transient. So transient that it fostered rather than dispelled the memory of that childish wish he'd made that night more than five years before.

That was it, of course. Months seemed a wink and years a breath because he viewed them so. And—

The door swung open and Carole came across the rug, holding a glass of warmed milk.

"You should be in bed," he scolded.

"So should you," she answered, "yet I see you sitting here. Do you know what time it is?"

"I know," he said.

She settled on his lap as he sipped the milk. "Galleys done?" she asked. He nodded and slid an arm around her waist. She kissed his temple. Out in the winter night, a dog barked once.

She sighed. "It seems like only yesterday, doesn't it?" she said. He drew in a faint breath. "I don't think so," he said.

"Oh, *you*." She punched him gently on the arm.

"This is Artie," said his agent. "Guess what?"

Owen gasped. "*No!*"

He found her in the laundry room, stuffing bedclothes into the washer. "Honey!" he yelled. Sheets went flying. "It's happened!" he cried.

"What?"

"The movies, the movies! They're buying *Nobles and Heralds!*"

"No!"

"Yes! And—get this now—sit down and get it—go ahead and sit or else you'll fall!—they're paying *twelve thousand, five hundred dollars* for it!"

"Oh!"

"And that's not all! They're giving me a ten-week guarantee to do the screenplay at—*get* this—*seven hundred and fifty dollars* a week!"

She squeaked. "We're rich."

"Not quite," he said, floor pacing, "but it's only the beginning, folk, *on*-ly the beginning!"

October winds swept in like tides over the dark field. Spotlight ribbons wiped across the sky.

"I wish the kids were here," he said, his arm around her.

"They'd just be cold and cranky, darling," Carole said.

"Carole, don't you think—"

"Owen, you know I'd come with you if I could; but we'd have to take Johnny out of school and, besides, it would cost so much. It's only ten weeks, darling. Before you know it—"

"Flight twenty seven for Chicago and Los Angeles," intoned the speaker, "now boarding at Gate Three."

"So *soon*." Suddenly, her eyes were lost, she pressed her wind-chilled cheek to his. "Oh, darling, I'll miss you so."

The thick wheels squeaked below, the cabin walls shook. Outside, the engines roared faster and faster. The field rushed by. Owen looked back. Colored lights were distant now. Somewhere among them, Carole stood, watching his plane nose up into the blackness. He settled back and closed his eyes a moment. A dream, he thought. Flying west to write a movie from his own novel. Good God, a veritable dream.

He sat there on a corner of the leather couch. His office was capacious. A peninsula of polished desk extended from the wall, an upholstered chair parked neatly against it. Tweed drapes concealed the humming air conditioner, tasteful reproductions graced the walls and, beneath his shoes, the carpet gave like sponge. Owen sighed.

A knocking broke his reverie. "Yes?" he asked. The snugly sweatered blonde stepped in. "I'm Cora. I'm your secretary," she said. It was Monday morning.

"Eighty-five minutes, give or take," said Morton Zuckersmith, Producer. He signed another notification. "That's a good length." He signed another letter. "You'll pick these things up as you go along." He signed another contract. "It's a world of its own." He stabbed the pen into its onyx sheath and his secretary exited, bearing off the sheaf of papers. Zuckersmith leaned back in his leather chair, hands behind his head, his polo-shirted chest broadening with air. "A world of its own, kiddy," he said, "Ah. Here's our girl."

Owen stood, his stomach muscles twitching as Linda Carson slipped across the room, one ivory hand extended.

"Morton, dear," she said.

"Morning, darling." Zuckersmith engulfed her hand in his, then looked toward Owen. "Dear, I'd like you to meet your writer for *The Lady and the Herald*."

"I've been so anxious to meet you," said Linda Carson, nee Virginia Ostermeyer. "I loved your book. How can I tell you?"

He started up as Cora entered. "Don't get up," she said. "I'm just bringing you your pages. We're up to forty-five."

Owen watched her as she stretched across the desk. Her sweaters grew more skinlike every day. The tense expansion of her breathing posed threats to every fiber.

"How does it read?" he asked.

She took it for an invitation to perch across the couch arm at his feet. "I think you're doing *wonderfully*," she said. She crossed her legs and frothy slip lace sighed across her knees. "You're very talented." She drew in chest-enhancing air. "There's just a few things here and there," she said. "I'd tell you what they were right now but—well, it's lunchtime and—"

They went to lunch; that day and others after. Cora donned a mantle of stewardship, guiding him as though he were resourceless. Bustling in with smiles and coffee every morning, telling him what foods were best prepared at dinner and, fingering his arm, leading him to the commissary every afternoon for orange juice; hinting at a p.m. continuance of their relationship: assuming a position in his life he had no desire for. Actually sniffling one afternoon after he'd gone to lunch without her; and, as he patted her shoulder in rough commiseration, pressing against him suddenly, her firm lips taking their efficient due, the taut convexities of her indenting him. He drew back, startled. "*Cora.*"

She patted his cheek. "Don't think about it, darling. You have important work to do." Then she was gone and Owen was sitting at his desk, alarm diffusing to his fingertips. A week, another week.

"Hi," said Linda. "How are you?"

"Fine," he answered as Cora entered, clad in hugging gabardine, in clinging silk. "Lunch? I'd love to. Shall I meet you at the—? Oh, alright!" He hung up. Cora stared at him.

As he slipped onto the red leather seat he saw, across the street, Cora at the gate, watching him grimly.

"Hello, Owen," Linda said. The Lincoln purred into the line of traffic. This is nonsense, Owen thought. He'd have to try a second time with Cora. The first discouragement she'd taken for nobility; the gesture of a gallant husband toward his wife and children. At least she seemed to take it so. Good God, what complication.

It was lunch together on the Strip; then, later, dinner. Owen trusting that enough hours devoted to Linda would convince Cora of his lack of interest. The next night it was dinner and the Philharmonic; two nights later, dancing and a drive along the shore; the next, a preview in Encino.

At what specific juncture the plan went wrong Owen never knew. It gained irrevocable form the night when, parked beside the ocean, radio playing music softly, Linda slipped against him naturally, her world-known body pressing close, her lips a succulence at his. "*Darling.*"

He lay starkly awake, thinking of the past weeks; of Cora and of Linda; of Carole whose reality had faded to the tenuous form of daily letters and a weekly voice emitting from the telephone, a smiling picture on his desk.

He'd almost finished with the screenplay. Soon he'd fly back home. So much time had passed. Where were the joints, the sealing place? Where was the evidence except in circumstantial shards of memory? It was like one of those effects they'd taught him at the studio; a *montage*—a series of quickly paced scenes. That's what life seemed like; a series of quickly paced scenes that flitted across the screen of one's attention, then were gone.

Across the hotel room, his traveling clock buzzed once. He would not look at it.

He ran against the wind, the snow, but Carole wasn't there. He stood, eyes searching, in the waiting room, an island of man and luggage. Was she ill? There'd been no acknowledgment of his telegram but—

"Carole?" The booth was hot and stale.

"Yes," she said.

"My God, darling, did you *forget*?"

"No," she said.

The taxi ride to Northport was a jading travelogue of snow-cottoned trees and lawns, impeding traffic lights and tire chains rattling over slush-gravied streets. She'd been so deadly calm on the phone. No, I'm not sick. Linda has a little cold. John is fine. I couldn't get a sitter. A chill of premonitions troubled at him.

Home at last. He'd dreamed of it like this, standing silently among the skeletal trees, a mantle of snow across it roof, a rope of wood smoke spiraling from its chimney. He paid the driver with a shaking hand and turned expectantly. The door stayed shut. He waited but the door stayed shut.

He read the letter that she'd finally given him. *Dear Mrs. Crowley*, it began, *I thought you ought to know. . . .* His eyes sought out the childish signature below. *Cora Bailey.*

"Why that dirty, little—" He couldn't say it; something held him back.

"Dear God." She stood before the window, trembling. "To this very moment I've been praying it was a lie. But now. . . ."

She shriveled to his touch. *"Don't."*

"You wouldn't go with me," he charged. "You *wouldn't* go."

"Is that your excuse?" she asked.

"Wha'm I gonna do?" he asked, fumbling at his fourteenth Scotch and water. *"Wha'?* I don' wanna lose 'er, Artie. I don' wanna lose 'er an' the children. Wha'm I gonna do?"

"I don't know," said Artie.

"That dirty li'l—" Owen muttered. "Hadn't been for her. . . ."

"Don't blame the silly little slut for this," said Artie, "She's just the icing. You're the one who baked the cake."

"Wha'm I gonna do?"

"Well, for one thing, start working at life a little more. It isn't just a play that's taking place in front of you. You're on the stage, you have a part. Either you play it or you're a pawn. No one's going to feed you dialogue or action, Owen. You're on your own. Remember that."

"I wonder," Owen said. Then and later in the silence of his hotel room.

A week, two weeks. Listless walks through a Manhattan that was only noise and loneliness. Movies stared at, dinners at the Automat, sleepless night, the alcoholed search for peace. Finally, the desperate phone call. "Carole, take me back, *please* take me back."

"Oh, darling. *Come home to me.*"

Another cab ride, this time joyous. The porch light burning, the door flung open, Carole running to him. Arms around each other, walking back into their home together.

The Grand Tour! A dizzying whirl of places and events. Misted England in the spring; the broad, the narrow streets of Paris, Spree-bisected Berlin and Rhone-bisected Geneva. Milan of Lombardy, the hundred crumbling-castled islands of Venice, the culture trove of Florence, Marseilles braced against the sea, the Alps-protected Riviera, Dijon the ancient. A second honeymoon; a rush of desperate renewal, half seen, half felt like flashes of uncertain heat in a great, surrounding darkness.

They lay together on the river bank. Sunlight scattered glittering coins across the water, fish stirred idly in the thermal drift. The contents of their picnic basket lay in happy decimation. Carole rested on his shoulder, her breath a warming tickle on his chest.

"*Where has the time all gone to?*" Owen asked; not of her or anyone but to the sky.

"Darling, you sound upset," she said, raising on an elbow to look at him.

"I am," he answered. "Don't you remember the night we saw that picture *A Moment or Forever?* Don't you remember what I said?"

"No."

He told her; of that and of his wish and of the formless dread that sometimes came upon him. "It was just the first part I wanted fast, though," he said, "*not the whole thing.*"

"Darling, darling," Carole said, trying not to smile, "I guess this must be the curse of having an imagination. Owen, it's been over seven years. *Seven years.*"

He held his watch up. "Or fifty-seven minutes," he said.

Home again. Summer, fall and winter. *Wind from the South* selling to the movies for $100,000; Owen turning down the screenplay offer. The aging mansion overlooking the Sound, the hiring of Mrs. Halsey as their housekeeper. John packed off to a military academy, Linda to private school. As a result of the European trip, one blustery afternoon in March, the birth of George.

Another year. Another. Five years, ten. Books assured and flowing from his pen. *Lap of Legends Old, Crumbling Satires, Jiggery Pokery* and *The Dragon Fly*. A decade gone, then more. The National Book Award for *No Dying and No Tomb*. The Pulitzer Prize for *Bacchus Night*.

He stood before the window of his paneled office, trying to forget at least a single item of another paneled office he'd been in—that of his publisher the day he'd signed his first contract there. But he could forget nothing; not a single detail would elude him. As if, instead of twenty-three years before, it had been yesterday. How could he recall it all so vividly unless, actually—

"*Dad?*" He turned and felt a frozen trap jaw clamp across his heart. John strode across the room. "I'm going now," he said.

"What? *Going?*" Owen stared at him; at this tall stranger, at this young man in military uniform who called him Dad.

"Old Dad," laughed John. He clapped his father's arm. "Are you dreaming up another book?"

Only then, as if cause followed effect, Owen knew. Europe raged with war again and John was in the army, ordered overseas. He stood there, staring at his son, speaking with a voice not his; watching the seconds rush away. Where had *this* war come from? What vast and awful machinations had brought it into being? *And where was his little boy?* Surely he was not the stranger shaking hands with him and saying his good-bys. The trap jaw tightened. Owen whimpered.

But the room was empty. He blinked. Was it all a dream, all flashes in an ailing mind? On leaden feet, he stumbled to the window and watched the taxi swallow up his son and drive away with him. "Good-bye," he whispered, "God protect you."

No one feeds you dialogue, he thought; but was that *he* who spoke?

The bell had rung and Carole answered it. Now, the handle of his office door clicked once and she was standing there, face bloodless, staring at him, in her hand the telegram. Owen felt his breath stop.

"*No,*" he murmured; then, gasping, started up as, soundlessly, Carole swayed and crumpled to the floor.

"At least a week in bed," the doctor told him, "Quiet; lots of rest. The shock is most severe."

He shambled on the dunes; numbed, expressionless. Razored winds cut through him, whipped his clothes and lashed his grey-streaked hair to threads. With lightless eyes, he marked the course of foam-flecked waves across the Sound. Only yesterday that John went off to war, he thought; only yesterday he came home proudly rigid in his academy uniform; only yesterday he was in shorts and grammar school; only yesterday he thundered through the house leaving his wake of breathless laughter; only yesterday that he was born when winds whipped powdery snow across—

"Dear God!" Dead. *Dead!* Not twenty-one and *dead;* all his life a moment passed, a memory already slipping from the mind.

"*I take it back!*" Terrified, he screamed it to the rushing sky. "I take it back, I never meant it!" He lay there, scraping at the sand, weeping for his boy yet wondering if he ever had a boy at all.

"*Attendez, M'sieus, M'dames! Nice!*"

"Oh my; already?" Carole said. "That was quick now, children, wasn't it?"

Owen blinked. He looked at her; at this portly, grey-haired woman across the aisle from him. She smiled. She *knew* him?

"What?" he asked.

"Oh, why do I talk to you?" she grumbled. "You're always in your thoughts, your thoughts." Hissing, she stood and drew a wicker basket from the rack. *Was this some game?*

"Gee, Dad, look at *that!*"

He gaped at the teen-aged boy beside him. And who was *he?* Owen Crowley shook his head a little. He looked around him. *Nice?* In France again? What about the war?

The train plunged into blackness. "Oh, *damn!*" snapped Linda. On Owen's other side she struck her match again and, in the flare, he saw, reflected in the window, the features of another middle-aged stranger and it was himself. The present flooded over him. The war over and he and his family abroad: Linda, twenty-two, divorced, bitter, slightly alcoholic; George, fifteen, chubby, flailing in the glandular limbo between women and erector sets; Carole, forty-six, newly risen from the sepulcher of menopause, pettish, somewhat bored; and he himself, forty-nine, successful, coldly handsome, still wondering if life were made of years or seconds. All this passing through his mind before Riviera sunlight flooded into their compartment again.

Out on the terrace it was darker, cooler. Owen stood there, smoking, looking at the spray of diamond pinpoints in the sky. Inside, the murmuring of gamblers was like a distant, insect hum.

"Hello, Mr. Crowley."

She was in the shadows, palely gowned; a voice, a movement.

"You know my name?" he asked.

"But you're famous," was her answer.

Awareness fluttered in him. The straining flattery of club women had turned his stomach more than once. But then she'd glided from the darkness and he saw her face and all awareness died. Moonlight creamed her arms and shoulders; it was incandescent in her eyes.

"My name is Alison," she said: "Are you glad to meet me?"

The polished cruiser swept a banking curve into the wind, its bows slashing at the waves, flinging up a rainbowed mist across them. "You little idiot!" he laughed. "You'll drown us yet!"

"You and I!" she shouted back. "Entwining under fathoms! I'd *love* that, wouldn't you?"

He smiled at her and touched her thrill-flushed cheek. She kissed his palm and held him with her eyes. *I love you.* Soundless; a movement of her lips. He turned his head and looked across the sun-jeweled Mediterranean. Just keep going on, he thought. Never turn. Keep going till the ocean swallows us. *I won't go back.*

Alison put the boat on automatic drive, then came up behind him, sliding warm arms around his waist, pressing her body to his. "You're off again," she murmured. "Where are you, darling?"

He looked at her. "How long have we known each other?" he asked.

"A moment, forever, it's all the same," she answered, teasing his ear lobe with her lips.

"A moment or forever," he murmured. "Yes."

"What?" she asked.

"Nothing," he said. "Just brooding on the tyranny of clocks."

"Since time is so distressing to you, love," she said, pushing open the cabin door, "let's not waste another second of it."

The cruiser hummed across the silent sea.

"What, *hiking*?" Carole said. "At *your* age?"

"Though it may disturb you," Owen answered, tautly, "I, at least, am not yet prepared to surrender to the stodgy blandishments of old age."

"So I'm senile now!" she cried.

"*Please,*" he said.

"She thinks you're *old*?" said Alison. "Good God, how little that woman knows you!"

Hikes, skiing, boat rides, swimming, horseback riding, dancing till sun dispersed the night. Him telling Carole he was doing research for a novel; not knowing if she believed him; not, either, caring much. Weeks and weeks of stalking the elusive dead.

He stood on the sun-drenched balcony outside Alison's room. Inside, ivory-limbed, she slept like some game-worn child. Owen's body was exhausted, each inadequate muscle pleading for surcease; but, for the moment, he was not thinking about that. He was wondering about something else; a clue that had occurred to him when he was lying with her.

In all his life, it seemed as if there never was a clear remembrance of physical love. Every detail of the moments leading to the act were vivid but the act itself was not. Equally so, all memory of his ever having cursed aloud was dimmed, uncertain.

And these were the very things that movies censored.

"Owen?" Inside, he heard the rustle of her body on the sheets. There was demand in her voice again; honeyed but authoritative. He turned. Then let me *remember* this, he thought. Let every second of it be with me; every detail of its fiery exaction, its flesh-born declaration, its drunken, sweet derangement. Anxiously, he stepped through the doorway.

Afternoon. He walked along the shore, staring at the mirror-flat blueness of the sea. It was true then. There was no distinct remembrance of it. From the second he'd gone through the doorway until now, all was a virtual blank. Yes, *true!* He knew it now. Interims were void; time was rushing him to his script-appointed end. He was a player, yes, as Artie said, but the play had been already written.

He sat in the dark train compartment, staring out of the window. Far below slept moon-washed Nice and Alison; across the aisle slept George and Linda, grumbled Carole in a restless sleep. How angry they had been at his announcement of their immediate departure for home.

And now, he thought, and *now*. He held his watch up and marked the posture of its luminous hands. *Seventy-four minutes.*

How much left?

"You know, George," he said, "when I was young—and not so young—I nursed a fine delusion. I thought my life was being run out like a motion picture. It was never certain, mind you, only nagging doubt but it dismayed me; oh, indeed it did. Until, one day—a little while ago—it came to me that everyone has an uncontrollable aversion to the inroads of mortality. Especially old ones like myself, George. How we are inclined to think that time has, somehow, tricked us, making us look the other way a moment while, now unguarded, it rushes by us, bearing on its awful, tracking shoulders, our lives."

"I can see that," said George and lit his pipe again.

Owen Crowley chuckled. "George, George," he said. "Give full humor to your nutty sire. He'll not be with you too much longer."

"Now stop that talk," said Carole, knitting by the fire. "Stop that silly talk."

"Carole?" he called. "My dear?" Wind from the Sound obscured his trembling voice. He looked around. "Here, *you! Here!*"

The nurse primped mechanically at his pillow. She chided, "Now, now, Mr. Crowley. You mustn't tire yourself."

"Where's my wife? For pity's sake go fetch her. I can't—"

"Hush now, Mr. Crowley, don't start in again."

He stared at her; at this semi-mustached gaucherie in white who fussed and wielded. "What?" he murmured. "*What?*" Then something drew away the veil and he knew. Linda was getting her fourth divorce, shuttling between her lawyer's office and the cocktail lounges; George was a correspondent in Japan, a brace of critic-fêted books to his name. And Carole, Carole?

Dead.

"No," he said, quite calmly. "No, no, that's not true. I tell you, fetch her. Oh, there's a pretty thing." He reached out for the falling leaf and toppled from his chair.

The blackness parted; it filtered into unmarked greyness. Then his room appeared, a tiny fire in the grate, his doctor by the bed consulting with the nurse; at the foot of it, Linda standing like a sour wraith.

Now, thought Owen. Now was just about the time. His life, he thought, had been a brief engagement; a flow of scenes across what cosmic retina? He thought of John, of Linda Carson, of Artie, of Morton Zuckersmith and Cora; of George and Linda and Alison; of Carole; of the legioned people who had passed him during his performance. They were all gone, almost faceless now.

"What . . . time?" he asked.

The doctor drew his watch. "Four-oh-eight," he said, "a.m."

Of course. Owen smiled. He should have known it all along. A dryness in his throat thinned the laugh to a rasping whisper. They stood there, staring at him.

"Eighty-five minutes," he said. "A good length. Yes; *a good length.*"

Then, just before he closed his eyes, he saw them—letters floating in the air, imposed across their faces and the room. And they were words but words seen in a mirror, white and still.

Or was it just imagination?

Fadeout.

Technical Adviser

BY CHAD OLIVER

The success of such films as Stanley Kubrick's 2001 has made the S.F. story a popular vehicle for today's film producers—as long, of course, as actual space exploration doesn't overtake their efforts! Chad Oliver, a prominent writer in the genre, seems to have somewhat predicted it all in the following story—which he in fact wrote some ten years ago!

Gilbert Webster, slouched down in a soft chair at the conference table, radiated a distinctly fluid impression that he was on the verge of cascading away into a puddle on the rug. His long, thin face wore a funereal air, as though he were perpetually preoccupied with World Problems. As a matter of strictly objective fact, however, he happened to be thinking about his incipient ulcer.

"You are not a corpse, Webster," stated the patient voice of Daniel Purdy Bell. "Let's sit up and play Man."

Webster flowed into a more orthodox posture and cocked an eyebrow at the producer. "Whom are we impressing today, Purdy? If it's the League again, I left my Eagle Scout badge in the washroom—"

"Don't play dumb, Webster. Just be yourself. Dee Newton is due here any minute." Purdy Bell paused significantly. "*Dr.* Newton has a Ph.D."

"Oh, *Dr.* Newton!" exclaimed Webster in awed tones. "Is he bringing his gravity with him?"

Bell sighed. "Brief him," he told Cecil Kelley, the director.

"Technical adviser on the science fiction deal," Kelley explained shortly. "Physicist. Used to write the stuff. Won't interfere with your script except for the science angle—"

"Never mind, Cecil," Webster interrupted, lifting his hands in surrender. "I was only kidding—you know, a joke. Like in an egg."

Cecil Kelley shot him a look reserved for subspecies.

"It's no joking matter, Gil," said Purdy Bell, his face very tanned under his snow-white hair. "In this business you've got to keep up with the times. Science fiction is big right now, and it's going to get bigger. You can't pass off fool's gold for the genuine article, not today. People know too much. *Valley of the Moon* has got my name on it, and it's going to be Scientifically Accurate right down the line from Atom to Zygote. That's what Newton is for—nice Joe, too; speaks English, got his feet firmly on the ground. . . ."

The buzzer on the table burped apologetically and Bell flipped a switch.

"Dr. Dee Newton, sir," announced a voice like distilled honey.

"Send him in," said Purdy Bell.

Dee Newton didn't look like a scientist. Of course, Gilbert Webster admitted to himself, such a thought raised the question of just what a scientist *did* look like. No doubt they came in all sizes, like Space Cadet hats. Nevertheless, they shouldn't, somehow, look like Dee Newton. Newton was a rotund, cherubic little man, nattily dressed, who seemed to be bubbling with silent laughter that percolated just below the surface. Webster liked him on sight.

"I'm not the man to waste words, Dr. Newton," said Purdy Bell when the introductions had been completed. "I'll run through the broad outline of *Valley* and you see what you think of it. Remember, what we're after is Scientific Accuracy—you don't have to pull any punches for *us*."

"Fine," beamed Dr. Newton, obviously pleased. "Admirable."

"Here's the set-up: *Valley* is going to be class, in colour, with a good, sound story of a misunderstood guy who finds both himself and the girl he loves in the dark reaches of Outer Space." Purdy Bell paused, in deference to Infinity. "Two ships have already reached the moon, you see, but have not been heard of since they landed. Something happened to them *after* they got there. This film deals with the Third Flight, sent by the U.S. Army to find out what happened to them."

"Martians, of course," chuckled Dee Newton.

"Of course," agreed Purdy Bell. "What else? There's no air on the moon—as I guess you know, Newton—so that rules out any moon people. Accuracy! That's what this business needs more of."

"Agreed," said Dee Newton, lighting up a virulent black cigar.

"Yes," said Purdy Bell. "Now—it all starts off with a bang, to hook the audience right from the beginning. This third job barely clears into Outer Space when she runs smack into trouble with a capital T—a blazing meteor swarm, great in Technicolor. The ship twists and turns, piloted by this guy nobody thinks is any good, and just barely manages to. . . ."

"Whoa," objected Dee Newton, waving his cigar like a fiery sword. "That won't do, I'm afraid."

"Something—ummm—wrong?"

"You might say that, yes. In the first place, Purdy, the chances of running into a meteor swarm in space between here and the moon are almost zero—the ship has a better chance of getting smacked on the noggin than you would have in your own backyard, but not much. And if the meteors *did* happen to be around, they wouldn't be blazing in a vacuum. No friction. In the second place, that's not a World War I Spad you're flying out there—it's a space-ship, jet-controlled. You'd do well to curve it in an arc at all in that short a time, much less do stunts in it."

"Hmmm," observed Purdy Bell. "Well, that's what we want— Accuracy! I tell you—suppose we cut it down to *one* meteor, just sort of glowing, and blast it out of the way. No fancy rays, of course; just some sort of radar-directed artillery—"

"No dice." Dee Newton smiled sadly. "At those speeds you couldn't hit the Empire State Building with a howitzer. Why not just forget the meteors?"

"No can do." Purdy Bell got to his feet and began pacing the room, the eyes of the three men following him like spectators at a tennis match. He jabbed his finger, six-gun fashion, at Newton. "That meteor may be just a chunk of rock to you, but to me it's Visual Appeal. Man versus the Unknown—in terms that the dumbest popcorn chewer in the third balcony can sink his teeth into, and no pun intended. The meteor stays in."

"You said you wanted accuracy," the physicist shrugged. "I've nothing against space opera, God knows—used to write it myself —but I don't see why it can't be *realistic*."

"Well," said Purdy Bell, "we'll see."

Gilbert Webster smiled sourly. Purdy had *meteor* written all over him in indelible letters a foot high. Webster went back to thinking about his ulcer while Newton and Bell haggled over the costs of technical accuracy on set, and then jerked back to attentiveness when Newton shot off on a new tangent.

"Look here, Purdy," Dee Newton said, banging his pudgy fist on the polished table. "Don't you realise that space travel is almost in our grasp today? You can't just throw a fake set together on chicken feed and get by with it. These things cost money."

"I am aware of that," Purdy Bell assured him. "But I'm not in the gambling racket; an investment has to show returns. This business of building these fantastic sets over and over again. . . ."

"Wait a minute," Dee Newton breathed, bouncing to his feet and standing there stock-still. "Wait—a—minute. Why do we *have* to go on faking these shots and rebuilding our sets? *Why?*"

"Ummm? I don't quite follow you."

Newton sat down again and leaned forward intently, eyes flashing with excitement. "Look here," he said. "How would you like to clear about 15,000,000 bucks on this picture?"

Purdy Bell smiled tolerantly.

"Look," Newton persisted. "Dammit, can't you see? I said that space travel is almost within our grasp, and it *is*. What it lacks is financing. Now, the government doesn't seem to be pushing it—and what's the other source of big-time financing?" He paused, then answered his own question: "Hollywood."

Purdy Bell's smile vanished. "You mean—"

"Exactly." Newton was breathing very fast now, his hands shaking. "You give me $4,000,000 and *we can go to the moon and shoot the picture there.* We can keep it strictly hush-hush; the very first shots of the moon will be in *your* picture!"

"Four million dollars. . . ."

"Million shmillion! Purdy, I thought you were a businessman. Why, man, you'll get the biggest audience in history—an exhibitors' paradise—it can't miss. Don't you understand? *It can't miss!*"

"You mean—film it on location," faltered Purdy Bell.

"On the *moon,*" amplified Cecil Kelley.

"Well, I'll be damned," said Gilbert Webster.

One year later, a toy in fairyland, the ship rode a tongue of white flame into space. Ahead of her, waiting, hung the moon.

Gilbert Webster surveyed the interior of the club room with quiet satisfaction. Comfortable modern chairs and couches in a soft pattern of contrasting greens were arranged snugly in the chamber and a neat chromium bar functioned against the far wall. There were no windows. The air was fresh and clean, vaguely pine-scented, and a green light set into a black check panel signified that the automatic pilot had everything under control.

Dee Newton smiled anticipating his thoughts. "It's real," he said.

Webster shook his head. "I *knew* that space travel was a possibility," he said, downing the last of his scotch and ice. "I believed in it, have for years. But it all went off with such precision, such clockwork! And artificial gravity and everything—more like a luxury liner than a pioneering vessel—"

Dee Newton puffed happily on his cigar. "That's one thing about a spaceship," he pointed out. "Either it works or it doesn't and there just isn't much in between. Why be uncomfortable when you don't have to be? I just used what knowledge I had, cut a corner or two with some notions of my own, and there you are—or more precisely, *here* we are. The ship is a bit unorthodox in some respects, but what's the difference?"

Gilbert Webster looked at the soft green wall that stood between him and nothing. "I've got to hand it to you, Dee." He paused.

"*Dee*— I've been meaning to ask you about that name. Where'd it come from?"

The physicist hesitated, chewing on his cigar. "Long story, Gil," he said apologetically. "I'll try to cut it short. The D was originally short for Danton, and I always sort of felt like a fugitive from the French Revolution. Never could keep Danton and Robespierre straight anyhow, and the D just naturally evolved into *Dee*, which same I am stuck with." He smiled engagingly. "One of those things."

Cecil Kelley stuck his head into the club room then, and Webster was surprised to note the flush of enthusiasm on the director's face. Around the studios, it was legendary that Kelley hadn't really been impressed with a picture since *Gunga Din*, and before that there was a gap that ran all the way back to Charlie Chaplin's *City Lights*.

"Shooting in the control room," he advised them. "Come kibitz."

Dee Newton bounded to his feet, hot on the trail of technical flaws. Gilbert Webster uncoiled himself more slowly, not entirely elated at the prospect of hearing his own dialogue mouthed by Linda Lambeth and the current bobbysox dreamboats. In the best of times trying to construct a workable script from one of Purdy Bell's "out-lines" was not his idea of Paradise.

He followed the two men out of the club room and through a narrow metal corridor. It was hard to believe, in the cosy club room, that you were thousands upon thousands of miles in the middle of nowhere. Here, with the great emptiness whispering from the walls and the vertigo tugging at your stomach, it was different.

You didn't doubt it here.

The control room was buzzing with activity. A sound effects crew had switched on a transcription of a screaming jet, which was intended to represent the noise of an atomic drive, inasmuch as the actual drive devised by Newton was unimpressively subdued. Prop men had already fitted a dummy instrument panel over the real controls, in order to supply the thumping relays, knife switches, rheostats, knobs, buttons, televiewers, spark gaps, and multi-coloured flashing lights that were conspicuously lacking in the genuine article.

Webster shook his head. Purdy Bell—who had judiciously elected to cheer them on from the safety of Mother Earth—even had to fake the real thing in the interests of Scientific Accuracy, which was an interesting exercise in semantics. But it was understandable enough, and Purdy *did* know his business, and had a private bank to prove it. It was just that he knew science in the same way that he knew Roman history—he had made a picture about it once. When Webster had ventured to suggest to him that perhaps Nero had not set fire to Rome at all, but had in fact been busily engaged in trying to put it *out,* Purdy had almost had him banished for heresy.

Dee Newton looked daggers at the phony control panel and waved his cigar at Webster. "Why can't they play it straight?" he demanded. "They've got such a wonderful opportunity; this idiocy isn't *needed.*"

"The popcorn all tastes the same, you know," said Gilbert Webster. "Sometimes I wonder why I don't just open the airlock door and step outside."

"There's no air out there, darling," protested Linda Lambeth, overhearing the last part of Webster's remark. "You couldn't breathe."

"That's the idea," Webster replied, watching her fluttering eyebrows without interest. Linda was a beautiful woman, by Hollywood standards, but a few years past her prime and beginning to acquire a certain desperate glamour. She had been written into the script on Purdy's orders; she was the lovely female reporter in love with The Guy That Nobody Understood. Webster had had nightmares visualising a Purdy Bell Special in which Linda bathed in Martian goat's milk, but the great man had spared him that final *coup de grâce.*

Kelley clapped his hands together for order. "Okay," he said. "Let's take that discovery scene and let's get it right. This is a take."

The room cleared as if by magic, and Gilbert Webster found himself seated on the sidelines next to Dee Newton. He relaxed, taking a secret satisfaction in the fact that his body was able to assume positions never intended for the human organism, and settled back to watch. The alchemy of drama never failed to fascinate him, even though the raw product you saw with your eyes was by no means what would later appear on the screen replete with music and special effects. There was silence now, except for the toned-down whistle of pseudo-atomics. Four men and Linda Lambeth took their places on the set. The men, for some obscure reason no doubt connected with Visual Appeal, had shapeless flour sack garments over the top halves of their uniforms—Purdy presumably remembered *Dawn Patrol* and wanted to protect his actors from flying oil. Linda was in a neat correspondent's uniform, as befitted a young girl reporter going to the moon.

"Okay, now," said Cecil Kelley. "You've just spotted it on the view-screen. *React!* Don't just stand there. You're up against the Unknown, your lives depending on a guy you have no confidence in. Set? Action. . . ."

Shadows blanketed the control room with crisscrosses of anxiety. Frosted stars swam in a deep black viewscreen. Somewhere, a high-toned radar *beep* whistled insistently at electronic intervals that were drawing inexorably closer together. A lieutenant, his face haggard, sank down next to the pilot.

"It's no use," he said flatly. "The computer doesn't *make* mistakes."

Linda registered Fear.

"That does it," said the grey-haired colonel, crumpling a chart into a wad in his fist. He shot a despairing look at the pilot. "To come all this way and then to. . . ."

"If only we could *do* something," breathed Linda Lambeth. "I don't understand—why must we just sit here and take it? *Why do we have to die?*"

"Extended parabola of the space-time co-ordinates," the old colonel explained rapidly. "There's only one man who could get us out of this alive." He looked at the pilot. "And *he* doesn't happen to be with us."

For a long moment, the pilot did not speak. Then, slowly, he lit a cigarette. His voice was steady in the hum of the atomics. "Stand by for turnover," the pilot said.

The *beeps* from the radar came faster and faster.

"But the *orbits*," protested the lieutenant. "It's a *collision* orbit."

"Stand by," the pilot said.

"You—you haven't got a chance," whispered the old colonel.

"He'll do it," gritted Linda Lambeth. "He'll *do* it."

The radar *beeps* coalesced into a keening whine.

"Steady," said the pilot. "Look out, meteor—here we come!"

The atomics erupted into a rising roar.

"Cut!" yelled Cecil Kelley. "That's fine."

"Come on," said Gilbert Webster. "Let's have another drink." Why couldn't they be just a little more realistic? What harm could it do?

"The fate of the artist, my boy," Dee Newton said, reading his mind. "The fate of the artist."

The ship's forward breaking jets flared into atomic life. The cold face of the moon watched them come, impassively. Staring into the viewscreen, Gilbert Webster filled his eyes with what he saw.

"How long?" he asked quietly.

"Soon, my friend," said Dee Newton. "Very soon."

"Just think," gushed Linda Lambeth, "we're going to land on the *moon*."

"Someone should really say something appropriate," an actor said, in sepulchral tones that hinted he was just the right fellow for the job. "This is a momentous occasion in the long history of mankind, an occasion which I feel sure will. . . ."

Gilbert Webster nudged Newton and together they slipped away from the voice, retiring to the bar where they could not hear. Newton excused himself and headed for the control room. Webster was alone, and it was just as well. There are some moments that cannot be shared.

Webster's heart pounded with a clean excitement he hadn't known since he was a youngster in Vermont. They would have to land a camera crew first, of course, and then the ship would have to take off and land again, in order to get pictures of the landing. It would consume a lot of fuel, but Newton said their supply would be sufficient.

There was no sensation of discomfort. The moon filled the screen. . . .

Webster tensed himself. Soon—very soon—man would be on the moon. And all because of a space opera! *Space operas or wars,* he said to himself. *One or the other. You pays your money and you takes your choice.*

There was a low whine and a sudden thump.

Silence.

The ship had landed.

The door of the airlock clamped shut behind him. Gilbert Webster felt the cold silence of the moon press down on him, sealing him in. It made him feel oddly heavy, despite the slight gravity. The five men of the camera crew, standing uncertainly with their equipment, were grotesque caricatures of life—living jokes stuffed in spacesuits and turned loose on the moon.

"I don't know about the rest of you," he said aloud, "but I'm scared stiff."

"Man's first words on the moon!" one of the cameramen chuckled. "Take that down for posterity."

"Nothing to worry about," Dee Newton's voice rasped in his earphones. Newton was handling the initial landing party, while Kelley directed the actors for the ship landing, inasmuch as this end of things was purely a technical one. "Come on—we've got fifteen minutes to clear the blast area."

Webster followed the squat figure across the desolate lunar plain. He had a sudden impulse to reach up and touch the stars, so near did they seem. Stars, brushing his fingertips. . . .

Walking was a pleasure in the light gravity and the men had no trouble carrying equipment that would have broken their backs on Earth. Looking back, Webster could see that the ship that carried them between the worlds had already dwindled against the close lunar horizon.

"Okay," said the physicist finally. "Let's get setup—we don't want to miss this."

Webster checked his special suit watch. Five minutes to go.

Newton had adjusted the automatic controls to lift the ship off the moon and bring her back again after an interval of half an hour. Nothing, he said, could possibly go wrong. Still, Webster worried. It would be disconcerting, to say the least, if the ship failed to return.

Thirty seconds.

"Okay," said Dee Newton. "Start the cameras."

The special cameras went into action as the crews activated the tracking mechanisms. A spot of white flame flickered around the ship's tail and a brief shudder shook the ground. The ship hesitated uncertainly for a moment, and then lifted on a column of fire. The complete absence of any sound at all gave Webster the creeps: it was like watching a silent film of Niagara, with tons upon tons of foaming water crashing down on the black rocks below, without a murmur, without a sound.

"What a picture," murmured Gilbert Webster.

"They're tracking her perfectly," said a cameraman's voice.

"Fine," said Dee Newton, and whistled three times into his suit mike. The whistles hurt Webster's ears, and he opened his mouth to protest. Or, rather, he *tried* to.

His mouth wouldn't open.

Out of the corner of his eye he saw that the cameramen, too, had frozen into immobility. Dee Newton, smiling cheerfully and evidently quite in command of the situation, balanced himself comfortably in his bulky space suit and began to hum *How High the Moon*, with bop interpolations.

Somewhere in space, the ship from Earth began her slow turnover for the return to the moon.

Within minutes, circular vehicles running on tractor treads came crunching over the rocks and whisked silently up to their position. Gilbert Webster just stared, unable to move a muscle, feeling like the man who casually dug up a live dinosaur out of his backyard. The machines stopped and spacesuited figures clambered out briskly. Webster could see distinctly red features on the faces behind the plastiglass helmets. His stomach took a long dive into nowhere.

It just couldn't be, his mind illogically insisted. Not his own plot, the oldest chestnut in the business, really *happening*. It was like finding a banker actually trying to poison a waterhole in Texas. It couldn't be——

But it emphatically was.

What was it that Newton had said so long ago? "*Martians, of course.*"

A confused jumble of thoughts chimed through his brain. So the Martians were telepathic—naturally. They *would* be. Webster wasn't surprised. Nothing surprised him any more.

Congratulations, Dee!

Stupid fools, most of them. Never suspected. . . .

Wonderful!

Newton waved at Webster and grinned. "Degrading business, this space opera," he said aloud. "But think of it—a really new twist at last! *A space opera with real live Earthmen in it!*"

Webster felt very ill.

"Don't worry, my friend," Newton said, reading his thoughts again. "I have plans for you, lad—big plans. I want accuracy in my pictures, and I like you. You've spent your whole life on Earth, while I only skimmed the surface. I want you for my technical adviser later—you won't be harmed, I assure you. We'll do 'em up brown together!"

Here she comes, the telepathy resumed. *Remember, no killing; We want no trouble with the SPCA. Stick to the paralysis, and we can use them all over again in other pictures.*

Linda Lambeth would be in heaven, Webster thought irrelevantly. One of the seven human women on Mars. . . .

The ship from earth eased down on her stern jets and settled on the lunar plain. The airlock door swung open. As indicated by Webster's own script, spacesuited figures clambered down a metal ladder, brandishing phony ray pistols in their gloved hands.

The Martian cameras worked feverishly. Webster wanted to groan, but couldn't.

"Rich, rich!" bubbled Dee Newton. "This is rich!"

Webster had to admit that it was. The Martian actors launched themselves from the rocks and advanced across the moon's surface, their paralysis beams mowing down the Earthmen like scythes going through wheat.

It was beautiful.

Webster took it all in, and was surprised to find that he felt quite good. Happy, even. It wouldn't be so bad, really. Technical adviser for a Martian film company, working under a stickler for accuracy like Newton! What if he was a Martian—Webster wasn't prejudiced, and it might even be a chance to do the job right at last. Webster didn't much care who the job was done *for*. Idly, he wondered how Ray Bradbury would go over with the Martians, and the more he thought about it the better he liked the idea.

"They can't be any worse than people," he thought cheerfully, and when they released him to walk he followed the Martians willingly to their ship.

It was one year later and it felt like ten.

Gilbert Webster surveyed the set of *Down To Earth* with a feeling of horror. Dee waddled up, a rather globular mass of reddish protoplasm in his native state, and Webster grabbed him in dismay.

"But my God, Dee!" he exploded. "You say you want accuracy, and then you have your women going around New York with bare breasts. Civilised women haven't done that since Crete!"

The thing that had been Dee Newton smiled sadly. "I know, dear boy," he said with infinite patience. "It isn't *quite* strictly accurate, but what can I do? The audience knows that these people are supposed to be mammals, and how else can I show it in dramatic visual terms?"

The Screen Game

BY J. G. BALLARD

J. G. Ballard has been described by The Times Literary Supplement *as "one of the most sensitive and enigmatic novelists of the present day". His novels—and in particular* The Crystal World—*have established him as the country's leading Science Fiction and Fantasy writer with an unrivalled imagination and compelling style. Ballard's interest in film making is well illustrated in this story of an experimental film unit on location in a setting of dreams and nightmares. . . .*

Every afternoon during the summer at Ciraquito we played the screen game. After lunch, when the arcades and cafe terraces were empty and everyone was lying asleep indoors, three or four of us would drive out in Raymond Mayo's Lincoln along the road to Vermilion Sands.

The season had ended, and already the desert had begun to move in again for the summer, drifting against the yellowing shutters of the cigarette kiosks and surrounding the town with immense banks of luminous ash. Along the horizon the flat-topped mesas rose into the sky like the painted cones of a volcano jungle. The beach houses had been empty for weeks, and abandoned sandyachts stood in the center of the lakes, embalmed in the opaque heat. Only the highway showed any signs of activity, the motion sculpture of concrete ribbon unfolding across the landscape.

Twenty miles from Ciraquito, where the highway forks to Red Beach and Vermilion Sands, we turned onto the remains of an old gravel track that ran away among the sand-reefs. Only a year earlier this had been a well-kept private road, but the ornamental gateway lay collapsed to one side, and the guard-house was a nesting place for scorpions and sand-rays.

Few people ever ventured far up the road. Continuous rock-slides disturbed the area, and large sections of the surface had slipped away into the reefs. In addition a curious but unmistakable atmosphere of menace hung over the entire zone, marking it off from the remainder of the desert. The hanging galleries of the reefs were more convoluted and sinister, like the tortured Gothic demons of medieval cathedrals. Massive towers of obsidian reared over the roadway like giant stone gallows, their eroded cornices streaked with iron-red dust. The light seemed duller, unlike the rest of the desert, occasionally flaring into a sepulchral glow as if some subterranean fire-cloud had boiled to the surface of the rocks. The surrounding peaks and spires shut out the desert plain, and the only sounds were the echoes of the engine growling among the hills and the piercing cries of the sand-rays wheeling over the open mouths of the reefs like hieratic birds.

For half a mile we followed the road as it wound like a petrified snake above the reefs, and our conversation would become more sporadic and then fall away entirely, resuming only when we began our descent through a shallow valley. A few abstract sculptures stood by the roadside. Once these were sonic, responding to the slipstream of a passing car with a series of warning vibratos, but now the Lincoln passed them unrecognized.

Abruptly, around a steep bend, the reefs and peaks vanished, and the wide expanse of an inland sand-lake lay before us, the great summer house of Lagoon West on its shore. Fragments of light haze hung over the dunes like untethered clouds. The tires cut softly through the cerise sand, and soon we were over-running what appeared to be the edge of an immense chessboard of black and white marble squares. More statues appeared, some buried to their heads, others toppled from their plinths by the drifting dunes.

Looking out at them this afternoon, I felt, not for the first time, that the whole landscape was compounded of illusion, the hulks of fabulous dreams drifting across it like derelict galleons. As we followed the road towards the lake, the huge wreck of Lagoon West passed us slowly on our left. Its terraces and balconies were deserted, and the once marble-white surface was streaked and lifeless. Staircases ended abruptly in mid-flight, and the floors hung like sagging marquees. A maze of twisted corridors, the summer house tilted into the desert sand like a huge contorted orchid.

In the center of the terrace the screens stood where we had left them the previous evening, their zodiacal emblems flashing like heraldic serpents. We walked across to them through the hot sunlight, and for the next hour we played the screen game, pushing the screens along their intricate pathways, advancing and retreating across the smooth marble floor.

No one watched us, but once, fleetingly, I thought I saw a tall aloof figure in a blue cape hidden in the shadows of a second-floor balcony.

'Emerelda!"

On a sudden impulse I shouted to her, but almost without moving she had vanished among the hibiscus and bougainvillea. As her name echoed away among the dunes I knew that we had made our last attempt to lure her from the balcony.

"Paul." Twenty yards away, Raymond and Tony had reached the car. "Paul, we're leaving."

Turning my back to them, I looked up at the great bleached hulk of Lagoon West leaning into the sunlight. Somewhere, along the shore of the sand-lake, music was playing faintly, echoing among the exposed quartz veins. A few isolated chords at first, the fragments hung on the afternoon air, the sustained tremolos suspended above my head like the humming of invisible insects.

As the phrases coalesced, reminding me of the tragic events of the previous summer, I stepped towards the dunes at the edge of the lake. Unlike Raymond and Tony, I knew what would bring Emerelda from her balcony. One night, two months earlier, I had driven alone to Lagoon West, and waited for her among the screens. Suddenly I heard feet racing towards me, but unable to restrain myself I ran back to my car. As I drove off I caught a final glimpse of a white distraught face watching me from the colonnade.

Then, too, I had heard the same music playing, the threnody of the dying sculptures, and I remembered when we had first played the screen game at Lagoon West, and I remembered the last tragic battle with the jewelled insects, and I remembered Emerelda Garland. . . .

I first saw Emerelda Garland the previous summer, shortly after the abstract film company arrived in Ciraquito and was invited by Charles Van Stratten to use the locations at Lagoon West. The company, Orpheus Productions Inc.—known to the aficionados of the cafe terraces such as Raymond Mayo and Tony Sapphire as the 'ebb tide' of the *Nouvelle Vague*—was one of those experimental semi-amateur units whose output is solely destined for a single rapturous showing at the Cannes Film Festival, and who rely for their financial backing on the generosity of the many millionaire dilettantes who apparently feel a compulsive need to cast themselves in the role of Lorenzo de Medici.

Not that there was anything amateurish about the equipment and technical resources of Orpheus Productions. The fleet of location trucks and recording studios which descended on Ciraquito on one of those empty August afternoons looked like the entire D-Day task force, and even the more conservative estimates of the budget for *Aphrodite '70*, the film we helped to make at Lagoon West, amounted to at least twice the gross national product of a central American republic. What was amateurish was rather the complete indifference to normal commercial restraints, and the unswerving dedication to the highest aesthetic standards.

All this, of course, was made possible by the largesse of Charles Van Stratten. To begin with, when we were first co-opted into *Aphrodite '70*, some of us were inclined to be maliciously amused by Charles's naive attempts to produce a masterpiece ("after all," Raymond Mayo would say, excusing Charles' latest gaucherie, "he is the last of the new vogue"), but later we all realized that there was something strangely touching about Charles' earnestness and single-mindedness. None of us, however, was aware of the private tragedy which drove him on through the heat and dust of that summer at Lagoon West, and the grim nemesis waiting for him behind the canvas floats and stage props.

At the time he became the sole owner of Orpheus Productions, Charles Van Stratten had recently celebrated his fortieth birthday, but to all intents he was still a quiet and serious undergraduate. A scion of one of the world's wealthiest banking families, in his early twenties he had twice been briefly married, first to a Neapolitan countess, and secondly to a Hollywood starlet, but the most influential figure in his life was Charles' mother. This domineering harridan, who sat like an immense ormolu spider in her sombre Edwardian mansion on Park Avenue, surrounded by dark galleries filled with Rubens and Rembrandt, had been widowed shortly after Charles' birth, and obviously regarded Charles as Providence's substitute for her husband. Cunningly manipulating a web of trust funds and residuary legacies, she ruthlessly eliminated both Charles' wives (the second committed suicide in a Venetian gondola, the first eloped with Charles' analyst), and then herself died in circumstances of some mystery at the summer house at Lagoon West.

Despite the immense publicity attached to the Van Stratten family, little was ever known about the old dowager's death—officially she tripped over a second-floor balcony—and Charles retired completely from the limelight of international celebrity for the next five years. Now and then he would emerge briefly at the Venice Biennale, or serve as co-sponsor of some cultural foundation, but otherwise he retreated into the vacuum left by his mother's death. Rumor had it—at least in Ciraquito—that Charles himself had been responsible for her quietus, as if revenging (how long overdue!) the tragedy of Oedipus, when the dowager, scenting the prospect of a third liaison, had descended like Jocasta upon Lagoon West and caught Charles and his paramour *in flagrante*.

Much as I liked the story, the first glimpse of Charles Van Stratten dispelled the possibility. Five years after his mother's death, Charles still behaved as if she were watching his every movement through tripod-mounted opera glasses on some distant balcony. His trim youthful figure was a little more portly, but his handsome aristocratic face, its strong jaw belied by an indefinable weakness around the mouth, seemed somehow daunted and indecisive, as if he lacked complete conviction in his own identity.

Shortly after the arrival in Ciraquito of Orpheus Productions, the property manager visited the cafes in the artists' quarter, canvassing for scene designers. Like most of the painters in Ciraquito and Vermilion Sands, I was passing through one of my longer creative pauses. I had stayed on in the town after the season ended, idling away the long empty afternoons under the awning at the Cafe Fresco, and was already showing symptoms of secondary beach fatigue—irreversible boredom and inertia. The prospect of actual work seemed almost a novelty.

"*Aphrodite '70*," Raymond Mayo explained when he returned to our table after a curb-side discussion. "The whole thing reeks of integrity—they want local artists to paint the flats, large abstract designs for the desert backgrounds. They'll pay a dollar per square foot."

"That's rather mean," I commented.

"The property manager apologized, but Van Stratten is a millionaire—money means nothing to him. If it's any consolation, Raphael and Michelangelo were paid a smaller rate for the Sistine Chapel."

"Van Stratten has a bigger budget," Tony Sapphire reminded him. "Besides, the modern painter is a more complex type, his absolute integrity needs to be buttressed by substantial assurances. Is Paul a painter, in the tradition of Leonardo and Larry Rivers, or a cut-price dauber?"

Moodily we watched the distant figure of the property manager move from cafe to cafe.

"How many square feet do they want?" I asked.

"About a million," Raymond said.

Later that afternoon, as we turned off the Red Beach road and were waved on past the guardhouse to Lagoon West, we could hear the sonic sculptures high among the reefs echoing and hooting to the cavalcade of cars speeding over the hills. Droves of startled rays scattered in the air like clouds of exploding soot, their frantic cries lost among the spires and reefs. Preoccupied by the prospect of our vast fees—I had hastily sworn in Tony and Raymond as my assistants—we barely noticed the strange landscape we were crossing, the great gargoyles of red basalt that uncoiled themselves into the air like the spires of demented cathedrals. From the Red Beach—Vermilion Sands highway the hills seemed permanently veiled by the sand-haze, and Lagoon West, although given a brief notoriety by the death of Mrs. Van Stratten, remained isolated and unknown. From the beach houses on the southern shore of the sandlake two miles away, the distant terraces and tiered balconies of the summer house could just be seen across the fused sand, jutting into the cerise evening sky like a stack of dominoes. There was no access to the house along the beach. Quartz veins cut deep fissures into the surface, and reefs of ragged sandstone reared into the air like the rusting skeletons of forgotten ships.

The whole of Lagoon West was a continuous slide area. Periodically a soft boom would disturb the morning silence as one of the galleries of compacted sand, its intricate grottoes and exquisite carved colonnades like an inverted baroque palace, would suddenly dissolve and avalanche gently into the internal precipice below. Most years Charles Van Stratten was away in Europe, and the house was believed to be empty. The only sound the occupants of the beach villas would hear was the faint enigmatic music of the sonic sculptures carried across the lake by the thermal rollers as they played softly to each other in the darkness.

It was to this landscape, with its imperceptible transition between the real and the super-real, that Charles Van Stratten had brought the camera crews and location vans of Orpheus Productions Inc. As the Lincoln joined the column of cars moving slowly towards the summer house, we could see the great canvas hoardings, at least two hundred yards wide and thirty feet high, which a team of construction workers were erecting among the reefs a quarter of a mile from the house. Decorated with huge abstract symbols, these would serve as backdrops to the action, and form a fragmentary labyrinth winding in and out of the hills and dunes.

One of the large terraces below the summer house served as a parking lot, and we made our way through the unloading crews to where a group of men in crocodile-skin slacks and raffia shirts—then the *de rigueur* uniform of *avant-garde* film men—were gathered around a large, heavily jowled man like a perspiring bear who was holding a stack of script-boards under one arm and gesticulating wildly with the other. This was Orson Kanin, director of *Aphrodite '70* and co-owner with Charles Van Stratten of Orpheus Productions. Sometime *enfant terrible* of the futurist cinema, but now a portly barrel-stomached fifty, Kanin had made his reputation some twenty years earlier with *Blind Orpheus,* a neo-Freudian, horror-film version of the Greek legend. (According to Kanin's interpretation, Orpheus deliberately breaks the taboo and looks Eurydice in the face because he wants to be rid of her—and in a famous nightmare sequence which projects his unconscious loathing, he becomes increasingly aware of something cold and strange about his resurrected wife, finds that she is a disintegrating corpse!).

As we joined the periphery of the group, a characteristic Kanin script conference was in full swing, a non-stop pantomime of dramatized incidents from the imaginary script, anecdotes, salary promises and bad puns, all delivered in a rich fruity baritone. Sitting on the balustrade beside Kanin was a handsome youthful man with a sensitive face whom I recognized to be Charles Van Stratten. Now and then, *sotto voce,* he would interject some comment that would be noted by one of the secretaries and incorporated in Kanin's monologue.

As the conference proceeded I gathered that they would begin to shoot the film in some three weeks time, and that it would be performed entirely without script. Kanin only seemed perturbed by the fact that no one had yet been found to play the Aphrodite of *Aphrodite '70,* but Charles Van Stratten interposed here to assure Kanin that he himself would provide the actress.

At this eyebrows were raised knowingly. "Of course," Raymond

murmured. "*Droit de seigneur*. I wonder who the next Mrs. Van Stratten is?"

But Charles Van Stratten seemed unaware of these snide undertones. Catching sight of me, he excused himself and came over to us.

"Paul Golding?" He took my hand in a soft but warm grip. We had never met but I presumed he recognized me from the photographs in the art reviews. "Kanin told me you'd agreed to do the scenery. It's wonderfully encouraging." He spoke in a light, pleasant voice absolutely without affectation. "There's so much confusion here it's a relief to know that at least the scenic designs will be first-class." Before I could demur he took my arm and began to walk away along the terrace towards the hoardings in the distance. "Let's get some air. Kanin will keep this up for a couple of hours at least."

Leaving Raymond and Tony, I followed him across the huge marble squares.

"Kanin keeps worrying about his leading actress," he went on. "Kanin always marries his latest protégé—he claims it's the only way he can make them respond fully to his direction, but I suspect there's an old-fashioned puritan lurking within the cavalier. This time he's going to be disappointed, though not by the actress, may I add. The Aphrodite I have in mind will outshine Milo's."

"The film sounds rather ambitious," I commented. "But I'm sure Kanin is equal to it."

"Of course he is. He's very nearly a genius, and that should be good enough." He paused for a moment, hands in the pockets of his dove grey suit, before translating himself like a chess-piece along a diagonal square. "It's a fascinating subject, you know. The title is misleading, a box-office concession, the film is really Kanin's final examination of the Orpheus legend. The whole question of the illusions which exist in any relationship to make it workable, and of the barriers we willingly accept to hide ourselves from each other. How much reality can we stand?"

We reached one of the huge hoardings that stretched away among the reefs. Jutting upwards from the spires and grottoes, it seemed to shut off half the sky, and already I felt the atmosphere of shifting

illusion and reality that enclosed the whole of Lagoon West, the subtle displacement of time and space. The great hoardings seemed to be both barriers and corridors. Leading away radially from the house and breaking up the landscape, of which they revealed sudden unrelated glimpses, they introduced a curiously appealing element of uncertainty into the placid afternoon, an impression reinforced by the emptiness and enigmatic presence of the summer house.

Returning to Kanin's conference, we followed the edge of the terrace. Here the sand had drifted over the balustrade which divided the public sector of the grounds from the private. Looking up at the lines of balconies on the south face, I noticed someone standing in the shadows below one of the awnings.

Then something flickered brightly from the ground at my feet. Momentarily reflecting the full disc of the sun, like a polished node of sapphire or quartz, the light flashed among the dust, then seemed to dart sideways below the balustrade.

"My God, a scorpion!" I pointed to the insect crouching away from us, the red scythe of its tail beckoning slowly. I assumed that the thickened chitin of the headpiece was reflecting the light, and then saw that a small faceted stone had been set into the skull. As it edged forward into the light, the jewel burned in the sun like an incandescent crystal.

Charles Van Stratten stepped past me. Almost pushing me aside, he glanced towards the shuttered balconies. He feinted deftly with one foot at the scorpion, and before the insect could recover had stamped it into the dust.

"Right, Paul," he said in a firm voice. "I think your suggested designs are excellent. You've caught the spirit of the whole thing exactly, as I knew you would." Buttoning his jacket, he made off towards the film unit, barely pausing to scrape the damp husk of the crushed carapace from his shoe.

I caught up with him. "That scorpion was jewelled," I said. "There was a diamond, or zircon, inset in the head."

He waved impatiently and then took a pair of large sunglasses

from his breast pocket. Masked, his face seemed harder and more autocratic, reminding me of our true relationship.

"An illusion, Paul," he said smoothly. "Some of the insects here are dangerous. You must be more careful." His point made, he relaxed and flashed me his most winning smile.

Rejoining Tony and Raymond, I watched Charles Van Stratten walk off through the technicians and stores staff. His stride was noticeably more purposive, and he brushed aside an assistant producer without bothering to turn his head.

"Well, Paul," Raymond greeted me expansively. "There's no script, no star, no film in the cameras, and no one has the faintest idea what he's supposed to be doing. But there are a million square feet of murals waiting to be painted. It all seems perfectly straightforward."

I looked back across the terrace to where we had seen the scorpion. "I suppose it is," I said.

Somewhere in the dust a jewel glittered brightly.

Two days later I saw another of the jeweled insects.

Suppressing my doubts about Charles Van Stratten, I was busy preparing my designs for the hoardings. Although Raymond's first estimate of a million square feet was exaggerated—less than a tenth of this would be needed—the amount of work and materials required was substantial. In effect I was about to do nothing less than repaint the entire desert.

Each morning I went out to Lagoon West and worked among the reefs, adapting the designs to the contours and colors of the terrain. Most of the time I was alone in the hot sun. After the initial frenzy of activity Orpheus Productions had lost momentum. Kanin had gone off to a film festival at Red Beach, most of the assistant producers and writers had retired to the swimming pool at the Hotel Neptune in Vermilion Sands, and those who remained behind at Lagoon West were now sitting half asleep under the colored umbrellas erected around the mobile cocktail bar.

The only sign of movement was that of Charles Van Stratten, roving tirelessly in his white suit among the reefs and sand-spires.

Now and then I would hear one of the sonic sculptures on the upper balconies of the summer house change its note, and turn to see him standing beside it. His sonic profile evoked a strange, soft sequence of chords, interweaved by sharper, almost plaintive notes that drifted away across the still afternoon air towards the labyrinth of great hoardings that now surrounded the summer house. All day he would wander among them, pacing out the perimeters and diagonals as if trying to square the circle of some private enigma, the director of a huge Wagnerian psycho-drama that would involve us all in its cathartic unfolding.

Shortly after noon, when an intense pall of yellow light lay over the desert, dissolving the colors in its glazed mantle, I sat down on the balustrade, waiting for the meridian to pass. The sand-lake shimmered in the thermal gradients like an immense pool of sluggish wax. A few yards away something flickered in the bright sand, a familiar sudden flare of light. Shielding my eyes, I found the source, the diminutive promethean bearer of this brilliant corona. The spider, a Black Widow, approached on its stilted awkward legs, a blaze of staccato signals pouring from its crown. Then it stopped and pivoted, revealing the large chiselled sapphire inset into its skull.

More points of light flickered. Within a moment the entire terrace sparkled with jewelled light. Quickly I counted a score of the insects —turquoised scorpions, a purple mantis with a giant topaz like a tiered crown, and more than a dozen spiders, pin-points of emerald and sapphire light lancing from their heads.

Above them, hidden in the shadows among the bougainvillea on her balcony, a tall white-faced figure in a blue gown watched.

I stepped over the balustrade, carefully avoiding the motionless insects. Separated from the remainder of the terrace by the west wing of the summer house, I had entered a new zone, where the bone-like pillars of the loggia, the glimmering surface of the sand-lake, and the jewelled insects enclosed me in a sudden empty limbo.

For a few moments I stood below the balcony from which the insects had emerged, still watched by this strange sybilline figure presiding over her private world. I felt that I had strayed across the margins of a dream, onto an internal landscape of the psyche projected upon the sun-filled terraces around me.

But before I could call to her, footsteps grated softly in the loggia. A dark-haired man of about fifty, with a closed, expressionless face, stood among the columns, his black suit neatly buttoned, looking down at me with the impassive, lustreless eyes of a funeral director. The shutters withdrew upon the balcony, and the jewelled insects returned from their foray. Surrounding me, their brilliant crowns glittered with diamond hardness.

Each afternoon, as I returned from the reefs with my sketch pad, I would see the jewelled insects moving in the sunlight beside the lake, while their blue-robed mistress, the lonely, haunted Venus of Lagoon West, watched them from her balcony. Despite the frequency of her appearances, Charles Van Stratten made no attempt to explain her presence. His elaborate preparations for the filming of *Aphrodite '70* almost complete, he became more and more preoccupied.

An outline scenario had been agreed on. To my surprise, the first scene was to be played on the lake terrace, and would take the form of a shadow ballet, for which I painted a series of screens to be moved about like chess-pieces. Each was about twelve feet high, a large canvas mounted on a wooden trestle, representing one of the zodiacal signs. Like the Kafkaesque protagonist of *The Cabinet of Dr. Caligari,* trapped in a labyrinthine nexus of tilting walls, the Orphic hero of *Aphrodite '70* would appear searching for his lost Eurydice among the shifting time stations.

So the screen game, which we were to play tirelessly on so many occasions, made its appearance. As I completed the last of the screens and watched a group of extras perform the first movements of the game under Charles Van Stratten's direction, I began to realize the extent to which we were all supporting players in a gigantic charade of Charles' devising.

Its real object soon became apparent.

The summer house was deserted when I drove out to Lagoon West the next weekend, an immense canopy of silence hanging over the lake and the surrounding hills. The twelve screens stood on the terrace above the beach, their vivid heraldic designs melting into blurred pools of turquoise and carmine which bled away in horizontal layers across the air. Someone had re-arranged the screens to form a narrow spiral corridor. As I straightened them, the train of a white gown disappeared with a startled flourish among the shadows within.

Guessing the probable identity of this nervous intruder, I stepped quietly into the corridor. I pushed back one of the screens, a large Scorpio in royal purple, and suddenly found myself in the center of the maze, little more than an arm's length from the strange figure I had seen on the balcony. For a moment she failed to notice me. Her exquisite white face, like a mask of Florentine marble, veined by a faint shadow of violet that seemed like a delicate interior rose-work, was raised to the canopy of sunlight which cut across the upper edges of the screens. She wore a long full-trained beach robe, with a flared hood that enclosed her head like a protective bower. One of the jewelled insects nestled on a soft fold above her neck, its light winking in the dim blue shadows of a jade scarab hanging like a dagger between her breasts. There was a curious glacé immobility about her face, investing the white porcelain skin with an almost sepulchral quality, the soft down which covered it like grave's dust. The fine nose and chin, and long sinuous pillar of the neck, had a marked translucence, as if she had spent her entire life in the shadows far from any sunlight.

"Who—?" Startled, she stepped back, the insects scattering at her feet, winking on the floor like a jewelled carpet. She stared at me in surprise, drawing the hood of her gown around her face like an exotic flower withdrawing into its foliage, then, conscious of the protective circle of insects, lifted her chin and composed herself.

"Sorry to interrupt you," I said. "I didn't realize there was anyone here. I'm flattered that you like the screens."

The autocratic chin lowered fractionally, her head, with its swirl of blue hair, emerging from the hood. "*You* painted these?" she confirmed. "I thought they were Dr. Gruber's. . . ." She broke off, tired or bored by the effort of translating her thoughts into speech.

"They're for Charles Van Stratten's film," I explained. "*Aphrodite '70*. The film about Orpheus he's making here." I added: "You must ask him to give you a part. You'd be a great adornment."

"A film?" Her voice cut across mine. "Listen. Are you sure they are for his film? It's important that I know—"

"Quite sure." Already I was beginning to find her dissociated personality extremely exhausting. She seemed to exist on several levels simultaneously. Talking to her was like walking across a floor composed of blocks of varying heights, an analogy reinforced by the squares of the terrace, into which her presence had let another random dimension. "They're going to film one of the scenes here. Of course," I volunteered when she greeted this news with a frown, "you're free to play with the screens. In fact, if you like, I'll paint some for you."

"Will you?" From the speed of the response I could see that I had at last penetrated to the center of her attention. "Can you start today? Paint as many as you can, just like these, don't change the designs." She gazed around at the huge zodiacal symbols looming from the shadows like the insane murals painted in dust and blood on the walls of a Toltec funeral corridor. "They're wonderfully alive, sometimes I think they're even more real than Dr. Gruber. Though—" here she faltered "—I don't know how I'll pay you. You see, they don't give me any money." She smiled at me like an anxious child, then brightened suddenly. She knelt down and picked one of the jewelled scorpions from the floor. "Would you like one of these?" The huge flickering insect, with its brilliant ruby crown, tottered unsteadily on her white palm.

Footsteps approached, the firm rap of leather on marble. "They may be rehearsing today," I said. "Why don't you watch? I'll take you on a tour of the sets."

As I started to pull back the screens I felt the long fingers of her hand on my arm. A sudden mood of acute agitation had come over her.

"Relax," I said. "I'll tell them to go away. Don't worry, they won't spoil your game."

"No! Listen, please!" The insects scattered and darted as the outer circle of screens was pulled back. In a few seconds the whole world of illusion was dismantled and exposed to the hot sunlight.

Behind the Scorpio appeared the watchful face of the dark-suited man. A thin smile played like a snake on his lips.

"Ah, Miss Emerelda," he greeted her in a purring voice. "I think you should come indoors. The afternoon heat is intense and you tire very easily."

The insects retreated from his black patent shoes. Looking into his eyes, I caught a glimpse of deep reserves of patience, like that of an experienced nurse used to the fractious moods and uncertainties of a chronic invalid.

"Not now," Emerelda insisted. "I'll come in a few moments."

"I've just been describing the screens," I explained.

"So I gather, Mr. Golding," he rejoined evenly. "Miss Emerelda," he called.

For a moment they appeared to have reached deadlock. Emerelda, the jewelled insects at her feet, stood beside me, her hand on my arm, while her guardian waited, the same enigmatic smile on his thin lips. Then more footsteps approached, the remainder of the screens were pushed back and the plump well-talcumed figure of Charles Van Stratten appeared, his urbane voice raised in greeting.

"What's this—a story conference?" he asked jocularly, then broke off when he saw Emerelda and her guardian. "Dr. Gruber? What's going—Emerelda, my dear?"

Smoothly, Dr. Gruber interjected. "Good afternoon, sir. Miss Garland is about to return to her room."

"Good, good," Charles exclaimed hurriedly. For the first time I had known him he seemed unsure of himself. He made a tentative approach to Emerelda, who was staring at him fixedly. They gazed at each other, and then Emerelda drew her robe around her and stepped quickly through the screens. Charles moved forward, uncertain whether to follow her, then gave up helplessly.

"Thank you, doctor," he muttered. There was a brief flash of patent leather heels, and Charles and I were alone among the screens.

On the floor at our feet was a single jewelled mantis. Without thinking, Charles bent down to pick it up, but the insect snapped at him,
and he withdrew his fingers with a wan smile, as if accepting the
finality of Emerelda's departure.

Recognizing me with an effort, Charles pulled himself together.
"Well, Paul, I'm glad you and Emerelda were getting on so well.
I knew you'd make an excellent job of the screens."

We walked out into the sunlight. After a pause he said: "That
is Emerelda Garland, she's lived here since mother died. It was a
tragic experience, Dr. Gruber thinks she may never recover."

"He's her doctor?"

Charles nodded. "One of the best psychiatrists I could find. For
some reason Emerelda feels herself responsible for mother's death.
She's refused to leave here."

I pointed to the screens. "Do you think they help?"

"Of course. Why do you suppose we're here at all?" He lowered
his voice, although Lagoon West was deserted. "Don't tell Kanin
yet, but you've just met the star of *Aphrodite '70*."

"What?" Incredulously, I stopped. "Emerelda? Do you mean that
she's going to play—?"

"Eurydice." Charles nodded. "Who better?"

"But Charles, she's. . . ." I searched for a discreet term.

"That's exactly the point. Believe me, Paul,"—here Charles smiled
at me with an expression of surprising canniness—"this film is not
as abstract as Kanin thinks. In fact, it's sole purpose is therapeutic.
You see, Emerelda was once a minor film actress. I'm convinced the
camera crews and sets will help to carry her back to the past, to the
period before her appalling shock. It's the only way left, a sort of
total psycho-drama. The choice of theme, the Orpheus legend and
its associations, fit the situation exactly—I see myself as a latter-day
Orpheus trying to rescue my Eurydice from Dr. Gruber's hell."
He smiled bleakly, as if aware of the slenderness of the analogy and
its faint hopes. "Emerelda's withdrawn completely into her private
world, spends all her time inlaying these insects with her jewels,
with luck the screens will lead her out into the rest of this synthetic

landscape. After all, if she knows that everything around her is unreal she'll cease to fear it."

"But can't you simply move her physically from Lagoon West?" I asked. "Perhaps Gruber is the wrong doctor for her. I can't understand why you've kept her here all these years."

"I haven't kept her, Paul," he said earnestly. "She's clung to this place and its nightmare memories. Now she even refuses to let me come near her."

We parted and he walked away among the deserted dunes. In the background the great hoardings I had designed shut out the distant reefs and mesas. Huge blocks of color had been sprayed onto the designs, superimposing a new landscape upon the desert. The geometric forms loomed and wavered in the haze, like the shifting symbols of a beckoning dream.

As I watched Charles disappear, I felt a sudden sense of pity for his subtle but curiously naive determination. Wondering whether to warn him of his almost certain failure, I rubbed the raw bruises on my arm. While she stared at him, Emerelda's fingers had clasped my arm with unmistakable fierceness, her sharp nails locked together like a clamp of daggers.

So, each afternoon, we began to play the screen game, moving the zodiacal emblems to and fro across the terrace. As I sat on the balustrade and watched Emerelda Garland's first tentative approaches, I wondered how far all of us were becoming ensnared in the strange world of Charles Van Stratten, by the painted desert and the sculpture singing from the aerial terraces of the summer house, and the sand-reefs with the barbed mouths like the vents of some volcanic hell. Into all this Emerelda Garland had now emerged, like a beautiful but exquisitely nervous wraith flitting among the sunlit phantoms of a noon-time dream. First she would slip among the screens as they gathered below her balcony, then, hidden behind the large Virgo at their center, would move across the floor towards the lake, enclosed by the shifting pattern of screens, now and then revealed as a corridor opened and pivoted.

Once I left my seat beside Charles and joined the game. Gradually

I manoeuvred my screen, a small Sagittarius, into the center of the maze, there found Emerelda in a narrow shifting cubicle, swaying from side to side as if entranced by the rhythm of the game, the insects scattered at her feet. When I approached she clasped my hand for a moment and then ran away down a corridor, her gown falling loosely around her bare shoulders. Then, as the screens once more reached the summer house, she gathered her train in one hand and disappeared among the columns of the loggia.

Walking back to Charles, I found a small jewelled mantis nestling like a brooch on the lapel of my jacket, its crown of amethyst melting in the fading sunlight.

"She's coming out, Paul," Charles said. "Already she's accepted the screens, soon she'll be able to leave them." He frowned at the jewelled mantis on my palm. "A present from Emerelda. Rather two-edged, I think, those stings are lethal. Still, she's grateful to you, Paul, as I am. Now I know that only the artist can create absolute reality. Perhaps you should paint a few more screens."

"Gladly, Charles, if you're sure that. . . ."

But Charles merely nodded absently to himself and walked away towards the film crew.

During the next days I painted several new screens, duplicating the zodiacal emblems, so that each afternoon the game became progressively slower and more intricate, the thirty screens forming a huge multiple labyrinth. For a few minutes, at the climax of the game, I would find Emerelda in the dark center with the screens jostling and tilting around her, the sculpture on the roof hooting in the narrow interval of open sky.

"Why don't you join the game?" I asked Charles. After his earlier elation he was becoming impatient. Each evening as he drove back to Ciraquito the plume of dust behind his speeding Maserati would rise progressively higher into the pale air. He had lost interest in *Aphrodite '70*. Fortunately Kanin had found that the painted desert of Lagoon West could not be reproduced by any existing color process, and the film was now being shot from models in a rented studio at Red Beach. "Perhaps if Emerelda saw you in the maze. . . ."

"No, no." Charles shook his head categorically, then stood up and paced about. "Paul, I'm less sure of this now."

Unknown to him, I had painted a dozen more screens and early that morning hidden them among the others on the terrace.

Three nights later, tired of conducting my courtship of Emerelda Garland within a painted maze, I drove out to Lagoon West, climbing through the darkened hills whose contorted forms reared in the swinging headlamps like the smoke-clouds of some sunken hell. In the distance, beside the lake, the angular terraces of the summer house hung in the grey opaque air, as if suspended by invisible wires from the indigo clouds which stretched like velvet towards the few faint lights along the beach two miles away.

The sculptures on the upper balconies were almost silent, and I moved past them carefully, drawing only a few muted chords from them, the faint sounds carried from one statue to the next to the roof of the summer house and then lost on the midnight air.

From the loggia I looked down at the labyrinth of screens, and at the jewelled insects scattered across the terrace, sparkling on the dark marble like the reflection of a star-field.

I found Emerelda Garland among the screens, her white face an oval halo in the shadows, almost naked in a blue silk gown like a veil of moonlight. She was leaning against a huge Taurus with her pale arms oustretched at her sides, like Europa supplicant before the bull, the luminous specters of the zodiac guard surrounding her. Without moving her head, she watched me approach and take her hands. Her blue hair swirled in the dark wind as we moved through the screens and crossed the staircase into the summer house. The expression on her face, whose porcelain planes reflected the turquoise light of her eyes, was one of almost terrifying calm, as if she were moving through some inner dreamscape of the psyche with the confidence of a sleepwalker. My arm around her waist, I guided her up the steps to her suite, realizing that I was less her lover than the architect of her fantasies. For a moment the ambiguous nature of my role, and the questionable morality of abducting a beautiful but insane woman, made me hesitate.

We had reached the inner balcony which ringed the central hall of the summer house. Below us a large sonic sculpture emitted a tense nervous pulsing, as if roused from its midnight silence by my hesitant step.

"Wait!" I pulled Emerelda back from the next flight of stairs, rousing her from her self-hypnotic torpor. "Up there!"

A silent figure in a dark suit stood at the rail outside the door of Emerelda's suite, the downward inclination of his head clearly perceptible.

"Oh, my God!" With both hands Emerelda clung tightly to my arm, her smooth face seized by a rictus of horror and anticipation. "She's there . . . for heaven's sake, Paul, take me—"

"It's Gruber!" I snapped. "Dr. Gruber! Emerelda!"

As we re-crossed the entrance the train of Emerelda's gown drew a discordant wail from the statue. In the moonlight the insects still flickered like a carpet of diamonds. There I held her shoulders, trying to revive her glazed, expressionless face.

"Emerelda! We'll leave here, take you away from Lagoon West and this insane place." I pointed to my car, parked by the beach among the dunes. "We'll go to Vermilion Sands or Red Beach, you'll be able to forget Dr. Gruber forever."

We hurried towards the car, Emerelda's gown gathering up the insects as we swept past them. Then I heard her short cry in the moonlight and she tore away from me. I stumbled among the flickering insects, from my knees saw her disappear into the screens.

For the next ten minutes, as I watched from the darkness by the beach, the jewelled insects slowly moved towards her across the terrace, their last light fading like a vanishing night-river.

I walked back to my car, and a quiet, white-suited figure appeared among the dunes and waited for me in the cool amber air, hands deep in his jacket pockets.

"You're a better painter than you know," Charles said when I took my seat behind the wheel. "On the last two nights she has made the same escape from me."

He stared reflectively from the window as we drove back to Ciraquito, the sculptures in the canyon keening behind us like banshees.

The next afternoon, as I guessed, Charles Van Stratten at last played the screen game. He arrived shortly after the game had begun, walking through the throng of extras and cameramen near the car park, hands still thrust deep into the pockets of his white suit as if his sudden appearance among the dunes the previous night and his present arrival were continuous in time. He stopped by the balustrade on the opposite side of the terrace, where I sat with Tony Sapphire and Raymond Mayo, and stared pensively at the slow shuttling movements of the game, his grey eyes hidden below their blond brows.

By now there were so many screens in the game—over forty (I had secretly added more in an attempt to save Emerelda)—that most of the movement was confined to the center of the group, as if emphasizing the self-immolated nature of the ritual. What had begun as a pleasant divertimento, a picturesque introduction to *Aphrodite '70*, had degenerated into a macabre charade, transforming the terrace into the exercise area of a nightmare.

Discouraged or bored by the slowness of the game, one by one the extras taking part began to drop out, sitting down on the balustrade beside Charles. Eventually only Emerelda was left—in my mind I could see her gliding in and out of the nexus of corridors, protected by the huge zodiacal deities I had painted—and now and then one of the screens in the center would tilt slightly.

"You've designed a wonderful trap for her, Paul," Raymond Mayo mused. "A cardboard asylum."

"It was Van Stratten's suggestion. We thought they might help her."

Somewhere, down by the beach, a sculpture had begun to play, and its high plaintive voice echoed over our heads in the bright air. Several of the older sculptures whose sonic cores had corroded had been broken up and left on the beach, where they had taken root again. Now and then, when the heat gradients roused them to life, they would emit a brief strangled music, fractured parodies of their former song.

"Paul!" Tony Sapphire pointed across the terrace. "What's going on? There's something—"

Fifty yards from us, Charles Van Stratten had stepped over the balustrade, and now stood out on one of the black marble squares, hands loosely at his sides, like a single chess-piece opposing the massed array of the screens. Everyone else had gone, and the three of us were now alone with Charles and the hidden occupant of the screens.

The harsh song of the rogue sculpture still pierced the air. Two miles away, through the haze which partly obscured the distant shore, the beach houses jutted among the dunes, and the great fused surface of the lake, in which so many objects were embedded, seams of jade and obsidian, was like a huge segment of embalmed time, from which the music of the sculpture was a slowly expiring leak. The heat over the vermilion surface was like molten quartz, stirring sluggishly to reveal the distant mesas and reefs.

Suddenly the haze cleared abruptly, and the spires of the sand-reefs seemed to loom forwards, their red barbs clawing towards us through the air. The light drove through the opaque surface of the lake, illuminating its fossilized veins, and the threnody of the dying sculpture lifted to a climax.

"Emerelda!"

As we stood up, roused by his shout, Charles Van Stratten was running across the terrace. "Emerelda!"

Before we could move he began to pull back the screens, toppling them backwards onto the ground. Within a few moments the terrace was a melée of tearing canvas and collapsing trestles, the huge emblems flung left and right out of his path like disintegrating floats at the end of a carnival.

Only when the original nucleus of half a dozen screens were left did he pause, hands on hips, his loose blond hair catching the sunlight, panting on his swaying legs.

"Emerelda!" he shouted thickly.

Raymond turned to me. "Paul, stop him, for heaven's sake!"

Striding forward, Charles pulled back the last of the screens. We had a sudden glimpse of Emerelda Garland retreating from the in-rush of harsh sunlight, her white gown flared around her like the broken wings of some enormous fabled bird. Then, with an explosive flash, a brilliant vortex of light erupted from the floor at Emerelda's feet, a cloud of jewelled spiders and scorpions spat through the air and engulfed Charles Van Stratten.

Hands raised helplessly to shield his head, he raced off across the terrace, the armada of jewelled insects pursuing him, spinning and diving onto his head. Just before he disappeared among the dunes by the beach, we saw him for a last terrifying moment, clawing helplessly at the jewelled helmet stitched into his face and shoulders. Then his voice rang out, a long sustained cry on the note of the dying sculptures, lost on the stinging flight of the insects.

We found him among the sculptures, face downwards in the hot sand, the fabric of his white suit lacerated by a thousand punctures. Around him were scattered the jewels and crushed bodies of the insects he had killed, their knotted legs and mandibles like abstract ideograms in some futuristic myth, the sapphires and zircons dis-solving in the light.

His red swollen hands were filled with the jewels. The cloud of insects returned to the summer house, where Dr. Gruber's black-suited figure was silhouetted against the sky, poised on the white ledge like some miniatory bird of nightmare. The only sounds came from the sculptures, which had picked up Charles Van Stratten's last cry and incorporated it into their own self-requiem.

". . . 'She . . . killed'. . . ." Raymond stopped, shaking his head in amazement. "Paul, can you hear them, the words are unmistakable."

Stepping through the metal barbs of the sculpture, I knelt beside Charles, watching as one of the jewelled scorpions crawled from below his chin and scuttled away across the sand.

"Not himself," I said. "What he was shouting was 'She killed—Mrs. Van Stratten.' The old dowager, his mother. That's the real

clue to this fantastic menage. Last night, when we saw Gruber by
the rail outside her room—I realize now that was where the old
harridan was standing when Emerelda pushed her. For years Charles
kept her alone with her guilt here, probably afraid that he might be
incriminated if the truth emerged—perhaps he was more responsible than we imagine. What he failed to realize was that Emerelda
had lived so long with her guilt that she'd confused it with the person
of Charles himself. Killing him was her only release—"

I broke off to find that Raymond and Tony had gone and were
already half-way back to the terrace. There was the distant sound
of raised voices as members of the film company approached, and
whistles shrilled above the exhaust of cars.

As the bulky figure of Kanin came through the dunes, flanked
by a trio of assistant producers, their incredulous faces gaping at the
prostrate body, the voices of the sculptures faded for the last time,
carrying with them into the depths of the fossil lake his final *cri de
coeur*, the last plaintive echoes of the death-song of Charles Van
Stratten.

A year later, after Orpheus Productions had left Lagoon West and
the scandal surrounding Charles' death had subsided, we drove out
again to the summer house. It was one of those dull featureless afternoons when the desert is without lustre, the distant hills suddenly
illuminated by brief flashes of light, and the great summer house
seemed drab and lifeless. The servants and Dr. Gruber had left, and
the whole estate was beginning to run down. Sand covered long
stretches of the road-way, and the dunes rolled across the open
terraces, toppling the sculptures. These were silent now, and the
white sepulchral emptiness was only broken by the hidden presence
of Emerelda Garland.

We found the screens where they had been left, and on an impulse
spent the first afternoon digging them out of the sand. Those that
had rotted in the sunlight we burned in a pyre on the beach, and
perhaps the ascending plumes of purple and carmine smoke first
brought our presence to Emerelda. The next afternoon, as we played

the screen game, I was conscious of her watching us, and saw a brief gleam of her blue gown among the shadows.

However, although we played each afternoon throughout the summer, she never joined us, despite the new screens I painted and added to the group. Only on the night I visited Lagoon West alone did she come down, but I could hear the voices of the sculptures calling again and fled at the sight of her white face.

By some acoustic freak, the dead sculptures along the beach had revived themselves, and once again I heard the faint haunted echoes by Charles Van Stratten's last cry before he was killed by the jewelled insects. All over the deserted summer house the low muted refrain was taken up by the statues, echoing through the long empty galleries and across the dark moonlit terraces, carried away to the open mouths of the sand-reefs, the last dark music of the painted night.

Death Warmed Over

BY RAY BRADBURY

Hollywood, as anyone who has been there recently will tell you, is not what it used to be. The myriad sets and studios that used to echo to the sound of films in production are now mostly silent or disappearing to be replaced by new industrial developments. The streets where tourists waited patiently for a glimpse of the stars are now lined with sightless parking meters—and the restaurants where the movie moguls dined are supermarkets and parking lots. It is a town of ghosts; the ghosts of great stars and great films. In their wake, however, has come television, the small screen mass-media entertainment that is relentlessly destroying all memories of the great days of the Hollywood myth. Spare a tear, then, for what has passed—and in particular for all the great horror films which are so much a part of the Hollywood Nightmare. For they, too, are not what they used to be, as Ray Bradbury so poignantly shows here.

Once each year, a small fête occurs at my local Hollywood television studio. I am invited for my annual love match with the new producers and vice-presidents, who shake my hand, dine me well and cry:

"Ray, tell us about your horror-film T.V. special!" I then describe the kind of extraordinary Halloween show I would like to write and produce some fortunate season.

Finished, the producers throw confetti, shout Huzza!, call me genius and promise to call tomorrow.

They never call again. Until the next year, or the year after, when I am asked to recite my piece for a newer, fresher face.

This year, lacking an audience, I'm telling *you*. Quite simply: I love and revere the old horror films. I do not care what your snob psychologist fears for their effect on the young.

To me, Dracula, Frankenstein's Monster and the Mummy are only good, tonic and superb. Before God and country, I will defend them. And not out of late camp sentiment, either. It is not so much nostalgia that moves me, but practical hair-ball psychology.

But before calling down the lightning to strike and the Wolf Man to sick your professional alarmists, allow me to sketch in my one-hour TV special. Imagine this:

It is night in a small Midwest town. Autumn and a good wind and the city-hall clock edging toward 12. Along the dark and empty Main Street comes a man, myself, walking with a brisk cloud of autumn leaves rustling at my heels. Before a deserted theater, I glance up at the broken marquee bulbs that read: LON CHANEY IN "THE PHANTOM OF THE OPERA." BELA LUGOSI IN "DRACULA."

Even as I watch, the bulbs begin to flicker on and off. I peer at the dusty foyer. The ticket booth is empty. A spider web covers the round glass hole where you chat through at the ticket seller. As I approach, a spider hung at the web's center skims down to the brass cashier plate. A ticket jumps with a cough of dust into my hand. All to itself, the theater door hushes open.

I hesitate. The autumn wind blows a scuttle of those dark leaves about my knees. I enter the dim and totally deserted theater. My feet are soundless in the heavy carpeting.

I survey the Gothic interior, the uninhabited seats, the opera boxes, the chandelier like a vast constellation of tears above, the dust-throttled Wurlitzer organ below.

"You're late," a voice calls, softly.

The town clock strikes midnight.

"No. Just on time."

I move down the aisle.

"Are we all here?"

A second whisper makes me glance up at the right-hand box. The Phantom of the Opera, pale-masked, is there. We nod. I sit.

"Please to begin."

The wind from out in the autumn night blows those dark leaves chittering on the air. The leaves beat dryly at the heavy velvet portieres, then strike at the projection booth.

Flying in through the projection-room windows, they drop one by one by one in the projector. The fierce bright bulb blinks on. And we see that these are not autumn leaves at all, nor insects or bats, but fragment of film that flick, shutter, fall frame by frame into place. Their images flash across the velvet abyss. The waiting ghost screen shapes up forms and spirits. Voices whisper from beyond time.

With the Phantom asking questions and myself trying for answers, we begin *The Beneficial Results of Horror Films* or *Why Dracula?*

And during the next hour, we would watch and comment on such pictures as *Nosferatu, Vampyr, Dr. Jekyll and Mr. Hyde* (comparing, perhaps, the performances of John Barrymore in the double role in the Twenties, Fredric March in the Thirties and Spencer Tracy in the early Forties). Inevitably winding up with *Murders in the Rue Morgue, The Mummy, The Bride of Frankenstein* and, maybe, for mere peevishness and perversity, *King Kong.*

Repeatedly, we would ask, Why tolerate the horror film? What good is it? What does it mean? Why, for a short time, did we make fine ones? Why do we rarely make the excellent ones anymore? Who today can equal the quality of such films as *Isle of the Dead, The Body Snatcher, The Cat People* or *The Curse of the Cat People?*

By my simple listing of these naïve titles, I sense I have alienated and lost some of you. Good riddance. Those remaining expect answers to the questions posed. And they all must deal with civilization and death.

When we, the human race, were very young, death was immediate. We had no time to think on it. We collided with it, had it done to us, did it to others, stayed to be slaughtered or ran to lick our very real wounds. Life was short, sometimes sweet, more often brim full of panics and living nightmare. Death, always a mystery, was embodied in real actions that lay no further off than the campfire rim or the edge of the cave. Its spirit lurked in the very fire itself that, momentarily tamed, gave warmth, but uncontrolled might burn a thousand miles of forest in a night. Death, as well as life, lurked in everything we could see, hear, smell or touch in those terrible twilights and impossible dawns.

Then, when the nit-picking ape named himself quite possibly human and left knuckle marks in the jungle dust on his way to brick cities, we walled out real death. Death still happened, of course, but we had more time to speak of it, to consider that blank bottomless abyss.

And from these night chats came raw mythologies about that great mouth that eats us all. We reared up folk tales, religious dreams and finally short stories, novels and motion pictures to help us make do with the incurable and inescapable emptiness into which each must fall one day soon or late.

Our opinion of death is not much different today than on those darling afternoons in primitive times when, as ax-wielding dentists, we cracked the fangs of the sabertooth. Very simply, we do not approve of death. We hate the rules he plays by. He must be cheating. He always wins.

Somewhere along the path, we named this thing that stops our breath. We saw animals sleep away, humans go silent, and knew that the stuffs were gone, the lightning bolt come out of the body, returned to earth and sky. The soul, the *élan,* whatever it was, indescribable, had done an even more indescribable thing: disconnected itself, vapored off. We called it death and finally even gave death a gender. We spoke not of it but of he who comes with the scythe and emptied hourglass.

Even Popes, in Baroque splendor, had tombs reared with winged skeletons and scythes harvesting the marble air, to show that if the great in all their pomps must fall, the small must surely follow.

What were we doing? Naming the unnamable. Why? Because man by his very nature must describe. The names change from generation to generation, but the need to name goes on. We were picturing the unpicturable. For, consider, does death have a size, shape, color, breadth, width? No, it it "deep" beyond infinity and "far" beyond eternity. It is forever incapsulated in the skull we carry, a symbol to itself, behind our masking face.

Our religions, our tribal as well as personal myths, tried to find symbols then for the vacuum, the void, the elevator shaft down which we must all journey and no stops evermore again. We had to know. We had to lie, and accept the lie of labels and names, even while we knew we lied, for we had work to do, cities to build, children to rear, much to love and know. Thus we gave gifts of names to ward off the night some little while, to give us time to think on other things.

The skeleton as symbol of death and inhabitor of tales moves among the races of the world. Death as creature, death as masculine being, reaper of souls, fills that void, gives us a thing to see, hear, smell and touch.

The business of the fine horror film, then, could be summed up as follows: For 90 or 100 minutes the writer, producer, actor says to the pale customer: Instead of the void, the unknown, the unnamable, allow us for a little while to name names, rear up shapes. Tonight the Prince of Darkness walks among you. We hold him high, shake his bones. We fan his wings, expose his teeth. His shadow quakes your seat. Is he not magnificent, is he not beautiful? Shiver sweet agonies from this encounter.

But then, behold, at the penultimate moment, as death moves to cull you in, with camera and story and swift-edited art, we hand you yet another symbol: a cedar stake.

Death lies before you. The afternoon grows late. Now, here in the tomb, before the nightshades rouse up death disguised as Dracula, strike!

So you, the acting, as well as acted-upon, audience, seize the cedar stake, place it against the dread heart of Dracula and strike it, once, twice, three times with a sledge!

Bang! The echoes flee! Bang! The echoes run. Bang! The echoes die.

And Dracula is dead.

And for some little while this night, death, why, he is dead, too.

And with a great sigh, having bested the void two falls out of three, having buried the void in cedar shavings and wolfsbane, you leave the theater and, smiling, make your way home. At the price of a splendid lie, an incredible myth, you have borrowed a cup of immortality. Tomorrow, perhaps, you will find it mere water, bacterial and possibly fatal. But tonight, through the transmutation of materials, through light and power, through film and imagination, you are larger, stronger, more powerful, more beautiful than death.

These are the stuffs of dreams that went to make the best old horror films. How rarely today do we bother to act out the most solvent, the most creative and therefore our most curative dreams.

We have fallen into the hands of the scientists, the reality people, the data collectors.

I do not for a moment demean their function. They are the vital necessaries without which we would remain ignorant. We need as much information about our universal situation as can possibly be found.

But once found, data must not remain data. Fact fused to fact must become more than those facts.

The horror film began to kill itself off when it began to explain itself. Fantasy, like the butterfly, cannot stand handling. Touch the wing the merest touch, brush some of that powder with finger tips and the poor thing won't fly again. You cannot explain a dream. The dream exists. It is. It cleanses itself. It is the mountain spring that, traveling dark distances underground, purifies itself. We do not know all the reasons. We will never know. But the modern horror film, by merely cutting back a man's skull bone to show us his transistorized Grand Guignol stage, all miniaturized in the frontal lobe, bypasses the dream to capture and kill with facts, or things that appear as facts.

So the pure, delightful, strangely life-enhancing terror of *Frankenstein*, where we make the Monster and it acts at one remove from us so we can watch and learn from it, becomes the modern robot-brute of *Our Man Flint*. We stare incredulous as high I.Q. modern man Flint roughly escorts his enemy into a public toilet, sits him on the bowl and cuts his throat, while toilet tissues fall in a dreadful snow about his feet.

Instead of imagination, we are treated to fact, to pure raw data, which cannot be assimilated, which cannot be digested. And, as most of us have already guessed, we already know the "facts" of our position as humans in this world. We do, indeed, know the facts of murder, torture, sickness, greed and death. We do not have to have the facts repeated in crude detail. Those who offer us the cut throat or the asphyxiated face stuffed in a plastic bag offer only reportage and not their reactions, their philosophy, about that reportage.

So the modern "horror" film, be it *Our Man Flint* or *Charade,* merely hands us a larger hair ball and demands that we cat-sick ourselves trying to eat it whole rather than dislodge it. We are asked to devour but are given no chance to vomit.

For what is sickness? Sickness is a way of becoming well. That is all it is. If we remain sick, we die. And any art that teaches only fact is a sick art and will sicken us and finally kill us or itself.

As I have said often to friends in affiliate art fields, your trouble is *you* want to give everyone polio. *I* wish to give them polio vaccine. One destroys. The other sickens us but to make us whole.

What are we saying here? Let me recapitulate. The basic facts of man's life upon earth are these: You will love. You will not be loved. People will treat you well. People will treat you badly. You will grow old. You will die. We *know* this.

You cannot tell a man that death and age are after him again and again all his lifetime without freezing his mind ahead of the reality. He must be told these truths by indirection. You must not hit him with lightning. You must polarize the lightning through transformers, which are the arts, then tell him to grab hold of the one-cent Electrocute Yourself for a Penny Machine. His hair may stand up, his heart beat swiftly as he juices his veins. But the truth, thus fed, will make him free.

Count Dracula, Baron Frankenstein, Dr. Jekyll and his friend Mr. Hyde, Dorian Gray and his portrait are all such agents of freedom. They take on the problems of mankind and, by shaping them in symbols, enable us to act our feelings toward death, the strange evil in man that has provoked us from the Garden gate to the edge of space, and the mystery of our love in the midst of envy and destruction.

Any horror film that lingers only on that cedar stake plunged into the grisly heart of a vampire loses its chance to transcend raw fact. The symbolic acts, not the miniscule details of the act, are everything.

For the time being, we must wait in the wings with the Phantom while *Virginia Woolf's* horror tale is acted out, even more frightening in some ways. For, while Count Dracula cannot be seen in a mirror, even as we watch, the four tormented men-boys in *Who's Afraid of Virginia Woolf?*, they are themselves invisible. They do not exist, even to themselves. They were never born. So they can never die. They are raw fact and only fact, which has no significance. Fact without interpretation is but a glimpse of the elephants' bone yard.

How much longer will American jackdaw intellectuals run about collecting reality, holding it up, declaring this to be the truth? One hardly dares guess. But a day must come when we turn full about to our intuitions, our collective creativity, our full rounded sufferance and digestion of facts to give us a full philosophy.

Meantime, we will have to suffer the book-burning intellectuals who, like Dr. Spock, fear Batman without having seen him; Dr. Wertham, who finds murder under every comic book; and the librarians who won't allow the *Oz* books on their shelves because "they are not good for children."

A new generation will scramble the sick bones of this one. And the health and strength of that generation will be built on the old ability to fantasize. To fantasize is to remain sane. The moment we hand over this tool to our bullying intellectuals of left or right, the sabertooth will come over the transom even as we lock the door.

Beneath our suitings, man the hairy anthropoid stands. Inhabiting cities, he saves up assassinations and rapes most foul, in order to be human. He cannot forever save hair as one saves string. The great bramblebush will choke him to death. He needs *Dracula*, then, and *Frankenstein* as depilatories. It is as simple as that.

The puritans are ever with us. The new scientific intellectual puritan will deliver us from evil, he says, by denying all of Edgar Allan Poe, Nathaniel Hawthorne and the headless horseman.

There is a scene in one of my *Martian Chronicles* where rocket men, come to Mars, sense there the fleeing spirits of all our best fantasy writers. Hid deep in the Martian hills, victims of the computer-data-fact-collecting age, the shades of Dickens and his Christmas Ghosts, Poe's falling House of Usher, Baum's Emerald City of Oz wait to be summoned back by a greater age of tolerance. A new age that will take raw fact in one hand and transcending intuition in the other. Only with a grasp on each rein can man move forward in space and time.

These characters of our needful dreams have been exiled not only by our blind intellectuals but by an even worse species of commercial fool, your fly-by-night on-the-cheap producer of such stillbirths as *The Monster of Blanket Beach* and *I Was a Teenage Werewolf*. With canned laughter, or unintentional humor outcropped from vulgarity, they have driven our monsters off. The jackal has, indeed, bested the werewolf.

To these I say: Give us back our small fears to help us cure the large. We cannot destroy the large death, the one that takes us all. We need a tiny one to be crushed in our hand to give us confidence. The complete and utter truth, completely known, is madness. Do not kick us off the cliff and send us screaming down to that. For God's sake, give us our morsel of poisoned popcorn to munch in the cinema dark.

May the day be soon in coming when the bright critics who damn Disneyland, for instance, without ever having seen it, and the money-grubbing Munchkins who laugh all the way to the bank are equally banished from the wild strange gift of night we find in motion-picture houses, leaving this art form to people who, stationed between the extremes, know how to shape the dream.

And on that day, not distant, the orang-utan of Poe will vault from the shadows and stuff the doctoral nonsense wrong side up the chimney. The clockwork men and their dusty facts will lie unscrewed on the jungle floor. Kipling's Phantom Rickshaw will run them down. The very Emerald City they tried to dynamite will, falling, bury them with intuitions. And man the fact collector, hand in hand with man the secret creator, will move forward in one body, sensing and beautifully guessing.

Then we shall call the ghosts home and the dead will return to teach us about death. Dracula will fly the night and the mad Baron will pull that switch that should best be pulled only by God. Mr. Hyde will sprout hair only to lose it, only to sprout it yet again. And Dorian's portrait will grow old, then young, then old again forever, and so cycle in cycle, fact circling dream and dream circling fact, Man, not the one thing but many, will continue his journey out of the Garden, on his way to becoming a thing he cannot now name nor know nor guess, but wish upon.

The motion picture projector stops.

My TV special on horror films is over.

The small autumn leaves of film fly out the projection-room window into the night.

The lights come slowly on.

The great opera chandelier shivers above me, as if struck a blow with a sledge. It threatens to fall. I wait. The tremble of glass subsides.

I walk to the far exit. I nod to the high box, where the Phantom moves his hand in a shadowed farewell.

The doors fall shut.

I walk along the dark street, accompanied by those autumn leaves that nibble my shoes.

I turn the corner. The leaves settle. I am gone.

PULL CAMERA BACK ALONG THE EMPTY STREET.

IF YOU MUST HAVE A COMMERCIAL, INSERT IT HERE.

THE END.

THE END